DISTANT CHOICES

Brenda Jagger

FAWCETT CREST • NEW YORK

A Fawcett Crest Book
Published by Ballantine Books
Copyright © 1986 by Brenda Jagger

Library of Congress Catalog Card Number: 86-28608

ISBN 0-449-21346-3

This edition published by arrangement with William Morrow and Company, Inc.

Manufactured in the United States of America

First Ballantine Books Edition: June 1988

PRAISE FOR BRENDA JAGGER AND HER SWEEPING HISTORICAL NOVELS

Also by Brenda Jagger
Published by Fawcett Crest Books:

DAYS OF GRACE

A WINTER'S CHILD

A SONG TWICE OVER

To my husband, Philip
and my daughters
Claudia, Vanessa and Alex,
as always

One

The two daughters of Matthew Stangway attended his wedding with outward composure and an inner variety of emotions ranging from mild embarrassment to downright fury.

The young ladies were similar only in age and hardly knew each other, Miss Katharine Stangway being the child of her father's first marriage; Miss Oriel Blake the child of sin. *His* sin, in fact, with the woman he was now taking to wife, a discreet and decidedly elegant Mrs. Evangeline Blake who, although passing herself off as the widow of a Captain Blake whom no one had ever heard of and certainly never met, had—by the look of it—been Matthew Stangway's mistress, at some clandestine address or other, these twenty years.

Mrs. Evangeline Blake indeed, who, when last seen in Matthew Stangway's neighborhood of the Gore Valley, had been Miss Evangeline Slade. A young lady—could it really be twenty years ago?—of fashion and good breeding without a penny in her pocket, who had come north, like many others, to find, among the new industrial rich of this new and most glorious age of power-driven industrial machines, a wealthy and, if at all possible, an agreeable husband. And who, having failed in her first endeavor and taken herself off in what everyone supposed to have been disgrace, had come rushing north again to lay her claims to Matthew Stangway— whatever they may be—before his first wife had been decently cold in her grave.

It was therefore, perhaps, unfortunate that the two young ladies were driven to church, that wedding morning, in the

1

same festive, white-upholstered landau, the daughter of the
bride, Miss Oriel Blake, erect and tall and sufficiently lovely
to startle not a few of her onlookers by the clear blue of her
eyes, the smooth, pale silver-gold of her hair, a long-limbed
grace that was almost statuesque, and a composure—it was
generally felt—considerably in advance of her twenty years.
The daughter of the bridegroom, Miss Katharine Stangway,
startling no one unless with the unusual tidiness of her dress,
her thick, dark, regrettably unruly hair smoothed down and
hidden, today, beneath a large hat which one might have supposed her to have borrowed from her mother. Had one not
known, of course, that the entire wardrobe of the late Mrs.
Stangway had been distributed, at least a year ago, to charity.

A most awkward, unpredictable, often far from goodhu-
mored girl, Miss Kate.

A most polished, personable, thoroughly delightful young
lady, Miss Oriel Blake.

"You are going to be the best of friends," Miss Blake's
equally polished mother had told them, some weeks ago,
when first they met. To which Miss Blake was understood to
have replied most correctly, "Of course, Mama." While
Kate—one heard—had fixed both mother and daughter with
one of those dark, half-scowling, half-smiling stares of hers
and had not even had the grace to nod her head. A denial
which might have won her some sympathy had she had the
good sense to be seen brooding over her own mother's grave,
instead of going off by herself to walk the moorland above
the Valley, which would have been unacceptable at any time
but a perilous place now, strewn with the raucous encampments of navvies come to build the railway, so that every
groom and footman in her father's service had had to miss
his dinner that night and join the search for her.

An escapade which had rapidly dried up the stream of invitations to tea-parties and sewing-parties, gossip-and-gig-
gling parties to which all motherless girls were entitled, no
high-principled matron of the Gore Valley caring to risk her
own daughters in too close contact with one who had been
found, well after midnight, sitting cross-legged on a rock in
the middle of a wilderness teeming with rough and unlettered
men.

But there had always been a streak of the wilderness in
Kate—one had tried hard enough to deny it—something of
the delicate yet quite possibly sharp-toothed woodland crea-

ture in her sudden movements, and in the brittle-boned angles of her skinny body which wore clothes, and expensive ones too, as if it did not find them natural. As if, perhaps, a wreath of oak leaves and berries and wild poppies would have suited her better than the safe, cream straw hat which some other, *responsible* person had chosen for her.

Yes. There was something disturbing about Kate. Something uneasy, or untamed, just beneath the none too neat and tidy surface. Something pagan, in fact, although the Gore Valley did not like the word and never used it, preferring to do away with such fanciful notions altogether and call her undisciplined, awkward, badly brought up.

Just as there could be no doubt at all that Miss Oriel Blake had been very well brought up indeed. An immaculate young person with not a wrinkle to be seen on the skin-tight sleeves of her gown or her cream kid gloves, the folds of her wide, ivory-colored skirt spreading all around her in fragrant, spotless profusion, every hair of her smooth, fair head exactly in its appointed position, framing her face in an intricacy of coils and ringlets which gleamed—in the opinion of several young Gore Valley gentlemen—like spun silver.

Truly a delight to the eye, Miss Oriel, a shade too tall, perhaps, to suit every taste—Gore Valley gentlemen being, in many cases, of only moderate stature—but with a calmness of manner, a serenity, an air of rather cool but decidedly good breeding which had made her the subject of much admiring comment.

One could not imagine Miss Oriel Blake, for instance, running off to wander, all alone, on the desolate and dangerous moorland, no matter what the provocation. One could not, in fact, imagine Miss Blake doing anything but the right and proper thing at the most appropriate moment. And doing it quietly, calmly, and very well.

Which had come as a surprise to many, since she was, after all, the daughter of a woman whose reputation had never been altogether beyond suspicion, a woman who may or may not have been legally married to this unknown Captain Blake who, indeed, may or may not have existed. Whereas no one among the two or three hundred persons who made up what the Gore Valley considered to be "Society" could be in any doubt as to the validity of Matthew Stangway's first marriage or the resulting legitimacy of Kate, his daughter.

In short, Kate Stangway with her tangled woodland hair in

which no one would have been surprised to find a stray sprig
of gorse or heather, a wisp of goose grass or a thistle, had
been born within the very strictest bonds of wedlock, a ceremony to which at least a hundred gentlemen of substance
and their worthy ladies could still bear witness. While Miss
Oriel Blake of the fine, silver chignon, the discreet and highly
civilized scents of rose and jasmine, the soft hands with their
pink, polished nails, the sweet voice saying only pleasant
things, had nothing but her mother's word to rely on.

Poor Miss Oriel, in a world where, unless one happened
to be fabulously rich, it was essential, above all things, to be
respectable.

Poor Kate, who was rich enough to be married but probably not to be forgiven for her eccentricities.

Did either of them realize—the Gore Valley had been wondering for a month or more—what storms and tempests, what
mighty domestic hurricanes and niggling little showers of
cold rain might well lie ahead?

But there was no sign of apprehension or dismay on the
charming face of Miss Oriel Blake as she got down from the
carriage and, smiling with the correct degree of courtesy to
left and right, went sailing into the church like a serene and,
just possibly, a shade too confident swan. No apprehension
in Kate Stangway either, that anyone could see as, forgetting
the volume of her new gown and the number of quilted petticoats she had been made to wear beneath it, her leap from
the carriage-step became a scramble. Although, being sure-
footed, neat-footed when it suited her—were not moorland
goats and foxes?—she soon corrected her balance, smiling
not in greeting, one felt, but with a kind of amusement one
knew to be impertinent, as if she thought her father's wedding—and all his guests—tedious and tame and faintly ridiculous.

An annoying girl, Miss Kate, and not looking her best
either beside silvery, statuesque Oriel as they walked together
down the aisle and then separated, one to the bridegroom's
side of the church, the other to the bride's, Kate flopping
down on her prayer-stool, it was noticed, and missing it by
inches so that she landed on cold stone and remained there,
her head clutched in her hands with a fervor considered excessive in one who had never been devout; Miss Blake kneeling slowly and surely on her red velvet cushion in an attitude
of not too passionate prayer, quite sufficient for the occasion.

A hushed, speculative moment with every critical eye fixed gimlet fashion on the bent heads and young, slender backs of Matthew Stangway's daughters. Oriel, who had glided swanlike in her self-possession, prolonging now her pose of religious devotion until she could trust herself to hide the bitter anxiety—from which she had always suffered—that someone in that hostile congregation might pierce her polished shell and *"find her out."* Kate, careless, impudent, taking her life—and her father—as casually as every changing breeze, pressing hot palms against her eyes and *burning* now, in full view of her father's friends—had they only been aware of it—with a very far from casual outrage, a by no means careless grief. And Matthew Stangway himself, standing halfway between them, waiting for his bride, the woman Gore Valley Society had known so well, twenty years ago, as Miss Slade.

Evangeline.

The same woman. And not much altered, either, by these twenty years which, one supposed, could not all have been kind to her. The same long, slender figure, the same porcelain-pale skin and silver-pale hair as her daughter, coiled most becomingly, as she had always coiled it, on a neck that still had the drooping, swaying grace of a willow. The same pale blue eyes with a sparkle of laughter and a chip of ice set deep in each one, the same voice, light and playful as springtime, and every bit as lethal—when she chose—as a well-aimed knife-thrust. And she had often chosen to be deadly.

Among those privileged upper few hundred of the Gore Valley no woman had ever liked Miss Evangeline Slade, while of the men whose heads she had turned in the old days few had had a good word to say for her once the spell had faded. A lovely woman, none could deny it. But tricky. Inclined to be scornful when caught off guard. And not always quite so clever as she ought to have been about concealing, from the heights of her own good breeding and aristocratic, albeit penniless connections, how thoroughly she had despised the very men she had been trying so hard to marry. Most of them now present in the congregation, local giants of trade and commerce with their sensible wives, twenty years older and richer and all of them quite wise enough—in view of Matthew Stangway's exalted position in the community—to accept his bride exactly as he chose to present her. The respectably widowed Mrs. Blake—no matter what anyone *really* thought about it—who, on this crisp, cold morning in perhaps the fiftieth year of her age, was to become Mrs. Stangway of High Grange Park, a noble house with a noble fortune attached to it, coming from mines and quarries and the dowry of the lady, now deceased, who had been Mrs. Stangway before her.

"*Charming* woman," murmured the congregation, rising to its feet as she entered the church, a smile on every face and rather more than a good idea in every shrewd, suspicious heart that when she had bolted so suddenly from the Valley all those years ago it had not been to accept the convenient proposal of one Captain Blake, but to hide herself away in secret to bear Matthew Stangway's child.

Charming woman. Schemer. Fortune-hunter. Calculating adulteress. Her calculation being that, in view of his wife's indifferent health and his own sense of duty, she would manage to coax him or inveigle him or shame him into marriage without too much trouble—one day.

How shocking. How terribly cold-hearted. How very like Evangeline Slade to wait twenty years, with the sleek patience of a pedigree cat, for another woman to die.

Yet now that she had succeeded, now that Matthew Stangway *had* deigned to make an honest woman of her—and a very rich one—how could one openly condemn her without forgoing the pleasure of observing, at very close quarters, all the heartless and wicked and highly entertaining things one felt absolutely certain she now meant to do? How could one decline to call on her, or send one's butler to the door with a curt "Not at home" when she herself came to call, without giving up the poignant thrill of hearing, at first hand, how the Stangway daughter, or Matthew Stangway's two sisters, might be getting on with her?

Badly. One knew it would be badly. Therefore one had expressed oneself delighted to attend the wedding and whatever came after it at High Grange Park, knowing, in any case, how little one's opinions counted with Matthew Stangway, a man who had long ago ceased to consider anyone's convenience but his own.

A handsome man, of course, he had always been that, of a dark, distinguished bearing and cold, somewhat empty eyes who, since he grew rich enough to afford his whims and fancies, had indulged himself to the full. Fine wines, thoroughbred hunters, a London gunsmith and a London tailor, a diamond in his cambric shirt-frill, fur rugs in his carriage, women, as and when they took his fancy, no matter what his thin, eccentric, quite recently deceased wife had had to say about it. Never much, one felt. Nor—it was generally believed—would he have listened if she had.

Would this new wife—this old mistress—fare any better? Or was Matthew Stangway about to turn foolish now, in his middle age, with love?

There came a mighty flaring of the organ, bringing the bride, as lovely as ever and probably just as treacherous in the dove-gray velvet with the swansdown muff and hem she had thought appropriate to her station, the triumph in her light eyes shadowed by a hat of gray gauze and feathers, pearls in her ears, a cluster of them pinned to the fall of white lace at her neck, her wide skirts flowing like water from a supple waist any woman half her age might envy.

Glorious Evangeline, savoring her victory like vintage claret.

Yet, as he turned to watch her progress down the aisle toward him his mind was so far removed from passion that he could not even retain its memory. He had desired her once, of course, when they had first met in those youthful, greedy years of his poverty, when he had owned nothing but the decaying shell of his ancestral home, his pride, his fastidious determination to live as a gentleman, his arrogance and his temper and the enormity of his desire for Evangeline Slade, as poor and proud and well-born as himself and just as urgently, as *ruthlessly*, in need of a "good marriage." Two high-bred fortune-hunters from the same stable, equally disdainful of the quarry they were hunting.

"I am a Sussex Slade," was the first thing she had said to him.

"I am a Yorkshire Stangway."

Two ancient families growing even poorer, every year—every generation—more hard-pressed to support themselves in the state befitting their rank as "landed gentlemen"; until Matthew's father and Evangeline's father had had nothing to bequeath their son and daughter but the same piece of advice. To go out and find money, wherever it could be had, through marrige.

How ironic that they had found each other.

She—a girl whose grandfather had been on easy terms with the Duke of Wellington—had taken a post as secretary-companion to a banker's widow in the Gore Valley town of Hepplefield eight miles away—in those days—from Matthew's still rural village of High Grange. And they had been drawn together instantly by many things, not least their shared contempt for Hepplefield's shopkeepers, merchants, industrialists, for anything which could be bought and sold since the things *they* valued could only be inherited. For anything and everything tainted by the vulgar hand of trade, although they were both ready to grasp that hand, of course, and squeeze it as dry as Hepplefield's choking, mercantile dust.

In those self-conscious, middle-class drawing-rooms where all the furniture had been brand-new and visibly expensive, all the women wearing their virtues and their pretensions as rigidly as they wore their whalebone stays, Evengeline's had been the only voice he had recognized. A woman of his own kind. *His* woman. And, for a while, nothing else had mattered. Yes—the roof at High Grange Park might be letting in the rain, the home farm in need of extensive repair, his two sisters even more in need of husbands which only a dowry apiece could buy. But how could he sell his name and status to a girl of the alien newly rich and lose Evangeline? He could not. For a while. Until he had fully acknowledged the flaw in his own nature which would have made him hate her, when passion cooled, if he had found himself trapped with her beneath that leaking roof, his coat and all his aspirations threadbare.

He had therefore shrugged his shoulders, hardened his mouth which had been quite hard enough to begin with, and married the thin, dry, slant-eyed, vaguely foreign daughter of Josef Kessler, wool merchant of Hepplefield and Bradford, thus ridding himself of the need to worry about frayed cuffs and collars or broken roof-tiles ever again. A marriage of convenience. A bad joke, it had seemed to him, on the day not long after when coal had been discovered beneath his land, making him a rich man in his own right.

Coal. That most "gentlemanly" source of riches, requiring no sordid commercial practices on his part, no greater personal involvement than the appointing of a pit-manager, as one appointed a gamekeeper to look after one's grouse-shoot and hand-rear one's pheasant. An excellent fellow, as it turned out, who had managed to situate his slag-heaps and his pit-wheels well away from the manor and village of High

Grange, throwing up an unkempt sprawl of workers' cottages on what, in Matthew's boyhood, had been Low Grange Wood and Low Grange Meadow. A hell-hole now, he supposed—if one cared to look at it closely, as he certainly did not—which meant no more to him than a source of revenue.

Of considerable wealth, in fact.

Although too late, of course. And not only for him and Evangeline, but for his sister Letty who had made only a very mediocre marriage, and for his sister Maud who, somehow or other, had never married at all, having grown too dignified, perhaps, or simply too old for passion. Which had been far from the case with Eva, his thin, dry Kessler wife, the heiress of Hepplefield wool barons who, despite the careful repressions of her education, had loved him, for a while, with a fire and a ferocity he had found astonishing.

Not welcome, either.

Poor Eva. Fierce and possessive and burned almost to a cinder by her own entirely unexpected sensuality, until he— embarrassed by a desire he could not reciprocate—had felt obliged to reprimand her for it, pointing out to her in cool, precise language, the unladylike nature of her excess. Making it very clear to her that this frenzy of hers had no part to play in their contract.

He had hurt her, of course. But he had seen no help for it. And she had paid him back by growing thinner and drier and every day more peculiar, withdrawing from all the social and domestic concerns proper to womanhood, so that in the end all that had mattered to her had been her paint brushes and easels and those garish caricatures she had called her "Art."

Ghastly daubs, which he hoped his sister Maud still had kept safely under lock and key in the attic—all as excessive, as positively embarrassing as Eva's own younger self. Paintings, each one of enormous size, throbbing color, which still haunted him—although he would never of course admit it— as an accurate record of those tarnished, *offended* years of avoiding Eva's passions and somehow stifling his own as he had watched Evangeline offering herself to anyone who could free her from her own trap of poverty, as Eva Kessler had rescued him from his. Clever Evangeline. The belle of every ball. The bridesmaid who outshone every bride. High priestess of elegance and wit and fashion who, every season, attracted a new worshiper to her shrine. And—every season— lost him. Not to some rival goddess of greater fascinations but to one tame and tedious schoolroom chit after the other whose father—like Eva's—could endow his child with the powerful charm of money.

Desperate Evangeline.

Yet Matthew Stangway, a gentleman by now of worth and distinction and acquisitive habits, had continued to want her. After ten years of living first with Eva's awkward hungers, then her enmity, finally her blank-eyed indifference, he had felt entitled to have her. And in the vulnerable thirtieth year of her age, when her last possible fiancé had deserted her for the heiress to a Gore Valley spinning mill, she had finally surrendered to him.

His woman at last. And what a year—or perhaps only half a year—of exultant, savagely indulged passion that had been. What an explosion of sensuality on his part at least; an acceptance, rather, on hers, of his carnal nature which, if she could not share it—and he had quickly realized she could not—she could most decidedly arouse, excite, taunt and tease and enrage. And did so. Could lead him, with her purring smile, to every frenzied physical extremity until, not in the least to her chagrin or surprise, she had conceived what she had intended to be his son.

The only child he would ever be likely to have, too, by the thin, overstrung look of Eva. His heir, therefore, this son of Evangeline's. Already, in her mind and his, she had set the wheels of legal adoption in motion; while even a daughter would have to be lavishly provided for.

So Evangeline had told him.

"Matthew, my darling, I fear I have rather become your lifetime responsibility now. I—and my little encumbrance. Have I not? What luck you are so well able to afford us."

Once again, too late. Had she kept him waiting too long so that the reality of her had failed to match his expectations? Or was it simply that his heart had grown too cold, too fastidious, ever to be fully satisfied? Or had it always been so? Very likely.

He had sent her to France to have her child in traditional, furtive luxuriousness. After which, when she had reminded him artfully, expensively, of her claims on his attention, he had established her in a series of country cottages or city apartments as they took her fancy, visited her as and when she took his, grown accustomed to her and been unfaithful to her as he had always been with Eva.

And even the child had been a disappointment. Not the son he had been promised but a girl who could offer him nothing in the way of interest or companionship. And when, two years later, Eva had finally produced a child herself, that had been a girl too, meaning—as every man of substance knew—responsibility without pleasure, substantial cash payments in the form of dowries leaving the family for the benefit of other men.

Daughters. Would anyone choose to have them? And he had paid little attention to either. None at all, in fact, to Miss Oriel Blake, beyond establishing her in her false identity and paying handsomely—Evangeline had seen to that—for her upkeep both at home and at all those select schools for "young ladies" to which her mother had kept on sending her.

A polite stranger to him, Miss Oriel Blake, addressing him as "Mr. Stangway" whenever he had been obliged to spend a restrained half-hour in her company.

"Are you quite well, Miss Blake?"

"Yes. Quite well, thank you, Mr. Stangway. My mother has just stepped out for a moment. She asks me to say she will not be long."

Had the girl realized, even after a liaison of such long standing, that it was still Evangeline's policy to keep him waiting, keep him guessing, keep him always a little unsure not only as to her whereabouts but as to the state of her heart? Did the girl realize there had been a liaison at all? He had not the faintest notion. And although he had now lived for eighteen years under the same roof as Eva's daughter, he did not pretend to know her any better. His Kessler daughter with her sallow skin and dark, disconcerting stare, so very like Eva who, to Evangeline's intense disappointment—why deny it?—had failed to die in childbirth, although she had taken little interest in the child thereafter, beyond handing him a list of names which he had at once rejected. Artemis, she had wished to name her daughter. Or Lalage. Ondine. Gaia. The Lord knew what other pagan nonsense. "Katharine," he'd ordered curtly, tearing her list neatly in half and consigning both pieces to the fire, before the servants got a look at them. "Katharine," his sister Maud had firmly seconded. His mother's name. Plain Kate, acceptable everywhere. And Kate it had been, with Maud's name, as the child's godmother, to follow it. Katharine Maud. Yet even then, looking down at the slant-eyed, brittle-boned changeling in the Stangway cradle, it had struck him, uneasily, that Lalage, or Ondine, would not have gone much amiss.

Eva's child, soon forgotten by Eva who had forgotten everything in her last years but her compulsion to record in impossible colors the scenes and faces of her life. Becoming a distant, disgraceful, paint-smeared figure, rarely emerging from her work-room in the attic, leaving the care of her daughter to his sister Maud who had taught her—he supposed—what any young lady needed to know. Not a great deal, in his judgment. A little music and drawing. Some embroidery and dancing. French within reason and a suitably watered-down version of history unlikely to turn the head. How to serve tea and press flowers and make herself agreeable to gentlemen. Accomplishments notably lacking in his daughter Kate but which anyone with half an eye could find in their smooth and polished abundance in Miss Oriel Blake.

His daughter too. Did she know it?

"Darling—of course not." Evangeline had appeared scandalized at the mere idea of such a thing. "One must have respect for the truth—naturally—I do so agree. But such a *burden* sometimes—don't you think? Rather more—perhaps? —than our innocent little lamb could carry. And—innocence apart, my love—these young girls do chatter so, one to another, like a flock of little starlings, heads all together. And we could not have her telling *our* secrets, after all, to today's best friend, who will be tomorrow's enemy for sure. No. She is Miss Blake. And so long as I remain Mrs. Blake, her widowed mother, then I—Matthew, my dearest love—have my reputation to think of . . ."

He had remained, therefore, remote from this eldest daughter of his. A distance which suited him. Although he was marrying her mother today for her sake. Or so he told himself. So Evangeline had told him, repeatedly, after Eva's death, wasting no time and making no bones about it either, since she had waited so long.

"We shall observe the necessary proprieties, of course— shall we not, Matthew, my darling?—by waiting a twelve-month more. And then, just as soon as we are all out of black gloves, you may ask me to marry you. What could be more natural after all? A widow and a widower, no longer so young as they used to be, each with a darling daughter. So suitable, Matthew . . . ? I had better move back to Hepplefield at once, so that the whole town may bear witness to our meeting again, after so many years apart. You will be able to find me a suitable house, I know, my darling—not too grand, not too small, just right . . . *Do* see to it, Matthew."

Had there been a hint of desperation in her? A stark dread, at this eleventh hour, of losing her final chance? He believed so, although it had not influenced him greatly. He was marrying her because he chose to acknowledge the obligation. Because—in bleaker terms—there was nothing else, nothing whatsoever, he wanted to do. Let her have her triumph, then. The prestige of his name. The comfort of his fortune. What remained of his passions—very little. Hardly anything at all. Let her have it. She had earned it. And what real difference could it make to him?

Fascinating, scornful, suddenly fragile Evangeline, who by still wanting so many things, so urgently, thus exposed her own weakness. Did she know how totally his own capacity to hope, to enjoy, even to desire, had deserted him? Or how comfortable he was, these days, with his own indifference?

Of course. She knew it very well. Yet, as she reached his side at the altar the thought uppermost in her mind was that she had come here, this bright, cold morning, not to be sentimental but to be married. And if a girl of her daughter's age—or Eva Kessler's daughter's age—might expect the two to go together, Evangeline knew they did not.

Dear Matthew. Still handsome but as cold—these several years past—as a marble statue, and as empty.

"My dearest, I truly believe we were made for one another," she had murmured to him the other evening, in the hearing of his sister Maud, on purpose to infuriate this woman who had always been her enemy.

"Indeed—my love—I believe we were," he had answered, his cynical eyes passing from Maud, who believed him to be in the grip of a renewed infatuation, to Evangeline herself who—having no taste at all for physical passion—was much relieved to find that he was not. But she had heaved a sigh nevertheless and breathed a few meaningless whispers into his ear, to further annoy his devoted sister Maud who could not know that his long infatuation had actually ended, perhaps not on the very day but certainly within a few months of having possessed her. At about the time, she shrewdly supposed, that she had managed to conceive his child.

A gamble, of course. But with her thirtieth birthday leering on her horizon such a gamble had seemed quite justified. It would not be the first time, after all, that a Slade had risked everything on the turn of a card. And what had there been to lose but a lifetime of genteel drudgery as a paid companion with nothing to hope for beyond a fifty-pound "remembrance" in her employer's will? The sin of adultery, if committed in sufficient luxury, must surely be better than that? A coolly considered decision. A cool hand, too, with which she had written her dramatic note of surrender to her lover. "Matthew, my darling—come to me. Take me."

And so he had taken her, a flirtatious, possibly unscrupulous, yet nevertheless immaculate virgin of thirty, as if they had both been eighteen, his ardor coming as a great shock to her, almost an indignity, until she had realized the power it gave her. And then there had been Oriel; the love-child, born, she readily admitted, when love—such as it had ever been—was drawing to a close, but whose very existence entitled her mother—at the very least—to a comfortable home of her own. Her own carriage, too. Her own status, albeit false, as the dashing widow Blake who, in the course of her wanderings from one spa town, one seaside resort, one country house visit to another, had made many friends. Once, in the black year of Eva Kessler's pregnancy, she had considered marrying one of them. But Eva's child had not been the son Evangeline had dreaded, only this skinny, nut-brown little Kate who could be no threat to her—no threat to her own polished pearl of a daughter either—and she had decided to wait.

The waiting was over now. The wedding service had begun. And with it the intense joy she expected to feel, every day of her life now, in showing these worthy citizens of the Gore Valley just what it would mean to deal with Mrs. Stangway of High Grange. A lesson they would begin to learn soon enough. Tomorrow morning, very likely, when her husband's spinster sister Maud, who had kept his house for thirty years and brought up his wife's daughter, let it be known that the household keys and accounts, the guest list and the menu book had been taken from her.

Nevertheless, "Dear Maud," she murmured, as she stood, half an hour later, on the church porch among her wedding-guests, the focus of all eyes, as she so dearly loved to be. "Dear Maud." And she bent forward through a shaft of winter sunlight to kiss the cheek of a woman of her own age who looked—Goodness, how very pleasing—*at least* ten years

older. Maud Stangway, straight-backed, thin-lipped, over-
bearing in her manner and exceedingly decided in her opinions who, having found no one grand enough to marry had
married no one, remaining with her brother as first lady of
High Grange Park and Low Grange village. Maud—who
would be an autocrat without authority tomorrow.

And then, having kissed Maud twice for good measure,
"Dear Letty . . ." enthused Evangeline, reaching out to take
the hands of her husband's younger sister. "The pretty one"
they had called her in the old days when—for a month or
two—she had been Evangeline's "very dearest, sweetest
friend," her most reliable source of invitations to High
Grange until Maud had spotted the use Evangeline was making of her as a stepping-stone to Matthew, and put a stop to
it.

Letty had written Evangeline a letter, dictated by Maud.
"I think it unwise for our friendship to continue, in fairness
to us all . . ." Meaning, "Unless you stop tempting my
brother to marry you instead of Money, then who will I ever
find to marry me?"

And who had she found, even when the coal revenues had
started to come in, but a country parson, well-born of course,
but good for little else that Evangeline could see beyond the
fathering of Letty's—how many was it?—ten, or eleven children. A whole tedious tribe of them, in any case, all with
that elongated, washed-out greyhound look of overbreeding,
forever scuttling in and out of High Grange Park where
Evangeline had already come across them far too often, con-
suming quantities of cakes and tea from the best china,
lounging all over the drawing-room in the best chairs, staying
on to dinner whenever their doting Aunt Maud chose to invite
them. At least four times a week by Evangeline's reckoning.

And even as she smiled with warm affection at their
mother, she had made up her mind to put a stop to that.

"Dear Letty—how wonderful that we are sisters now, as
well as friends . . ."

Poor Letty, it seemed to Evangeline's sharp eye, in every
sense of the word. Poor in that chilly little vicarage of hers
with its threadbare, overcrowded gentility. Poor in her hopeless little husband who could barely afford to clothe all those
children, much less establish the boys in suitable professions
and get the girls decently married. Poor in the loss of her
looks—with the best will in the world one could hardly help

noticing it—her face sadly shrunken and faded, her figure, which had once been so neat and trim, saggy and puffy now, so that one could hardly tell, any longer, whether she happened to be pregnant or not. Poor in her nerves, too, by the look of it, her chin being rather apt to quiver and her eyes to fill with tears without warning and for no specific reason that Evangeline could see.

Was she tearful now as Evangeline took her in an exquisitely condescending embrace? Remembering perhaps—as Evangeline herself was remembering—how she and Maud had once let it be known that they could accept no invitations to parties of any kind if the dubious Miss Evangeline Slade was also to be a guest. Thus bringing Evangeline's social engagements in the neighborhood to an effective close.

Now here was Letty, the "pretty one," an old woman at forty-five; and Maud, the "clever one" with nothing in the world but a "spinster sister's" pension to call her own. And here was Evangeline at fifty, with the best of her life still before her, holding her court already in the churchyard among those false friends who could no longer afford to be her enemies.

Despite her outward composure, the cool courtesy of her voice and her manner, Evangeline Stangway was ablaze with a fierce joy that had nothing whatsoever to do with her husband.

She did not even look for him among the crowd—*her* crowd—as he stood back cynically, wryly, to watch her play the role for which she had undoubtedly been created. The wife of a rich man.

"Congratulations, Papa. Is that what one says?" His daughter Kate spoke from behind him, startling him as she often did, so that he was frowning—by no means unusually—as he turned to look at her.

"Ah—Kate."

"Yes, Father. Kate." Was she reminding him of her existence? Kate, his Kessler daughter, with those black Kessler eyebrows, wide forehead, sharp, birdlike nose, the overcrowded, *clever* Kessler face which he had always found—displeasing.

"Thank you for your good wishes, Kate," he said.

"And what does one do now, Papa? Congratulate the bride?"

She was being insolent, of course. But then, she often was,

usually with Maud who had always dealt with her, harshly he
supposed, knowing Maud, although he had never interfered,
finding it better—more convenient, at any rate—not to notice.

He nodded. "I believe so."

"Oh—good." She bounded away, coltish, skittish, haphazard, the sudden focus of several dozen pairs of interested
eyes as she came face to face with Evangeline.

"Dear child . . . ?" And Matthew Stangway, with a cool
spurt of amusement, interpreted the message of his wife's
outstretched arms. "Dearest Kate, you must think of me as
a mother now." Nor did he fail to note the masterly fashion
with which she concealed her annoyance when Kate, with
what looked like an excess of awkward enthusiasm, heartily
kissed Evangeline's proffered cheek and, at the same time,
managed to dislodge her elegant gauze and feather hat.

No easy matter, since Evangeline was the taller and had
an expert way with a hat-pin. An expert ear, too, for the few
discreet titters from her "well-wishers" who knew how easily a woman with her hat askew can be ridiculous.

"Oh dear—I am so sorry . . ." Kate's hands, in what
looked like their eagerness to make amends, were tugging
the hat to an even more drastic angle, badly ruffling its feathers and Evangeline's with them, Matthew had no doubt at all.

"Please—don't trouble," said Evangeline.

"No trouble," said Kate. "Oh—absolutely not . . . We
can't have you looking such a fright . . ." And perhaps she
would have had the hat off altogether and several strands of
Evangeline's smooth hair tumbling down with it had not another pair of hands swiftly intervened.

"*Do* allow me," murmured his *other* daughter, Miss
Blake, moving Kate aside with so little fuss, setting the hat
and the awkward moment with it so swiftly to rights that even
Matthew Stangway felt obliged to admire her expertise.

"There, Mama. You are quite lovely again."

"Thank you, my darling." They smiled at one another
with quiet satisfaction.

"Are you acquainted with my daughter," inquired
Evangeline of everyone around her, bringing Oriel forward
and, without appearing to do so, pushing Kate back.

Astute Evangeline. And polished, immaculate, highly accomplished Oriel. But when it came to marriage—wondered
her father—would the silver hair, the clear blue eyes, the cool
serenity, even the dowry he knew Evangeline would prevail

upon him to give her, be compensation enough for the questions concerning her birth which even Evangeline would be unable to answer?

He doubted it. Which seemed a pity, since she had everything in her to make a man happy: whereas it would take a desperate man indeed to risk himself with Kate.

"Come—everyone." Evangeline was calling them all together, eager now to go and take possession of the home for which she had waited so long.

"Come, Maud—and Letty. Come, children . . ." And then, with the air of a woman who has suddenly mislaid her gloves. "Come, Matthew . . ."

Where was he?

"Here, my love."

Smiling, he handed her into her wedding landau, tucked a fur rug carefully around her knees just as if she were precious to him, even kissed her hand. Bells rang. There seemed to be a flurry of snowflakes mixed with dried rose-petals in the air. He saw that his sister Letty, surrounded by her progeny, was shedding tears; his sister Maud standing as rigid and stern as a soldier on parade. His daughter Kate scowling and scuffing her new kid boots on a stone. His daughter Oriel making pleasant conversation with strangers, her gloved hands neatly clasped together, saying—he felt certain—only the most appropriate thing.

Did any of them realize that he had seen the dawn of this, his second wedding day, with no more joy than his first? That all he really wanted from these women—daughters, sisters, wives—was to be left alone?

Did any of them understand that?

Only Evangeline.

"Welcome to your kingdom, my darling," he said.

Two

Maud Stangway gave up the keys to High Grange Park with a steady hand, a fixed smile, and venom of a most lethal nature in her heart, thus abandoning a reign which had been as long as it had been absolute.

"What a noble-hearted creature she is," the Gore Valley had been saying of her these thirty years, enjoying a spasm of self-righteousness at the sight of this handsome and, at one time, perfectly marriageable woman sacrificing herself on the altar of family loyalty. Since *somebody*, after all, had been needed to make good the shortcomings of her brother's wife and bring up his difficult daughter. Poor, brave Maud, they said, who had remained single, the better to do it.

But, in fact, she had been a perfectly happy woman, finding in her strict control of the house, the estate, and all within it, the very things she most desired from the married state without any obligation to suffer the caresses of a man. A physical indignity from which her brother's domestic misfortunes had spared her.

For thirty years High Grange Park, the house she preferred above all others, had been hers in everything but name. Her sister Letty's children, living so conveniently nearby at High Grange vicarage, had—in everything but the distasteful task of giving them birth—been hers too. Letty being so much in the habit of taking Maud's advice that she was uneasy about choosing so much as a new shawl without it. While Letty's husband, the Reverend Rupert Saint-Charles, had never seemed to mind who chose the schools his sons attended, or found the money to dower his daughters so long as he was not called upon to do so himself. A *hopeless* couple, Rupert and Letty. Therefore Maud had taken them in hand, for their own good of course, so thoroughly and so naturally that—for as far back as anybody could remember—nothing had been done at High Grange, either at the Park, the vicarage, or in the village itself, unless Maud approved it, gave her permission, or had ordered it, in the first place, herself.

A state of affairs which suited both her brother Matthew, who did not wish to be troubled with domestic matters, *and* her sister Letty, who had no head for them: Letty's children— for whom she had never had much head either—being left gladly, quite naturally, to Maud. And had Maud's ''other'' niece, Kate, shown the same appreciation, then matters at High Grange Park may well have been easier. But Kate— neglected little cuckoo in the Stangway nest—had never seen in Maud the role of virgin-mother which she had been quite ready to play. She had a mother of her own, after all, her manner had always seemed to imply. A mother who prowled the attic all day, perhaps, talking to her paint brushes, but a mother nevertheless; which had led her to question—often and rudely—why she should need, or in fact pay attention to an aunt? An attitude which had soon turned Maud's ministrations to slaps, her words of wisdom—so eagerly absorbed by Letty's children—to reprimands, orders, threats; leading her finally to pursue a policy not so much of bringing Kate up as keeping her under some sort of control. A harsh policy, growing harsher as Kate continued to resist it, during which she had done her best to instill into the child a proper sense of shame and fear. Shame, that is—although the actual words were never spoken—at being the daughter of so odd and un- happy a mother. And the fear that she might come—unless she mended her ways—to resemble her.

''If you wish to be loved then you must deserve it,'' had been Maud's favorite maxim to all her charges, bringing her a steady stream of little gifts, embroidered purses and slip- pers and flattering little water-colors from Letty's daughters, posies of flowers and ''secrets'' from Letty's sons; nothing from Kate but a blank stare, an insolent half-shrug of a brittle shoulder, a raised eyebrow which said mutely, but as plain as day, ''Aunt Maud—what a tedious fool you are.''

Difficult moments, these, when Maud—for years now— had been forced to wrestle with her conscience, warding off, as best she could, the evil—for she knew it to be that—of

wishing a human life away. Yet there were times, nevertheless, when she was angry enough or honest enough to succumb to the temptation. For if Kate had never been born then
how simple, how natural, how *right* it would have been for
Matthew to make Letty's eldest son his heir. Thus elevating
to the rank of master of High Grange Park and Low Grange
Colliery a young man who was his mother's darling and the
apple of his Aunt Maud's determined eye.

How fitting. How fervently—before the shock of Eva's unexpected pregnancy—had Maud and Letty prayed for that. A
dream shattered first by the appearance of Kate and then, to
somewhat more serious effect, by Evangeline whose arrival
as mistress of High Grange began with a flourish, the new
Mrs. Stangway expressing herself tolerably satisfied with the
bedroom and dressing-room prepared for her own use, and
with the accommodation provided for her personal maid, but
somewhat puzzled by the room "dear Maud" had thought
suitable for her daughter.

"Oh dear . . . ." she murmured, pausing on the threshold
as if waiting for someone to tell her it was all a mistake.
"How small .. ."

"How *pretty*, Mama." Oriel came forward at once to pour
balm on troubled waters in the same practiced manner in
which she had rescued her mother's wedding hat.

But Evangeline, turning to Maud with the bright, brisk
smile of mistress to head-parlormaid, had not the least intention of being pacified.

"Dear Maud—my daughter is so very good-natured, I am
sure you have noticed it?"

"Yes, indeed."

"And so much inclined to consider the feelings of others . . ."

"I dare say."

". . . that she often allows her own feelings to be set aside.
An attitude of unselfishness in which . . ."

"I am sure you have trained her well, Evangeline."

"I have done my best. The room is too small, Maud."

"It is of exactly the same proportions as Kate's." Evangeline looked puzzled again, as if wondering what Kate could
possibly have to do with it.

"Poky," she said. "And dark. A window like a prison
cell. *Really,* Maud."

"Mama," murmured Oriel, moving across the fourteen

feet or so of rose-patterned carpet to glance out of the perfectly adequate window. "There is a carriage on the drive. A landau with—I think—a coat of arms. And two ladies in it. *Rather* dignified . . ."

"I wonder?" said Evangeline. "Lady Merton?"

And by the time Evangeline had taken tea with her caller *not* Lady Merton, alas, the coat of arms having had no existence outside Oriel's imagination—Oriel had quietly installed herself and all her dainty possessions, her hair-brushes with their mother-of-pearl backs and spotless bristles, her lace-trimmed petticoats and chemises, her winter wardrobe of fine, pale woollen dresses, her summer wardrobe of white lawn, sprigged muslin, crisp cotton, her evening wardrobe of ice-blue silk mousseline and cream-colored satin, her strands of pearl and coral, her silver-topped bottles of toilet water, her dozens of pairs of gloves to suit every occasion—wrist-length gloves in white kid, pastel suede, embroidered Spanish leather, elbow-length gloves in white or black silk, ribboned gloves, riding gloves, net mittens, gloves of lace and knitted silk and velvet—all neatly placed in an appropriate drawer with her ivory glove-stretcher.

"I see you have made yourself at home," said Maud, who had been excluded—sweetly but firmly—from Evangeline's tea-party.

"Yes. It seemed best." Oriel's light blue eyes were polite but very steady.

"Although somewhat against your mother's wishes."

"Oh—I think she will be pleased to see I have got everything in and will be quite comfortable."

But Evangeline, as Maud knew, had been far less concerned with her daughter's comfort than with making a demonstration of her own authority. And now, having demonstrated it, her daughter might take the perfectly well-proportioned, prettily furnished room or not, as seemed best to her. Which was, Maud realized, exactly what this irritatingly self-possessed girl had just told her.

"You are satisfied then, Miss Blake?" Maud, spoiling for a fight, rather hoped she was not. For if she could find evidence—*now*—that the daughter was as tricky and greedy and flighty as the mother, then she would feel justified in striking out at her, and beating her, as she had failed to do with Evangeline, to her knees. An impulse of savagery instantly foiled by Oriel's sweetly spoken "Yes—perfectly, Miss Stangway."

"You are sure you wouldn't want—well—*my* room, perhaps? It is large and overlooks the rose-garden. Don't hesitate to ask for it. Your mother would not." Maud's temper was rising.

"How kind you are, Miss Stangway."

And even Maud, with her prickly self-esteem, her senses tuned so finely to detect the least hint of insult or disobedience, was not certain whether Oriel was goading her or paying a compliment.

"Kind?"

"To be so concerned. But there is really no need to pay *too* much attention when Mama makes a fuss about me. Where I am to sleep, or where I am to sit at dinner, or making sure my name is on every invitation. Things like that. I am her only child, you see, and we have been very much together. I suppose it worries her that I might feel neglected. And so she takes *extra* care—perhaps even more, sometimes, than might be needed."

Oriel smiled encouragingly, serenely, inviting Maud—it rather seemed—to join her in a little conspiracy to protect Evangeline from the affectionate overflow of her own maternal heart.

"Are you *explaining* your mother to me, child?"

"Oh no." Oriel looked as if such a liberty had never crossed her mind. "I simply did not wish you to think me disobedient, by settling myself in, after what Mama said. When she sees I am happy then it will all blow over. These things almost always do."

"You are very loyal, Miss Blake."

"Oh—am I? How kind of you to say so."

And a shade too composed, too clever by half for the taste of Miss Maud Stangway who spoke sharp words that same afternoon to her sister Letty on the subject of Evangeline Slade's daughter, warning her that still waters of this type would be likely to run exceedingly deep.

"I believe, Letty, that we would do well to keep her away from Quentin." The name of Quentin, of course, being that of Letty's much-favored eldest son.

"My dear," Letty was predictably horrified. "Do you mean she might—well—turn his head?"

"I do. Should she find it in any way to her advantage. She

would not lose her own head, either. One may be very sure of that. Like her mother before her.''

Still waters. Calm waters. Treacherous waters, perhaps, in which any young man she decided to lure there might drown.

But, contrary to all appearances, Oriel Blake walked through the first weeks of her new life on eggshells, a delicate process to which her old life had thoroughly accustomed her, each careful step accompanied by a careful word—the *right* word—and her calm, if never too radiant, smile. A pose of quiet self-confidence which had so far managed, during the twenty years of her life, to deceive everybody. Except—that is—herself.

''You are fortunate in your daughter,'' the Gore Valley told Evangeline. ''So accomplished—so very pleasant . . .'' So beautiful too, although the Gore Valley, of course, was not given to making statements such as this.

''Quite the pearl beyond price,'' muttered Maud, very tight-lipped, deciding, since every jewel must surely have its flaw, to keep a sharp look-out for this one.

''Such a comfort,'' sighed Letty Saint-Charles, who found little in her own life to comfort her.

To which Evangeline nodded her elegant head and Oriel calmly smiled.

It was her defense against the world, that smile, whenever—as often happened—the world seemed to threaten her. An effective barrier, she had found, between her real self and the constant upheavals of her childhood which seemed to have taken place in removal-vans, post-chaises, and the domestic storms regularly created by Evangeline, with whom no maid or governess ever stayed for long, ''Mrs. Blake'' being inclined to ask far too much for far too little wages, so that no matter how sorry one felt for ''the child'' one had really no alternative but to pack and go.

They had packed, therefore, all Oriel's nurses and nannies, one after the other, and taken their leave, sometimes without a word, sometimes with an unleashing of sentiment from which, in order not to recoil, she had hidden herself away behind her smile.

''My poor child, what is to become of you?''

''Oh—I am quite well, thank you, nanny.''

And then, having waved a fond farewell, there had been an equally warm welcome when, the next day or the day after, the new nanny—or, as she grew older, the new governess—came bustling through the door. Not always in the best of tempers.

"I had expected your mother to be here to meet me."

"Yes. Of course." She had learned, at a very young age, to protect her mother's reputation by lying to her mother's domestic staff. "And so she would have been had she not been called out so urgently. She asked me to apologize. I have put the kettle on."

"*What!* A child of your age playing so near the fire, with hot water. What are you thinking of?"

"Why, nanny—of making you a cup of tea."

And, as she spoke the gentle, soothing lies, Oriel—no stranger to fire and hot water at any age—would offer her smile as a token of her good intentions, a guarantee that she would brush her hair and her teeth each night, would keep her pinafores clean, would ask no awkward questions, and—although this was not immediately understood—would answer none.

"Will your mother be long, then?"

"Oh—I'm afraid I can't say. She has gone to visit a friend who has been taken ill . . ." So that if Evangeline did not happen to return until very late that night, or not at all, there would be no need for further explanation.

Oriel the peace-maker, the smoother of sharp-edges and awkward corners, no trouble to anyone, who, when she outgrew her final governess, had set off without complaint in the company of strangers, on hazardous coach journeys which had taken her to the school in Carlisle, the school in Penzance, the school in Paris, the school in Florence. Returning in the summer holidays always to a different address. A new house, a new town, new furniture more often than not, always new servants. Sometimes to be greeted by her mother, but just as likely to find only an indifferent parlormaid waiting to tell her that Evangeline had been called away. By Matthew Stangway, she had presumed, smiling at that too. And when she finally and quite suddenly admitted to herself that he was her father the shock had been so slight that she realized she had known it all along.

"Mr. Stangway is our special friend," Evangeline had always told her. "Should we find ourselves in any little difficulty it is to him we should turn. So comforting."

"Yes, Mama."

"It is essential, you know, my love, that one should have

a measure of gentlemanly protection. Women of our sort, after all, were not created to be self-reliant. And since your dear father is no longer here to be relied upon, then he would surely have wished us to be grateful to Mr. Stangway . . . ?''

"Of course, Mama.''

No more had ever been said, maintaining a fiction which had become the natural fabric of Oriel's life, an essential part of the shell, glossy and smooth as pearl on the outside, somewhat sharper-textured within, which had, from a very young age, enclosed her. So that she had found nothing incongruous in the lectures her mother regularly gave her on the subjects of good conduct, virtue, and morality.

"One must not only be good and clever, my love,'' Evangeline told her, "one must be *seen* to be so. In fact, one must be seen to be a great deal better and a great deal brighter than anybody else. An earl's daughter, perhaps, can afford to be somewhat stupid or peevish or to have her little whims—can even afford a little misdemeanor every so often. But when one is not quite the daughter of an earl . . . Well then—one has to be very, very good sometimes—well nigh perfect, in fact, to be thought even good enough. One has to positively shine like a star—alas—if one wishes to be seen at all. One has to run rather fast, in fact, in order not to stand still, if one happens to lack—well—you know, darling—rank, and position, and bundles of money in the bank. Or the bank itself, of course, which would be even better. *Do* remember that.''

She had remembered.

"And one more thing, my darling . . .'' Evangeline's eyes had been cool and clear, her voice infinitely serene. "One must speak the truth, of course. Everybody knows that. Just as everybody knows there are some things of which one does not speak at all. A lady never tells her age, for instance, nor expresses any particular opinion about anything controversial. Not in public, at any rate, she does not. Therefore offending no one. Just as one offers no details of one's private life—*so* vulgar—and certainly never inquires such details of others. One keeps one's privacy strictly where it belongs—to oneself. It is not telling lies. Just good manners. You do see . . . ?''

"I see, Mama.''

She had remembered that too.

"Mrs. Blake is much afflicted with the migraine,'' she had

told a new and particularly sharp-eyed parlormaid during those uneasy weeks after Eva Stangway's death when her bereaved husband had seemed in no haste to make firm promises about taking another bride.

"My mother is most unwell," she had told Matthew Stangway himself when he had called in answer to the third or fourth letter Evangeline had artfully penned him. And, leading him to the darkened bedchamber, the anguished bedside, she had left him to endure the reproaches of a woman who, while accusing him in fading tones of ruining her, had certainly made up her mind to ruin him should he fail to see the error of his ways.

"You *are* going to marry me, Matthew?"

"Am I, Evangeline?"

Oriel had tiptoed away, not caring to hear more, never doubting for a moment that her mother would prevail. And the next morning the migraine was gone, Evangeline weakened rather becomingly by pain but sitting up in bed to partake, quite heartily, of her tea and toast nevertheless.

"Oriel darling, you will hardly believe it, but our dear, old Mr. Stangway has asked me to think about being his wife . . ."

"And shall you accept him, Mama?"

Evangeline, her eyes gleaming, her mouth lifting at its corners with her purring smile, had savored the question at her leisure. As Oriel had known she would.

"Ah well—who knows? We have been acquainted for so long and I suppose the poor man is lonely, now, in that positive palace of a house with his cranky old sister. Perhaps it would be a kindness."

"Very likely, Mama."

"Oh—do you think so? It would mean moving north, of course."

"We have moved so many times, Mama."

"Indeed. But only to pleasant places. Whereas Hepplefield . . ." She shuddered. "And I suppose it would have to be Hepplefield, to begin with. Such a grim, gray place, you cannot imagine. Full of gray-minded people too, who would feel obliged to burn me at the social stake if I dared to marry him before his first year of mourning is through. Thank goodness it is *he* who has suffered the bereavement, not I, since women are expected to mourn for so much longer. Two years in black and then another year in lavender. Quite horrid. So

I fear we will have to put up with a small house in Hepple-field, my dear, for a while before the wedding. Quite ghastly. Although Mr. Stangway's village of High Grange is rather delightful . . .''

Oriel had not found it so. Not really a village at all, in her eyes, with the dark smudge of industrial Hepplefield visibly looming in the distance and Low Grange Colliery only just hidden by a screen of low hills and wide-spreading chestnut trees. The sky, to the south, pierced by a growing line of factory chimneys and stained an unhealthy, sulfurous yellow by the smoke they generated so that even on days of sun and high white cloud to the north—beyond the grouse moors of Lord and Lady Merton—the direction of Hepplefield, would seem a foggy day.

"Oh dear," Evangeline had murmured. "But then—I suppose this is the price one pays for progress. And all that comes with it. But the garden is just as I remember it—thank heaven the wall is so very high. Only look at the peacocks on the lawn. And the house is lovely. Well—Oriel, darling—isn't it?''

Uncomfortable, Oriel thought, on the occasion of her first visit—some few weeks before her mother's wedding—when, in her best ice-blue silk with its watered-silk sash and ribbons, she had sat, a restrained guest, in her father's drawing-room, facing the hostility of his sisters; Miss Maud Stangway who, she quickly guessed, would have preferred death by torment to speaking one true word of welcome; and Mrs. Saint-Charles, "Miss Letty" the servants still called her, who talked of nothing but the brilliance, the virtues, the golden prospects of her own eldest son.

A fussy, faded, fidgety little woman, Oriel had judged "Miss Letty," her flowered mousseline dress several shades too light for her and several sizes too big, her thin hair arranged, around her aging countenance, in a brave attempt at the girlish ringlets of thirty years ago, her expression absent, not quite paying attention to anything one said to her until suddenly, her ears catching the sound they had been straining for, she clasped her hands ecstatically together and cried out, "Here is Quentin—my son." As if he had been the sole purpose of their visit, the one, indeed the only person who could possibly be thought worth waiting for.

To his mother, Letty Saint-Charles, disappointed in her life and with little faith in her husband, her son Quentin was that person, her eyes very clearly seeing no one else from the moment he entered the room, her ears rejecting every voice but his, her mind aware of nothing but the impression he was creating. While even the sharp, shrewd eyes of his aunt, Miss Maud Stangway, were observed to be glowing with a satisfaction deep enough to merit the name of pride.

"This is *Quentin*," said Letty breathlessly, meaning "*My* Quentin. My hope for the future. My pride and joy."

"My first nephew," said Maud, meaning just as clearly "The eldest male of the Stangway line, after Matthew who will not live forever. And after Letty's husband, who doesn't count. The *head* of the family, therefore, in due course, if I have *my* way." And she had smiled, very far from pleasantly, first at Evangeline who had long passed her final hope of bearing a son, and then at Oriel, the girl-child it could not possibly be worth her brother Matthew's while to publicly acknowledge.

So this was Quentin.

Evangeline had offered a languid hand. "Delighted—charmed—dear Quentin. *So* like your father . . ."

"Like Rupert? Oh no—I hardly think *that* . . ." cried Letty in anguish.

"Possibly," Maud said crisply. "But with the Stangway nature . . ."

"Not the name, though," murmured Evangeline so faintly, in such the barest whisper that, unless one particularly wished to do so, one had no need to hear.

"How do you do, Mr. Saint-Charles?" Oriel had quickly inquired, her voice expertly covering her mother's in case anyone *did* feel obliged to take up the challenge.

"How do you do, Miss Blake." The voice was neutral and restrained, the handclasp brief and no warmer than politeness demanded, the eyes clear-sighted, she felt no doubt, but of a color too nondescript—or too subtle, perhaps—to be remembered. Not a handsome young man by any standards having, indeed, the same elongated, overbred greyhound look as the Reverend Saint-Charles, his father, and the four or five of his brothers she had already met. Although, unlike them, he was immaculate in every detail of his dress, a "laundress's miracle" she knew Evangeline would call him, of starched white linen and dark-gray, vaguely clerical broadcloth.

Did he intend, perhaps, to replace his reverend and somewhat ineffective father at the vicarage? But his ardent mother soon dispelled any notion of that.

"You will have heard," she told Evangeline, "of his honors degree from Cambridge and of all the high opinions—truly golden opinions—his tutors had of him? Yes, I know Matthew will have told you all about it. And of the letters I had, from Cambridge, telling me how they expect great things of him in the future—in absolutely any direction he might choose to apply himself. Such a *true* scholar, they said. A real academic yet with a flair for such things as mathematics and business—which so rarely go together . . ."

"Mother . . ." Had Quentin Saint-Charles, in his attempt to restrain his parent, noticed the amusement in Evangeline? Or did he, perhaps, feel a shade uncomfortable about accepting Letty's adoration in the presence of his brothers and sisters who, although sitting nearby, were as far removed from her attention as if they had been in Timbuctoo?

"Mother—I am sure Mrs. Blake has no interest . . ." But Letty, on this one topic, was well-nigh unmanageable.

"Of course she has—for she knew you as a baby when she was still living as companion to that old widow woman in Bishop Blaize Street—can it be twenty-four years ago? Indeed it must, since you will be twenty-five this month. And she must often have wondered how you were getting on. Have you not, Evangeline?"

Evangeline, for a moment, had looked puzzled, as if at a loss to understand how Letty could suspect her of any such thing. And then—as an act of kindness, her manner implied—she nodded her head.

"Yes, Letty dear—*so* often."

Letty, despite her billowing, flowering skirts, her fringed shawl, her lace cap and mittens, her several dozen petticoats, had looked quite naked in her triumph.

"There you are, Quentin. He is always imagining people do not wish for news of him—when it is no such thing. A day never passes without somebody coming running to me to sing his praises. One could blush to hear it—except that it is all so true. So Mrs. Blake will be very pleased to hear how well you are getting on with Mr. Price. Titus Price, Evangeline—Matthew's lawyer—you certainly know him. Quentin has quite taken over his practice . . ."

"*Mother!*"

But Letty, swept on by this one passion of her life, this one devotion, was unabashed.

"But *yes*— you must allow me, Quentin dear, to be just a little better informed, sometimes, than you are yourself. And Mr. Price is grateful to me, Evangeline—he said as much— for pointing Quentin in his direction. 'Dear Mrs. Saint-Charles, I only wonder how I ever managed without him . . .'" —he said that to me only the other afternoon when I happened to meet him in Piece Hall Square. Sharp as a box of carving knives, he called you, Quentin—a phrase which even I, who had not heard it before, could easily understand to be a compliment. Since with lawyers it must be the sharper the better—surely?"

"Oh—surely." Evangeline's voice had rippled with the amusement of a purring cat.

"Quentin will do very well for himself," said Maud, intending everybody—particularly Evangeline—to take her word for it.

"Poor Letty," Evangeline had remarked airily as she and Oriel were being driven back to their lodgings in Hepplefield. "To hear her prattle on, one would think she had no other son but this marvelous Quentin. When, in fact, she has five others and nearly as many daughters. How his brothers must hate him. And his father too, I dare say—if he can find the energy."

"I suppose so, Mama.

"Did you hate him, Oriel?"

"Hardly . . ."

Wrapped in the aura of his mother's hysterical devotion it had been difficult even to see him clearly; just a tall, pale young man with those oddly transparent eyes, saying only what one wished to hear, watching his own advantage, guarding his back, taking all the precautions to ensure his own survival that Oriel took herself, but, in his case, taking them coldly. And sharply, she supposed, like those carving knives his employer had spoken of. Could her mother be thinking of him as a possible son-in-law?

"He has no money, Mama, and no position," she quickly said, such things, in Oriel's experience, being the warp and weft of marriages.

"Exactly, my darling. Which is why his mother, and his dear Aunt Maud, are so anxious to get him some. His Uncle Matthew's money and position, in fact, which can only be done by marrying him to Uncle Matthew's daughter—our little Kate. Thus making him master of everything his Uncle Matthew has put together—except my widow's portion—whenever Uncle Matthew should happen to die. And even before that sorry event—well—such a marriage would not suit *us*, of course, Oriel—would it, darling? *We* should not be pleased to have Letty running in and out of High Grange Park as if she owned it—backed up in everything by Maud, who thinks it all belongs to her in any case. You do see, dearest—I know—that one has to give such constant thought to one's own position. And just what would my position be—or yours—should Letty's razor-sharp Quentin become master of High Grange? No—no—we must apply ourselves to finding Kate a husband rather more sympathetic to *our* cause than that. It does not shock you—does it, my darling?—to hear me making my little arrangements for a comfortable widowhood even before I have quite become a wife?''

"Of course not, Mama.''

For what, after all, had ever shocked Oriel Blake, brought up in the midst of Evangeline's necessities, guarded by her polished shell, her air of distant serenity, her smile?

"Good girl.'' Evangeline had expected no less. "Then—since you will be very much in the company of Kate Stangway, and Quentin too, I suppose, from now on, should you hear the very faintest tinkling of wedding bells you will be sure to let me know? Absolutely at once.''

It was neither an order nor a request, simply a statement of the alliance formed, for their mutual survival, by their two closely related selves. Not a bond of affection precisely but an acknowledgment that their lives would always be bound to run, more or less smoothly, together. "I *am* fortunate in my daughter,'' agreed Evangeline, whereas to Oriel such matters as good fortune or bad became irrelevant before the simple truth that Evangeline was the only mother she had.

Not perfect, of course. But then, who *was* perfect, whose motives *were* entirely spotless, what *would*, indeed, have become of Evangeline during those haphazard years of waiting and wandering if—with Oriel's help—she had not taken such good care of herself? And since it could never be considered proper in a daughter to judge a parent in any case, Oriel had taken up residence at High Grange Park with her eyes wide open, her ears alert, her senses as finely tuned as Maud's and

her mother's to pick up the faintest nuance of anything which
might prove a threat to herself and Evangeline.

A path of eggshells, many of them treacherous and sharp-
sided, which she had been treading—head high, back straight,
calmly smiling—for the whole of her remembered life, her
careful, watchful feet taking her through her mother's new
home smoothly, causing no ripples, no stir. And it was soon
clear to her that the true stranger in the house of Matthew
Stangway was Matthew Stangway himself.

The house, when he inherited it, had been old and bare
and in decay. Her mother, she knew, had taken a certain
pleasure in telling her that. The roof had leaked, the resulting
damp causing damage to priceless antique Chinese wallpa-
pers, and to even more priceless tapestries woven by medieval Stangway hands as decorations for the great hall. The
carpets had been full of holes, torn no doubt by booted and
spurred Stangway heels, but a constant danger, nevertheless,
to any running servant who caught a foot in them. The drawing-room chairs had sagged, the stairs—of which there were
several, the house having been added to without any particular plan, to suit the varying needs of the generations—had
all creaked. There had been loose boards in places along the
unlit rabbit-warren of upper corridors which had caused
somebody or other to turn an ankle every day of the week.
A fungus had appeared in a sinister patch along the wall of
the Long Gallery, between the portrait of a Stangway Master
of Foxhounds in strident hunting pink, and a Stangway
"younger son" in hair powder and brocade, who had seen
service with the East India Company. Even the weaponry
above the fireplace in the hall had started to rust, the massive
family silver to lose heart and begin to blacken.

Eva Kessler's dowry had put an end to all that but only in
accordance with the decree of Eva Kessler's father—shrewd
wool merchant of Hepplefield, Bradford, and Hamburg—that
since he, in effect, would be paying the bills, then *his* taste
should prevail. And, to suit his own nature, he had chosen
rich, important pieces of furniture which would hold their
value, velvet chairs with massive claw-and-ball feet and a
great deal of carved mahogany, china in substantial quantities
fresh from its Dresden makers, crystal which bore no mon-
ogram but the aura of Kessler gold, a grand piano of impres-
sive proportions which had necessitated some alterations to

the drawing-room, and which only his daughter knew how to play.

He had torn out old woodwork and old banisters, no matter how many generations of Stangway hands had brushed against them, and put in new. He had refused to pay out the fortune it would cost to restore the wonderful hand-painted Chinese pagodas and mandarins and concubines on the drawing-room walls and had had the whole room replastered and done over in fashionable, by no means guaranteed to last a century, watered-silk. He had cured the spreading fungus in the Long Gallery and hung watered-silk on the walls there too, replacing, everywhere, the iron wall-brackets and their guttering candles with crystal chandeliers to match the ones he had had specially brought over from Bohemia for his own house in Hepplefield.

He had created, in the antique shell of the Stangway home, a luxurious, impersonal, possibly salable—had the necessity ever arisen—hotel, as alien to Matthew Stangway as the Kessler woman he had married. But by the time the coal revenues had started to come in and he could have afforded to throw out all the silk and crystal and millmaster's mahogany and go back to the oak and pewter and musty tapestries of his childhood, somehow both the disgust and the desire had failed him. And he had left well enough—if one could call it that—alone.

The house belonged to him, of course. Not he to the house. And his assembled family—Evangeline and Oriel now among them—were spared only carefully rationed measures of his time throughout the day. Ten minutes for those who wished to join him for breakfast in the South parlor, although Evangeline, from the start, had seen no reason to change her habit of breakfasting—on tea, hot lemon juice, dry toast—in bed. A further ten minutes in the afternoon, two or three times a week, as a concession to Evangeline's quite natural desire to give her tea-time guests at least a glimpse of conjugal felicity. An often uncomfortable quarter of an hour in the drawing-room before dinner, should he happen to be dining at home. Dinner itself, during which he had little to say and no apparent disposition to listen. A few moments more for anyone who could catch him alone after the port and cigars on his way to the gun-room where he often spent his evenings. Apart from which one saw him, by appointment only, in the square, heavily paneled book-room, rich with the odors of tobacco and the gold-tooled volumes of the classics, bound in dark brown leather and all of them unread, which had been provided—as decoration it seemed—by Josef Kessler.

Or else, in cases of some urgency, one inquired his whereabouts from his nephew, Quentin Saint-Charles, who, apart from his invaluable services to his Uncle Matthew's solicitor Mr. Titus Price, appeared to hold some kind of unofficial appointment as private secretary to the master of High Grange himself.

"And where would my husband be hiding this fine afternoon, Quentin my dearest?" Evangeline would inquire, to be informed in precise although possibly not always truthful accents that "Uncle Matthew" was busy that day inspecting a horse, or the ledgers of Low Grange or was most urgently engaged in the business of promoting the railway which, as most people agreed, was badly needed in the Gore Valley.

"And when will he return?"

Glancing ceremoniously at his watch, his cold, light eyes unblinking, Quentin would name the exact hour. The first one, of course, that came into his head.

"What a *treasure* you are, dear Quentin. I must tell your mother to count me among the ranks of your admirers. She will be so delighted."

The pale eyes did not flicker. "I try to be of service, Aunt Evangeline."

But Evangeline's early days as mistress of High Grange were too rosy with triumph to be spoiled by the absences of the man who had shared her bed and paid her board and lodging for over twenty years. Or by the cool presence of his nephew, either, whose measure she had quickly taken. A young man as unscrupulous as herself, she judged him, and for very much the same reasons. Born with a cutting intellect, fastidious tastes, driving ambitions into a family who could not afford him, so that he would be obliged to fight every bitter inch of the road—as she had—to attain those lofty, powerful, expensive things to which he felt himself entitled.

She understood that. Had he been *her* son she would have known, far better than Letty or even Maud, how to scheme and contrive for him, how to cut corners and cut throats, if necessary, on his behalf. Just as now—since he was not her son and owed her no share of his victories—she would cut the throats of his ambitions, one by one, should they threaten her own.

Yet for the moment, with Matthew alive and well and showing no inclination to interfere in her domestic arrangements, his daughter Kate safely uncommitted to anyone in marriage, her own dear Oriel always there to be relied on, no thought of Quentin Saint-Charles could mar Evangeline's satisfaction on the morning she called the Stangway upper-servants together—butler, cook, head-parlormaid—and told them, in the presence of Maud, that, from now on, there would be many changes, the tone of her light voice suggesting clearly that *any* change, in the muddle she had uncovered, could only be an improvement. "A little organization is all it takes, I do assure you. And so we shall have organization. Set the wheels running more smoothly—generally lift up our standards. Heaven knows we can only be the better for it. And in no time at all we shall have everything going like clockwork again. You may take my word for it. You will all come to me, of course, without the least hesitation, the moment any little difficulties arise. And should I happen to be not at home or engaged otherwise, you may take instructions from my daughter, Miss Blake . . . Oh yes . . ." And she directed a dazzling smile at Maud. "My daughter is young, you might think, to be burdened with such responsibility. But she has lived very much in the great world—as not all unmarried ladies have been privileged to do—and knows exactly how to go on. My daughter is absolutely to be relied upon."

"So-like-you-in-every-way," jerked out Maud, as rigid, in her fury, as a marionette.

"Oh dearest—how sweet of you to say so—I am so pleased. But just let me say one thing more—to Cook this time. Dear Mrs.—Loudon, isn't it?—oh, *Lowther*, I do beg your pardon. Dear Mrs. Lowther—thank you for a truly succulent roast beef last night—and Wednesday night too, I seem to remember—and the vegetables so very fresh from the garden, I feel certain. So plainly dressed too, which—I absolutely agree—may be quite the thing for healthy young appetites such as—well, every single one of the many Misses Saint-Charles and their various brothers. They *did* tuck in, I noticed. But the guests I shall be inviting from now on will be rather less famished—my dear Mrs. Lowther—and considerably more discerning. You will see to it, I know, and get out your more adventurous recipes? Delicacy, I think, rather than just—bulk?''

Maud, a stainless virgin in her physical inclinations but a warrior-mother in her heart, watched the offended Mrs. Lowther withdraw and then turned at once to Evangeline, who certainly awaited her.

"Do I understand that my Saint-Charles nephews and nieces—your husband's close family—are no longer welcome here?"

Evangeline smiled very slowly, visibly wondering what Maud would dare to do about it if they were not.

"My dear—of course they are welcome. Although perhaps not quite so often and absolutely not *en masse*. One rather fears to overwhelm one's other guests. Do you suppose that Lowther woman can cope? I find her menus uninspired, to say the least."

"She has been here, without complaint, for fifteen years."

"Really?" Evangeline was clearly surprised that Matthew, at least, had been able to bear it. "Then perhaps she would be glad to make a change. No doubt a simpler household would suit her best. Is there anything else you particularly wished to say to me—Maud dear?"

"There is."

"Ah—yes?"

"It simply occurs to me that—since you are set on giving some share of household responsibility to your daughter—that you should do the same to Kate. It will be *her* house, one day, after all."

Evangeline smiled. "Dear Maud," she said. "Did you really think I had forgotten that?"

Indeed, who could forget the whirlwind that, descending on the household at breakfast time, would continue to blow hot and cold, fast and furious, throughout the day. Kate, bringing chaos in the untidy folds of her skirts, strewing hairpins and ribbons and odd wisps of fur and leaf and feather in her wake, mud on the soles of her shoes, the hem of her dress damp and torn and coming down. Where *had* she been?

"Up a tree, Aunt Maud."

"Are you being insolent, child?"

"I expect so."

She usually was. Indiscreet too, unpredictable, full of nervous fits and starts. So like her mother, thought Letty who

did not really wish to be unkind, and Maud to whom un-
kindness came fairly naturally.

"Can't stop a moment, Aunt Letty. I'm just off to Arabia
on a camel."

This, spoken at the top of her voice, in Letty's drawing-
room one day at tea-time, with half the parish gossips looking
on, elderly spinster ladies, most of them, with nothing else
to do but remember how restless and careless Eva Kessler
had been, how prone to sit like an awkward schoolboy, twisting her thick, dark hair in an irritable hand, and then go
suddenly rushing off, like Kate, with no proper explanation.

By camel to Arabia! Letty, shuddering slightly, could well
imagine Eva Kessler saying something like that. Could imagine her doing it, if Matthew had not managed, through the
years, to restrain her to a point where—at least—there had
been no more embarrassing remarks and hectic comings and
goings. Just the disconcerting, *listening* silence into which
she increasingly fell, her eyes half-closed, her mouth muti-
nous, or sarcastic.

Like Kate. What a terrible, tormenting, tragically *essential*
wife she would be to Quentin.

"Do sit up, Kate dear," Letty reprimanded her one day in
the South parlor at High Grange. "A lady never leans her
back against the back of her chair."

"Why not, Aunt Letty?"

"Oh—" Letty had never been a match for her. "It is just
that no lady ever does. It is how one tells a lady apart from
someone who is—well—*not* so . . . ."

"Oh. I see." Kate, in this mood, always sounded agreeable. "Thank you, Aunt Letty. I had not realized it was so
easy. Being a lady, I mean."

"Dearest . . . ?"

"Yes. What a relief. Knowing all one has to do is not lean
on chairs . . ."

"Kate." They had all known, of course, that Maud would
intervene. "You are insolent again. Go to your room and stay
there."

"Oh . . ." Kate's dark, fine-boned head tilted to one side,
making a decision where none—surely?—ought to be needed.
Since it was a standard punishment, after all, to which young
persons in general, and Kate Stangway very much in particular, were quite accustomed.

"I don't think I will," she said.

"Are you defying me, child?" No one—except Oriel perhaps—quite believed it. But once again the dark head tilted to one side, slowly considering.

"Do you know, Aunt Maud, I believe I am. Perhaps I won't go to my room. And what I wonder—yes, really I do—is how you can make me?"

She was not the only one who wondered, Letty appearing shocked and definitely tearful, Evangeline very much amused, Oriel appearing to notice nothing amiss as Maud rose to her feet, her back taut and dangerous as a hot poker, knowing full well—as they all knew—that she could not let this pass.

"What can I do? I can inform your father, for one thing. In fact I feel I must do so . . ."

"Oh, Aunt Maud." Kate sounded almost disappointed, as if she had expected Maud to do better than that. "Tell my father? And what will *he* do? Tell you to deal with me yourself—as he always has—as you always have . . ."

"Yes. And it has never been a pleasure, Kate."

"No, Aunt Maud. It hasn't. I agree with that."

No one in the tense, astounded parlor had ever heard a young lady speak with such defiance, such open contempt, to an adult. Letty, indeed, had not thought such a thing to be possible, while Evangeline simply remarked, with some satisfaction, that no one had ever spoken like that to *her*.

Nor to Maud either, until now, in this too public place, with Letty absolutely relying on her to deal with it, Evangeline hoping smugly that she could not, the parlormaid, who had just come in with the tea-tray, standing there all agog. And that dark, Kessler stare asking her, all over again, the same question.

"I don't think I will go to my room. And if that's what I decide, how can you compel me?"

And for good measure Kate got to her feet, reminding Maud that although not tall and with no weight anywhere about her, she was, nevertheless, too strong now at just eighteen, too agile, too *fierce*, perhaps, to be picked up—screaming, she well remembered—and carried upstairs to be locked away, without a candle, behind her bedroom door. Or to be led there, blanched by temper and horror—since she was afraid of the dark—with Maud's hard fingers pinching her ear.

She put her hand to her ear now, recalling the tugging pain: and smiled.

"I rather think—Aunt Maud—that I shall go where I please."

Because not even Maud Stangway, in all her wrath, could really order the footmen to take, one by the shoulders, one by the ankles, their master's only legitimate child and bear her—kicking, no doubt, and caterwauling—away. They all knew that.

"I pity you, child," Maud hissed at her, goaded by the sheer weight of her mortification, to cruelty.

"No—no—Aunt Maud. I don't think so."

But Maud, seasoned campaigner, came back at her now like a whiplash. "*Anyone* would pity you, Kate. In fact everybody does so. Burdened as you are by such an inheritance . . ."

And as Letty caught her breath in alarm—for Quentin's sake—at this reference to Eva Kessler's madness, and Evangeline fanned herself with a leisurely hand, Kate shrugged her thin shoulders and did one more thing not expected of a young lady. She grinned.

"Ah yes—my inheritance—you mean this house, of course, don't you, Aunt Maud? And the pit. And all my mother's money."

Steadily rather than defiantly she gathered up her torn skirts and left the room, not oversetting anything but leaving behind her the impression that she had.

"You have done your best with her, Maud dear," said Letty. "You have nothing with which to reproach yourself."

"My word," said Evangeline archly. "How very fortunate this makes me feel, since *my* daughter has never caused me one moment of anxiety." And crossing the room in high glee, she sat down with a sudden shriek of alarm on the pincushion, sharp side up, left by Kate in what everyone knew to be Evangeline's favorite chair.

Oriel retrieved the pin-cushion and, awhile later, came upon Kate in the empty November garden, sitting like a cat in a pool of late sunshine, her back against a mossy wall, her knees tucked up to her chin. A schoolroom pose of dreaming into a guarded nursery fire had it not been for the sharp little breeze stirring through dry leaves, the low gray aspect of the winter sky.

"Kate . . . ?"

"So it is."

Had she been crying? But Oriel knew better than to ask any such thing.

"Are you not well?"

"Oh—a headache, I think. Unless the evil of my disposition is slowly poisoning me. Or Aunt Maud."

Nothing, of course, could have induced Miss Oriel Blake, in her pale blue woolen dress, to sit on the ground. Nor did she particularly like the look of the low wall with its covering of slippery moss. Yet just the same, not liking to tower above Kate who was smaller and thinner and far more vulnerable than her calm and careful self, she gathered her own skirts together gingerly and sat, in silence for a while, until Kate, very abruptly, said, "Did I win a victory just now, Oriel? Or make a fool of myself?"

"You may have done yourself harm."

"Made an enemy, you mean? Of Aunt Maud? That was done long ago—the first time she held out a charitable hand to feed me and I bit it . . . You would never have done that, Oriel, would you?"

"No." Oriel smiled. "I would have lacked the courage."

"You may have had more sense. I've watched you, Oriel, defending yourself by being always beyond reproach."

"And I've watched you, setting out to be a thorn in their sides. They won't like you for it."

"Does that matter? Being liked?"

"It makes life easier."

And they were both surprised, sitting there in the sharp-toothed, irritable wind, how easily they passed the restraints of politeness to a point where they could talk to each other.

"Is that what you want? An easy life?" And because Oriel had never quite dared to examine her desires too closely—in case there should be too wide a gulf between desire and probability—she quickly threw back the question.

"What do *you* want, Kate?"

"Oh—" The thin shoulders rose jerkily in a shrug. "To set off for Arabia on a camel."

"*Kate.*"

"Oriel—I mean it. There—or anywhere else, so long as it is far away and I can go alone. Or without Aunt Maud, at any rate. And failing that, I'd like—oh, wildly ambitious things, like not feeling uneasy at dinner if father happens to be there. Not feeling sick whenever I have a set-to with Aunt Maud. Not marrying Quentin."

"Does he want to marry you?"

"No." The reply came with another shrug and the return of her wide, boyish grin. "He wants to be rich and influential and to get away from all his hopeless brothers and sisters. I think he may want to get away from his mother, too. I suppose one can sympathize with that. So—taking into account my Kessler money and my Stangway money—marrying me to get it is a sacrifice he's quite ready to make."

"Kate . . ." Oriel, to her great astonishment, felt an urge, which almost overcame her, to reach out and touch, to ruffle the thick, unruly hair with an affectionate—a *sisterly*— hand, and then, with her own calm, quick fingers, to smooth out its tangle, tuck every haphazard wisp in place with a secure hair-pin, a prettily arranged knot of ribbon. Scarlet, she thought, against the heavy tresses which would gleam raven-black, she felt certain, with some regular brushing. And what a tiny waist Kate would have if one gave her a wider skirt to show it off, instead of the skimpy rag she was wearing that looked like a hand-me-down with its disgracefully bedraggled hem.

"They make me do my own mending," Kate said, as Oriel's eyes remained speculatively on her gown.

"So I see. If you leave that skirt in my room tonight I'll tidy it up for you."

"Why?" Kate's eyes, shooting wide open, looked suddenly hungry for a truthful answer.

"Because I would like to. Will they make you marry Quentin?"

"Aunt Maud and Aunt Letty will do their best. My father will not care. He tends not to care. It is really what he *does*. Not caring, I mean. And poor, brave Quentin, of course, will grit his teeth and march to the altar like a human sacrifice . . . and then they will all come and live here happily ever after. Except me, of course. I don't expect to be here. And what about you, Oriel? Men must always be falling in love with you. Who are you going to marry?"

And leaning forward a little, reaching out once again, Oriel spoke a cold truth into the wind.

"Falling in love is not marrying, is it? When it comes to wives, men are very careful and I—well—I shall not find it easy."

She would find, instead—as her mother had done—a host of ardent beginnings which would founder, she supposed, one after the other, on the hurdle of those questions which could not be answered, those loose ends which even in her mother's agile hands could not be tied.

She bit her lip.

"I suppose you know . . ." Kate said. "That—well—you and I?—I suppose you realize . . . ?"

"No," Oriel said gently, raising her hand palm outward to push the words away. "I know nothing about it. And neither do you. Much the best way."

"Do you believe that?"

"Of course. I have to live in the world as I find it, Kate. And I am not in the least suited, you know, to travel by camel."

Kate grinned again. "So you will just have to make sure of a comfortable coach and horses—as best you can."

And this time Oriel did reach out, smiling as she placed the tips of her fingers on the tousled crown of Kate's head, a butterfly touch, soon gone.

Dear little sister. Dear little hurt, offended soul. Words she could never bring herself to speak. She knew that.

"Give me your skirt to mend," she murmured instead. "We can't have you catching your heel and falling off your camel."

They had *not* said:

"My mother was a madwoman—or so they tell me—prowling the attic in a filthy artist's smock and painting insulting portraits of my father, who hated her. Which means that I might go mad and be hated too. So they say. How that terrifies me."

Or: "I am the illegitimate child of a scheming woman who used me—and still uses me—to lay claim to your father. Which means—in this strait-laced, self-righteous world—there is no place for me. No man to marry me. Although my mother will offer me in turn to every man who approaches, as she once offered herself. How I dread that."

They had not said: "We are sisters, with more, perhaps, than a casual tie of blood between us." Yet, beyond all question, they were in no doubt that they had heard and accepted every word.

Three

The Gore Valley was, for the most part, prone to some excitement the following spring, at the launching upon its sturdy scene of two new events, the rise of Mrs. Evangeline Stangway to the head of local society and the arrival of that modern miracle the railway. The dazzling Mrs. Stangway being welcomed by all it seemed, even by those hoping for the pleasure of seeing her fail; the railway causing far more serious and therefore even more diverting disagreement between those who wanted it—the industrialists and shopkeepers for instance—and those of a more traditional mind who did not.

A time of harsh resentment—absolutely no less—by all those to whom the railway appeared in no way a blessing. By the owners of canals, for instance, who risked serious damage to their trade in the conveying of heavy goods from industrial centers to the sea. By the landlords of coaching-inns in remote situations who, without the stage-coaches and the mail-coaches, the constant demands of travelers for bed and board and fresh horses, would see their livelihood, like the roads themselves, fall into decay. By "landed gentlemen" who, ever since the truth of what a railway actually meant had burst upon them, had set up a great caterwauling, quite often shot-gun in hand, that the infernal machines would startle their horses, disrupt the seasonal habits of their grouse and pheasant, scare off the foxes and thus ruin the hunt. By local farmers who maintained, just as stubbornly, that engine sparks would set fire to their crops and sour the milk in their cattle, causing them to abort. By certain clergymen of a pu-

44

ritanical persuasion who, being concerned above all things
with the preservation of the Sabbath, had seen in the proposed use of trains for the quick delivery of mail, a most
pernicious temptation to Sunday travel.

By Lord Merton of Merton Abbey, the greatest land-owner
in the area, whose estates included the only moorland ridge
through which the track could effectively be tunneled to join
the main-line to Leeds and who, although quite seeing the
advantage of the railway in getting himself, and his guests,
from the House of Lords or his club in St. James's Street, up
to Merton for the grouse-shooting in a few hours flat, had,
nevertheless, declined disdainfully and absolutely to allow
the foul-mouthed, iron monsters a foothold on his land.

"By all means," he had said, "run the trains to Hepplefield." Why not? Since Hepplefield, already tainted by its
factories, its steams and damps and its eternal blanket of
yellow fog, would hardly notice the addition of another metal
monster or two. No, there was nothing to spoil in Hepplefield, nor in the blasted heath around it. Nor anything that
Lord Merton himself particularly valued in the market town
of Lydwick, since the land thereabouts belonged mainly to
his cousin, who had been living abroad these twenty years.
Lydwick, therefore, might have its station and Cousin Eus-
tace his profit from the sale of the acreage to build it on, with
Lord Merton's blessing. But the parkland and woodland of
Merton, the deep meadows in the valley bottom watered to a
lush emerald by the River Gore, the neat farms and cottages,
even the desolate, rock-strewn upland that was Merton Ridge,
must remain undefiled.

No. Railways could never be the business of a gentleman.
An attitude in which Lord Merton remained unshaken, joining a great many of his fellow peers in their apprehension
about the effect these trains might have on the working classes, the opportunity offered to them by this cheap new trans-
port *to move about*, to congregate together, in fact, for the
airing of grievances and the plotting of treason. A possible
and very rapid mustering of subversive elements within the
population which could never be done effectively by stage-
coach at a rate of fifteen or so passengers a time, and at a
cost, from the rebellious North to London, of what amounted,
for a working man, to a full year's wages.

And the railways were only asking a penny a mile.

Lord Merton opposed it, therefore, and encouraged his

acquaintances, their tenants, servants and hangers-on to do the same, the Valley's "landed gentry" happily turning a blind eye to any gamekeeper who happened to take a shot at a railway engineer, mistaking him—*of course*—as he bent down in the long grass to do his measuring, for a rabbit. These "mistakes" occurring so regularly and with such painful accuracy that the first surveyor had abandoned the work altogether, while the second had employed a bare-knuckle prize-fighter to walk the route with him.

But the survey had been completed nonetheless, and parliamentary sanction eventually obtained to break into the Valley at Merton Ridge, thus proceeding through Lydwick, High Grange, and Low Grange toward Hepplefield, every millmaster on the way putting forward his claim to a station as near as possible to his factory door or a branch-line to take him and his merchandise to the precise spot where it was most profitable for them both to be. And when work finally began a great deal of the credit seemed due—and not only in the opinion of his mother—to Quentin Saint-Charles, who, it was generally believed, had earned more in legal fees, that one year, from railway business than his employer, Mr. Titus Price, had earned in twenty.

An astute young gentleman indeed, Mr. Quentin Saint-Charles, who had known, by instinct one could only assume, how to plunge into that sea of complex legal negotiations which even the whisper of a railway appeared to generate, and emerge not only unscathed but with his hands full of gold. So young too—and so *supple*—to have settled the prickly consciences of the Sabbath Day Observers by working out a timetable by which no train would arrive at any Gore Valley station during the hours of their church services, thus making it easier for them not to notice. So clever of him, too, to have tempted Lord Merton—who ought really to have been above temptation—with the offer of a special branch line to Merton village, thus giving his lordship an extremely pretty little station of his own and saving him the trouble of fetching his grouse-shooting guests by gig from Lydwick. Very clever. Even though it had been rumored, of course, that what had really put an end to his lordship's lobbying in the House of Lords to defeat the Railway Bill and his sudden decision to sell land to it instead, had been another offer—also through Mr. Saint-Charles—of at least ten times more, cash in hand, than those bleak moorland acres at Merton Ridge could ever have been worth to anybody else.

He had appeased the farming community too by pointing out to them that their milk could be moved by rail to Hepplefield at a speed which would entitle them to call it fresh and encourage suspicious city housewives to drink it. Which had been far from the case up to now. He had even gone to London, in the company of railway directors and high-ranking engineers, to present the Gore Valley's case to the Palace of Westminster, and had dined, one glorious evening, at Lord Merton's house in Grosvenor Square. An occasion to which his mother could never refer without tears of pride and joy, leaving his Aunt Maud to inform anyone who might wish to hear that, as a result of all this excellent work and the prospect of more richly deserved successes to come, his employer, Mr. Titus Price, had offered him a partnership.

A young man, then, who knew how to cut his coat in cloth of every shade of opinion and wear it to his own best advantage. A young man whose evident self-esteem Evangeline would not have cared to encourage by giving a special "railway dinner," at which he would unavoidably be among the guests of honor, had she not seen her own advantage very clear. Quentin had dined in Lord Merton's house in London, admittedly as one of a large party and on railway business rather than as a personal friend. But he *had* dined there, nevertheless, which—since Letty was clearly not up to it—would make it quite natural for her to return the invitation on Quentin's behalf. And rather difficult, moreover, for his lordship to refuse if she also invited a sufficient number of railway personnel, since he had used some of that shocking purchase price for Merton Ridge to become a rather major shareholder of the railway himself.

And although Evangeline anticipated no difficulty in making herself Queen Regnant of High Grange and its rather too near neighbor of Hepplefield, and was already a most welcome visitor in the upper echelons of Lydwick and several very pleasant "gentlemen's residences" in the villages beyond, she had failed so far to attract so much as a sign of recognition from Merton Abbey. Not that the Mertons were much in residence, being not only the greatest land-owners in the Gore Valley but the fortunate possessors of a castle in Scotland, a hunting-box in Leicestershire, a villa in Monte Carlo, a tall, Grecian-pillared house in Grosvenor Square, coming up to Merton only for Christmas, or to shoot grouse in August, with one or two brief visits in between. Great people, in fact. Very great, who might possibly condescend to invite the first lady of High Grange to one of the over-crowded impersonal receptions they gave at the Abbey, every five years or so, when they happened to remember their duty of *noblesse oblige* to the local gentry and the better half of Hepplefield.

It would not do for Evangeline.

"Lady Merton has never accepted an invitation to any house in the neighborhood," Maud told her acidly. Nor, in-deed, did she accept Evangeline's, fearing, perhaps, to open a floodgate if she did, thus making her visits to Merton wea-risome with the importunities of local squires. But Lord Mer-ton, who was pleased with his railway station since it was not just everybody who had one and had found it quite a talking point at his club, agreed not only to eat Evangeline's dinner but to have his two daughters and any friends they felt inclined to muster, to join him at High Grange for the mu-sical reception to follow.

A triumph indeed. Very nearly a social miracle. A "foot-in-the-door" of Merton Abbey, at any rate, no matter what she had to do to contrive it.

"Could it be," murmured Matthew, wicked tongue in cheek, "that his lordship has a guilty conscience? Goodness me, how middle-class."

But Evangeline, so long as his lordship sat at her table for all to see, did not care if he had become inflicted with a social disease or had lost his wits.

Cook, of course—whose name she managed never to re-member—would have to go. Cook went, to be replaced by a cadaverous woman from a domestic agency in Manchester who brought her own two kitchenmaids with her and was sufficiently secretive and superior to inspire at least a measure of confidence in Evangeline.

"I think, perhaps, nine courses, Mrs.—er, Widdop? Does that dismay you?"

"By no means, madam. And will madam be requiring two choices of soup, or three?"

Evangeline was pleased, although she settled for two soups only, a creamy, complicated asparagus, a clear beef essence heavily laced with sherry, and two fish courses, plain but perfect salmon or deviled whitebait, spreading her entrées to include beef olives, dainty little rabbit quenelles, lobster cutlets a vol-au-vent of sweetbreads and mushrooms in red wine, followed, as a fourth course, by a choice between a roast of lamb or plump capons garnished with ham and parsley and green peas.

The game dishes, of course, would be a problem. No larks until July. No woodcock or grouse until August or September. But there would be quails, she supposed?

"Certainly, madam."

"Ah yes," she sighed. "One seems hardly ever to be without them. So you will do something to them—well—a little out of the ordinary, I am sure, Mrs.—Widdop? Will you not?" While as for the sweets, a good, rich syllabub and some kind of chocolate pudding full of cream and vanilla could usually be relied on to please gentlemen, while the ladies might enjoy an orange water ice, a whisper of meringue, such fruit as might be in season. Or, better still, fruit that was not in season and could, therefore, announce itself as having been fetched, at great cost and inconvenience, from some distant greenhouse.

Oriel, of course, would decorate the table, her mother knowing no lighter hand, no keener eye than hers when it came to swathing ivy and mosses around the table silver, making garlands and posies of flowers; nothing more exotic than daffodils, redcurrant, and forsythia, she supposed, at this time of year, which Oriel would transform into nests of blossom and foliage in which to set the place-cards and menus, written in her elegant copperplate, and—naturally—in French.

And then, when the ladies had taken their coffee, the gentlemen their port, Evangeline would lead her dinner-guests to mingle with the company she had invited "for the evening": a little music in the hall, a few violins, a piano across which she had draped an antique shawl, the drawing-room left open and the chairs arranged for conversation, the library arranged for cards, a tasty little supper on the *interesting* side of midnight of oyster patties, lobster salad, cold fowl, various highly complicated trifles, a great deal of claret-cup and champagne. A feast, a frolic, of which the sole purpose was to make Lord Merton's first taste of High Grange so agreeable that he would come to sip and sample it again. And bring his wife.

Dress—needless to say—was an immense preoccupation.

"It would be rather interesting," she murmured to Oriel,

"if we could wear identical gowns, you and I—or very nearly. A positive froth of gauze for the skirt and almost no bodice to speak of. Bare shoulders just rising out of the foam—very enticing. Me in black and you in white. Yes? But too daring—alas—for the Gore Valley. Or, at least—until one knows the Mertons rather better. So—perhaps silvery gray with pearls? For me, that is."

Inviting several Hepplefield dressmakers to attend her at High Grange, she made her selection and ordered a "modest" dress of silver tissue, a flowing skirt which gleamed and swayed, a bodice which covered but did not conceal the wineglass stem of her waist, the full breast, the regal arch of her back.

"I expect you will think it too plain," she said on the day the dress was delivered, posing before Oriel who knew it to be no such thing, and Kate who did not seem to notice.

"Beautiful, Mama."

"Yes. And what do *you* think, Kate dear?" Kate looked at her, frowning, honestly considering.

"I'll tell you . . ."

"Please do."

"It looked like nothing at all when it came out of the box . . ."

"And now?"

It was an enchantment, a display of wickedly enticing skill which would make other women appear overdressed, full-blown, dismally run-of-the-mill. They all knew it. Was Kate so unwilling, then, to admit the fascinations of her stepmama? Evangeline gave her purring smile, moving imperceptibly so that the skirt rippled and glinted, releasing a scent of magnolia.

"You look magnificent," Kate snapped at her. "How do you do it?"

"Oh—my dear—" Evangeline was amused and very well satisfied. "One learns to know oneself. One creates an illusion. *Now*—let me create one for you. Both of you. White, of course. What else? And you must make the most of it while you can, for the time is not long. It ought to be forbidden, in my view, to any woman over twenty-five. Oh yes—for I have seen no one past that age with the teeth or the skin to cope with it. The bloom fades, my children—so 'gather ye white dresses while ye may' is my advice to you. *White*—with hints of pastel. The only thing."

For Oriel, certainly. But the same billowing yards of white silk, the same frills of fluted chiffon which made Oriel appear to be moving at the center of a graceful cloud, seemed somehow to engulf Kate, to become a burden she carried unwillingly so that, from the first fitting, the frills, the puffed sleeves, the vast skirt looped up at the hem with white rosebuds over white chiffon, seemed to droop, and then to wilt, with her spirits. She did not like the dress. But because she did not know why, she kept silent, grew inattentive, lost interest entirely, so that she was late for her fittings, awkward in the dressmaker's hands, and, on one occasion, did not come at all.

"Then we must proceed without her," said Evangeline, who had been doing exactly that from the start. "One assumes—one hopes—although with Kate one can never be certain—that she may have some little ideas of her own about the trimming. But since she is not here to express them then—well—yes—white on white, I think is best. So just do it like my daughter's . . ."

"Mama." Oriel had been waiting for her opportunity. "Is it necessary for us to be dressed alike?"

Evangeline smiled. "Oh yes, dear. Very necessary."

"Why, Mama? Since we are so different to look at, it seems—unfair."

"Unfair? To whom?" Evangeline smiled again. "Not to you, dear Oriel."

"No, Mama. *Not* to me. People are bound to notice."

Evangeline's eyes narrowed and then opened wide with a sudden, feline gleam. "Yes, Oriel. Exactly. People *will* notice. And what will they see? That I have spent exactly the same on both dresses, down to the last silk ribbon and the last seed-pearl on the bodice—should anyone care to count them. That I have not favored *my* daughter . . ."

"You have favored me, Mama."

"Of course I have." Evangeline was crisp, now, with impatience. "Naturally. It is called the art of survival. Or just plain common-sense. You know that as well as I. So let us say no more about it. There is a great deal still to do. I am not quite happy with the table plan. If you could write out a list of who is to go in to dinner with whom and give it to Matthew, so he can learn it and get everybody together with the right partners at least ten minutes before dinner is announced, then that would be a help. I simply cannot bear to see people hanging around like lost sheep, not knowing with whom they are supposed to walk to table. So sloppy. Do see to it, Oriel.''

The guest list itself had not been the work of a moment.

"Dear Evangeline is giving a dinner for Quentin," breathed Letty to all her acquaintances, as if Evangeline had experienced a sudden conversion to the true faith.

"My brother, Matthew, is entertaining some railway people," Maud declared bluntly to several friends of her own who had not been invited, knowing she had been asked herself only as the inevitable spinster "sister-at-home," and to balance the ratio of male to female caused by the absence of Lady Merton.

Not that Evangeline intended Maud to walk in to dinner with Lord Merton, of course. Nor with the famous railway engineer Mr. Morgan de Hay, who was far too interesting and important a gentleman to be wasted on Maud. Nor with the railway contractor, Mr. Garron Keith, either, who, being newly rich and consequently rather common, might prove a difficult dinner partner and had better be left to Oriel. Kate, of course, would partner Quentin. There seemed no help for it and no great harm in it either from Evangeline's always well-calculated viewpoint, since she was well aware by now both of Kate's aversion to her cousin, and at Quentin's cool tolerance of her. Which left two very self-important, enormously wealthy directors of the railway company who could partner each other's expensive wives, and a third director, apparently a bachelor, less affluent or perhaps simply less inclined to mention it so often, who could partner Maud. Letty and Rupert Saint-Charles she decided to place together to save anyone else the bother of putting up with them. Matthew, of course, would give his arm to Mrs. Morgan de Hay as the most notable lady present, which would leave the great engineer himself to . . . ? Oriel? The obvious choice. Certainly it would have to be a member of the family, for Mr. Morgan de Hay, now that engineers were becoming so very much the fashion, had developed a most precise opinion of his own worth. Who else, therefore, would do him sufficient honor but a daughter of the house? Oriel. Or Kate, whom Evangeline neither trusted nor wished to bring forward. Or Evangeline herself, who would be far too fully occupied with Lord Merton. Oriel, then. Although it meant the inconvenience of finding some other female for the contractor, the difficult Mr. Keith. Someone of only moderate consequence about whom there was no need to worry should the man offend her.

"It will have to be one of Letty's dreary daughters," she told Oriel. "The eldest, I suppose, so as not to cause a revolution. Is her name Constantia? Oh—is she the married one? Absolutely *not*, since Letty would expect me to invite the husband as well. Susannah, then. A perfect goose, as I recall, who will be scared silly—or sillier—by this Mr. Garron Keith, who is—well—not the kind of man she is used to seeing at the vicarage. Nor the kind of man I am particularly anxious to see here, to be strictly honest."

"Then why invite him, Mama?"

Evangeline shrugged light shoulders, dismissing the very sizable Mr. Garron Keith, who had arrived only very recently with his army of laborers, his picks and shovels, his kegs of gunpowder, his teams of heavy horses, to blast his way through Merton Ridge into the Valley and lay down the track as far as Hepplefield, as a mere irrelevance.

"Because, my dear, since it *is* a railway dinner, one hardly knew how to exclude him. One even felt that if one did so he just might arrive in any case. He has that kind of air about him."

"Poor Susannah."

"Indeed. She will not have the least idea how to talk to him. One of Letty's little lambs to the slaughter, I fear. Unless—yes, I will sit you on Mr. Keith's other side, Oriel, so that you can rescue her from him, every now and then, and *him* from total boredom, I dare say. Although you must take care not to neglect Mr. Morgan de Hay, who is altogether a gentleman, and will feel entitled—one rather imagines—to your full attention. You will manage it all very smoothly, dearest. I am not in the least worried about you."

"Thank you, Mama."

"Thank Heaven," said Kate, coming to Oriel's room on the great evening, "that I only have to contend with Quentin, who will just ignore me. I have come to see how lovely you look."

Very lovely, in fact, with the graceful white dress floating around her, her bare shoulders with a bloom on them like cream velvet, the startling contrast of a black velvet ribbon around her long neck, clusters of pearl and jet beads in her ears, black ribbons and pearl pins in the complicated coils

and ringlets of her silver hair which, piled high on the crown
of her head, made her even taller, even more of a fine-boned,
pure-bred swan than ever.

"Oriel—you—are—so—beautiful." Kate, giving each word
a separate emphasis, was stating a fact, telling a truth, her
keen, dark eyes staring, assessing, in a way Oriel had found
unnerving until she had realized it was the way in which other
people examined a work of art. A garden statue, she thought
wryly, in cool marble which could be animated at will—not
always *her* will, either—to write place-cards and arrange
flowers, to share herself evenly between two difficult dinner-
partners who might flake off little pieces of her as they chose,
since it was only marble after all.

"Thank you, Kate."

"Lord, don't thank me. I didn't make you beautiful. You
do it yourself, don't you? I mean—well, yes, you have lovely
fair hair and big blue eyes and good skin, but so do lots of
other people and they don't look like you. You have something *else*, Oriel. Do you know what it is?"

"Oh—one creates an illusion . . ."

Kate wrinkled her nose. "Your mother says that."

"My mother *does* that."

"Yes. But not you. I think it's something you *have*."

"Like the measles?"

"Well—maybe. But I wish *I* had it, that's all. I don't know
how I ought to look, or how I want to look. I just know I'm
wrong. I don't know which dress I ought to be wearing—
except that it shouldn't be this one."

Oriel, slowly and calmly, looked at the dress, taking in the
white ribbons and white beading on white silk, the pure elegance which was, at the same time, too big and too civilized, too pale, too much the stuff of classical garden statues
for Kate.

"Well—yes," she said, as if it had just this minute
occurred to her. "Perhaps it does need a little something . . . ?"

"I know." Kate had no hesitation. "It needs you inside
it."

"Well—let's see . . ." Oriel, moving slowly, apparently in
deep contemplation, opened a drawer and began to look
through it very much at random until, finding the very thing
she had put there to be found, she made an exclamation she

hoped Kate would mistake for surprise, and produced a sash in vibrant, scarlet satin.

"This might do it, Kate. What do you think? I had it once on a dress of mine—oh, ages ago . . ."

It was, of course, brand new, purchased by Oriel a week ago in Hepplefield when, having managed to evade her mother's scrutiny long enough to slip unobserved into the silk mercer's shop, she had been caught coming out and, in response to Evangeline's desire to know what she was up to, had told a swift tale of ribbons glimpsed in the window which, on closer examination, had proved not to match. A breathless moment.

"Indeed?"

She did not think her mother had believed her. But the shop had been crowded, making a discreet inquiry difficult, and Evangeline, who would have been far more likely to suspect her daughter of wishing to snatch a few moments alone with a young man than of helping Kate, had let it pass.

And now here it was, long and very wide, the vivid fabric reducing Kate's waist to fairytale proportions as Oriel quickly wound it around her, its fringed ends making a swirl of wild scarlet to the hem of her dress, an odd effect, perhaps, but one which, instead of whispering "Evangeline" now boldly stated "Kate." Or would do so, in a minute or two, when Oriel had done with her.

"I have some scarlet ribbons somewhere too, I seem to remember—oh yes—what luck. We'd better have you all to match, I suppose."

And, having deliberately chosen to wait until this last moment when there would be no time for anyone—Maud or Evangeline—to send Kate back upstairs to change, Oriel, working quickly now, brought out ribbons, combs, pins, brushed out the fussy, far too girlish ringlets into which Evangeline's maid had dressed Kate's hair, and piled it, instead, as high and smooth as she could on Kate's suddenly Oriental head, the weight of it lengthening her eyes, heightening her cheekbones, the coarse dark hair itself turning to ebony as Oriel threaded the chignon through with scarlet satin and scattered it with glowing, enameled pins like a swarm of fireflies.

"There. That's better."

Not beautiful, perhaps. But, more distinctly than ever,

could be heard that statement of identity. *Kate*. No other woman in the room tonight would look like her.

"Kate . . . ?"

But, staring at herself in Oriel's long mirror, Kate did not move, wholly intent upon her own reflection, her slanting eyes black in the candlelight, her pointed, finely carved face a warm bronze against the vivid contrast of scarlet and white, her head, with its high-crowned ebony hair that of a young and very fragile Egyptian Pharaoh, disturbingly neither entirely female nor male.

"I think," she said, as drowsily as a sleepwalker, "that I look quite nice . . ."

"Yes, Kate. You look quite nice."

Dear little sister, "nice" is not the word for you. Nor "little" either, in your bold, bright scarlet. If we have created your illusion now—together—then I am happy for you. And happy for me, if I have found a real use for all my precious, drawing-room talents at last. Dear sister.

The words of her mind only, quickly suppressed as Kate swung around and caught her hands in a grip fierce enough to hurt.

"*Why?*"

And her voice, like her hot, dry hands, seemed explosive with an emotion from which Oriel instantly retreated into the defense of laughter.

"Good heavens, Kate, such a fuss about a few yards of satin . . ."

"Why, Oriel?"

"Whatever do you mean?"

"I mean you never wore scarlet in your life—did you? I mean you didn't just *have* this sash and these firefly pins and ribbons lying in a drawer. I mean you went down to Hepplefield behind your mother's back . . ."

"Kate—you really ought to know me better than that. *Me*—the very soul of obedience . . ."

". . . and bought them with your pin-money, which *means* you must have done without something yourself, since I know they don't give you much . . ."

"Yes, indeed. Such a sacrifice." Oriel's voice was light, her eyes deliberately teasing, although behind them she was well aware of the sting of tears. "I went without my dinner for a fortnight. Don't you see I am half-starved?"

But the starvation was in Kate, the fierce hunger for affection, a need frozen by her father, unnoticed perhaps by her mother, which came pouring out of her now like a hiss of anguish.

"Don't *you* see, Oriel—don't you—that no one has ever taken trouble before . . ." And because she was on the very brink of saying "Oriel, I love you," Oriel smiled, shook her head, clicked her tongue, and scuttled once again—as a matter of some urgency this time—into laughter.

"What nonsense. Aunt Maud is always troubling you."

"I'll never forget this, Oriel. I never will."

Dear little sister, little again now in your need to be loved. Very small in your fear that because these first giants in your life, your father—and mine—and his dry sister, have never loved you, that it means you are not fit to be loved at all. That because they have rejected you then the whole world must follow suit. I know. I understand. But—just the same— don't leave yourself so undefended, don't open yourself so wide at the first touch. Don't wear your heart on your sleeve like this—dear little sister—or somebody will surely break it. I know. Believe me. I understand.

"What a goose you are, Kate," she lightly said.

Four

They went down to the drawing-room together, Oriel safely intact inside her fine, pale shell, Kate's crackling excitement converting itself into the entirely natural and wholesome glow of a young woman about to make an entrance and knowing she is looking her best. Kate. Not Eva Kessler's daughter, nor that awkward, ungrateful thorn in the side of "poor, long-suffering Maud." But Kate Stangway, at ease in her own skin at last.

A revelation.

"My word," murmured Evangeline. "Busy little hands *have* been at work, I see. Kate dear—is it really you? Or one of those illusions we were speaking of?"

"Very nice," said Matthew Stangway going through the motions of looking them both over without seeing either, even when Kate stepped directly in front of him in her swirl of scarlet and snow-white and made him a low curtsy.

"What is the matter?" he demanded sharply, not expecting, one felt, that it could be anything pleasant.

"Just—good evening, Father."

Her voice was bright and perfectly steady, but she was really crying out to him "Look at me, Father. Notice me." Was she even asking him to love her? Oriel thought so.

"Good evening, Kate," he said.

She smiled, nodded, and moved on.

"Good evening, Aunt Maud." And this time the tilt of her high-piled, ebony and scarlet head was plainly inquiring "And what have *you* to say to me?"

58

"Just remember what I told you," snapped Maud; a token reprimand.

"What was that, Aunt Maud?"

"Not to disgrace yourself again by eating cheese. No lady ever does so in public. And no game either. It lingers on the breath."

Once again Kate smiled, nodded, and moved on.

"Hello, Aunt Letty."

"Oh—Kate." Letty, in bunchy chiffon with lace frills and a great many lace-edged bows, gave a startled little jump, rather as if Kate had bitten her. "You have done your hair differently, dear, haven't you?"

"I have, Aunt Letty. Don't you positively adore it?" Letty blinked, startled once more. "Yes—yes, dear. Indeed. Very nice. Very—well . . ." "Foreign" was the word she was searching for, "strange" the word which sprang into her mind. Followed by "odd," like Eva, who had had some foreign blood in her somewhere, one seemed to remember. "Is it not rather too *straight*, dear?" she murmured feebly, her own concept of beauty being the pretty pink and white of her own girlhood.

"I am not the curly kind, Aunt Letty."

"Oh—I see—" Had Kate said something rude? Without at all knowing why, Letty felt sure she had. Ought she, perhaps, to issue a reprimand? Oh dear—how difficult it all was. But then, miraculously, as the door opened again to admit Quentin, her spirits lifted to a height where none of it—whatever it was—could possibly matter. "Quentin—*dearest*—we have been waiting for you."

"With bated breath," murmured Evangeline.

"Quite so," said Kate and, carefully picking up her skirts, she very deliberately moved her bold scarlet satin, her firefly-studded head, *herself*, as far away from him as she possibly could.

Little sister, learn to bend, as I do. Learn to sway with every wind. Because what happens to winds? They blow themselves out, don't they? And then—if you're not brittle and broken—you can get up again. To sway with the next one. And the one after. Like me.

But as the guests began to arrive, Oriel's tasks were too many and various to allow her to keep watch on Kate. Mr. Morgan de Hay, the railway engineer, taking it for granted during the half hour before the announcement of dinner that her attention belonged entirely to him. Miss Blake, he believed, would be most anxious to hear his views on industrial architecture? She heard them. *"Do* please go on," she breathed, knowing there was every likelihood of it, her eyes wandering, without appearing to do so, to see if her mother needed help with Lord Merton who had turned out to be an unremarkable little man with the same, washed-out, well-bred greyhound look as Letty's husband, the Reverand Rupert Saint-Charles. Except that his lordship, of course, was very rich and very powerful and had the added fascination of being thought somewhat too rakish and high-living to suit the taste of Queen Victoria's young, and rather pious, husband.

"The girl was right as ninepence," Oriel heard him braying to Evangeline—*"the girl"* she assumed being England's reigning queen—"until she got herself mixed up with the Coburgs. Jolly little thing, she used to be, just like her royal uncles—God rest the scoundrels—until Albert the Good came along and turned the whole palace into something between a chapel and a nursery. Never go to court myself nowadays, Mrs. Stangway, if I can help it . . . ."

Unless, of course, the good Albert no longer cared to invite him?

He was telling the story of his little "set-to" with the Prince Consort for the fourth time when dinner was announced and, giving his puny arm to Evangeline, he looked up at her with weak-sighted admiration, reading clearly in her eyes—Oriel noticed—the message that he was not really the tedious, undersized man most people took him for, but a glowing young Adonis, eight feet tall at the least.

"Shall we go in?"

It was the signal to take one's partners, Matthew giving his weary arm to Mrs. Morgan de Hay who seemed also to be in a state of excitement about her husband's industrial expertise.

"Oh—Kate?" said Quentin, detaching himself from the circle of railway directors with whom, in a serious tone, he had been discussing only the most serious of issues. Money, thought Oriel, and the strategy, the manipulations, the sheer cunning required to make it; and have his share of it too. And now he had remembered the girl he had long thought of as a financial foundation on which to build.

"Kate—are you coming?"

She came, placed her hand on his immaculate sleeve, her

eyes fixed straight ahead of her as if everything that animated them had been, most efficiently, snuffed out. Small again, abrupt and awkward, as she would be if she became Kate Saint-Charles.

They went in.

Taking her seat between the famous Mr. de Hay and the apparently *in*famous Mr. Garron Keith—if the rumors concerning his troublesome gangs of laborers were anything to go by—Oriel expected neither pain nor pleasure, Mr. de Hay being no more self-important, finicky, fond of the sound of his own voice, and dazzled by his own wit, than any of the other gentlemen she was used to meeting in "good society." While Mr. Keith, the contractor, although not really a gentleman at all, having risen, one heard, from the ranks of those same wild hordes of navvies, those vagabond laborers presently terrorizing the neighborhood of Merton Ridge, had nevertheless behaved quite well so far, having made an adequate show, in the drawing-room, of listening to Susannah Saint-Charles' timid enthusiasms for her parish charities and the restoration fund for her father's church organ, subjects which—it had been clear at least to Oriel—could not possibly interest him.

A very large man, Mr. Keith, both in his voice and in his dress, his evening clothes, she judged, having cost more than those of any other man at the table—including Lord Merton, who might well have inherited his along with his ancestral acres—not only in the amount of cloth needed to cover his exceedingly broad shoulders but in its quality, the lace-edged profusion of his shirt-frill and the diamond pin it flamboyantly sported, the jewels in his cuff-links, the weight of his gold watch chain and the various charms and medallions—also in massive gold—hanging from it. A display of jewelry, a *use* of it, in fact, as a deliberate announcement of wealth and status which she had seen before only in a gipsy, or—now that she came to think of it—in the burly, strapping navvymen one met nowadays making their way toward the site of the Merton Ridge Tunnel. Navvymen "on the tramp" someone had told her, coming on foot from their last employment, which may have been any hundred of miles away, sleeping rough in hedges and ditches, living off the land on what they could poach or beg or steal, yet arriving at Merton, nevertheless, shabbily resplendent in scarlet velveteen jackets, pale moleskin trousers, a jaunty cock's feather in every hat-band, a dangle of lucky charms in various shiny metals gleaming on the front of every checked or flowered or otherwise gaily patterned shirt.

And, like them, Mr. Keith—beneath his costly black broadcloth and his fancy shirt-frill—seemed a man well able to endure extremes of heat and cold, whose shrewd brown eyes did not dazzle in the sun, whose head, with its tight chestnut curls, did not ache, nor worry overmuch—she decided—about anything beyond the amassing of his own fortune, the satisfaction of his own pleasures, the arranging of his public and private affairs so that *his* will—and his only—should be done.

Which—in all fairness she felt bound to admit—was an aim shared in full by Mr. de Hay, by Matthew Stangway, by Quentin Saint-Charles, by all men, in a man's world, who saw every reason to have their way, and ample means of getting it.

The meal began, Susannah talking brightly of nothing at all as "etiquette" demanded, Mr. Keith making noncommittal grunts in her direction during the soup, while even through a liberal helping of salmon he allowed his official partner to talk *at* him without offering her any greater offense than silence. Yet here, it seemed, his good manners ended and, once his place had been heaped with more beef olives than Oriel believed the Stangway butler had ever before served to one person, his glass refilled with claret, he suddenly turned his back on Susannah's timid efforts to entertain him and said, loudly enough to startle Mr. de Hay who was toying absently with a lobster cutlet, "And how do you pass your time, Miss Blake?"

She was startled too, but the words came automatically, rising at once from the store of correct social formulas she had learned to suit every occasion. "Very pleasantly, Mr. Keith." No more should have been necessary to remind him of one of Society's most essential and elegant commands. One did not indulge in general conversation at the dinner-table, her duty, therefore, being exclusively to Mr. de Hay, Mr. Keith's to the lady he had brought in with him.

Mr. Keith did not care to be reminded.

"So what pleases you, Miss Blake?"

"A great many things." She had made her voice rather cool, as cool, in fact—remembering her mother's warnings—as she dared. He took no notice. Nor did he seem aware, or did not wish to be aware, of Mr. de Hay's stare of pained surprise, or the very evident alarm in Susannah who had undergone so strict a training in the rules of "etiquette" that she had not even imagined they could be broken.

"Mr. Keith . . ." she murmured faintly, mentally tugging at his sleeve. He took no notice of that, either.

"What things?" he demanded of Oriel, leaning his bulk toward her so that Susannah disappeared behind him and she had little choice but to abandon Mr. de Hay to his lobster and *deal* with this intrusive, annoying man as quickly as possible.

"I play the piano, Mr. Keith. I paint in water colors. I am very fond of flowers and gardens—of growing things. I help Mama . . ." The portrait, in a few calm words, with just a hint of frost behind them, of a "young lady at home," ending in a manner which ought to have told him that she had no more, just now, to say. Bidding him, in fact, to mend his manners for his own sake as well as hers if—as his expensive coat implied—he wished to climb even a rung or two of that precarious ladder of "Good Society."

He smiled at her, very widely, his size blocking her view of the many things on which her mother had asked her to keep an eye, his head too close to hers, invading the little space of air around her which she liked to call her own, a man who, no doubt having clawed his way to fortune in a manner these other *gentle*men could not even imagine, did not feel able to afford the luxury of standing back and asking for what he wanted—her attention, just now, it seemed—but demanded it, took it, *snatched* it away from all competitors, all rivals, and would—she suspected—fight hard and probably dirty should he decide to keep it. A suspicion which—since no angry words must ever be spoken at her mother's table, no one allowed to leave it in a huff or, in Susannah's case, in tears—caused her considerable alarm.

"Do you ride, Miss Blake?" He was smiling at her again, still leaning too near, his chestnut-brown eyes far too openly admiring and far too precise as to what it was in her they admired the most.

"Yes, I ride, Mr. Keith—whenever I can."

"And do you drive in your carriage?"

"Yes—of course."

"In a high-crowned hat with a feather? And a lace parasol?"

Was he mocking her? It was quite possible.

"I have a lace parasol."

"A white one?"

"Yes. And pale blue . . ."

"I thought you might."

What *was* he saying? *Really* saying, behind the wide smile, the speculative glances? His eyes on her pale skin told her the answer so clearly and so suddenly that she blushed, thus deepening her smile.

"There is something—intriguing," he said, "about a young lady riding by in her carriage, holding up her parasol so the sun can't get at her complexion, and taking sidelong glances at the world outside it, every now and then . . ."

Intriguing, perhaps, to men who stood by the roadside with picks and shovels in their hands, doffing their caps as the carriages went by and staring sometimes at the girls who did not stare back but might glance occasionally, if "Mama" should not be looking. Girls from another universe? Was that it? Girls of "good family and sheltered upbringing"—silly little ninnies, most of them, if he only knew it—who formed part of all the things it took more than money to conquer. On a quick wave of sympathy, a confused impulse to "put things right" although she could not imagine him admitting to anything being wrong, she experienced a rare loss of words.

She was, for the first time in her life, in the presence of a "self-made" man and could readily admit that she was finding him too much for her. Too large and hard and heavy, taking up too much space and light and air, working her so hard that she could almost feel guilty about returning him to plain, timid Susannah.

Although it *had*—absolutely—to be done, of course.

"Don't let him fluster you, Miss Blake," advised Mr. de Hay very languidly. "These contractors, you know . . . One learns to deal with them. A necessary evil."

"Evil doesn't bother me," Mr. Keith said, *very* pleasantly. "And as for the 'necessary'—yes, de Hay, we both know I'm that."

"Dear fellow . . ." Mr. de Hay sounded most agreeable. "So is the north wind. It comes and goes. Which—my dear Miss Blake—is just what these contractor chappies tend to do. Here today, with a dozen brass bands playing, and no-where to be found tomorrow when one goes to inquire about little things—like the completion date they were so quick to promise.''

"As you can never find a famous engineer," said Mr. Keith almost cordially, "when the good firm land he tells you he's routed the line across turns out to be swamp, and he can't understand what you mean about extra time and money for drainage.''

"They blow hot and cold too," murmured Mr. de Hay, his eyes closed. "Just like the wind."

"Aye." Mr. Keith sounded somewhat less cordial. "And if all those drawings and blueprints and calculations of yours got blown clean away, I reckon I could still blast and line a tunnel and lay the tracks in the right direction. I stand to make more money at it too.''

"And lose it quicker," murmured Mr. de Hay as if he were talking to himself.

The arrival of the next course came, it seemed to Oriel, in the very nick of time.

"The lamb," chose Mr. Keith, his tone implying, "And plenty of it.''

Mr. de Hay took a dainty amount of capon with a pink curl of ham, Susannah Saint-Charles missing out this course entirely, her face forlorn, her drooping, defected pose that of the eternal wallflower as she gazed at her empty plate, tears—one felt—not far away.

"Mr. Keith," said Oriel, seeing she had no choice but to abandon Mr. de Hay and Susannah who could both be trusted to behave, and give her mind to this man who all too evidently could not. "Do tell me . . ."

"Yes, Miss Blake?"

What on earth did she wish to know? What *safe* topic could she introduce? "Where is it you come from? Newcastle?"

"Yes. Or near enough." He did not seem inclined to specify.

"And have you always been involved with railways?"

"*Always*, Miss Blake?" His smile reminded her—although it did not seem to worry him—that while she was just approaching twenty-one he was already four years or so, she estimated, into his thirties. "The first one came in not more than twenty years ago, Miss Blake, and that was only the Stockton to Darlington—about nine miles of it. You'll be interested in railways then, will you?"

"Oh yes. I find them fascinating."

She had given him a license to talk about himself and therefore, with luck, should have no more trouble.

"Fascinating?" He smiled and, exploiting his license to the full, moved his chair—to the mutual consternation of the butler and poor, abandoned Susannah—an inch or two closer to hers. "That's not the word I'd use. Commonsense, more like. Or a keen eye to a solid profit—like those few canny Quakers in Darlington who had the sense to trust George Stephenson's wild tales about replacing horses with locomotives, and wooden rails with iron."

"Really?" she breathed, scarcely listening.

He nodded. "Really. Just a lad from a pit village in Tyneside—George Stephenson—who taught himself to read after he'd done his shift underground."

He did not say "Like me," although, her attention caught now, she heard it in his voice, saw it in the wry quality of his smile.

"I admire that, Mr. Keith."

"I'm sure you do. So he built the Stockton to Darlington with Quaker money. Eight miles an hour it used to run, rising to fifteen downhill. Slow enough to jump on and off again without paying, if you happened to be a lad the age I was. And not too much chance of getting caught either—although they *did* arm the guards at one time, with shotguns. I don't forget it."

"Did they take a shot at you, Mr. Keith?" For all her good intentions, she rather hoped so.

"I don't recall them hitting me."

"I'm so glad."

"Aye. So that's how it began. A few Quaker merchants in Darlington who wanted a quick way of getting their heavy goods nine miles or so to the sea. And now, twenty years later, there's not much short of 3,000 miles of track up and down the country. A revolution, they call it."

And one, moreover, requiring a gang of vagabonds—he freely admitted it—who, belonging nowhere, would be ready to travel anywhere the job demanded. Hard laboring men who commanded—and deserved—high wages and, not being much inclined by nature to anything Miss Blake would recognize as family life, found little else to do with their time and money but drink. Particularly at sites like Merton Ridge, miles from anywhere, with nothing but rocks and grass and the never-ending Yorkshire mist and drizzle for company. He supposed Hepplefield, with its gin shops and dog-fights and appropriate female company would suit them better, next year or the year after, when the line extended so far.

"I am sure you are right," murmured Oriel with all her voice, only half her mind now, the other half strictly on the alert to pick up any signs of distress from Mr. de Hay, so that a sudden interruption from Susannah Saint-Charles almost alarmed her.

"I do hope, Mr. Keith," said Susannah, her voice coming in a breathless flurry, forced out of her not by choice but by conscience, "that you will provide decent living accommodation for those poor men at Merton Ridge. One hears such terrible stories of—of overcrowding and squalor—and—and of depravity too . . ."

For a moment he looked as surprised as if a sparrow had suddenly alighted on the table and pecked his hand. But then, glancing at her earnest little face, he sighed.

"Ah yes—I see . . ." He had, it seemed, encountered women of this social-reforming, soul-saving type before. And *plain* women—his raised eyebrow implied—invariably flat-chested and thin-lipped and mousy, at that. "Yes, Miss Saint-Charles. Quite so. But right now I'm afraid there's no question of accommodation of any sort at Merton Ridge. And won't be, either, until I can get some cart-roads put in. Four miles of them, to be exact, from his lordship's village to the site of what I expect his lordship will be thinking of as *his* tunnel . . ."

"Why is that, Mr. Keith?" asked Oriel and Susannah in unison, Oriel seeking to remind Susannah that the last thing one ought to do at a dinner-party was begin any kind of serious conversation, Susannah too overwhelmed by her own crusading conscience, her own great daring, to care.

"Because—" and perhaps he sounded a little too patient, "until I have cart-roads I have no way of getting carts across Merton Moor. Therefore no way of transporting the tools of my trade, which are picks and shovels and wheelbarrows, iron bars, barrels of gunpowder, bricks and mortar. Cumbersome things—which could also be said of the materials to build my navvy huts. But when I do . . . Well, Miss Saint-Charles, what would *you* consider to be decent accommodation?"

"Why—indeed . . ." The subject, at best, was indelicate and it was clearly costing the vicarage-bred Susannah a great effort to speak of it. Yet since a duty was something which had to be *done* she squared her narrow shoulders and swallowed hard. "I would think a military-style arrangement for the single men. A kind of—barracks, I think. And entirely separate accommodation for . . ." she gulped quite painfully once again, ". . . for *families*."

He had no pity on her. "For married couples, you mean? There'll not be many of them. If any at all."

Blushing a deep, damp red, she bit her lip, yet compelled—as perhaps those seeking martyrdom are compelled—to go on.

"But there will be—women?"

"There surely will. My men will be hereabouts for a year or two, maybe longer. The ones who have women will bring them. Which seems—well, *reasonable* enough to me. You wouldn't want to see all those poor girls abandoned, would you, Miss Saint-Charles? And as for those who are presently 'single' as you call it, they'll make their own arrangements just like they always do—locally."

They would create havoc, in fact, in the villages of Merton and Dessborough and High Grange, not even the market town of Lydwick nor the great city of Hepplefield itself being safe from them; humiliating the men and seducing the women as one had heard only too clearly they had done elsewhere, drinking, brawling, carrying off foolish young virgins who, in some cases—as even Susannah knew—would be more than willing.

"Children," she said weakly. "I expect there will be a great many?"

"I expect so."

"But that is terrible, Mr. Keith, don't you see . . ."

"Hardly my business, Miss Saint-Charles." And hardly *her* business either, his tone implied, to question the domestic arrangements, no matter how irregular, of *his* men.

"I follow the standard practice, Miss Saint-Charles. I build huts as near the site as I can, big enough to house a dozen. I take one man, who has a regular woman, as my main tenant and whether that woman—the hut landlady—chooses to sublet to single men or men who aren't exactly single . . . Well—if you'd ever met a navvywoman on pay-night, Miss Saint-Charles, with a pint of gin inside her, you might not care to ask too many questions about her marriage-lines."

"I hope," said Susannah, gritting her teeth so that her chin trembled, "that I should do my duty."

A serious conversation indeed. It would not do. And, catching an inquiring glance from her mother who would certainly expect her to put a stop to it, Oriel said, very brightly, "And will you be staying in the neighborhood yourself, Mr. Keith—to supervise?"

"Yes—on and off—I will." His attention was hers again, instantly. "I have contracts to complete as far north as Carlisle and big ones to begin elsewhere in Yorkshire. Five or six years' hard labor in this region if things go well. Eight or nine if they don't. And since I follow the work, like the navvies, this valley might be a good place to settle until the work's done. It may be time—even high time—to make a proper home for my children."

He was married then. She was infinitely relieved about it.

"I lost my wife," he said crisply, "some years back."

"I am so sorry." It was the plain truth. Very sorry indeed if it meant—as it surely did—that he was on the look-out for a replacement, someone, she judged, who could be considered a step up that slippery social ladder yet whose chances in the marriage-stakes had been sufficiently damaged in some way to make her accept a far from socially advantageous husband like himself. Plain girls without dowries, like Susannah. Or pretty girls with questionable backgrounds, like herself.

"Susannah," she murmured, "how sad for Mr. Keith to be bringing up his children alone."

"I expect," said Susannah who, as a vicar's daughter, was on easy terms with self-sacrifice, "that they are a comfort to him."

"Not that I've noticed," declared Mr. Keith quite cheerfully, his eyes, lingering on Oriel's bare shoulders, indicating that the comforts of fatherhood were not the ones he most appreciated.

"Are they sons?" she said just a shade tartly, feeling sure they would be. Big, unruly boys with grazed knuckles and a scattering of cuts and bruises, as he would have been himself. Insolent, lounging, staring boys, little braggarts full of wild schemes and coarse language, created exactly to their father's image.

"One boy. Two girls," he told her. "You'll be fond of children, Miss Blake. Aren't all women?"

"Oh—some more than others, I think. Susannah—I know—

adores all children. Whereas I have had so little to do with them . . ."

He looked straight at her, she thought, with the same warm appreciation, the same insolent delight as he had bestowed on the roast lamb.

"That ought to be remedied, Miss Blake." The appearance of a dish of quails and plovers made an answer happily unnecessary, enabling her to turn to Mr. de Hay with a far more dazzling smile than she would otherwise have felt him to be entitled.

"Do try the quail, Mr. de Hay. It is a very special recipe . . ."

Mr. Keith had eaten every morsel which had been placed before him and drunk every drop. Mr. de Hay, most correctly, had left a little of every dish on his plate and enough wine to "show" in every glass. Susannah, again correctly, had picked like a nervous sparrow. Kate, directly opposite, had eaten almost nothing at all, staring, her eyes out of focus, into hostile space, drugged by boredom, in pain with it, her face vacant and strange and showing, never more plainly, its Kessler heritage.

Catching her eyes, Oriel smiled at her, conveying encouragement, the clasp of an understanding hand. *Never mind, little sister. One ordeal is like another, in that they all come to an end sooner or later. Don't worry, Kate. And don't stare like that, as if nothing, anywhere you look, seems quite real to you. Don't play into their hands. Don't wilt before Quentin. Fascinate him. Let him see you as Young Nefertiti, as you saw yourself upstairs in your mirror. Fascinate them all and take your pick. You can if you try.*

"You must sample the chocolate pudding, Mr. de Hay— Mr. Keith—" she said. "We are rather pleased with it."

"A *soupçon* merely," murmured Mr. de Hay. Mr. Keith firmly declared "I will."

The sweets were taken away and Evangeline, with a graceful, half-reluctant movement, rose to her feet, signifying the withdrawal of the ladies so that the gentlemen might smoke and drink their port and brandy and pass, as last, to those serious topics considered unsuitable for ladies. Business and politics, Oriel supposed, certainly in the case of Quentin. Stories of a coarse nature, perhaps, from gentlemen of such differing social status as Lord Merton and Mr. Keith. A supercilious silence from Matthew Stangway.

Her father? She could not think of him as such. "Kate," she called out as they left the room. *Certainly* her sister. But Kate had fled instantly upstairs to avoid the fuss of greeting new arrivals, those who had not been thought interesting or important enough to attend Evangeline's dinner, and those who had not thought her dinner grand enough for them. Another batch of Quentin's brothers and sisters, whose names Evangeline made a point of never quite remembering, a few local squires and merchants from Hepplefield who made a show of remembering *her* just a shade too well. And then— the prize of the evening—Lord Merton's two daughters who, despite their exceedingly superior manner, their die-away airs and graces and the reputation which had followed them up from London, of being rather "fast," could easily have been mistaken for any of the Misses Saint-Charles, accompanied by a young man who lit an immediate spark of animation, of recognition almost, in Evangeline.

"Our cousin—Francis Ashington," said Dora Merton, speaking very nearly through a yawn. "And terribly famous, don't you know. Been all over India dressed as a native. And all over Syria and Arabia too, pretending to be an Arab. The Royal Geographical Society think the world of him. Lectures for them, you know—and has articles in all the magazines. You will have heard of him, I expect—Mrs.—er—Stangway?"

Evangeline had not. Yet somewhere, it seemed to her, she had *seen* him. No doubt Oriel would remember.

"Mr. Ashington, how do you do? This is Miss Blake—my daughter."

For a moment Oriel recognized him too and then the resemblance—as resemblance it could only have been—faded, or eluded her, leaving her a clear view of a man who was, quite simply, the most handsome she had ever seen. Not— and she *did* realize this—that he was really any more beautiful in face or figure than the other men who, from time to time, had briefly attracted her. It was just that none of *them* had moved her like this. None of them had seemed so wonderful to her and at the same time so familiar that she might well have known him intimately and happily at some other level of experience, somewhere else. Or had simply dreamed him into her reality.

She knew that her throat had gone dry, her stomach tight

with anticipation. She knew herself to be at a threshold in her life, face to face with a vital door.

"Mr. Ashington . . ."

"Miss Blake."

He was very dark, a man who could easily have passed for an Indian, she supposed, his skin tanned not to leather like Mr. Keith's but to smooth amber, his eyes almond shaped and deep set and very nearly black in color, an air of something essentially exotic about him while, at the same time, he was unmistakably an English gentleman. Immensely civilized. Courteous and restrained. Beautiful.

Oriel Blake, behind her fine, pale shell, was mesmerized.

"Ah—there you are." Lord Merton, in need of Evangeline to convince him all over again of his new-found wit and extra inches, had soon grown restless, declining a second glass of port, stubbing out his cigar, and declaring his intention of joining the ladies, thus obliging the rest of the smoking-party to do the same.

"There you are Mrs. Stangway—and that young dog of a nephew of mine with you. Very decent of you, Francis, to bring Dora and Adela. You'll have met him before, I reckon—my cousin Celestine Ashington's boy? Beautiful woman—something like yourself, Mrs. Stangway—although dead and gone now, of course, more's the pity, like all the Ashingtons. Except this young scoundrel. Quite the hero, don't you know—soldiering and adventuring all over India and the Lord knows where else. Lost in the desert—nearly died of thirst. Twenty bouts of fever—or was it twenty-one? Reported dead in all the papers. My wife, who was very fond of his mother, shedding tears. And then he turns up again, looking like a scarecrow, with nothing in his head but going off again to some Holy City or other, where they'll kill a white man as soon as look at him. Told him straight, Mrs. Stangway—or my wife did—to come home first and find himself a wife. There's been an Ashington at Dessborough Manor as long as we've been at Merton. And if he's the last, then it's his plain duty, before he disappears into the wilds again, to get himself an heir. Introduce him to your daughter, Mrs. Stangway. I'd give him either one of mine except that Dessborough's only a small property, not grand enough by half to suit them. Or their mother." Lord Merton, despite his refusal of that last glass of port, was quite drunk, a matter of which his daughters, who thought him ridiculous in any case, took only moderate notice.

"Really, Papa," reproved his elder daughter Adela who was almost engaged to be married to another cousin, the one who would eventually inherit her father's title, Lord Merton having no sons.

"Do hush, Papa," said Dora, his younger, who, since she could not be Lady Merton had made up her mind to be a duchess.

The ladies, who had been called upstairs to the attention of Evangeline's maids, returned—all except Kate. The gentlemen returned too, filling the room with the clatter of coffee cups and the anticipation of champagne. Card tables were arranged in the book-room. Violins began to play in the stone-flagged hall.

"Francis . . . ?" Dora Merton beckoned to her cousin who, although not rich enough to marry, was exactly the kind of man with whom—while waiting to be a duchess—she thought it would be most exhilarating to fall in love.

But he was looking at Oriel, and did not see her.

Quentin Saint-Charles approached with cool affability, expecting an introduction and wishing to know where Kate was hiding.

Oriel, her mind full of Francis Ashington, did not know.

Mr. Garron Keith, the railway contractor, stood for a while, his bulk filling the doorway, watching her until she looked at him with what she did not realize to be mute appeal. *Please go away. Don't intrude and spoil this—well—whatever one can call it. Please don't break this spell for me. There may never be another.*

"Oriel, what ought I to do?" asked Susannah Saint-Charles very pink and flustered. "There is Mr. Keith over there looking like thunder—because of all the things I said at dinner, I suppose, about his poor navvies. Ought I to go over and apologize?"

"Yes," said Oriel. "Please."

But by the time Susannah, wearing her most resolute expression, reached the doorway, Mr. Keith had gone.

They went together to the hall to listen to the violins although her senses were too enraptured by the simple presence of this man to take in a note of music. Nor did she taste the champagne beyond a prickling sensation on her tongue which did little to ease her parched throat.

She was not part of the company. She was with Francis Ashington. Amazed and enchanted. Still shaken. Yet managing nevertheless, to perform, as smoothly as she always did, the basic acts of smiling at him, answering his questions, asking him the requisite details of his life in India, his journeys, his home at Dessborough, his family, whether or not he was glad to be in England again.

"I find it strange," he told her. "The colors seem wrong." And when she did not understand him, he drew her aside, so as not to disturb the musicians, and explained himself to her.

"I was taken out to India as a child and grew up with Indian colors—hot pink and flaming scarlet and a wonderful, smoldering orange all around me—and all together, more often than not. So now, sadly perhaps, it is all these muted English colors which seem foreign to me. And, to be honest with you, I don't think my ears are quite tuned, as yet, to these violins. Perhaps they would sound better if we went up to the Long Gallery? I may find them sweeter, at a distance."

Smiling, moving very slowly, she went with him, knowing herself to be in a blaze of excitement as vivid as any of those Oriental pinks and scarlets, no matter how much she might look like a placid English swan, not a feather unruffled. It did not even occur to her to wonder how he knew the way to the portrait gallery.

"I ought to tell you," he said, "that I used to come here, sometimes, in childhood."

"Before India?"

"Ah, no. There was nothing *before* India. I was sent back to England to school, of course . . ."

"Of course."

"And since my father was a cousin of some sort—although rather distant, I think—of Mr. Stangway's . . ."

She caught her breath. So that was it, the hint of something in him which had seemed familiar. The candle-flame of a resemblance which, the moment he spoke to her, had been snuffed out. The dark, aquiline, faintly sardonic looks of the Stangways, seen here in their portraits and in Matthew Stangway. Her father. But with a warmth, an excitement in life's adventure, a joy in living that was not in Matthew.

"I see," she said.

"What do you see?" He smiled at her. "I know what I see, Oriel. May I call you that—since we are, to some extent, related?"

She nodded, still mesmerized, the forward movement of her long neck so slow that it could have been a lovely, lingering bow of submission.

"Francis . . . ?"

"Yes, Oriel. What a golden name. You are the girl we all dream of in India. Do you know that? You look like an April day."

"An English April?"

"Of course. There *is* no April, worth speaking of, anywhere else."

The gallery was empty, lit only by the candles from the hall below, the air heavy and a little dusty, very still, his lean, alert body standing a correct six inches away from her yet touching her, nevertheless, like a breath. Silence spreading between them and around them like gently lapping water, closing them in together until—harshly—it was broken.

"Francis Ashington—is that you?"

And Oriel could have clapped her hands over her ears to shut out the ugly sound of that stridently intruding voice, those trespassing footsteps shattering her quiet dream.

Dora Merton, she supposed.

But it was Kate—her own Kate—who emerged suddenly from the shadows in a vivid swirl of scarlet and white, her strange, uptilted eyes aglitter, her overstrung body vibrating with an urgent rhythm that caught the breath and held the eye.

"Francis Ashington."

"Yes?" He turned to her with immediate courtesy, his eyes which had been full of cool, green April blinking a moment in her tempest of color.

"We met once. You won't remember. I was just a little girl. I know all about you. I've read every word you've written for the papers. I didn't *know* you were here. I could hardly believe it."

She believed it now. Francis Ashington, soldier, poet, explorer. And standing on tiptoe as if poised for some erotic flight, she offered her hands to him and the whole of her naked, overflowing heart. The man who had done everything, who *was* everything she had ever dreamed of. The man who had not only set off for Arabia on a camel but who had arrived there. And come back again. To her.

Five

It was true that he had come home to find a wife. A perfectly sensible undertaking in view of his marked liking for the world's jungles and deserts and any other wild places which offered a more than average chance of shortening his lifespan. And, as the last of the Ashingtons of Dessborough, a small but ancient property within both driving and walking distance of Merton Abbey, it was no more than his simple duty, before going off again to court death by thirst or fever or the bite of a poisoned arrow, to marry some suitable young woman and get Dessborough an heir.

Someone calm and dependable who would not mind being left to cope alone with her husband's manor and village, the many ups and downs of his land and his tenants, the raising of his children, while he set about making a name for himself in the field of reckless endeavor. Someone he could rely on not only to keep the manorial wheels smoothly turning in his absence but, when he did come home, to provide the cheerful tranquillity he needed to translate his adventures into enduring, and hopefully lucrative, prose.

Oriel.

None better. And Evangeline, understanding in a flash that Francis Ashington had been sent to her from Heaven, set swiftly to work. He was, quite simply, everything she had ever dreamed of, both as a husband for her daughter and a son-in-law for herself. No impoverished cleric or academic or "younger son" who would have nothing to offer, in exchange for Oriel's perfectly reasonable dowry, but a respectable rather than a noble name. No city merchant or coarse-grained opportunist like Mr. Garron Keith, seeking to improve his social status. But a gentleman of education, good breeding, and *property* whose unconventional way of life so far, moreoever, might well incline him to overlook the irregularities of Oriel's birth. Handsome too, although this, in itself, made little difference to Evangeline to whom a positively evil countenance would have been a small price to pay for the single, glorious fact of his relationship to the Mertons.

His father had been the second Ashington son, packed off to India to save the reputation of lovely Celestine Merton who, having lost rather more of her virtue than anyone had suspected, had felt obliged to run off and marry him at sea, giving birth to her son Francis in Calcutta not quite nine months later. A scandal which, swiftly crossing the ocean, had endured until a succession of family bereavements had made Francis Ashington Dessborough's heir.

"My wife was very fond of his mother," Lord Merton had told Evangeline, those few words echoing in her mind like the sound of doors opening, not only to Merton Abbey where the young Ashingtons would be received by right, but to London and Monte Carlo and all the other exalted circles where Lady Merton, a woman of far less brains and beauty than Evangeline herself, received famous opera singers, artists, ministers of state and, once his lordship's tiff with Prince Albert had been mended, might well be entertaining prim and proper young Victoria herself.

And who better to show just how that tiff could be resolved, just how that fierce and fertile little queen might best be coaxed to eat her dinner at the Merton table, than Evangeline? It was a prospect which made her daughter's marriage to Francis Ashington of great advantage to one and all.

"I want Francis Ashington for Oriel," she told Matthew bluntly. "Do you object?"

"Why should I?"

"Because it will cost you money."

"My dear—" he shrugged and smiled. "So I would imagine. And rather a lot of it, I think, to satisfy the Mertons who will expect to be consulted and can be counted on to have their say. Not that he will be obliged to listen, of course. He is a free man and may do as he pleases."

"He will marry Oriel."

"If that is what you wish, my love, then I expect he will."

"And you will pay whatever is necessary?"

"My dear wife," he bowed to her, "if I refused would you allow me to know peace ever again?"

Returning his bow, she gave him the lingering, purring smile which once—he remembered with neither pain nor pleasure—had so enchanted him. "Cheer up, my darling," she said. "You will look so very well at the altar beside Mr. Ashington when you give the bride away. He is so like you in appearance. Or rather, so like you used to be, dearest, before the world became such a wearisome place to you. Ought you, perhaps, to be flattered that a man with your young face can so move our daughter?"

"Is she so moved?" He had seen no sign of it. But then, it was not his policy to look too closely at either of his daughters, growing ever more convinced that the only decent thing he could do for either was to leave them alone. And if all he had to give them was his indifference then, at the very least, he had no demands to make, no burdens to impose on their time or their emotions, no restraining cries of "Do this—or that—for me. You are neglecting me—or letting me down." He saw no sense, no point, in caring for them. Nor did he wish them to care for him. Although he could see little chance of it in a girl so like Evangeline; a girl like Eva.

"When the affair is sufficiently advanced," he said, "I will have Quentin draw up a marriage settlement. You may negotiate the terms with him yourself, whenever the time seems ripe to you."

"Thank you, my darling. And will dear Quentin give me everything I ask for?"

"Ah—" he smiled and bowed again. "One may—I think—assume he will not. Or not without a fight. And a certain amount of bargaining, perhaps, since there is a great deal they would all like me to do at the moment in the matter of school fees etcetera for Quentin's brothers. I expect he will take his opportunity to get something for himself out of everything he allows to you. But you will enjoy the encounter, my love. You see how solicitous I am, as always, of your pleasure. And since, in this case, Quentin will be defending family money which he does rather tend to think of as *his*, you might well have to struggle hard and long. Such a treat for you. And a treat for me, of course—I don't deny it— simply watching you . . ."

"And will you agree to whatever I obtain?"

"I will."

"Without question?"

"Naturally. As you—I am sure, my love—will agree in your turn to whatever *he* obtains from me when he marries Kate."

"My darling—of course I will. You have my word."

And although the dazzling quality of her smile told him she had not the least intention of keeping that word, he understood, nevertheless, that she had accepted the inevitability of Quentin as the future master of High Grange; a prospect which would seem far less grim to her if she could take refuge whenever she pleased with her married daughter at Dessborough Manor, or—far better still—with her friend Lady Merton in London or Monte Carlo.

It was part of the game they played. A game far more satisfying to Matthew, nowadays, than any act of love, far more exhilarating to Evangeline than such acts had ever been.

"You do realize, Evangeline, my darling," he purred to her with a quite demonic reassurance, "that when I am gone my nephew Quentin—Kate's husband by then—will look after you? I would not wish you to suffer any anxiety about the future. Quentin can be trusted absolutely to supply you with—well—such things as might seem appropriate for a widowed lady . . ."

This was part of the game too.

"Such things," she murmured, purring very expertly in her turn, "as Quentin might consider appropriate? A cottage on the estate as a dower house, perhaps, and an invitation to the squire's table on Easter Sunday and Christmas Day?"

They both expected her—one way or another—to do much better than that.

"On top of whatever income I leave you, of course," he almost whispered, having no intention of letting her know how much, or how little, that was likely to be.

"Of course." It was a rule of the game that she must accept the challenge. "Although are you quite certain, Matthew, that Quentin and Kate will really marry?"

"Dearest—how else could he be master here?"

"Indeed. Yet—just the same—with his legal practice doing so well through his railway connections, and with Lord Merton asking him to keep an eye on his affairs . . . Or had you not heard about that? Quite a golden prospect, according to Letty, and for once one can hardly disagree. So golden, in fact, that one wonders whether he may still think it worth his while to take on—well—a wife who will not be much help to him. Or much comfort.''

His smile did not falter. "My dear," he said crisply, "I married her mother.''

Her smile was at its most radiant and alluring. "But you were never an ambitious man, my darling. You have never wished to make your mark on the world—have you? Like Quentin.''

The game, at least that day, was hers.

Yet, nevertheless, although her assessment of Quentin's abilities had been quite accurate, she had perhaps underestimated the size of his domestic burdens; four younger sisters for whom dowries would have to be found, five younger brothers who would have to be established, somehow or other, in business or the professions; a mother and aunt who adored him to distraction; a father who did not like him at all but who was more than content, nevertheless, to leave everything to him. The estate of High Grange, its neighboring colliery, the money Kate would inherit on her twenty-fifth birthday from the Kesslers, were therefore of such vital importance to him that he made his long-awaited move to obtain them a few days later, proposing by the simple method of announcing, "I would like you to get into the habit of keeping a proper appointments book, Kate, as Oriel does. It would save a great deal of confusion and the possibility of giving offense, when we are married.''

She was standing in the South parlor, her hair hanging loose down her back as it should not have been at that advanced hour of the morning, looking as if she had just got out of bed or, more accurately, had scrambled through a hedge of brambles, an untidy bundle of old letters and invitations in her hands, many of them unread, all of them unanswered, through which she was frantically sorting for proof that she had *not* received a note from Quentin's married sister Constantia inviting her to a tea-party in honor of Constantia's new baby. And, therefore, could not be guilty of rudeness in not only having failed to appear herself but to call for Susannah, who had badly wanted to attend and had waited a full, tearful hour at the vicarage for the Stangway carriage.

Susannah, too, had written a note confirming the arrangement to which Kate—of course—had not replied. Her mother—poor Eva—had never answered letters or kept appointments either, as Maud and Letty in their separate fashions were quick to remind her when Letty drove over to complain. And so Kate had run off to rummage through the desk into which she thrust all her correspondence, followed by Quentin who, being somewhat prickly about the respect due to his family, had come first to lecture her and then to propose. Not even a question which required an answer, but a statement of a hitherto unspoken reality. She was to be his wife. Everybody expected it. Everybody saw it, even, as the final, indeed the only solution, to the problem of Kate. And even had she known how to tell him of her fascination, her obsession even, for another man, she did not think he would have taken her seriously.

She had breathed no word of it to anyone else, nor given any sign, not even to Oriel who would only have cautioned her—she supposed—to dignity and discretion, warning her of the possibility of pain which, no matter how much it might tear and torment her, she wanted nothing better than to clutch to her breast. She had fallen in love with Francis Ashington in the way an initiate might walk into a holy fire, actively seeking to be scorched by it until every part of herself that was not the lover, the devotee, had been burned away.

Perhaps it was not a healthy feeling. *Almost* she could see that. Too intense, perhaps, too absolute to be good for her, or for anyone, although, her life so far having lacked any sight or sound or any hope of love, she did not feel in any way fit to judge. She had, quite simply, met him. Her heart had exploded, something with the force and brilliance of forked lightning had ripped through her senses, opening them to such desire for him that, in her total inexperience, she believed it could never diminish, far less that it could ever end.

Remembering the pit into which love—or so they said—had cast her mother, she had once feared her own capacity for emotion. Remembering the pained withdrawal, the flicker of disdain with which her father had invariably greeted any sign of feeling in anyone—particularly his wife—she had tried, very hard, often cruelly, rarely with success, to hide the vast joys and sorrows, the sweeping, ever-changing peaks and troughs which, from childhood, had boiled up, and then down again, in her bewildered heart.

She had been intensely and openly moved—once—by the colors and scents and sounds of every miraculous day, inclined to reach out and touch, to laugh with a huge delight when happy and, when miserable, to say so. A child to whom both rapture and agony came as easily and naturally as her need to look, to taste, to find out, to be heard and seen and to marvel—out loud and over and over—that anything so wonderful as the spring, the summer, the clear light of morning, the day's soft descent into evening, could ever happen again.

"The child, I fear, is somewhat given to excess." Such had been Maud's opinion, and Matthew's. Like mother like daughter, in fact. *Excessive;* which, in their cool translation, meant "embarrassing," "to be apologized for," "unlikely ever to be loved."

Nor had her mother been of any help to her. "Aunt Maud knows best, my dear. She always has. Do as she tells you. You will find it safer." Had Eva really been saying "Be warned by me." Or had it been: "Leave me alone, child. Don't worry me. I wanted *him*, to be his woman not just his legal wife and the mother of his child. So now that he rejects me why should I concern myself with you?"

She had not concerned herself, or so it had seemed to Kate. "Your father does not care for lively children." Kate, therefore, had schooled herself never to run to him with her eager inquiries, never to tug at his hand, never to chatter in his presence, never to clamor for a seat beside him in the carriage, or to attract his attention in any other way than by the careful art of not annoying him. Obeying, in fact, the rules laid down by Maud which, when they failed after all to win her his affection, had left her hurt and shuttered and difficult to handle.

"Your father sets great store, Kate, by ladylike behavior and strict obedience to the conventions."

A straitjacket into which she had forced herself for a while and then, finding no advantage, had shrugged off, emerging crushed, not without distortion, a few emotional bones certainly broken, a few others set at awkward angles, to live her real life in critical, often angry solitude. By day she was odd, willful, unrepentant. By night she dreamed of suffocation by earth and sand and mountainous feather pillows, or of striving to run on feet that were embedded in swamp.

Having long known herself to be unwanted, she had believed herself to be unattractive too until Oriel had shown her otherwise, and had almost resigned herself to a life with Quentin as the only possible alternative to a life with Maud,

until Francis Ashington stood before her, not in her dreams
of escape to Arabia—as he had escaped himself—but in the
flesh. And the very violence of her feelings made all her fear
of them irrelevant. If love killed her then, quite simply, she
would die, since what could her life mean to her now without
it? She believed, with all the fervor of a convert to some
devastating, all-devouring religious faith, that it could mean
nothing whatsoever. Francis Ashington was not only her love,
he was her hero, her guru, her savior, he was *herself* as she
wished to be. She had been caged all her life waiting not just
for liberty but for *him*, she could admit the possibility of no
other, to open the door.

And now, so full was she of her wild fire that Quentin's
cool voice came to her from a wholly alien level, very far
away. She did not want to hear him, did not want to see him,
her face hidden behind the tangled screen of her hair, her
manner so brittle, so breakable, so oddly terrified, that Quentin, his senses razor-sharp, his instincts professionally acute,
checked the step he had been about to take toward her and
remained perfectly still. Biding his time, perhaps, as those
who believe themselves to be stronger and surer, or to have
right on their side, often do.

"When we are married, you say, Quentin?"

"Yes, Kate. Soon, I think. Don't you?"

Was there no cross on her brow then, marking her irrevocably with the brand of Francis Ashington? Had she kept her
secret so well. Even through her tight-clenched panic she was
astonished to realize that she had.

"Why, Quentin?" Her voice was sharp, a little off-key,
taking him aback. "Why me?"

"Oh Kate—surely?" Surely she knew that. Surely she had
understood and accepted long ago—as Maud had told him—
the rights and reasons of their future together? Yet—in case
she had not—he was a lawyer after all, accustomed to awkward, unexpected questions, whose skill at making words
mean what it suited them to mean had never failed him yet.

"Because, for one thing—and of course there are other
reasons—I believe I can look after you."

There was a short, uneasy silence, something taut and immensely troubled in the air.

"Oh," she said. "I see. And am I so much in need of
care?"

"I think so. Like all women—surely?"

"No thank you, Quentin."

"I beg your pardon."

"No, Quentin."

Silence again, threaded as before with a dreadful tension which, although she knew it to be coming from the turmoil of her own body, she could not break. Perhaps it would strangle her as this aching for Francis, in the busy presence of Quentin, seemed to be strangling her. Unless it was her mad desire to shout her love aloud which was so painfully blocking her throat and restricting her breath. But she could not shout it to Quentin until she had found her way to shout it to Francis himself, until she knew for certain that when she began to follow him he would at least reach out his hand.

And, in the meantime, if Quentin should touch her she knew she would scream and scratch and utterly disgrace herself in the mad way they said her mother had once done, in a fit of jealousy over her father. Would she, in her turn, be exposed to jealousy? Was there something else still to come, in this perilous world of emotion? An even more scorching fire than this?

"Have I taken you by surprise, Kate?" Quentin's voice was quizzical. "You must surely know that I have always meant to marry you?"

"Yes. I know. Aunt Maud and your mother have often told me."

He smiled. "Ah yes. I see. Then you should take less notice of my mother, I think, and more of me. It may be her wish. And Aunt Maud's. But it is mine too."

"Not mine, Quentin."

"Kate, I do feel . . ."

"Not *mine*, Quentin."

She heard him sigh, very slightly, not even very much out of patience, being accustomed to conducting these conversations of man to child with his mother.

"Well, Kate, you are still very young and I suppose . . ."

"What? You suppose I don't understand what marriage is about? Perhaps not. Or not exactly. But whatever it is I know I can't do it with you . . ."

"Kate." She had startled him at last, embarrassed him even, and she sensed all too clearly how much he disliked it. "There is no need, I think, to be specific . . ."

"And I dare say you don't want to do it with me, Quentin. In fact I know you don't."

Silence. And then, very curtly, "I am asking you to *marry* me, Kate."

"No, Quentin."

And perhaps it was the pain in her voice which caused him to move toward her and then froze him in his tracks as, feeling herself menaced, she tossed back her hair, revealing a pair of wild eyes, a face pared to the bone with nervous agony, and hissed at him, "Don't harass me, Quentin—don't push me. I might have been able to face it once—before—I even thought I'd have to. But not now. Never—now. Don't you see, I'd rather *die* than marry you. And if you, or your silly mother, or your hateful Aunt Maud, try to make me— then that's just what I will do. *Die.*"

It seemed to her that he had turned to ice, that she was herself caught in some frozen block, embedded there chilled to the bone forever, until, with visible effort, she sprang forward and ran out of the room, across the hall, along one corridor and then another, to fling open a door and bolt for cover into the tranquil, fragrant room where Oriel was sorting out her ribbon boxes.

"Kate—what is it now?" She had been neglecting Kate lately, since Francis, and knew it, dreaming of him instead of keeping an eye on what was going on around her in this place she currently called her home, relaxing the guard she kept on her own back, and her mother's, and Kate's too, in a mood of rare self-indulgence. Had she missed something now, lost in her warm remembrances of every word Francis Ashington had spoken? Something she ought to have seen coming? With the alarm of those who are not often caught out she realized she had.

Kate flung herself across the bed, pressing her face into Oriel's pillows, her hands curling into fists which hurt by their very impotence.

"Oriel, I feel sick. Oh God—*sick.*"

"No you don't." Oriel had always found it best to deny nausea and, quickly soaking a handkerchief in lavender water, she laid it firmly, expertly, on Kate's forehead, expecting no miraculous cure from a square of cambric and a dab of perfume other than the calming effect of *something* being done.

"Sit up now, Kate, and stop thrashing about—you'll make yourself worse. It can't be so bad."

"Yes it is," her teeth were chattering. "I have refused him, that's all . . ."

"Quentin?"

"Who else? And in *such* a manner. I have called his mother a fool, and Aunt Maud a devil, and told him I'll die before I'll let him touch me. So now he'll have gone to tell them all that I said, and how crazed I looked when I said it—just like my mother. And you know what they'll all make of that when they go into a huddle with father—as soon as he gets home—to decide what's to be *done* with me."

Yes. She knew. There seemed no point in denying it.

"Do you hate him so much, Kate?"

Hate him? Once, perhaps. But she had hardly thought about him lately. He was simply a man who was not Francis, like all the others. A man who wished to keep her away from Francis. *That* was his only identity and as such, yes, she hated him.

"If only I had been calmer," she said.

"Yes," Oriel smiled. "I dare say it would have been better. But you weren't. And, at least, to have refused him like that means he probably won't ask again."

Which did not mean, of course, that he would not ask her father to compel her to change her decision, would not call up the wrath of the whole family against her so that, by the withdrawal of all her privileges, her use of the carriage, her few pounds pin-money, her little measure of freedom and air, she would live a virtual prisoner, frustrated and wilting, until desperation or simple boredom prevailed. And if that happened—as seemed highly likely—then Oriel, herself subject to the same restraints, did not know how she could really help her. Might it not even be in Kate's best interests to accept him now and have done with it, thus freeing herself from the awful bondage of girlhood, the authority of a husband allowing more dignity—it seemed to Oriel—or being easier to manage or easier to evade, perhaps, than Aunt Maud's? Marry and then "come to terms," "make an arrangement." Such, she knew, would have been Evangeline's advice.

It did not occur to her that Kate might be in love with somebody else. It did not occur to Kate that Oriel, behind her fine, pale shell, might be in love at all.

Sitting up cross-legged, disheveled, tossing back her hair and rubbing her eyes, Kate managed a shaky smile.

"So tonight, at dinner, they'll all have their knives into me. Unless, of course, I do something fatal and save them the trouble. Where does hemlock come from, Oriel?"

"A plant. I don't suppose it grows in the garden."

"Then I could always run away."

"I'd miss you."

"Oriel—tell me the truth—don't you ever want to run away yourself?"

"No, Kate. Because I know I have nowhere to go." Neither, she believed, had Kate. Marry and "come to terms." Marry and compromise. Compromise and survive. She had been ready to accept that compromise herself, thinking it inevitable. But now, with the golden dream of Francis Ashington filling her whole mind, she could not speak to Kate—of all people—of sordid convenience. Marry and "come to terms." But Francis Ashington had offered her a glimpse of marrying for love, the ultimate blessing which, since she could not give it to Kate, she would not flaunt before her. Indeed, how could she be so heartless as to parade her own possible—just possible—happiness before the near certainty of grief in store for Kate, who had had grief enough in her life—surely—from the start?

"I'll help you, Kate," she said. "Although—do you *know* what it is you want to do?"

And she was taken aback by the fervor, the thrill of absolute certainty in Kate's reply. "Oh yes. I know."

"Can you tell me?"

For a moment Kate's whole body seemed to tremble with the double effort of almost reaching out, almost confiding, followed by the sudden force of her withdrawal.

"No. No, I can't. There are some things—don't you see—that one can't speak of—one mustn't speak of—until they're certain—until they've *happened*. Things that matter too much . . ."

With her own fragile secret clutched tight in her heart how clearly Oriel understood. *Breathe no word of it. Or some jealous demon, listening just over your shoulder, will snatch it all away. So leave it unsaid, don't take the chance . . .* How well she knew.

But, for the present, there was Quentin to contend with and all those who, certainly by now, would have been summoned to his assistance, his outraged aunt and mother, his Uncle Matthew who, since Quentin suited *him* as a son-in-law, would be unlikely to show Kate any mercy. It would be a difficult evening, full of voices raised in horror and anger, hysterical tears, Kate locked in her room, not by Maud who could be defied but by Matthew who could not, while downstairs in the South parlor the talk would be of punishment and compulsion, the shocking insult to Quentin, and taking of proper steps to bring Kate to her senses or, if not, at least to ensure that she would do as she was told.

Kate was white-faced and tense by dinner time, walking downstairs with the mixed bravado and desperation of a woman going to her execution. Yet as she and Oriel entered the drawing-room together it was to encounter nothing more sinister than the quick up-and-down glance Evangeline bestowed as a matter of course on all females, proving that she, at least, had not yet heard Quentin's shocking news. Nor, it seemed, had Letty who was dining at High Grange that night. Nor even Maud, Quentin's favorite confidante, who, looking up from her needlework—busy hands becoming ever more essential to her these days—had no more serious reprimand than a curt "Kate—must you fidget so?" While Susannah, the most devoted of Quentin's sisters, who had been invited in compensation for the missed tea-party, talked of nothing but the navvy camp at Merton Ridge and the scandalous manner in which Mr. Garron Keith was permitting his laborers to *wallow*—no other word could describe it—in drink and depravity. Particularly now, with the cart-roads in and the huts erected, that the men had felt able to send for—or otherwise acquire—their female companions.

"Mr. Keith has crammed them into those huts like sardines I do assure you, in circumstances which cannot help but lead to—well—all manner of dreadful things, certainly fever. I have done my share of parish visiting in Hepplefield, as everyone knows, where the slums are quite as bad as anything to be found in Leeds, or even in Bradford. So no one ought to think me squeamish or naïve, as Mr. Keith seems to do."

"Certainly not, my dear," murmured Evangeline. "Does Mr. Keith not see that you are altogether a woman of the world?"

"I believe," said Susannah, in the tone of one making a revelation, "that he thinks me meddlesome."

Evangeline looked shocked. "Good heavens . . ."

"Yes. But, just the same, if it is meddlesome to point out

to him the evils which he can surely remedy then I see no
help for it. And I have never in my life seen so unruly a place
as Merton Ridge has become. Had our curate, Mr. Field, not
been with me when I went to distribute those extracts from
the Gospels then I believe I would have lacked the courage
to proceed. Children in swarms, of course, running wild, and
speaking so roughly one felt almost grateful not to quite understand them. And all the women smoking clay pipes and
lounging and sprawling in their doorways—their legs quite
apart. Or brewing beer for sale and then carrying it in buckets
on poles across their shoulders, like milkmaids, to the men
as they worked. I felt obliged to speak to Mr. Keith about
that, although I made little impression. He merely said digging is thirsty work and, considering the state of our wells
and sewage channels, beer is safer to drink than water.''

Would her mind have been so full of Merton Ridge and
Mr. Garron Keith had she known of the insulting rejection
suffered by her brother? And when Quentin himself came into
the room, instead of making the announcement then and there
as Kate had feared, he said his usual good evenings in his
usual bloodless manner, accepted his mother's adoration with
no more than his usual, only partially veiled disdain, and
began a discussion on the coolness of the spring and the
subsequent late flowering of the apple blossom.

Very clearly he had told no one as yet.

"He is playing cat-and-mouse with me," muttered Kate,
her stomach tightening to a nausea that was quite visible to
Oriel. And what a clever cat, to Kate's already exhausted
mouse, he seemed to be, prolonging her agony so skillfully,
so cruelly, that in the end she might well break down, confess, and beg for her punishment.

Now. And get it over.

Yet the "now" would very evidently be of Quentin's
choosing. After dinner, perhaps, when he and Matthew would
retire to the book-room to discuss those entirely male mys-
teries of "business" in the world outside.

"Uncle Matthew—I have a most shocking matter to report
to you . . ."

"Good Lord—my dear boy—we can't have this. In fact we
won't have it. Send for Maud. Maud will see to her."

Dinner that night was sparse—Evangeline seeing no reason
to waste the substance of her larders on her in-laws—and

silent, even Susannah abandoning her latest tale of Merton Ridge when she realized no one was listening.

But, the uncomfortable meal over, although Quentin and Matthew did retire to the book-room with an air clearly marked "serious matters," Maud—that expert in the bringing of wayward girls to just retribution—was not sent for, remaining at her place by the coffee tray from where she issued no more than the standard number of official reminders to Kate about her posture, her slovenliness, could she not condescend to pay just a *little* attention to what was being said to her, and why did she seem to be finding it so hard to swallow? Was something the matter with her throat?

"Diphtheria, I expect," said Kate.

"Oh, my goodness," said Letty, thinking of the risk of infection to Quentin.

"Nonsense," said Maud, who subscribed to the theory that if one ignored a disease long enough it would go away.

"That is one of the things I fear most for the navvy children," said Susannah. "And the cholera, of course. And their constant exposure to so much really *foul* language which Mr. Keith condones because—he says—they are not likely to die of it."

"Is that Quentin coming?" muttered Kate, straining to detect his footsteps as intently, tonight, as his mother.

But when he came it was only to bring the information that his Uncle Matthew had gone to bed and to begin yet another bland discussion on the progress of the weather. A most accomplished, most immaculate cat stalking his frayed and hectic little mouse again.

Unable to bear the strain, Kate got to her feet. "I have a headache. I am going upstairs. Good night."

"Good night, Kate." He let her go without a tremor although he waited, Oriel noticed, until she was out of hearing before announcing that he must be going too, thus denying her the reprieve of knowing that he would say nothing now until tomorrow.

If reprieve it was.

"Good night," he said to the room in general, bowing slightly. "I may call tomorrow—perhaps in the afternoon. Or—if not—on Wednesday."

Were his words directed at Oriel, in further proof of his power to prolong Kate's agony, or end it, as and when he chose? Oriel thought so and, making swift, expert excuses, followed him into the hall, waiting at the foot of the stairs while he was given his hat and cloak and gloves, her manner apparently composed but, in reality most ill at ease since she believed herself to be dealing with a man who was cold and shrewd and devious; and merciless too, perhaps, when it concerned his self-esteem, his precious self-interest. And, after all, he had been insulted.

"Quentin . . ."

"Yes, Oriel? And what may I do for you?" Immediate courtesy, of course, she had expected, although the texture of it was like a needle-fine shower of ice.

"Quentin, what I want to say is actually none of my business. I do know that."

"Ah." She had also known how swiftly he would move in to the attack. "Then if you *know* yourself to be in the wrong perhaps you ought not to say anything at all. I am merely making a—suggestion—naturally."

Ice again, smilingly delivered, bitterly cold.

"It is about Kate."

"Yes, Oriel. I know."

And when she hesitated, wondering how best to explain why Kate disliked and feared him without implying that he was indeed dislikable and fearful, he said crisply, "Go on."

"Yes." Having set out to do battle, very much against her nature, she knew she had no choice but to proceed. "I am sorry, Quentin. I am not insensitive to your position in this. But I would like you to realize that Kate is most distressed . . ."

"But I do realize it, Oriel." Only in her mother had she seen so cold a smile. "In fact her distress is not in question. Only its cause eludes me."

"That should be obvious . . ."

"Do you think so? Then tell me—is it because she may have hurt my feelings? Or because she is afraid of being found out?"

She looked at him levelly, as calmly as she could which, to an onlooker, would have seemed very calm indeed.

"I think, Quentin, that allowances should be made. After all, she *is* only eighteen . . ."

"And you only twenty."

"That has nothing to do with it. My experience of life has been entirely different . . ."

"And your nerves are stronger."

"Perhaps I have had less to bear."

"Oh," he smiled at her, coldly it seemed, once again, "I shouldn't think so, Oriel. We all have our burdens. And our defenses."

"Exactly. And if you mean Kate's defenses are weak then I see no shame in that. Her life has not been easy . . ."

"Nor yours. Although mine, of course, has been most privileged—full of every advantage one could wish for at least twice over. I am sure you will agree with that."

Levelly, calmly, she stared at him again, the only device she could muster to conceal that she was, in fact, at a loss for words, needing a breathing-space to somehow gather together the threads of her attack which he had taken away from her, unraveled, dispersed.

"I am sorry, Quentin . . ."

"So you have said already."

"Yes. I know. But I think you will just have to make allowances. She has been brought up very badly and I don't see how one can blame her for it—since *she* didn't do the bringing up. And I don't know why you should expect her to be kind and gracious and considerate when no one ever seems to have been particularly kind to her."

"A most unusual theory, Oriel—although not likely to be popular, one would have thought . . ."

"I dare say. But nevertheless, Kate has suffered all her life—and suffered severely, I think—from the lack of anyone to appreciate her . . ."

"As you appreciate her, Oriel."

"Yes." Her gaze was truly level now, her voice steady. "I am very fond of her. That is no secret. I see qualities in her which have been very far from encouraged—which I think a great waste and a great pity."

He smiled, very briefly this time. "Then I dare say you will be pleased to know that the allowances you mention had already occurred to me and have been duly allowed for. Does that surprise you?"

It made her angry.

"In that case what *does* surprise me is that you have kept her in such cruel suspense all evening."

"What suspense, Oriel? By not telling her father, I suppose you mean?"

"You didn't tell him, then?"

"As it happens—no, I did not."

"Then—whether you think me a busybody or not—I am going to ask *when* you mean to do so?"

"Is it necessary that he should be told at all?"

And because he spoke the words coldly and curtly, like a reprimand, she thought for a moment that she had misheard him.

"I beg your pardon?"

"I said," and his voice was *very* curt now, "is it necessary to inform him? *I* see no need for it. You may tell her so."

She paused, drew breath. "Then—*yes*—I must apologize to you, I think."

"There is no need for that either."

Again she offered her level glance, uncertain of his motives but, if she had misjudged him, very ready to make amends.

"Nevertheless—I *do* apologize."

He gave the merest sketch of a shrug, containing a hint of dismissal, a faint but very potent measure of disdain. "As you wish, of course. But it might be rash, you know—or premature—to assume I am acting out of consideration for Kate. I may well have other reasons."

So, indeed, thought Kate, when Oriel went to her with the glad tidings. So thought Oriel herself; although, the crisis over, she was glad to return to her own quiet room, her own thoughts, her own happy though still very private astonishment at being in love.

She had never expected it, having made up her mind long ago to be content with her life's probabilities, wasting neither time nor tears nor effort in futile cravings. She was who she was, *as* she was, and must therefore accept her situation as naturally as the color of her eyes. Not with the calculation of Evangeline but as a simple turning of self-control into self-defense, coming to terms with her limitations in order not to be soured by them, safeguarding herself from the ravages of shattered hopes and unfulfilled desires by taking care never to hope or desire too much.

So she had reasoned, until Francis Ashington had swept her careful edifice of good sense away.

"I believe our Mr. Ashington has an eye for you," murmured Evangeline. How commonplace her mother's choice of words sounded to Oriel. How crude. And then, abruptly, how terrifying. "*Please*, Mama—don't breathe a word about it—to anyone. Please. It's too soon."

Don't startle it. Don't scare it away. Don't tempt those

*demons who must be flying everywhere around me now, those
jealous sprites who don't like to see us mortals too happy.
Don't attract their notice to me now.*

But how could she tell her mother not to meddle? Even in
the throes of her unexpected, irreplaceable, one and only
love, she clearly could not. Although, as the cool spring became a sudden, fragrant summer, she could not deny the
soundness of the strategy by which Evangeline, too delicate
a huntress ever to alarm her prey, merely created situations
for lovers' meetings and then stood back so that the lovers
might come together of their own accord, or not, as they
chose. When Evangeline invited Francis Ashington to dinner
she did not seat him next to Oriel but rather in a position
where he could best see the effect of candlelight on her pale
hair and shoulders, the pure lines of her profile as she turned
to smile at another man. When he joined them for picnics or
drives in the country, or expeditions to look at abbey ruins,
a few stones that were all that was left in the valley of Imperial Rome, a litter of white kittens at a distant farm, the
first lilacs or elderflowers or roses, she filled the carriage with
such a bevy of unattached femininity—untidy Kate, mousy
Susannah, high and mighty Dora Merton—that he had need
of skill and effort to separate Oriel from the throng. When
he, in turn, invited them to inspect his home at Dessborough,
she kept her own daughter rather better chaperoned than the
rest, allowing Kate to wander where she pleased, and Susannah to spend ten evidently excited minutes in argument with
Mr. Keith who happened to be passing by, but putting off
"to another day" Francis' suggestion of taking Oriel to look
at his rose-garden.

Yet the day came and she did go with him—alone although
not out of sight—to see the roses, smiling through the glow
of her deep contentment both in him and in this place to
which he belonged, this ancient house, this lovely, peaceful
garden, as he played the courtly game of selecting the flower
he thought most resembled her, ivory petals just ready to
open with a blush of deep cream at the heart. Rose Oriel. So
that when he sent a basket of them to High Grange the next
day both she and her mother knew they were intended as a
personal gift to her.

Rose Oriel, waiting to become the guiding spirit, the healing balm of that lovely, neglected garden and of the family
which ought soon to be playing there. Dare she allow herself

to believe it possible? Had her eyes been less dazzled she would have been able to judge more clearly. Yet why else should he seek her out in every gathering? Why else should he give a rose in his garden her name? She would have known exactly what to think had any other man behaved in that fashion, and had had no difficulty at all in understanding, at once, that Mr. Garron Keith admired her and had started to consider her—*at once*—as a possible mother for his children. And since Francis Ashington's need of a wife was equally pressing, then . . . ? Why not? *Why not?* When surely he could see her fitness for the task, could sense her desire for it, the warm ocean of her love for him. A summer sea without storms, calm, nourishing waters flowing through his life and the gloomy house he had inherited.

She had no way of knowing, of course, that he had never wanted the house and, had the inheritance not been thrust upon him, he would never, for one moment, have considered marrying Oriel Blake or anyone else. Indeed he would not even have met her since nothing but the sorry business of family funerals and an irritating sense of family loyalty which he had never quite managed to root out of himself, would have recalled him to England.

He was twenty-eight years old and had spent no more than a few scattered months of his life at Dessborough, his first conscious memories being the ripe odors and vibrant colors, the hot pinks and gold and burnt siennas, the passionate perfumes and spices of India. Impressions so deeply and dearly held that when, as a child of nine, he had been "sent home" to school, the taste of England had seemed very bland on his tongue, the scents and shades of his native land dull and damp and giving him no sense of belonging. England, not India, had been the foreign land. It still was. He had spent his schooldays longing for one thing only. To return. *Home.* To the vivid, tragic, profoundly compassionate land which so excited and moved him.

Home. To a commission, at first, in the Bengal Army, the careless privileges of a European officer in the service of the Honorable East India Company, polo and pig-sticking and junketing in the mess, mild flirtations with the ship-loads of young English gentlewomen who came out, every year, on what had been called the "fishing fleet" in search of husbands. A pleasant enough life, until India itself overcame him, his knowledge of Indian languages, his taste for Indian society, his ability to *become* an Indian, setting him apart from his brother officers.

And setting his brother officers decidedly and uneasily apart from him. Francis Ashington, a chap who had gone a shade too native, who spent too much time in the bazaar and the temple or squatting around the well of some outlandish village listening to a man whose claim to holiness seemed to be that he never cut his hair or his toe-nails. Letting the side down, rather, with his fakirs and gurus and dervishes, instead of drinking tea with his colonel's lady and playing croquet on her manicured lawn like the rest of them, pretending they were in England.

But social neglect by Europeans had troubled him so little that, finding the few hundred a year his father had left him more than enough to live on once he had shed the obligation to keep up "appearances," he had resigned his commission and disappeared into his own concept of the India he loved. A few miles away in distance but a thousand in spirit from tea and croquet on an imitation English lawn.

A time of living to the limits of himself, of exploration and self-discovery from which he had emerged, three years later, to publish the journal of his experiences, or such of them as he could bear to expose to the public view, and had become a minor celebrity. Francis Ashington, rum sort of a chap but likely to take the fancy of somebody in high places. Best keep on the right side of him, then. Best invite him to dinner, and all that. And it had been partly to escape the attentions of too many colonels' ladies, far too many romantic, impossibly innocent, overpoweringly English girls, that he had gone off again to the deserts of Syria and Arabia, wandering alone—which meant, of course, in Arab company—for so long that he had been reported dead, winning fame all over again by his sudden reappearance, bearded, emaciated, gaunt from a dozen bouts of fever, wanting nothing more than to set off again.

But now he had come back to Dessborough to perform what he had been brought up to consider as his duty, to marry and impregnate as quickly as possible a woman who would be a good mistress not for himself but for Dessborough, thus paying his debt to his ancestors by ensuring the continuance of their line. After which he could feel free to set out on his carefully planned journey to Mecca, the holy city of Mohammed forbidden on pain of death to all infidels where, disguised as one of Mohammed's faithful, it was his intention to kiss the Black Stone of pilgrimage and, should his disguise prove inadequate, be flayed alive for it. He knew of no other European who had survived the experience intact. He wished to be the first. Although this as he well knew, was not his true reason.

The most profound experiences of his life, the things which had molded him, moved him, and scarred him had all been Indian. He had only loved Indian women and had married one of them in his heart and his soul and in her traditions, in every way except the Christian ceremony which he had almost forgotten, her early death leaving a void in him which only danger, risk, the constant picking up of a lethal challenge—not another woman—could even partially fill.

Not such a woman as Oriel Blake, certainly, although he fully appreciated her beauty and her quality as well as his own good fortune in finding so soon the very girl—this calm and serious and very lovely Rose Oriel—who would be so perfect in every way for Dessborough.

Lord Merton, of course—his mother's cousin—had felt obliged to warn him about the question-mark hovering above Miss Blake's identity. Not that Lord Merton, who had sown his own wild oats in plenty, had any truck himself with all this middle-class prejudice against bastardy. Not he. Nor any of his old companions from the Prince Regent's day either, when nobody had blamed a fellow for following his natural inclinations. But what with the Prince Regent's young niece, Queen Victoria and her German Albert getting so prim and proper and so deucedly middle-class themselves—which ill became Victoria when one remembered the carryings-on of her father and uncles—it seemed worth mentioning. Lady Merton, who valued her place in court circles, had thought so, in any case.

But what could such things matter to Francis Ashington, squire of a small north country manor, whose moderate means and lack of political and social ambitions made the opinions of royalty irrelevant, and whose personal tastes inclined him, moreover, to a huge tolerance? A man whose first, much-loved, deeply-mourned wife had been the daughter of a silk merchant from Kashmir, a woman the Mertons would have found impossible to acknowledge as anything but a native and, therefore, a temporary concubine.

What concerned him was neither Miss Blake's illegitimacy

nor her lack of the princely dowry his name and station might have commanded elsewhere, but simply to discover whether or not that name and station were the ones she wanted. To be certain, in fact, that *she*, and not merely her mother, sincerely wished to see herself as the mistress of his house, the patroness of his village, and his wife.

Not the wife of his heart, of course. *That* had ended, three years ago, beside a flower-decked funeral pyre, scarlet and orange petals and the naked face of a woman burning all together beneath his crazed, suddenly too European eyes. His woman, the root and reason of his life, who had accepted her own death peacefully, easily, seeing it as the mere casting off of a worn garment in order to assume another. Leaving him only to await him, she had said, on another plane of existence in which he, that day and on all the days that followed, had never managed to believe.

Wife of his heart. Thank God—when one remembered the pain of it—that there could be no other. But Miss Blake—if she wished it—could be his wife of reason, of respect, of warm appreciation and content. The silver and ivory of her too pale for him, perhaps, as this land of England was too pale, too subtle, too civilized, too elusive, but beautiful nonetheless. It would be his pleasure to give her the life for which she had certainly been created and to share it with her whenever, and as best, he could. Rose Oriel, who would bloom equally in his presence or his many absences, nurtured by the very soil which so burdened him. She was the one, exactly right, perfect in all her moods and manners, just as Kate, the legitimate Miss Stangway, was so exactly wrong.

Although he had enjoyed Kate's company that spring and summer rather more and certainly more often than anyone may have realized, beginning one crystal-clear English morning in Merton Woods where no young lady, of course, ought to have been rambling—particularly now that Mr. Keith's navvies had poached the Merton estate clean of rabbits, driving his lordship's irate gamekeepers to set man-traps under the trees and in the long grass.

Assuming Kate to be ignorant of such things, he had warned her and even offered, somewhat reluctantly, to escort her back to her carriage, or her governess, or her gaggle of aunts and cousins from whom he supposed she had strayed.

"Don't trouble," she had said and, suddenly tossing her head, had plunged—he could think of no other word for it—

into the tangle of undergrowth where the traps were most likely to be concealed and gone dancing off, courting terrible trouble and laughing at it in a way he knew, from his own experiences, to be thrilling; leaving *him*, the great traveler, on the tame and tedious pathway.

Astounded, he had watched her for a moment and then, almost hearing the snap of metal jaws biting through her ankle, had rushed to catch up with her.

"Why?" he had demanded, sounding, he suspected, more like an elderly uncle than a man who had crossed the burning wastes of Arabia. "Why on earth did you do that?"

"Oh—why *not*?"

Why not indeed? Was that his own voice he could hear, or one dangerously akin to it, bidding her, as so often it had bidden him, to take the wild chance, to glorify life by risking it, to value each breath because it might be the last, so that eventually one could value it *only* because there might never be another? Surely this fragile, awkward girl could not be similarly addicted?

"Do you even know," he had waspishly inquired, feeling in honor bound to lecture her, "what would have happened if there *had* been a trap?"

And she—little minx—had lowered her eyes meekly, modestly and folded her hands like a good child at school.

"Might I have caught my foot in it?"

Was she mocking him? Of course she was. And because he could not—could he?—ruffle her hair and laugh at her, laugh *with* her, he had taken refuge in an entirely justifiable pulling of rank and seniority.

"You might. Which would have been painful at the very least and possibly lethal if you had been alone . . ."

But she knew that—damn her—knew it very well. Otherwise, without that fine appreciation of her peril, where would have been the fun? Had her addiction really gone so far? Dear God—and she was so slight and small, her bones so brittle, her narrow, nervous body having no more real stamina, real toughness in it, than a sparrow.

Urgently, uncomfortably, he had feared for her.

"But I was not alone, Francis. I expect you would have got me out and carried me home."

"I dare say. And what then?"

"At home?" Her pointed chin had risen abruptly, her long eyes glittering as if he had issued a challenge. "You mean what would my father say, or do? Oh—anything, I suppose, to cover his embarrassment.''

''Embarrassment?'' Hardly the reaction to be expected, surely, from Matthew Stangway should he see his daughter carried home, her leg a mangled ruin, in the arms of a bachelor who must clearly have been alone, at some stage, in the woods with her. Horror, more likely. Fury. Distress, perhaps. Certainly a good many pertinent questions.

''Embarrassment,'' she said, suddenly laughing at him. ''Well, of course, Francis, for Lord Merton's sake, don't you see? Because man-traps are illegal, aren't they? So how—if my father wants to go on inviting Lord Merton to dinner—could he admit to knowing he's been setting them on his land? Certainly my father's wife would never admit it. So they'd just have to put themselves to the bother of making up some story to account for my mangled leg, or my blood-poisoning, wouldn't they? Perhaps they could say I'd been bitten by a mad dog. I expect my father's wife could even arrange it.''

He shivered.

''Kate—were you afraid just now?''

''Oh yes.'' He understood it was the question she had been waiting for. ''Oh *yes*—very afraid. Terrified. Were *you*—in the desert?''

''Yes. Part of the time.''

The only part, in fact, which he could now remember, the rest of it—the safe part—leaving on his tongue the same bland, wholly alien taste of England.

''I've not heard you talk about it, Francis.''

''No.'' He preferred to talk to these alien people only of life's irrelevancies, the safe, *bland* topics of landed interests and the social calendar, weddings and christenings and the right number of invitations to dinner which had no meaning for him whatsoever. But, nevertheless, he found himself talking to Kate Stangway, on that day and others, a whole series of clear, cool English mornings when she, forgetting to be an English lady, would sit down on the grass, her head bare, her knees drawn up to her chin in the rapt posture of village lads squatting around an Indian well, listening to him—the guru, the master—with the fervent attention of a disciple.

''And what then, Francis? What *next*? Go on.''

She was excited by the very names of the cities he mentioned. Places of discomfort, some of them, to him, others only half-remembered. The strands of a magic carpet to Kate, a dazzling web to lift her and carry her . . . Where? Not far, it seemed to him, and not for long.

"Kashmir," she breathed, holding the exotic syllables on her tongue. "Lahore. Benares." And then, when he had shifted the location. "Samarkand—is it possible? Damascus. Petra. Oh Lord—how glorious. Have you really *seen* all of those—*walked* in them?"

She was thirsty for them, he could feel it in his own throat, parched dry by her simple longing for the name of Samarkand—Baghdad—Babylon.

"Mecca," she breathed. "The holy city. The Black Stone of the Kaaba."

He was still thirsty for Mecca himself. He understood. But he would go there—soon—would stand not just on fevered imaginings but on living, doubtless sore and bleeding feet, but *there*, before that fabled black stone with all the other pilgrims, the beggars, the holy ascetics, the fanatics who would murder him by joyful, horrible inches should he be detected as an Infidel.

Yes, he would be on his way before the year was out, just as soon as he had done his duty by Dessborough, whereas she—and with what a deep-felt spasm of sorrow he knew it—would go nowhere, except into the noose of convention which had always awaited her. The uniform destiny of women, eagerly awaited by some, unbearable to others who would have to bear it, just the same.

"What do you want from life, Kate?" he asked, knowing it would make no difference.

"Everything." The thirst again, scorching her now, reaching out to him. "Oh—not to *have* everything—of course not. But to go and take a look at it—to see, and find out, just what it is, and what other people do about it. *You* know."

He knew.

Tossing back her hair, she revealed a face so naked that he lowered his eyes, not thinking it right to look.

"I often dream," she said, "that someone is holding a pillow to my face."

Suffocation. Yes. That too he understood in her.

"Do you see who it is?"

"Oh yes. Sometimes one person, sometimes another. They usually kill me, too."

Did she die struggling? Very likely. Although, once again

it could make no difference. Certainly not to the dry, quest-
ing flame in her which would be snuffed out one way or
another. By the man they would find to marry her, he supposed, by the children her nervous body must surely be too
frail to bear, by the pillow of "Society" which, if all else
failed, could be relied on most effectively, he thought, to
smother her. Leaving nothing of her but a hollow twig.

Had he not heard something like that about her mother?

"Tell me," she said, "about Zanzibar—*all* about it. And
then—where else have you been? Jerusalem?"

"I have."

"Tell me."

The afternoon wore on.

"Oh Lord—is that the bell from Merton church?"

"It is."

"Oh Lord—oh *damnation*. I shall be late for tea now and
in as much disgrace for it as if I had stolen the crown jewels.
Three o'clock. Four o'clock. All this fuss about time. What
does it matter?"

"It passes," he said.

Poor Kate, who would bleed and burn and be devoured
whole, he supposed, by the monster "Society," unless someone forced her to conform to it. And since that could only be
done by breaking her hectic, too frail spirit, he did not wish
to see it.

Nor had he any real help to give her beyond feeding her
imagination with such of his traveler's tales as were fit for
her to hear, bearing constantly in mind that, although a rebel,
she was also very much a young English lady. Innocent,
therefore, and kept in deliberate ignorance of life's realities.
Sad and funny. Intriguing, too, at times although he was in
no mood to respond to the challenge in her and did not do
so. A girl born in the wrong skin, the wrong place, the wrong
time, as wrong in every way for his needs and purposes as
Oriel was right.

Frail, chaotic Kate. Desperate, thirsty soul. And, for all
his experience of the world and its women, he did not realize
she had fallen in love with him until she told him so.

Six

The Stangway carriage horses grew accustomed to the up-hill journey to Dessborough that summer, Evangeline ordering her coachman to drive slowly along the narrow, leafy lane approaching the village and then *very slowly indeed* through the village itself—a single, cobbled street, two rows of low, stone cottages, a squat, square-towered church almost black with age and the smoke which had begun to blow over, this last twenty years or so, from Hepplefield—so that the villagers, stout women who came with most obliging curiosity to their cottage doorways, old, quiet men and craggy, quiet young ones, might see the lovely face of Miss Blake, her daughter, and recognize it when she became their squire's lady.

An event, Evangeline reckoned, which would be proposed, anounced, and irrevocably settled by the summer's end. Thus her reason, two or three mornings a week while the fine weather lasted, for taking her carriage-exercise in the direction of Dessborough, doing no more than obey the urgings of the current Squire Ashington to call upon him and relieve the tedium of a poor bachelor just as often as she was able.

He had issued the invitation with deliberate gallantry, bowing over Evangeline's hand in a manner calculated to please; having learned these charming niceties to perfection at his public school and in his regiment.

"Do come and see me, Mrs. Stangway."

"Perhaps—perhaps . . ."

And, as she turned to go, he had taken the game of courtship a stage further by whispering, for *her* ears only, "And will you bring your daughter?"

Of course she would. But not every time and never alone, still forcing him to make a deliberate effort to be on his own with Oriel, and then, more often than not, frustrating it. Clearly there was to be no dalliance. If he desired Oriel's company, her mother signified, then he must declare himself honorably, concisely, and as soon as possible. Otherwise the Stangway carriage, every time he walked out of his front door to greet it, would remain—as on this particular July morning—full to the brim with ladies; the discreet and elegant Evangeline herself; Oriel in a flowing ice-blue gown and pale straw hat; Kate in one of the nondescript garments of her Aunt Maud's choosing; Susannah Saint-Charles in a garment cut from the same pattern and showing considerable agitation at the sight of Mr. Garron Keith, the railway contractor, who had ridden over, half an hour before, from the site of what was to be the Merton Tunnel, to answer complaints lodged by Squire Ashington of Dessborough and Lord Merton of Merton Abbey against his navvies.

And if Squire Ashington had not cared to invite the contractor indoors but had kept him talking outside on the gravel path, as he would have kept a gamekeeper, it seemed hardly surprising, now that it was no longer just a matter of poached rabbits—although that was quite bad enough—but a whole crop of sorry tales to tell of a nature wilder and far more wicked than anything these quiet regions had hitherto imagined.

Tales of Dessborough girls and Merton girls "molested" as they went about their rightful business, so that it was no longer safe to walk, even three or four together, in the lanes around the village. Tales of navvywomen swaggering hand on hip along the village street, smoking their foul pipes and shouting their foul language, pushing decent women aside at the pump and the dairy and terrorizing the children. Tales of navvymen invading the ale-house at Merton every night, swearing and fighting and offering money to honest men's wholesome wives and daughters. The truly awful tale of the Dessborough girl who had actually taken those wages of sin and, far from dying of the shame of it, had gone off to the navvy-camp at Merton Ridge to sin again, one presumed, with the man who had despoiled her.

And the girl had been entirely respectable, "walking out"

these three years past with a "hedger and ditcher" on the
Merton estate and with the required amount of household and
personal linen hem-stitched and ready in her "bottom
drawer." Dessborough and Merton had talked, the past
month, of little else. The nearby market town of Lydwick,
knowing itself to be the next station on the line, had shuddered. High Grange, its own station at least a year away, had
squared its collective shoulders for the attack, Miss Susannah
Saint-Charles of High Grange vicarage having taken it upon
herself to visit the Dessborough girl's abandoned parents
whose hearts, she had formed the opinion, might be in some
way mended should it turn out that their daughter had taken
up residence not with a seducer but a prospective husband.
Might such an outcome be possible? Susannah, little church
mouse with the heart of an eagle, had promised to inquire,
to beard the lion Mr. Keith in his den, if need be, and demand his intervention; or, at least, detain him when next she
saw him, just long enough to say a word—whispered perhaps—about his responsibility for the morals and immortal
souls of his workingmen.

He was here now.

"Oh—Mr. Keith . . ." Her mouth opened in silent re-
hearsal anticipating his impatience although, indeed, he appeared in no great hurry to mount his tall roan horse and
gallop away—not, she feared, like a gentleman who rides for
pleasure but a man who wishes to get very quickly to his
destination. He remained instead, quite calmly, on the broad
gravel drive as they got down from the Stangway carriage,
Evangeline and Oriel with an identical floating grace, Kate
catching her hem on the carriagestep because she could never
trouble to look where she was going, Susannah herself very
straight of back and clenched of jaw, taking care, above all,
to show no hoydenish glimpse of ankle as Kate had just done.

"Ladies—this *is* a pleasure," said Francis Ashington,
looking at Oriel.

"So it is," agreed Garron Keith, looking at Oriel too.

"Such a lovely day," murmured Evangeline.

They took a few moments, standing on the carriageway
bordered by overgrown beds of geranium and fuchsias and
small intensely fragrant roses, to agree with her, each one
passing comment on the glorious turn of the weather.

There came a pause, during which it was felt by some of
them that Mr. Garron Keith might think it time to go away.

"Mr. Keith is here," said Francis, very lightly, "to explain to me that one cannot make omelettes without breaking eggs. Or something to that effect. And is now on his way to tell Lord Merton the same, I rather think . . ."

"Oh—Mr. Keith . . ." began Susannah, seizing—or so she hoped—her chance.

"If Merton wants his railway station," said Mr. Keith, ignoring her, "then it takes navvies to build it. And if they go on the randy every pay day and make off with a few of his milkmaids then I reckon it's only to be expected. Considering my lads earn ten times better wages than they'd ever get digging Merton's ditches—and acquire a sight more muscle too . . ."

"And so much more skill," murmured Evangeline, "at snaring other people's rabbits."

Mr. Keith looked down at her, smiling but letting it be seen, nevertheless, that he had heard rather more than enough lately about stolen rabbits.

"The site at Merton Ridge is miles from anywhere," he said. "The men have to eat. I've been to Lydwick and Hepplefield and let it be known the kind of profits to be made from a stall or two up at the camp. But your local merchants seem a bit on the timid side, or maybe just hard of hearing. So far I've convinced a baker and a butcher to drive out twice a week. And, as I'm sure you all know, the men brew their own beer and distill their own gin in the huts. So—until the shopkeepers stir themselves—that's that. Because I'll have no tommy-shop on any site of mine."

"*Tommy*-shop?" Evangeline's voice hovered between amusement and the suspicion that he had led her to repeat a vulgar word.

"Yes, Mrs. Stangway. Tommy-shop. You won't know what that is, I reckon."

She smiled at him very sweetly, provoking him for what seemed to her the good and rather pleasant reason of sharpening her wits as a pianist would seize the chance to practice on a particularly grand piano.

"You may take it, Mr. Keith, that your reckoning is quite correct. *Do* enlighten us. You can see we are all agog."

For a moment he stared at her, insolently in her opinion, and then, evidently deciding not to overstep the mark this time, nodded his head.

"There are some contractors, Mrs. Stangway, who set up their own shop on site . . ."

"Are there *really*, Mr. Keith?" The yawn in her voice was audible, almost visible. "And—do you know—that sounds an excellent, even an obvious idea to me."

He nodded, curtly, once again. "Aye. I dare say. Except that such contractors only pay half their men's wages in cash and the other half in tickets for the tommy-shop. To be spent on moldy flour and rancid bacon at ten times the price they'd have to pay elsewhere. Which means the tickets won't go far enough and the lads have to use their cash—at the tommy-shop again. Which means nobody has a brass farthing left by Tuesday, more often than not, and so they all have to borrow out of next week's wages. And when the same thing happens the week after, they have to borrow again. So, by the end of a month or two they're working to pay off their debts—to the contractor."

"It sounds rather—inefficient—of them, Mr. Keith."

"It causes trouble, Mrs. Stangway. Because a man doesn't need a Cambridge education to know when he's being cheated. The lads soon realize the contractor is paying them with one hand and taking it back with the other."

"Indeed. But you, Mr. Keith, are evidently more tender-hearted than that."

"No, Mrs. Stangway. I've got more sense. A site with a tommy-shop has more frayed tempers, more drinking which leads to more brawls and more accidents—and more production lost because of it—than any other. I won't have it. Sub-contractors have a go at it now and again on my sites and I chase them off. So—as I've already told you—until your shop-keepers get out there and sell to my lads, then Lord Merton is likely to go on losing his rabbits. And his grouse and partridge as well, in season, I shouldn't wonder."

"That is scandalous, Mr. Keith."

"It's a fact, Mrs. Stangway. It's the price his lordship seems likely to pay for his station. Not *too* high, I reckon, if you take into account what he charged us for the land to build it on. Maybe he ought to look at it that way. And what I'm just about to ride over and tell him is that if he goes on setting man-traps in his woods and just one of my lads loses a leg with the gangrene because of it, then I'll sue him."

"Mr. Keith!" Evangeline, not only on Lord Merton's behalf but for the sake of her entire class and creed, was truly

scandalized. ''A man is entitled to protect his own p
erty—surely?''

''Not when it comes to maiming other men for life
isn't—on account of a rabbit stew. And—that apart—if it
happens and the man concerned turns out to be well-l
then his mates will see their own kind of justice done
brick or two through his lordship's stained-glass windows
dark night, for instance . . .''

''And, *of course*, you couldn't possibly stop them . .

''I may not even be in the neighborhood, Mrs. Stang
I have seven sites in full operation between here and Carl
I could be at any one of them.''

''You have—foremen?—one supposes.'' Evangeline w
kled her nose as she spoke the word, making a show of
ing it rather quaint even though, at close quarters, it m
well turn out to have a bad odor. ''Foremen?'' she repe
experimentally, as one does with a foreign and decidedly
gainly language.

''Yes. I have foremen.'' Mr. Keith, whose own odor
an aggressively expensive one of good cigars, top quality
oil, boot polish and leather, gave her a hard look. ''
who've come up through the ranks as I have myself—I d
hide it . . .''

''Ah—as to that . . .'' murmured Evangeline, conve
through her purring smile that, in her view, the concealr
of Mr. Keith's origins—so common, alas—would be im
sible.

He looked at her, very hard, again, his patience so c
ously near its end, the temptation so strong in him to
nounce the vulgar word, the damning insult she was invi
thus abdicating effectively and forever from his not yet
acquired status as gentleman, that Susannah Saint-Cha
interruption may even have been welcome.

''Oh, Mr. Keith—Mr. Keith . . .'' She had not really h
his conversation with Evangeline. She had simply been v
ing for it to end and now, when the pause came, she ru
in, already pink and agitated and breathless, ''Mr. Keit
must—I really must inquire about Sadie Clough—as I pr
ised her parents. Much as the subject pains and offends n
I must.''

Her words did not, for a moment, appear to register
meaning to him and then, turning slowly, he stared at he

a long moment, waiting quite deliberately it seemed until her blush had deepened from pink to a damp crimson.

"What did you say?" he asked, his tone making it quite clear that, whatever it was, he did not care.

Drawing in a deep breath, standing as tall as she could, which even then did not bring her to Garron Keith's broad shoulder, she began to recite quickly, while her courage and his patience should last, "Sadie Clough. The girl who was enticed away from loving parents by one of *your* laborers and is now living—in one of *your* huts on Merton Ridge—in a manner which is causing immeasurable distress to her father who is a churchwarden—and her mother who is—well—who keeps her house quite *spotless*. Will he marry her, Mr. Keith? Sadie, I mean."

Once again Mr. Keith took his time and quite possibly even his pleasure in watching the spread of her blush, before answering curtly, "I shouldn't think so."

"And there is nothing you can do—or *will* do? How terrible."

Terrible too, for Susannah, had Mr. Keith's temper slipped its leash and gone snarling for her throat. As seemed rather more than likely, until suddenly, almost shockingly, his scorn converted itself into a veritable battery of charm, turned full upon Susannah with a force that made her gasp for breath and clutch, quite visibly, at her decorum.

"Come now, Miss Saint-Charles," he said in a tone Evangeline would have called caressing. "Is it so terrible? For the girl, I mean?"

"Mr. Keith—she was to have been married . . ."

"Aye. So I hear. To one of these puny farmboys you grow hereabouts. A good, steady lad, they tell me—which might just be another set of words for dull. And these strapping buck-navvies of mine aren't dull, you know. Rough and ready, I grant you. But then, some of these girls from spotless homes and church backgrounds have a funny sort of craving for that. Wouldn't you think so, Miss Saint-Charles?"

And he smiled down at her, allowing his eyes to rove a little over the thin, childish, utterly virginal body, raising an amused eyebrow as if wondering just what *she* might make of a buck-navvy of her very own.

An act, of course, of deliberate cruelty, witnessed quite gleefully by Evangeline who saw no reason to end it; by Francis who could think of no tactful way of doing so; missed entirely by Kate who was far too busy with the immensity of her own emotions; taken note of with some understanding for both parties by Oriel.

What a nuisance you are, Susannah. What a holy fool. Yet, just the same, Mr. Keith, this is not kind—not even worth the poor impression you are making.

Stepping forward, she opened her white lace, silk-fringed parasol with a practiced hand and began to fan herself—making a pleasant little stir about it—with one lace-topped white glove. "My goodness, Mr. Keith, how hot it must be on Merton Ridge," she said as if carrying on a general conversation about the weather. "Although I have never been there yet . . ."

Instantly—as she had neatly calculated—the mouse Susannah was not only rescued from this giant alley-cat but—less happily, perhaps, in Susannah's own opinion—entirely forgotten by him.

"I should be delighted to take you there, Miss Blake. You have only to say the word."

"Thank you, Mr. Keith. You are very kind."

But she had not spoken the word he wanted, had not said "Tomorrow," "Next month," or even "One of these days," had simply distracted him, drawn his fire, and then, adjusting the angle of her parasol, looked around, in the manner of well-bred young ladies, for her mother.

"Mama, dear—you are standing in full sun."

"Heavens . . ." Evangeline's cry of alarm sounded altogether genuine. "So I am. And you too, my love. Francis, dear . . . I do feel . . ."

He came forward at once, a knight-errant to her service.

"My dear Mrs. Stangway, how unforgivable to have kept you standing here so long in the glare."

Not unforgivable, perhaps, she smiled to him, but certainly unwise, no porcelain-pale lady of fashion caring to turn—by such an oversight—the weatherbeaten color of a pedlar, or a fishwife, or a navvywoman.

And so, by Oriel and Evangeline's competent hands, the company was dispersed, Mr. Keith riding off on his tall, livery-stable roan mare, kicking up the gravel, on his way to take issue with Lord Merton, if he could be found, at his Abbey; Francis Ashington escorting the ladies with all due ceremony through the heavy iron-studded oak door of Dessborough.

The house was smaller than Matthew Stangway's High Grange Park and rather older, a tower of guard at its beginnings, into which the reigning squire would barricade himself at need to fend off the marauding Scots, and to which each generation of his ancestors had added a room, here and there, all of them small and low with thick walls and narrow mullions to conserve heat and keep out the worst of the Yorkshire weather. Rooms opening one from the other, the older ones stone-flagged and uneven, the more recent paneled in carved, blackened wood heavily scented with beeswax, their atmosphere quiet and dim, oppressive, furtive almost to Francis, yet speaking their welcome at once to Oriel as she moved easily across each threshold, sure of her direction, at ease with the house, quietly, profoundly content with it as she knew it to be content with her. The house and the woman, waiting both together with the same deep patience for the same man.

Allowing the others to fall behind, perhaps at Evangeline's contriving, Oriel was the first to cross the galleried hall and enter the drawing-room, the scents of wax polish, the musk of old tapestries, the freshness of garden flowers through the open window blending in her nostrils as she heard Francis whisper "Oriel—may I have a moment of your time—alone somewhere—today?"

"Yes, Francis." *Yes.* Her time and the whole of herself with it, so her slow, dreaming smile conveyed to him as she turned her alabaster head toward him, her body beneath the ice-blue gown made of alabaster too, he imagined, very cool and smooth to touch. And he knew he would be touching it very soon now. Rose Oriel, to be taken one fragrant petal at a time, a woman—a body—over which to dream and linger, to spend the whole of an erotic night, a dozen such nights, delicately drawing out her sweetness before penetrating the source of it. He would always treat her with courtesy and gentleness and go on wooing her long after she was won, if for no other reason than to provide the challenge he knew he needed and which ought surely to give a constant impression of her own value to her.

"How lovely you are," he said, a connoisseur as yet rather than a lover, by no means mad with desire—as he had been maddened once—but reassured by the stir of it in his obedient body, neither too urgent nor too violent but enough, he judged, to make its consummation very pleasant.

"Yes, so lovely. The loveliest girl in England." And because he had meant to say "I love you. Please marry me," and knew he *would* be saying it before the day was done, he smiled at her through a long, warm silence, enjoying her elegant head, her fine, cool body with no awareness whatsoever of the tumult he was stirring within it, not only of love and devotion and all her woman's tenderness but a dim, uncertain, yet growing—growing—desire of her woman's body for the male caress of his. The first hesitant acknowledgment of her sensuality which he—since she continued to meet his gaze with such composure, such a calm elegance of manner—missed entirely.

"Any man," he said, thinking how well that smooth elegance would suit the position of Dessborough's first lady, "would consider himself fortunate . . ."

Was it the beginning of a proposal? She smiled at him, her heart crashing violently against the wall of her chest, yet her expression remaining no more than attentive.

"Yes, Francis?"

She was inviting him to go on, offering the only encouragement a lady ought to give in these delicate circumstances. Rose Oriel, her heart on fire, yet waiting, as all her life she had waited, with the exquisite politeness of those who are never quite sure of their position. Waiting to be invited, to be included, to be *asked*, her heart already wildly crying out "I love you, Francis. Forever," her voice calmly pronouncing the correct formulas she had been taught—by Society, by Necessity—for the occasion.

"Oriel . . ." Should he settle it now by taking her in his arms and be discovered kissing her by her mother who, surely not far behind, would know exactly what to make of it? But no. This girl deserved a more thoughtful, more accomplished proposal than that.

"We must talk," he murmured and allowed her to see his regret as Kate and Susannah Saint-Charles came jostling each other through the narrow doorway, both of them exclaiming about the length of sari silk tossed over a chair by the open window.

"What is *that*?" demanded Kate.

"How pretty," said Susannah, sounding by no means certain, needing Maud, perhaps, to tell her whether it might, in fact, be gaudy: or even improper.

"One supposes it to be something Indian," said Evangeline, coming in behind them. "Have you been sorting out your souvenirs, dear Francis?"

He had come across it, in fact, that morning at the bottom of a storage chest, sent years ago, he supposed, as a gift from his mother to his aunt, the old squire's lady. Both women were dead now, the gift unused, forgotten, and he had taken it idly to the open window and held it to the light, wondering if he might make a gift of it to someone in his turn. Idly wondering, and then, with slow-building agony, remembering. A length of gossamer-fine silk shot through with gold and orange and the wild, hot pink which still touched raw places in his mind, the glorious flamboyance of India still faintly spiced with sandalwood, which looked so garish—he well knew—to these rain-colored English eyes.

So, for a while, had he remembered, suffered, and then, carefully, gently, had draped the silk across the chair-back, taking pains with its arrangement as he would have taken pains to seat a fragile woman. And he had left it there in the pale, northern sunshine, this mild, subtle season which passed for summer, knowing the garment to be empty, as were all other garments, since his wife's body had never touched it. Knowing himself to be empty since he would never touch that body again. Knowing, as the pain receded, that his own male body could desire other women no more than physically, desire and even enjoy them without betraying Arshad, without ceasing for one moment to acknowledge her as "the woman," all the rest remaining in a category which was neither higher nor lower but quite simply *not her.*

So, he supposed, would it always be. Arshad. The fierce need of her channeled now, since he could not be rid of it, into his need for the desert, the bare mountain, the forbidden city. The need for danger to replace the loss of love. And even so he would be a good husband to Miss Oriel Blake, would take her pure alabaster body with patience and tenderness and such skill in the erotic arts as he had acquired from women who were not ashamed of their sensuality, as he knew England's young ladies were taught to be. He would release her from her prudishness, if at all possible, give her children, and take pride in her fertility. And when she had had enough of childbearing he would inflict no more of it upon her. If he lived long enough to achieve contentment then he believed he could be content with her. And if he left his bones on the road to Mecca, as seemed more likely, then the future of his house would be safe in her pale, steady hands.

He *must* settle it today. He wanted it settled. He would give her the sari now as a personal token of his past and future, to take home with her until he should follow and claim it back again, with her inside it. A romantic piece of nonsense which might please her. Yet, as he picked it up, the gold threads glinting in the sunlight, he saw how badly some of them were tarnished, how raucously the vivid orange and burning pink shouted alien words—so deeply significant to him—at the ice-blue and cream and ivory of Miss Blake. No, it could give her no pleasure, this gaudy, dusty relic of a past he did not even wish her to share and so, in order not to embarrass her with it, he glanced quickly around him and tossed the silk, on impulse, to Kate.

"My goodness," said Evangeline. "What does one do with it?"

But Kate, by what could only be instinct, swiftly draped the sari around her, or draped herself inside it, so intimately did the thin body, the exotic fabric seem to fit together, the vivid, clamorous colors, the sudden release of sandalwood from the swirling folds filling the room with an alluring disturbance of other worlds, other moods and morals which had Kate—and Kate alone—at its heart.

"Have I got it right?" She was talking only to Francis.

"Oh—I think—near enough."

"I want an elephant to ride on," she said. "And a tiger to lead around on a golden chain, like a dog, Francis . . . ?"

"Of course," he said. "You shall have them."

"Now."

"Even sooner."

She laughed, the drab, beige dress of Aunt Maud's choosing disappearing entirely, growing pale and fainting away before the vibrant impact of India, all that was vibrant in her nature—so contrary to the drab, beige teaching of Aunt Maud—rising now like a torrent of hot rain to her dry surface, giving her the brief, riotous bloom of desert land touched by water.

Not for long, though.

"Kate, dear," murmured Evangeline, understanding the effect of ice on desert flowers. "Do I detect a smudge on your cheek? Here we are, dear—my handkerchief—if you have left yours in the carriage again, with your gloves. *Do* keep it.''

The moment passed. The visit with it. And, as the carriage from High Grange drove off into the by no means unattainable distance, Francis Ashington, obedient only to impulse, sent a swiftly penned note after it, requesting the permission of Mrs. Evangeline Stangway to visit her that evening, after dinner, on a matter very close to his heart.

The die was cast. He would be a fiancé tomorrow, a bridegroom the month after, a father as soon as may be. And even before that, as soon as his seed should be safely planted, he would have embarked on his journey to Mecca.

"He is coming to propose to you, Oriel," said Evangeline, having called her daughter to her bedroom to show her the letter.

"Yes, Mama. I think so."

"And may one assume it is what you want?"

Had she not said so? No. The longing was still too deep for words, the wonder of it too precious, too intense. But tonight—four hours away, then three, then two, then *almost* here—then she would speak of it. Tonight, when her life had been transformed, enriched, made magical, when he had lifted her from her uncertain perch at High Grange to the one place in the world, the one life she wanted. Going to her room, needing absolute silence, perfect solitude, she placed her hands lightly against the windowpane, the sunlight, as it filtered through them, seeming to symbolize the joy and love and deep contentment already in their grasp. Or very nearly. Tonight when he came to ask her to love him, to be wife, mistress, mother, friend, healer, entertainer, comrade, defender. Woman.

Yet dinner that night at High Grange was considerably delayed, Matthew Stangway, upon whose convenience all such arrangements depended, returning very late from some appointment in Hepplefield, thus obliging his wife and his cook and his entire household to wait for him. So that when Francis arrived with his bouquet of cream roses and his various speeches—to Evangeline, to Matthew, to Oriel herself—ready in his mind, the family were still at table and, in the opinion of the butler, likely to remain so for another hour.

But Mr. Ashington was, of course, expected. Provision had been made.

"Would you care to wait here, sir. Mrs. Stangway asks you to take your ease."

The door of the South parlor was held open, a tray with glasses and decanters of port and brandy placed at his disposal with a suitable array of sporting and political—safely High Tory—magazines.

"Mrs. Stangway will join you presently, sir." And privately, of course, since the family, once the meal was over, would adjourn to the drawing-room and the coffee tray, allowing Evangeline ample opportunity to grant him permission to marry her daughter and then send Oriel to him in this cozy little place while she conveyed the news to the others. Then, he supposed, there would be an interview with Matthew Stangway, a business meeting of dates and mutual finances during which he may, or may not, be told the truth about Oriel's birth. Not that it mattered a jot to him. He would take her as she was, for what she was, although having spent a few tedious mornings going through the estate account-books with his land-agent, he knew he could not afford the grand gesture of refusing whatever money came with her. Enough, he supposed, to salvage her mother's pride without causing fresh gossip by its excess. A delicate balance. A mere pittance, no doubt, compared to Kate's portion, something of an injustice to Oriel if she really was Matthew Stangway's daughter; except that Kate, of course, would always need more of everything. More care, more effort, more love, more money, more concentration, more time than he—since Arshad—thought reasonable, or safe, to invest in anyone.

And it was then, standing alone—surely alone—in the discreet, almost twilit atmosphere of Evangeline's parlor that solitude tore itself away from him, every nerve, every taut muscle within him straining through the shadows to the presence in the far corner, the distant swirl of color and odor forming, like a desert mirage—still distant through the gloom—into the body of a woman, the frail amber of her limbs, the fine, mystical purity of her mind, veiled in the gold and orange, the wild, hot pink of her sari.

His woman. The only woman to whom his mind and his heart had been joined at the same moment as his limbs. And although, as she moved slowly from her corner toward the civilization—not necessarily merciful—of lamplight and firelight, he knew her to be Kate, it was still Arshad—only Arshad—who drew him within her, as she had always drawn and held him, Arshad who possessed him.

Silence came, and stillness, a moment long and deep enough, it seemed, fatal enough, to take him—*at last*, he rather thought—across the barrier Arshad had told him of. *Yes*. Until, as always before, he blinked fiercely and shook his head.

"Kate?" And even then he could hear the question in his own voice, the hope still painfully whispering *Arshad, here I am.*

Was he even asking *Take me now. I'm ready*? Yet his words, as he had expected, came swiftly and—he even admitted—quite possibly to his rescue, from the European turn of his mind.

"Kate."

"Yes."

Of course it was. Kate. Yet even then, with the shadows still around her, how delicate, how smooth her awkward body seemed beneath the vibrant silk, how intense her face, and how dark, half-veiled as it was in the pink and gold of *his* country. Of *his* woman.

"Kate—" He felt a pressing need to get all this—whatever it was—in order. "What are you doing here?" Surely she ought to be at dinner? "Are you ill?" Yes. That must be it. Illness, which had set her face in these taut, well-nigh tragic lines beneath the swirling, the eternal sari.

"Yes," she said, "I suppose I am."

What had they done to her? Abruptly—as he cleared his head—it came to him that he had been expecting her to look like this one day, when it finally entered her head that this house, this room, this sofa, would be the final boundaries of her one and only and inescapable life, that there would be no adventurings in Arabia, no adventurings anywhere, no escape of any kind from these spinster aunts and stepmothers, this cold man her father, and that other cold man her cousin, who did not really want to marry her but would certainly do so, just the same. Was that it? Had they fixed the date for her marriage to Quentin Saint-Charles and sent Aunt Maud off to Leeds or Manchester to buy the wedding-dress? Rich white brocade, he supposed, pearl-encrusted and silk-embroidered, to announce her value as a bride, but which would suit her no better than the drab, plain beige in which they had dressed her today.

He did not want to see it. He would manage to be off on his honeymoon with Oriel, or away to Mecca, long before it happened.

"Kate—what can I do for you?"

"I waited here for you, Francis . . ."

"Yes?"

"I couldn't dine. I waited. I have to tell you . . ." And her voice, through the swirl of Oriental silk, might have been reaching him across the exotic scents and shades of a temple.

"Tell me . . . ?" And accustomed as he was to life's pains and perils, the hoarse whisper of her reply came to him as the greatest shock he had known.

"Francis—please—I know why you have come here tonight. And if they say I can't be your wife, that I'm promised to someone else, or that I'm—not fit, not *strong*—don't believe them. It's not true, Francis. I can marry you. And if they won't consent, then I'll come away with you, just like your mother did with your father. Yes—yes, I will. You have to know that. That's why I waited here—to tell you. To see you myself, first, before *they* saw you."

He had no voice, no breath, he had frozen to the marrow of every bone in his body and beyond, caught in the trap of her words and their impossible meaning and held there so tight that he could not even unfasten his eyes from her suffering face.

And of the intensity of that suffering—albeit still in the shadows—he had no doubt.

"Don't believe them, Francis. Don't let them send you away. Quentin did ask me to marry him, I admit it—but whatever he says, or Aunt Maud says, I refused him. Oriel knows I did. And as for the other—about my not being strong—let *me* tell you about that. Listen to *me*."

"Kate . . ." Struggling through shock, knowing panic could not be far away, he managed, nevertheless, to recognize how totally Kate had lost herself in her emotion—as totally he knew, without wanting to remember, as he had abandoned himself to Arshad—the power of it holding her before him, her desperation—he saw it clearly enough to hurt his eyes—turning the sari she still held around her, into a garment of sacrifice, the offer—and he wished quite desperately that he could not see this—into a heart seeking to be taken, or destroyed.

"Kate." And he heard with alarm the break in his voice, knowing it to be pity, dreading what she might make of it.

"I love you so much," she said. He believed her. He had seen love like this before and understood its absolute submission, an intensity of feeling he had thought to be Asian, never European: Arshad, whose surrender to him of her body and soul had been glorious because he had craved that velvet body and humbled himself, in sheer pleasure and thankfulness, before its spirit. And now here was Kate, standing before him in the grip of a love he had aroused by accident and never noticed, never intended, and with which he could not—absolutely could not—cope.

Nor, it occurred to him on a wave of anguish, could she.

"Yes, I love you, Francis. Lord—*how* I love you!" And once again, as her hoarse voice reached him, he found—with horror now—that the parlor had once more given way to the deeper intensities, the darker tragedies, the golden bliss of the land he thought of now, in itself, as Arshad.

"Kate . . ." Somehow he must restrain her, must save her some little part of the agony to come, must stop her—at once—from saying these things which, afterward, she would find so atrocious to remember. He must. Yet, no matter the effort, he could not force his voice past the barrier of pity and guilt, and fear he supposed—yes, fear—lodged in his throat. He had lost his nerve and, while he struggled desperately to retrieve it, he was helpless to prevent her from going so tragically on. And on.

"Yes, every day since that first day in the woods when I ran all among the man-traps just to make you notice me—yes, ever since then I've *thought* love to you, Francis. When did you begin to feel it? Not that day, I suppose—although I loved you then. That wild day of the man-traps. I knew I had to do something startling enough, hadn't I, so that you'd remember me—and remember me. But of course you knew that. Lord—how wild I really was that day. *Wild.* Dear God—I thought I understood wildness. I thought I'd been wild all my life. Until you came. Until our days in the woods with nobody knowing, just being there with you and feeling it happen—feeling us come together in our minds—*letting* it happen. And now I can hardly breathe for the love I feel. It fills me. It even terrifies me sometimes. Does it terrify you?"

"Yes," he said.

"And so, when you gave me the sari, I knew it would be

today. I came home on fire—I can tell you—*burning*. Wild
again. And then there was your letter to Evangeline, and the
way she smiled when she said you would be calling later on.
I understood. Lord—how I started burning *then*. That's why
I had to get to you first. It never seemed right to talk about
these things in the woods, so I never did. Quentin, I mean—
and the rest. They never seemed to exist there, so I forgot
them. Canceled them out, I think. But I knew I'd have to
explain tonight—myself—before *they* could tell you . . .
About Quentin. And about my mother. You have a right to
know.''

She had "canceled them out." Quentin, her mother, and
how much else? How, he wondered desperately, had it been
possible? How had she lived, this spring and summer, so
close to Oriel without understanding his real intentions? Had
she really been so engrossed in the weaving of her own romance, her eyes so dazed by the dream, the fairytale, that
she had missed even a hint of the reality? He believed so.
For Oriel, sweet soul of discretion, would have confided in
no one but her mother who was not the woman to count any
unhatched chickens in the presence of Letty or Maud. And
so they had all seen exactly and only what they had wished
to see, themselves mainly, their own desires, and "canceled
out" the rest.

What now? How much harm had he already done to this
girl who so terrified him with her fragility, her terrible innocence? How much guilt and shame could he carry with
him to Mecca?

"What about your mother?" he said gently, speaking to
an invalid, knowing, as he asked the question, that it had
already become impossible to proceed with his proposal to
Oriel. He could not do it. Could not—quite purely and simply—invite Kate to dance at his wedding and to live, very
probably forever, as a near neighbor to his wife. Such callousness was not in him. No, there could be no Rose Oriel
now. And if he regretted it—and he rather thought he did—
then so much the better. He would have to live out this night
as best he could, make whatever excuses he could lay tongue
to, and *leave*, early tomorrow, in disgrace if need be, to
make the final arrangements for his journey into Mecca.

His intentions had been good, their performance disas-
trous. He would be leaving Dessborough untenanted, Oriel
puzzled and disappointed he supposed, Kate in a condition

of mind he could not bear to contemplate. But Oriel, surely, was only fond of him? He was hardly more than fond of her himself. It was Kate's anguish that mattered.

Kate. And once again, as he leaned forward to catch the hot, dry scent of her, his eyes were possessed by the colors of Arshad around her face, the slight, amber-skinned body beneath the musky silk, waiting—it seemed—to welcome him back to the only real level of his life which had ever been vital, or even true. Arshad.

"Francis . . ."

And he regretted the reluctance with which he returned to her, forcing himself back into this place, this hour, the clamoring of this present. And of her.

"Yes, Kate."

"I have to tell you of my mother."

"Yes."

"Francis—she loved my father. But he had nothing to give her. Hatred would have been better than nothing, but he even kept that from her. Deliberately, I think. And dislike isn't much to live on. She couldn't live on it. They say it drove her mad."

"They?"

"Aunt Maud—and Evangeline—and others."

"Do you believe them? Is their judgment to be trusted?" Here at least he could help her.

She shook her head. "No. It suits them too well to think so. Perhaps she just had a kind of melancholy—a kind of deep disappointment she never could shake off. But if not— if they should be right, and if madness goes from mother to—to *me*, Francis . . . ?"

"It hasn't."

"How do you know?"

"I know." Although, in truth, looking at her fevered eyes he admitted, with the sense of picking up an extra burden, that he was not sure of it. And if the balance of her mind should be as fragile as her body, as easily broken as those brittle, restless bones then what a crime he had indeed committed. Of negligence perhaps, but just as terrible.

"It doesn't matter, Kate."

"Oh yes it does. It does. She was strange—my mother— but she was rich too. Which means there'd be no need for me to explain her to—to the other men who might want to marry me. 'Rich' would be all they'd need to know—since I inherit quite a lot one day. So they wouldn't care about the 'strange.' And—for them—neither would I. It wouldn't matter. But it matters with you, Francis. I want to be honest. And strong. Damn it, I want to be *perfect* for you.''

And he would have given a great deal—almost anything but the ultimate sacrifice of his freedom—to have been able to tell her that she alone, blessedly imperfect, was all he wanted. *I love you, Kate. Beyond any damage your mother or father may have done to you, beyond anything but the possession of your uniquely precious self. You are all in all to me.* She deserved a man who could say that to her. She needed it, he fully understood, as Arshad had needed it. Some man, somewhere in her future, who was not Francis Ashington.

"And one has to think, I suppose—one *has* to—about a child. That is part of it, after all—isn't it?''

This was terrible. Whatever it cost him, he must stop her now. But, her passion in full flight, she could not be halted.

"I want . . . Oh Francis, I know females are supposed not even to know about such things. But *I* know. *I* feel—well—as men feel—about loving you—wanting you to love me. *Wanting* you. So there's no reason to be shy with me because I'm only eighteen and I've never been anywhere in the world further than Manchester. I have eyes, after all, and dreams, and I understand, Francis. Yes, I do. And if I ought to be afraid of it—as they all say one should—then I just can't be. Not with you.''

She was offering him the love not only of her heart and mind now but of her body, as Arshad had done, a virgin not afraid but glorying in the riches she had to bestow, the joys to be learned and shared, bemused by her own sensuality. *Touch me, Francis.* He did not think she spoke the words although it hardly mattered with the clarion-call of her body, beneath the sari-silk, ringing loud in his head, setting up, along the complex pattern of his nerves, the familiar vibrations leading him, inevitably—as such calls always did, always had, he was not proud of it—to a wholly physical desire. A fierce thrusting urgency of it far beyond anything he had experienced this morning in the rather mannerly stirring of his body toward Miss Oriel Blake. A heat aroused in him not infrequently by the unexplored, the unexpected, the spice and peril of the unknown.

Caution, then. He knew he had need of it, for it would not

be the first time he had lost his head, briefly, over a chance encounter, a forbidden woman tempting him sometimes as greatly as a forbidden city. Except that he would burn for Mecca tomorrow, and the day after, the year after, whereas a woman who was not Arshad could not detain him long. And this girl, above all others, must not be used or deceived any more than he had already used and deceived her. Somehow he must find a way—*now*—to convince her that he loved her yet would be forced to leave her, to write her another romance in place of the one he was about to tear to shreds.

"I lead a terrible life, Kate. How can I ask any woman to share it?"

But he saw by the leap of excitement in her throat that he had merely taken another step into the trap.

"Ask me? I would follow you barefoot—don't you know that?—just to lead your life, even if I didn't love you. Francis—I loved your life—your adventure—your freedom—even before I met you. I was thirsty for that life. And then I was thirsty for you. Parched dry with wanting you, so that it was you and not the life that mattered. You became the adventure—the freedom. The miracle. I thought they would end up suffocating me, Francis—Aunt Maud and the rest. I knew—really—that I wouldn't be strong enough to stand against them alone. To get away. And then—you . . ."

Closing her eyes, throwing back her head as he had seen Oriental heads poised for sacrifice, she opened both her arms, the sari separating, sliding away, not even the satin English dinner-gown beneath it concealing the nakedness and intensity of her desire.

"Kate." Was that the name he had really called her? *Kate.* He was by no means certain of it.

"Yes, Francis. Oh—yes . . ." And even if he had never heard a voice making a total sacrifice to passion before, he could not have mistaken this one.

She was an English schoolroom miss with no more knowledge of the erotic arts than a new-fledged gosling. She was an odalisque glorying in her power to entice and arouse him, naked already in her own mind. And—to his horror—in his. Unless he moved away from her now, at once, then he would fall into her and drown. What an insane notion. Yet that was what he felt. Fall into her and drown, with the scent of her desire in his nostrils, the desperate odor of her need for him, his pity and tenderness for her, and the brutal fact that he now desired her too, choking him even before the water closed over his head.

Desire and drowning.

Touch me. Who spoke? What insane folly, *his* madness now, not her mother's, filling his mind as he put a hand on her shoulder and heard her moan out loud at his touch. A thrilling sound. He touched her again just to hear the long-drawn note of it, to feel the quivering of her shoulder blade beneath his fingers, to know how absolutely she was crying out to him to possess her. He was in deep water now, deeper, as, moaning again, she seized his hand and pressed it hard against her breast, giving herself and taking him in a act of simple unrestrained passion which mesmerized and thrilled him.

He was truly drowning now.

"Love me, Francis." She had claimed him and, the sari silk wrapping them both together, the whispering of another voice—another name, dear God—there, still *there* in his ears, he knew he had surrendered, her arm around his neck now, her mouth finding his and opening beneath it as if sexual love came quite naturally to her.

To him, in matters of sensuality, too.

What was he doing? For God's sake, had he taken leave of his senses? What *was* he doing? Kissing her and loving it, but not loving her. Harming her. A girl whose plight had moved him more than anything else he had encountered in this alien land. Being a damned fool. Certainly he was doing that, which would not have mattered too much in England had she been married or of a lower class, but which mattered a great deal with her. Mattered *to* her.

Stop it then. Make some damnable foolish, cruel excuse, play out a grand scene of renunciation: "I love you but this cannot be. I shall mourn you all my life." And *go.* But she had found his mouth again, was moaning now into his ear, had taken his hand and was guiding it, this time, between her breasts beyond the sari, so that his fingers were touching bare skin and the tiny, brittle bones of a bird.

Lovers drowning together, clinging, amidst the wreckage of good sense and reason, to the very limbs, the very needs which had provoked it, dragging each other down beneath a raging floodwater which, in the manner of such torrents, might drain away as quickly as it had arisen, marooning them—fatally perhaps—on dry land. And had Evangeline been the one to open the door upon them, then she, understanding none better the speedy evaporation of passion, would certainly have closed it again and kept it closed until some other plan of concealment had occurred to her. But, as the family came out from dinner and were being shepherded to the drawing-room by Evangeline—safely out of her way, so far as she knew—it was Letty Saint-Charles who, remembering the needlework she had left by the parlor fire, made a sudden dart for the door, wishing to get on with the shirt she was pin-tucking for Quentin; the sight which met her eyes causing her to shriek and fly out into the hall again as if she had witnessed murder being done.

As indeed she had. The murder of her hopes for Quentin, her ardent desire to see him established here as master of High Grange, which could only be achieved through marriage to this unstable, ungrateful, and now, it seemed, wanton girl. And it was of this she babbled and cried out to the family party still gathered in the hall, her meaning not clear to everyone, although Evangeline and Quentin, both grasping it at once, moved forward, for entirely different reasons, to restrain her.

"Mother—for Heaven's sake—do calm yourself. There is— *I am quite sure*—no need to make a fuss."

Very clearly, very forcefully, he wished Letty to be sure of it too, to have the sense to realize that he quite simply could not afford to find Kate in the arms of another man until *after* he had married her and secured her property for himself. "Mother, you must be mistaken. The poor light, I expect, which makes shadows . . ."

But sense and Letty had never gone much together.

"No, no, my dearest. I saw them plainly—and her dress in such a state as your father has never seen *my* dress in all these years . . ."

"To be sure," murmured Evangeline, the arch of her eyebrows conveying amusement, although no surprise, at the modest nature of vicarage lovemaking. "But Letty dear— forgive me—your nerves, of late, have been so agitated, so very often—such storms, which surely cannot be good for you. Do come and sit down, quite quietly, and take a glass of port—what could be better? You may leave the rest to me, which will turn out to be nothing at all, as Quentin has just told you."

"They were kissing," said Letty, defending, or so she

imagined, her best-beloved son. "And holding each other. It was disgraceful."

"Could she have been feeling faint?" suggested Quentin.

"I expect so," agreed Evangeline. "She *has* had a dizzy turn or two lately—several of them. You must all have heard her mention it. Oriel—have you not?"

But, behind her, Oriel had frozen to pale marble, Maud to granite, while Matthew, with an invitation to play whist in Lydwick after dinner, looked irritable and bored.

"Go and see to her," he told Maud, glancing rather peevishly down the hall where the butler was waiting to hand him his hat and gloves. But then, incredibly at this hour and with a game of whist in mind, he appeared to remember something—quite suddenly—which made him smile.

"Ah no, on second thoughts, my dear, perhaps *I* had better see to this particular matter myself."

"Matthew." Evangeline's voice was sharp-edged with warning. *Don't interfere. Leave this to me. I can salvage it.* To which he responded with a slight nod of the head, as one accepts a challenge, his eyes narrowing with a far from charitable amusement. And very little had amused him of late.

"Evangeline—my darling—if there is a man in my parlor kissing my daughter then surely it is my place to interfere? If only to inquire the exact nature of his intentions?"

Kissing *my* daughter, his eyes told her with cool enjoyment, when you expected him to be kissing yours. So, if your little schemes have gone awry—my love—then *do* permit me the pleasure of laughing, just a little, behind my hand. Surely you won't grudge me that, Evangeline?

He walked past her, still smiling, playing the master of his household with a light, malicious touch, aware—so very pleasantly—of her fury and Maud's, of Quentin's cleverly concealed frustration and Letty's terrible suspicion that she, with the best intentions, was somehow to blame for it; aware too of a stillness in Oriel, a suspension of breathing he understood to be painful. Was she piqued at the loss of a comfortable husband, or had she loved the man? He neither knew nor wished to inquire.

"Now then, Francis my dear boy," he said, leaving the parlor door open to allow his voice to carry, "by the look of things there must be something you wish to say to me?"

And all those who waited in the silent hall knew it could only be a proposal of marriage.

"This is—too much," said Maud.

"No doubt it could have been avoided," said Quentin, glancing coldly at his mother.

"I hardly think I am needed here," said Evangeline, turning with studied grace and walking, back straight, head very high, upstairs.

Oriel remained quite still, looking as if she might well stay in that same spot forever, until Matthew, and Francis, and a glowing, disheveled, wild-eyed Kate came all together through the parlor door.

"It seems we are to have a wedding," Matthew said.

"How splendid." That was Maud. While Letty, who always wept copiously at weddings in any case, burst into tears.

"May I offer my congratulations." Quentin's voice was no cooler than usual, the hand he offered to Francis perfectly steady, the kiss he placed neatly on Kate's cheek neither more nor less affectionate than the circumstances—had they been normal and expected—would have required.

"Oriel . . ." Kate's hands reached out eagerly, fiercely. Oriel, her friend who would rejoice with her. "Oriel—this is what I couldn't tell you—the thing that couldn't be told—you remember?—until it happened—Oriel?"

She remembered. She remembered other things, too, other confidences, other fears. Fears for Kate, not herself. *Dear little sister, don't wear your heart on your sleeve like this, or somebody may break it.* How odd, how ironic, that the heart to be broken—the guarded, careful heart—had been Oriel's own.

She did not think she could move. Yet because it had to be done, she moved, came forward, uncertain of her ability to speak until she opened her mouth and heard the correct formulas tripping from her tongue. The words one learned, like prayers she suddenly understood, to ward off the evils of "letting oneself down in public," the crime of failing to conceal that one had just lost everything one had hoped and cared for. Thereby losing one's self-respect. And she would be in desperate need of that from now on.

"Kate—how wonderful." Had no one noticed that her lips were trembling? Thankfully not. And then, because this too, this above all, was absolutely necessary. "Francis. I hope you will be very happy." She gave him her hand, spoke yet another formula, and then withered and died, it seemed to her, although he saw no outward change in her. Not that his eyes, just then, could see anything clearly through the humiliation, the self-disgust, the growing apprehension he was feeling.

Rose Oriel, pale cream and ivory, who would find a more steadfast heart than his to love her, he supposed, ere long. How badly had he hurt her? Less, he hoped, than he had hurt himself since—through his own folly—the things which really mattered, the freedom, the adventure, the journey to Mecca, were certainly lost to him now. For how could he leave a fragile soul like Kate to keep his house and bring up his children? He had known, for the last ten minutes, that he could not. Not this year. Or next year. By which time someone else would have got to Mecca and back before him: and he did not care to be second.

Not this year. Perhaps never. "I would follow you barefoot—don't you know that?" she had said to him. "Just to lead your life." How ironic, how cruel, if she had condemned him instead to lead hers. His blood ran cold within him—already—at the thought of it.

"Thank you for your good wishes, Oriel," he said. She smiled and continued to move, anywhere so long as it was away from him, finding herself in the South parlor where the act of love, the act of destruction perhaps, had just occurred, wishing to face it more intimately and doing so, retaining her calm until she saw the bouquet of roses left behind on the table. Pale, long-stemmed roses from Dessborough. Her roses. Why had he brought these particular ones to Kate? Or had they been the first that came to hand, just roses for a lady, any roses. And any lady too, it seemed.

The door opened behind her.

"Ah—Oriel."

"Yes, Quentin." Thank God, once again, for the formulas, the mechanical words that spoke themselves, the mechanical smiles acting as a shutter to the mind. Thank God, even, that it was Quentin, passionless and rigidly controlled who, although he had lost as much, in his fashion, tonight as she, would not rant and rave and make accusations like Maud and his mother. Her own mother, too.

"Oriel—are you—quite well?"

Anxiety, or mere curiosity? She could not tell.

"Of course. And you, Quentin?" For, after all, this affected him more nearly since everyone knew he had intended to marry Kate, whereas her own hopes of Francis had been secret—surely—from everyone? Surely? Unless *he* knew? She saw that he did.

"Of course," he said, smiling at her, his eyes like glass. "I am suffering merely from surprise. And you?"

"Possibly."

"From which I shall recover in good time to draw up the marriage-settlement and the list of bridesmaids. Shall your name be on the list?"

"Naturally."

Was he taunting her, or simply reminding her that if he could undertake the legal procedure of transferring the Stangway property—which should have been his—to another man, then she too could play her part at the wedding—which should have been hers—of another girl?

Of course she could.

And afterward? What then? She felt the shock of it, the dread of it, rising in a great tremor through every vulnerable part of her. Yes, it would be terrible. For when this numbness faded there would be pain and grief and a great fear—just now beginning—of never finding her way back to the state of resignation in which she had taken refuge before. She had taught herself to want very little. Francis had seemed to offer her the world. Nothing remained to her now but the obligation to endure its loss. The obligation to behave with good taste and dignity: even—perhaps especially—when others did not.

The cream roses caught her eye again. "Oh look—I believe Kate has left her flowers. I'll just run and take them to her . . ."

But raising his hand in a gesture somewhere, she thought, between restraint and congratulation, he smiled and shook his head. "No—no," he told her, his voice so quiet that later she thought it had been almost gentle. "No, Oriel. There is no need, I think, to go quite so far as *that*."

Seven

Evangeline recovered quickly enough from her husband's treachery in what she termed the "Ashington fiasco," accepting it, quite simply, as a round of their conjugal swordplay which he, this time, had won. Yet she experienced a depth of emotion most unusual to her, veering between anger and a positively maternal sorrow, that her lovely, her *perfect* daughter had lost the best matrimonial proposition ever likely to come her way, to Kate, Eva Kessler's daughter who ought never to have been born at all in her opinion, much less to have become—since September—Mrs. Francis Ashington of Dessborough, presently enjoying a lengthy honeymoon in Paris, the Merton's villa in Monte Carlo, and the Madeira home of an Ashington cousin in the hills above Funchal.

Evangeline could neither get over the injustice of it herself, nor allow Oriel to do so.

"Discretion is all very well, Oriel my love, but one can hardly help thinking it odd—certainly unfortunate—whenever one remembers, that here *you* are, with all your social and physical, and every other kind of perfections. And there is Kate, who has not an ounce of sense in her silly head, married and provided for and visiting *the Mertons*— her husband's cousins—and Heaven alone knows who else . . . How, do you suppose, could it happen?"

"It *has* happened, Mama."

"Indeed. And, Good Heavens, Oriel—how could you allow it? How could you? *Kate*—who cannot hold a candle to you in any shape or form—ever. Oh yes—I know her methods were crude and obvious from what one can gather. Lying in wait for him in Merton Woods and then throwing herself at him—physically—which is just what her dreadful mother would have done. But it succeeded, Oriel. Obviously the man is quickly aroused. But men *are*, dear. One supposed you would have known that."

"Yes, Mama."

"Ah—so you do know." And because she could not show her anger to anyone else, without giving the game away, she grew angry. "I am amazed. May one take it, then, that when the next man comes along you will put your knowledge into action? Just a whisper of encouragement, no more, my love, to make a man overstep the mark and then—hey presto— wedding bells and all the rest of it. Just like clever, scheming, thieving little Kate. Come now, dearest, you can hardly deny that she stole the man from you? Nor that it was devious and very cunning of her?"

No, she did not deny it. At least, not in words and certainly not to Evangeline. But, in her aching heart—and how bitterly and silently it ached throughout that autumn, that dreary approach to winter—she did not blame Kate for anything. Nor did she blame herself. She had behaved in what she understood to be the proper manner. She had obeyed the rules, had waited to be asked, while he—fully understanding those rules—had conveyed to her, quite clearly enough, the seriousness of his intentions. He had meant to ask her. Something had occurred to change his mind. And she could think of nothing more likely than some revelation about her background and parentage, made to him no doubt by the Mertons; the revival of some old scandal which he did not wish to see reflected in his own children. The very disaster which, in fact, she had always expected and before which her spirit, almost naturally, bowed. Of course. What was it in the Bible about the "sins of the fathers," and of the mothers too, on this occasion? No doubt Lady Merton would know. "*Miss Blake.* My dear boy, *who* is Miss Blake? Can any of us be certain? A bastard Stangway, perhaps. But, there again, one cannot help but wonder . . . ?" So Lady Merton might well have warned him, going on to suggest how much better it would surely be to take the real Miss Stangway with all her land and all her Kessler money, and then one would know *exactly* to whom one's children were related.

Such, she knew, would have been the advice of the Mertons and even of Evangeline herself had it not concerned her own daughter. Such was the way of the world. And if a man so enlightened, so fine, as Francis Ashington had declined, at the last moment, to take a woman the world condemned, then she saw little hope, in any direction, for the future. And since she could not blame the whole world for her troubles without sinking into an irrevocable bitterness and thus doubly destroying herself, it seemed best to blame no one at all. She could neither change what had happened nor run away from it. They would be there, Francis and Kate together, living their shared lives just a few miles away at Dessborough, within easy driving distance, easy dinner-party distance, no distance at all for Kate, in her terrible innocence, her certainty that Oriel must be overjoyed at her happiness, to invite her, day in day out, to be its witness, the young Mrs. Ashington's constant companion, the favorite aunt of her children.

Quite simply, and with a great deal of carefully concealed panic, Oriel knew she could not bear it.

There had been a short, intense engagement, a hurried wedding between a bridegroom who did not care for Christian ceremonies and a bride who still saw herself riding to church on an elephant, wrapped in musky, gold-threaded, orange silk. But, rather more appropriately, a white dress and a veil of Brussels lace had been duly provided, Maud overseeing the trousseau with an almost visible taste of ashes in her mouth, Letty withdrawing herself from the situation, very possibly on the instructions of her competent eldest son, by taking to her bed with a malady generally thought to be "convenient." A handy little upset to the nerves and to the stomach, brought on not only by the shock of discovering Kate in that lecherous, bare-bosomed embrace, but by Quentin's all too evident displeasure that she had seen fit to mention it. She had been championing his cause, after all. Why then did he look at her so coldly, freezing her constant attempts to explain herself with a clipped "Just so, Mama. Let us say no more about it."

"Quentin, you were not—not *fond* of her—surely? Dearest—you are worth a hundred of her—a thousand . . ."

"As you say, Mama."

"*Quentin*—oh my dear—could I have done otherwise?"

"No, Mama. You could not."

"And you could not possibly have wished—could you?—to marry a wanton?"

But he had wished to marry High Grange Park, the estate, the mines, the status of landed gentleman and the opportunities of professional advancement which accompanied it. She knew that very well. But at any price?

"Dearest—dearest—to be tied to such a wayward creature . . . No—no. It would have been too terrible. Too much to pay. Remember her mother."

"Quite so, Mama."

She saw that he did not agree with her. Had she, who loved him most, ruined his life?

"I am not well, Quentin. For some days now I have felt so—so very poorly . . ."

"Then would it not be best, Mama, to go to bed?"

She had obeyed him, and lay shivering for a day or two in the high, always chilly room she shared with her husband, Rupert Saint-Charles, distant cousin of an earl and an admiral, with his honors degree in the classics and his mild enthusiasm for ecclesiastical architecture, who had never been more to her than a *husband;* the best of the none too brilliant selection willing to save her from the disgrace of spinsterhood. Rupert Saint-Charles. She hardly knew him, rarely thought either of him or the children his vague and very brief, although very frequent, contact with her fully clothed body in the dark kept on so regularly producing. Except Quentin, her first-born son, to whom she had given all the rapture and adoration of her own romantic girlhood, which no knight in shining armor had ever come forward to claim. A store of love which, since she knew it would have embarrassed her husband, had been waiting intact, untouched, for her son. And being of a faithful disposition, she had lavished it wholly and exclusively upon him, leaving nothing to spare for the rest. Good children, of course, to be clothed and fed, taught their letters and their manners, but causing her no anxiety for the simple reason she had always been far too busy worrying over Quentin.

He had been the ultimate experience of her life, her true reason for living, and when her "nervous indisposition" turned out to be the all too familiar symptom of yet another little brother or sister on the way, it hurt her badly to see him greet the news with a curl of the lip which, in anyone else, she would have called a sneer.

Did he blame her for this too?

"Is it wise, Mama—at your time of life?"

She had blushed most painfully, not even liking to admit that her one darling child had so much knowledge of such things, much less that he might be capable of putting that knowledge into practice.

"Dearest—one takes what the Lord sends—surely?"

"Ah—yes."

And He would be sending this, her *last* child—please, *please* make it that—at the same time as her daughter Constantia's second. Constantia had been married for two years, Letty for twenty-seven, and since marriage and children were all really made in Heaven then one took what Heaven saw fit to inflict upon one. Of course one did. So had Letty instructed all her daughters, for unless one believed it, then how—she had often wondered—could any woman bring herself to carry on?

"Yes," she said bravely, hoping he would tell her it was something to be proud of. "I am to be Mama and grandmama both at once."

At High Grange it had provided a not unwelcome diversion from the forthcoming wedding.

"Does one offer congratulations, dear Quentin?" Evangeline had inquired very sweetly, breathing in to accentuate the nineteen supple inches of her own waistline as she often did when Letty was mentioned.

"Hardly to me, Aunt Evangeline. Possibly to my father."

"Oh—my dear boy—I doubt if your father will even notice the addition. Such a scholarly man, so deeply engrossed in designing all those pretty little cathedrals. Such a pity, I often think, that no one actually builds them anymore. What a blessing—I know he thinks so—to be able to rely so much on you, Quentin dear, when it comes to finding employment for all your brothers, and suitable young men for your sisters to marry. However are you going to manage it?"

Particularly now, she was really saying, when his best hope of establishing himself and the rest of his family in life was about to walk down the aisle with a man who neither needed nor valued High Grange as much as Quentin.

A bitter pill indeed for him to swallow, although nothing could have exceeded the correctness of his manner as, in his capacity as family lawyer, he explained the necessary financial settlements to Francis who was at pains not to seem too interested, and to Kate who, in her desire to follow her lover barefoot across burning deserts, had no interest at all.

"Kate—do pay attention."

"Yes, Quentin."

"Kate—it is important that you should understand."

"Quentin—Quentin—I know everything I want to know, and it has nothing to do with deeds of settlement, I do assure you."

Yet nevertheless, competently, coolly, saying no more and no less than was needful, Quentin performed his duty, as Oriel performed hers on that uneasy wedding morning when, in the lesser finery of a bridesmaid, she followed Kate down the aisle. For, although Evangeline might say what she pleased to Oriel about the plight into which her unwillingness to be seduced had led her, she would give no one else the opportunity for gossip. No. In Evangeline's book—and in Oriel's—one kept one's troubles to oneself. One wept, if one really *had* to, in private. But in the prying public eye one smiled. Appearances were what counted and so, with hemlock in the soul or a knife in the heart or both together, *one kept those appearances up*. One swallowed the hemlock as if it were honey, one ignored the knife and—when no one was looking—one mopped up the blood. Gracefully. One did not make of oneself—*ever*— an object of pity. Which was exactly the same as making oneself ridiculous. And about as shameful as appearing in public in one's chemise.

So believed Evangeline. So had she taught her daughter who, therefore, had consented graciously to act as bridesmaid and even to dress the bride's difficult hair which the maids could never manage. She had done her own hair very simply, a Grecian knot at the nape of her long neck with a red rose in it. Kate's colors, which Oriel herself had shown her how to wear. A splash of crimson flowers against bridal silk, a red rose in Kate's hair too, nestling among the coarse tresses which Oriel's skill had smoothed and burnished to ebony. A pair of ecstatic eyes, black with emotion, glimpsed beneath the lace veil, as sudden and disturbing as feline eyes caught peering by night in a beam of torchlight from a hedgerow.

A bride who moved in a trance toward her destiny. A hastily put-together little wedding otherwise, providing entertainment, it seemed, for no one but the bride's father, the elegant, sardonic Mr. Matthew Stangway, in whose eyes, as he led his daughter to the altar, could be detected a decided glint of amusement.

"Who giveth this woman . . . ?"

"I do." And with the greatest of pleasure, he seemed to be saying, his eyes straying very deliberately to Evangeline, whose only consolation about this sorry ceremony was that all of the Mertons had agreed to attend it.

It had been the most appalling day of Oriel's difficult life. An ordeal which offered her no comfort beyond the bare fact that it would end. It ended. And, for days afterward, she could not rid herself of the ache in her head, and in her bones, and in her heart. There seemed to be sand beneath her eyelids and a hungry hollow in her stomach which the food she kept on eating—and eating—to avoid sharp questions as to why she had lost her appetite never managed to fill. She was hungry and empty, her nerves raw, her mind heavy and easily distracted from everything but the need to heal herself, harden herself, before the honeymooners should come home again in the spring.

In October, a month after the wedding, she caught a severe chill, another in December, her coughs and sneezes obliging her to miss the Boxing Day Dance at Merton Abbey, somewhat to the chagrin of Lady Merton's middle-aged and disreputable, but nevertheless bachelor, brother who had glimpsed her out riding one day; and greatly to the annoyance of Evangeline who had not only worked hard to woo the Mertons—unashamedly using the weapon that her husband's daughter was now the wife of one of their cousins—but saw no reason to accept Oriel's judgment that Lady Merton's brother would remain lecherous and unmarried to the end of his days.

"You could get up—I would have thought, dear child—and make the effort."

The effort to be Lady Merton's sister-in-law, that is. And then there was always Lord Merton's heir to be considered, a sickly, short-sighted nephew with an unfortunate resemblance, perhaps, to Lord Merton's famous rabbits, which might be readily overlooked, thought Evangeline, when one took into account the many other things in his favor. The Mertons, of course, were expecting him to marry one of their daughters, to keep the estate in the family and give her the title, just as the Stangways had been expecting Kate to marry Quentin. But Adela Merton was very plain, her sister Dora by no means pretty, their cousin Timothy Merton—His Future Lordship—just as capable, one supposed, of losing his head over a clever woman as Francis Ashington had been.

Therefore, in Evangeline's opinion, her daughter would be well advised to rise up from her sick-bed and *try*.

"Are we not aiming a little higher than we ought, Mama?"

"Certainly. I would aim for Queen Victoria's Albert if I saw the least chance of him."

"Well—I am just a little tired, you know, Mama—at present."

"Nonsense. You cannot afford to be tired, my sweet child. None of us can."

But Oriel's eyes *were* red, her cough persistent, and when with Christmas over, she was still out of sorts and consequently out of looks, it seemed sensible to see what a change of air would do. Not London air, though, which Evangeline, as a result of her masterful charm, her exquisite skill in the social arts, had received an invitation to sample with the Mertons for a few days before their annual winter departure for Monte Carlo.

"I suppose, my dear, you had better go and see Miss Woodley."

"I think so too, Mama."

For the three most settled years of her childhood, Oriel had attended a school in Carlisle run by a Miss Woodley who, now retired to a cottage by Lake Ullswater, had several times had Oriel to stay with her. Times of personal stress, some of them, like this one, or merely times when the presence of a half-grown, and then full-grown, daughter had been temporarily inconvenient to Evangeline. Pleasant times all of them, cool nights on a mattress stuffed with sweet woodruff and lavender, quiet days in a garden overcrowded with herbs and old-fashioned plants where Miss Woodley, patient nurturer of violets and gilliflowers, firm guardian of hives and nests, healer alike of feline paws and broken wings, asked no questions, issued no invitations to dinner and accepted none, allowing her guests to eat—as she did—when they were hungry, to cry when they were sad, to talk or to be silent—as she did—when they pleased.

"Yes, Mama. I'll go to Miss Woodley."

It was an easy enough journey to Lancaster and then by coach to Penrith where Miss Woodley was to meet her, the rose-colored little town far busier than she had ever seen it before with the impact of the railway workers, the infamous navvies who had come here too, in their wild gangs, to dig and tunnel and blast the railway from Lancaster to Carlisle;

upward of ten thousand men descending with their spades and wheelbarrows on those close-knit, lakeland towns and isolated villages where strangers of any kind were rare and usually not more than two or three in number. Reflective academics mainly who came for the natural beauties of silent hills and silent water, so that the men—and more particularly the women—of the lake country had shuddered, as the earth itself shuddered, beneath the rough-handling of these brawling, beer-swilling invaders. Rootless and reckless every one of them, tearing the ground apart almost bare-handed, it seemed, to make their cuttings and their embankments with little more equipment than pick-axes and muscle and a certain very casual tossing of gunpowder which would take the track—hopefully in triumph—from the treacherous peat bog at Bolton-le-Sands to the mighty summit of Shap Fell, descending gloriously to Penrith and the final eighteen, only-steep-in-places miles into Carlisle.

Certainly the railway workings had changed courtly, harmonious Penrith: not the physical dimensions of the town but the feel of it, which, as Oriel got down from the stage that chilly February day, struck her as somehow off-key, as if she had arrived on the wrong day, perhaps, or not *exactly* in the place she had expected.

Miss Woodley was not there to greet her, either.

But the inn yard of the George was the one she remembered, the same low, red sandstone hostelry where Bonnie Prince Charlie had once spent the night, a hundred years ago, on his way from Scotland to fight the foreign king of England. No mistake, she realized, had been made, the coach rather late of course, the carriage horses and riding horses which had come to meet it striking fretful hooves on the cobbles, their breath visible on the cold air, ostlers and inn-servants shouting at one another as they always did above the din, the steaming coach horses being led off in one direction, their replacements clattering in from another, the livery-stable gigs in a great rush to pick up their passengers and baggage and get away before the coach from Carlisle—also late, she gathered—came in.

It was a scene to which she was well accustomed, except that this time, on this day, there was something more—somehow—about the bustle than the usual urgencies of journey's end. Something sharp-edged and taut—somewhere—which began to worry her, reminding her with growing discomfort that Miss Woodley, so famous for her absent-minded good humor, might not come, with her dog-cart, for an hour yet if something in her garden had caught her eye.

Ought she, perhaps, to go inside the inn and wait there? But, despite the rapid dispersal of the passengers from Lancaster, the inn still seemed full to overflowing, with local men, she noticed, cramming the doorways, talking, gesticulating, all at the same time and in a manner agitated enough to warn her that the presence of a lady would not be welcome. There could be no cause, of course, for alarm. Nothing—she firmly insisted—which need worry her in the least. Except the cold, perhaps, and the numbness of her feet in boots of well-cut but less than substantial calfskin, hardly likely to survive the ten miles or so of winter road to Lake Ullswater, should that turn out to be their destination.

Yes. A cold afternoon indeed, sharpening into a colder evening, the sky already darkening as the coach from Carlisle came in. And standing there, surrounded by her boxes, with very little money in her pocket, a definite threat of rain in the air, a threat of another kind—although she could not name it—hovering somewhere in the crowded, coarsened town very definitely *all* around her, she was exceedingly relieved to see a familiar face among the newly arriving passengers. Especially one set above a pair of burly shoulders with an air of authority about them quite sufficient to procure, for her use, a carriage from a livery-stable if necessary, and the wherewithal to pay for it. Mr. Garron Keith, on railway business, she supposed, looking enormous and prosperous and possibly just the man her situation best required, in a black greatcoat with caped shoulders and a high-crowned, curly-brimmed, quite dashing hat.

"Oh—Mr. Keith . . . ?" She had never been pleased to see him before but now, being sufficiently acquainted with life's emergencies to know the value of a suitable ally, and judging him very suitable indeed, she called out to him and waved her hand.

"Miss Blake?" Shouldering his way to her through the crowded yard, he looked astonished. "Not here by yourself, surely?"

"Oh no? Not really." For Evangeline never liked it known that she permitted her daughter to travel alone. "I am to be met . . ."

Lightly she explained her situation—very lightly—not

wishing him to see, or not quite at once, her awareness of
the tension in the air, an odd impression, rapidly growing,
that it would be as well to keep looking over her shoulder,
to tread warily, above all not to risk herself alone in these
familiar streets which now, because they *had* been so familiar, seemed to offer her a double menace.

Yet, having employed her "lightness" to its full effect, she
did not want him to think her a fool either.

"Has something happened, Mr. Keith?"

"Aye. I reckon so."

Something to do with the railway? An accident? She had
stood once before, in another country, at a place where people had died by blind chance, and felt this same menace.
And here, with so much gunpowder in the hands of men who
were famous for drinking their daily thirty or so pints of ale
apiece and who therefore could never be sober, disaster might
easily have occurred.

"An accident, Mr. Keith?"

"You might call it that."

"Is there danger?"

"Enough for me to get you out of Penrith *now*, my bonny
lass." And even as she made her protest—for form's sake
only—he was snapping hard fingers at the inn-servants and
ordering her boxes into his carriage.

"Your friend Miss Woodley won't be coming. The road
from Ullswater goes through Yanwath and the Yeomanry
won't let her pass. Not a woman alone. They've been killing
each other, I hear—or trying to—at Yanwath, since yesterday."

"They?"

He shrugged the massive shoulders upon which, with the
spark of Evangeline inside her, she had already decided to
rely.

"The navvymen. Who else? The Irish against the English.
Or the other way round. Not that it matters, since it's the
contractors who'll get the blame, when it's over. For not
keeping our flocks of lambs in order, I reckon."

Which was why he had come down, in haste, from Carlisle, having heard, among other rumors, that the English
navvies, having failed to drive the Irish off the site, were
bringing in reinforcements from Kendal and Shap Fell who
were already slipping past the Cumberland Yeomanry and
getting into Penrith.

"So there won't be a lodging-house safe in Penrith tonight if it has an Irishman in it. Nor a beer-house or a gin-shop that's ever served a drink to a Paddy. And when those pick-ax handles start to fly—well—I reckon it's no fit sight for a lady. You'll come with me, Miss Blake."

Where to? She saw no point in asking as he lifted her into the nondescript livery-stable gig and drove off with her, managing the horse with the rough skill of a coachman who had the Queen's mail to deliver. A man who had swung a pick-ax handle himself, she supposed, before railway money had put gold rings on his square-palmed hands and a gold watch-chain thicker than Lord Merton's across his well-fed middle. Not her ideal companion for a romantic Lakeland journey but a man who—that spark of Evangeline again told her—would be of far greater assistance than any romantic ideal just now.

"This is very kind of you, Mr. Keith."

He did not answer.

She tried again. "I hope I am not taking you far out of your way?"

He smiled down at her. "No, Miss Blake."

It hardly seemed enough. "Then—you were going, in any case, to Lake Ullswater? I did explain to you that my friend's house is on the far shores of the lake, between the bays of Sharrow and Howtown—didn't I? Is that in your general direction?"

He smiled again. "No, Miss Blake. My direction is Askham. The Queen's Head—a charming hostelry. I often stay there."

"But you will take me on—of course—to Ullswater." Very deliberately she had made a statement, allowing no question to be possible. *Of course* he would take her where she wished to go.

"I will take you to Ullswater," he said. "When I can."

The village of Yanwath lay two miles away. An empty road. A sudden taste of snow in the air. The early winter dark drawing in. The black sketch of a bird circling mournfully in a blackening sky. And then, some way ahead but fast approaching, appearing as suddenly as if they had risen from the ground, a crowd of short, thick-set men in flat caps or gamekeepers' feathered hats, flannel shirts in red and yellow, blue and yellow checks, moleskin trousers tied below the knee with string, a jaunty band of navvy men on the "randy," until one saw the shovels, the pick-axes with the sawn-off heads, the iron bars used on the line as rammers for blasting, lethal weapons every one in the hands of men who would not think too much, or too long, about using them. Men who drank ale in buckets, lived rough and usually in sin, cut off from "decent folk," like gipsies, like bandits, in their isolated camping places. Men with no roots, no loyalties, with no property of their own, no families of *theirs* cowering in Penrith, no reason, therefore, to worry just where the ax fell or the flame kindled. Fifty of them, Oriel counted, then a hundred. A battalion.

Suddenly not far away. Quite near. "Englishmen, by the look of it, from Shap and Kendal," said Garron Keith. "And Penrith has more Irish in it today than Dublin."

"Will they stop us?" She did not wish to sound too alarmed about it, although her mouth felt very dry, her skin oddly tender. Fear, she supposed, of an expressly physical nature to which she was not accustomed. Fear, not of insult but of actual injury, not of damage to one's pride and emotions, but of brute force.

Her skin crawling now, her stomach tightening very close to nausea, she forced herself to admit the possibility. Yes, it could happen. Anything could happen. And since there was absolutely nothing she could do to prevent it she might just as well straighten her back and make the only choice left to her; to behave badly or to behave well. No choice at all, of course. She would behave well. *Very* well, if she possibly could. At least that would be something.

"Will they stop us?" she murmured again, believing him well able to judge.

He shrugged his shoulder. "If they want to, then yes, I reckon they will."

"Do you know them?"

"I shouldn't think so. But they may know me. In which case they'll know I'm a Geordie, not an Irishman. It might help."

"Can you—help them?"

"To do what?"

She hesitated. "I think—to keep out of trouble." For, even through her fast-building panic, it seemed more than likely to her that these unguided, incoherent men were heading to punishment, deportation, prison, the gallows even, far more surely than to victory.

She saw him smile. "Trouble is what a navvy's made for, Miss Blake. They like it. Why else would they lead this life?"

"One hears—for the money?"

"What money?" Once again, although he kept his eyes on the road, his gaze as narrowed with calculation as a sailor squinting through strong sunlight on the sea, she saw him smile. "Money's not in it. There are ten thousand men up and down this line and I'll not be far out if I tell you they'll spend a thousand pounds on booze for every mile of track they lay down. And what I know for certain is that not more than a hundred will have a penny piece to take away, wherever it is they're going, when the job's done. That's the way they are."

And the road ahead was black with them now. Men who held their own lives cheap and so would have no care of hers.

"Are you afraid, Miss Blake?"

She straightened her back at an exceedingly proper angle.

"Yes. It would be foolish—surely—not to be?"

"It would. Especially—look over there . . ."

But she had already seen the smoke curling quite gracefully in the sky ahead of them, a cloud of it rising high and then spreading, drifting, from fires already growing cold.

"Damnation," he said. "They've been burning the Irish huts at Yanwath. And making free with Irish whiskey and Irish women, I reckon. There'll be no quarter now."

And whipping up the livery-stable horse, he took a sudden left turn at a speed which jarred every bone in her body and went hurtling along a lane so narrow that, unable to contemplate the possibility of some other vehicle coming from the opposite direction, she closed her eyes and clung to the edge of her seat with aching hands, her mind finding enough to occupy it with the immediate problem of keeping on her hat, not bursting into tears, not—absolutely not—being sick.

The gig stopped—eventually—in the yard of another inn surrounded, she thought, by miles of sleeping, undulating, empty land.

"This is Askham," he said. "The Queen's Head."

Was it also safety? She rather doubted it.

"Miss Blake." He looked amused. "What else can I do? You're an Englishwoman. And if you happened to meet a gang of Irish lads on the road somewhere between here and Pooley Bridge, who've just had their homes burned down and their women molested—one way or another . . . Well, I can't let you risk it, can I?''

"No, Mr. Keith."

"So you'll stay here and I'll send a message to your Miss Woodley. I reckon a boy could get through across the fells.''

"Thank you, Mr. Keith."

What else could she say? Nothing, she rather suspected, to which he would pay the least attention.

"So I'll just take you inside and get you settled. They know me here and so they'll look after you very well. And when I get back we'll have some supper together and talk awhile . . .''

"Where are you going?'' Her voice was sharper than she had intended, crying out, perhaps—she was not quite certain . . . *Don't leave me. I may not trust you. In fact, no, certainly not, I don't trust you. But at least I know who you are, and even if you harm me yourself—and I expect you might well try—you won't let any of these others, these strangers, come near me.*

Had she understood that much already? He nodded and smiled at her. "Not far. And maybe not for long. There's just a spot of railway business—you may have noticed—to attend to.''

The inn was low-beamed and very pleasant, full of the fragrance of wood smoke and the gleam of copper and brass, a caress of warmth and ease touching her, velvet-handed, as she entered, the landlady agreeing at once with Mr. Keith that the "young lady" must have every consideration, a small, firelit parlor of her very own to sit in behind a discreetly closed and very heavy door, hot water and towels, a deep, leather armchair made into a nest of welcome repose by large, fringed, dark red cushions, red plush curtains drawn across the window to make the nest warmer, cozier, more secret, even a glass of brandy which one could offer with perfect propriety to any young lady in shock. Dreadful, she thought it, wrinkling her nose, although having taken it like medicine, she found herself very drowsy and fell fast asleep, waking to find Mr. Keith back again, sitting with a whiskey bottle beside him, a glass in his hand, looking at her.

A strange, and very shocking, moment.

She had taken down her hair, anticipating a long wait with plenty of time to do it up again, and now, badly shaken by the very fact of being observed in the vulnerable act of sleep by a stranger, she shook it instinctively forward to hide her face like a pale curtain.

"Very pretty," he said.

She gave him a level stare, not unfriendly—since, in the circumstances, she doubted if she could afford to be *that*—but thinking it best, thinking it wise, to nip any familiarity firmly in the bud. And then, having delivered her reprimand, her sharp little rap on the knuckles of his possible desire to flirt with her, she followed it, in recognition of the service he had done her, with a slight smile.

"Are you forgiving me my trespasses, Miss Blake?" he said.

She ignored that.

"What has happened, Mr. Keith? Did you go back to Penrith?"

"I did. I'm not the only contractor on the site. There's Brassey's men, and Stephenson's men. So I thought I'd just go along and make sure my lads weren't the only ones clapped in jail . . ."

To keep them out of trouble after all, as she'd suggested?

"Did you find them?"

"Some of them. More or less the ones I'd expected. There's a breed of men you won't have come across, Miss Blake, who don't think they've had a good night out unless they can crawl home covered in blood. Their own or the other fellow's—it makes no difference. *They* were all there, of course. Wouldn't have missed it for the world. And now as many as I could round up, English and Irish alike, are back in camp at Plumpton or Yanwath—or what's left of it."

"That was—brave?—of you, Mr. Keith." She heard the question in her own voice, to which, without hesitation, he replied, "I reckon not. Commonsense, more like. Those men—whatever else they are—are good workers when they're not on the randy. And with this railway mania spreading all over the country, good labor is getting hard to find. Very hard. I've had look-outs posted, these six months past, on every main road between Lancaster and Carlisle, picking up likely lads on the tramp and getting them into the nearest beer-shop. The best place in the world to make sure they sign on with Keith, instead of Stephenson or Brassey. I've accepted a fixed completion date on this contract and it's going to cost me money if I don't meet it. So I can't afford to have too many of my lads in jail, you see."

"I see." And she might have smiled at his effrontery had she not feared to give him too much encouragement, being already aware that for every ounce of anything, or everything, one gave him he would help himself to a gallon.

"Do you know how the trouble started today?" she inquired instead.

He shrugged, his prizefighter's shoulders filling the high, wide-backed chair, his brown eyes and skin and hair looking vigorous, tough-fibered, enduring, his legs stretched out at ease on the hearthrug, one large, highly polished calf boot uncomfortably close, she abruptly realized, to her own narrow, pointed shoe. A proximity she did not relish, particularly when it occurred to her that it might be unwise to offend him by drawing her foot too obviously away. And, having decided she had better not move it, it suddenly dominated her awareness, the size of his foot and the heat she imagined to be coming from it menacing her own, so that it began to ache and tingle.

"How did it start?" he said. "Out of nothing—as always. An English ganger—that's a foreman, in your language—and an Irish navvy came to blows, it seems. The ganger told the man to put down his pick and pick up his shovel—or some fool thing. The man refused—I reckon he'll have forgotten why himself by now, so don't ask me. The ganger turned rough, the Paddy called on his mates, and the ganger got himself knocked about a bit. So *his* mates went down to Yanwath and set fire to the Irish huts. You saw them still smoking."

And there would have been women in those huts, and a great many children.

"Was anyone killed?"

"Hard to tell as yet." But by the tone of his voice she understood not only that he thought it likely but would not lose much sleep over it either way. "But there's a big Irish camp at Plumpton, and the lads there didn't take kindly to the fires at Yanwath. Which is why the call went out for English reinforcements from Shap Fell. Two thousand of them, they're saying, slipped past the Yeomanry into Penrith. Enough to smash up every lodging-house that ever housed an Irishman, at any rate. They were smoking the Paddies out into the street and beating them senseless—an hour or two back—until the soldiers, and a few others, got matters in hand."

A vicious conflagration indeed, she thought, to have arisen from a single spark between two men. "Is there always hostility of this kind?"

"There is." And, quite evidently, it was a normal part of the daily round to him. "Because the Irish work well and they work for less. Digging is what they've been brought up to. There's nothing else to do in Kilkenny or Donegal. And whenever their potatoes won't grow so well and they get hungry—which seems to happen every year or two—they come over to the construction sites and think they're millionaires the first time they draw a navvy's wages. Some of them even save their money and go home like kings. But most of them drink, like most of the English and most of the Welsh and the Geordies. And when a Paddy goes fighting-mad with booze, it's not easy to stop him. A man can get hurt making the attempt. And if he happens to be an Englishman it might sour his liking for the Irish. Although that's not really the root of it. I reckon men who live rough and hard with nothing much at the end to show for it, need somebody to blame who isn't one of themselves. A scapegoat. And the Irish look different enough and sound different enough to fit the bill. They never give me any trouble when they're on their own."

"And is it over now?" Was she asking him "Can I go now? Will you release me?" Glancing at his large, brown boot, gleaming arrogantly at her in the firelight, surely a fraction closer now than before, she rather thought so.

"To all intents and purposes. They've got the Irish penned in at Plumpton and the English at Yanwath with the soldiers in between."

"And Penrith?"

"A lot of broken glass and thick heads, and a few men in jail who won't remember what they did to get there, or why, when the beer runs out of them in the morning. Although I expect the magistrates will pack somebody off on a convict ship to Australia, just to set the rest a good example."

Remembering that Matthew Stangway and Lord Merton were both magistrates, she thought it very likely.

"And is it safe for me to go on to Ullswater now?"

"*Miss Blake.*" He acted out an expression of shock and alarm. "At twenty minutes past midnight. How could you think of such a thing?"

Her shock was entirely genuine. Was it possible she had slept so long? Yet the journey to Penrith had been very te-

dious, the coach cramped and airless beyond any possibility
of rest. She had been sleeping badly, too, since September.
And this room had been so warm, so snug. And there had
been the brandy.

"Heavens—I had no idea. What can I do about it . . . ?"

"Nothing." He sounded absolutely certain. "Miss Woodley knows you are here and understands the situation. She
was glad to see the boy I sent her, having thrown something
of a fit, it seems, when the soldiers turned her back halfway
to Yanwath. She knows there's still trouble here and there, in
patches, and won't be expecting you before—shall we say
noon, tomorrow?"

Was this reasonable, or likely, or even true? For she knew
he would lie to her very cheerfully if it suited him and show
no remorse, either, should his perfidy be discovered. Dangerous man. Devious man. Had he really saved her from the
perils of riot and arson or simply tricked her into exchanging
one hazardous situation for another? She was here alone with
him, after all, by his contriving, with no other word but his
to tell her it was unsafe to leave. A man from a world so
different from her own that she had no real way of judging
his disposition or—rather more to the point—just what he
might be likely to do next to her. A man who had once lived
rough and hard—he made no secret of it—like a gipsy, a
bandit. A *navvyman* beneath his pleated cambric shirt and
showy blue and silver brocade waistcoat, who, in this isolated
place, could be as tough and hard with her as he pleased.

"Your boxes are upstairs," he told her, "in the best front
bedroom. You must be hungry. I know I am. I've ordered
supper in here, by the fire."

Supper? Inn-servants coming with plates and dishes and
their own, unlikely-to-be-favorable opinion of a girl who
could be served cold meat and pickles and strong claret with
her hair hanging down. But when, instinctively, she began to
pin it up again, he said, "Leave it down. I like it."

"That would not be suitable, Mr. Keith."

"It is what I want, Miss Blake."

Indeed? She *was* in danger, then. A pang of alarm and the
awareness that she had really known it from the start struck
her both at once. Yet, nevertheless, she gave him a long, cool
stare copied exactly from Evangeline and, hoping he could
not see that her hands were trembling, began to dress her
hair into a low and very severe chignon, ramming each pin

in place very precisely and in a silence *she* did not intend to break.

"That does not suit you, Miss Blake."

"On the contrary, Mr. Keith. And, in any case, that is for me to say—surely?"

"I don't like it, Miss Blake."

"Really? But one cannot always have just what one would like. Have you never learned that?"

Through the glinting firelight he leaned forward and, with an air she felt to be impudent, raised his glass to her. "No, Miss Blake, I never have learned that lesson. And don't intend to. Not that you're the first to try and teach me, either. Maybe I'm a slow learner, but I've never managed to get it through my head. That and one or two other little matters. Like 'knowing my place,' for instance. And 'paying attention to my betters.' Well—so I would, if I could work out just who those 'betters' were. Or why. It may be glaringly obvious to you, Miss Blake. Not to me."

Draining his glass he set it down sharply on the table beside the whiskey bottle and then, as if something had just occurred to him, picked it up again and refilled it.

"Shall I tell you about myself?" He did not wait for her permission. "Aye—I reckon it might be best. I come from a pit village on Tyneside. Not a place you'd much care for. I've not been back there myself, lately, though I reckon I'd not find it much changed. They'll still be sending the lads underground to cut coal as soon as they're big enough. At ten or eleven they can usually manage a full shift, although my father set me off a bit earlier. Took me down with him when I'd just turned three, to sit and keep the rats off his dinner while he was working. That's quite usual. Even at Low Grange, where the Stangways get their money."

"I don't know anything about that, Mr. Keith."

"Of course not. They wouldn't see any reason to tell you. But that's the way of it. Families work as a team in the villages. So did mine. We all went underground together. My father cut the coal. Then he harnessed my mother to a coal-cart and she dragged what he'd cut from the seam to the shaft. Well yes, Miss Blake—because a woman on all fours is smaller than a pony and therefore better—it stands to reason—when it comes to crawling down narrow tunnels in the dark. And then we'd hoist it to the surface if the brat who was operating the winding gear could be bothered to turn his handle. My father coughed to death one night—it often happened. And then, about a year later, I grew an inch or two taller than the man in my mother's house—which made it harder for him to belt me every pay night. I belted him instead. Just once. But then, of course, I had to go. I was fourteen. It was the year they built the Stockton to Darlington, which makes me thirty-four now, as I expect you'll be wondering. And I found out that George Stephenson, who put in that line and built the first locomotive in the world to go with it, had started down a pit on Tyneside, like me. Except that instead of using his spare time learning how to smoke and keep down a bellyful of ale, and chase women, like the rest of us, he'd taught himself to read. I did the same—in Sunday schools, where there's always a good woman like Miss Susannah Saint-Charles ready to give a likely lad his chance. For reasons some of these 'good ladies' never acknowledge—and some of them do. I took my chances, Miss Blake—every one of them. Whatever they turned out to be.''

"Yes. I do believe you, Mr. Keith.''

He smiled at her.

"I'm very pleased to hear it. I worked hard for a long time, physically hard, lived rough and kept my eyes open. Because all it takes, Miss Blake, is to see a need. Any need. And, once you've seen it, to get in there fast and fill it, before anybody else can beat you to it. When the railway mania started, the need I saw was for labor. Not the kind that could ever be recruited in one locality. Men—in their hundreds of thousands—who'd be ready to follow the track as they laid it down. Rootless men who wouldn't go sloping off back to the farm to get the harvest in and leave my job half done. That was the need. I fill it better than some others because there's not a job the navvies do I haven't done myself and couldn't do again. So, when I go on site and tell them to move six cubic yards of earth apiece per shift they know *I* know it can be done. Which means when the great engineers like Mr. Locke and Mr. Isambard Kingdom Brunel and Mr. Morgan de Hay have their mighty projects on hand I'm certain to get my share. Because my men are more reliable than most. I pay them on time, you see, and they trust me.''

"Really, Mr. Keith?''

Once again, through the firelight, he raised his glass to her.

"I said the *men* trust me, Miss Blake. Maybe I wouldn't

make the same claim for women. I was married once, as you know. Men of the class I come from marry young because there's always a chance they may not live to be older. And, often as not, by the time they get to the altar there might well be a bairn on the way. My wife died eight years ago, just as the good times were starting. I have a girl of eleven and one of ten. The boy's eight now. You'll see the significance of that.''

"Yes." She nodded. Three children in four years born perhaps not in easy circumstances to a woman whose strength he may well have overestimated, taken for granted, until the last child—the boy—had drained it away completely. One did not have to live in a pit village or a navvy encampment to understand such things. One had only to think of Constantia Saint-Charles and a dozen like her. Had Mr. Keith loved his wife, she wondered? But eight years, she rather imagined, was a long time for such a man to mourn. Even to remember. Perhaps a long time for any man.

"I am so sorry, Mr. Keith." It was the thing one said—the correct formula—to a gentleman who happened to be a widower, although, in truth, she could not feel that Pity and Mr. Garron Keith had ever spent much time together.

"Sorry? For my wife? Yes—I'll allow that, I reckon. She'd have been a rich woman now, after all, taking her ease in her own carriage, and all the other little luxuries Miss Blake has been taking for granted all her life. Aye—'' He smiled suddenly. "And who knows how she'd have taken to all that? I'm not certain. But her daughters, now—they'll *have* to take to it. They're a different matter. I can handle the boy. But how do I set about teaching those scamps of mine to be young ladies? Can you tell me that, Miss Blake?''

Most assuredly she could tell him. "My friend, Miss Woodley," she said crisply, "ran an excellent school for young ladies in Carlisle. She would be pleased to recommend some similar establishment. Or, failing that, a good governess. There are several agencies. My mother would know.''

He allowed a moment to pass by during which she heard every sound in the room around her quite separately, the logs crackling, wood against black iron in the hearth, the inquisitive patter of rain on the close-curtained window, the slow, deep-chested, assertive breathing of Garron Keith who was playing with her now, she well knew it, with all the concentrated pleasure and lazy cruelty of a cat.

"And if your mother were here now," he said, "she would know very well—as you do—that it is not a governess I am thinking of."

Here too she had learned a formula, to be pronounced *absolutely at once* to any gentleman on the point of making an unwelcome declaration, thus saving embarrassment all round.

"Mr. Keith, I think it only right to make clear to you that I . . ."

"That you don't wish to be troubled by the impertinences of a common man? Do you have any choice, Miss Blake—just now—if I choose to trouble you?"

She got up, her legs far from steady yet enabling her, because she demanded that they should, to stand very tall, her voice strained but steady.

"Mr. Keith . . ." And this too was a formula, unoriginal, bland, not likely to afford her much protection but better, surely, than nothing at all. "I feel this conversation has gone far enough."

He stood up too, much taller, his eyes touching her with an appreciation she knew to be sensual, an enjoyment wholly and frankly of the appetite. "I used to see girls like you driving past in their carriages, Miss Blake, when I worked on the turnpikes. Mending the roads for your pleasure, ma'am . . ."

"How kind."

"So it was, when I remember the wages they paid me. But things change. Don't they?"

"Indeed." She was speaking words—she knew it—without regard for their meaning, any words so long as they sounded distant and cold. A defense she saw to be useless as his eyes touched her again, assessed her, decided.

"All right, Miss Blake. I'll tell you straight what I'm after. Marriage, my bonny lass. But you must know that."

"Oh dear." And it was Evangeline, as so often at times of crisis, who spoke within her. "I have been aware, from time to time, Mr. Keith, of your admiration, which I have been at some pains never to encourage . . ."

But the destructive phrase had no greater effect than to make him smile.

"I handled contracts to the value of two million pounds last year, Miss Blake, and made myself a handsome profit . . ."

"How very gratifying for you."

"And this year I shall do better still."

"I am sure you are to be congratulated."

"So I have bought a house in Lydwick, in your Gore Valley—since a man has to settle somewhere. A fine house, such as they call fit for a gentleman."

And he needed, along with his Turkey carpets and his crystal chandeliers, a lady to put inside it, a decoration for his dinner-table, a wife for his bed, a social mentor for his children. It was the compromise to which her life had long been leading her, a simple acceptance—in fact—to be paid, for the services she would render, in wages rather than in love.

"I can provide," he said, his keen eyes fixed on hers, "right handsomely. And if I should hurt you myself, as men do, I reckon, without meaning it, maybe without even knowing I had, then nobody else will hurt you. I can promise you that."

No other hand but his own, he was telling her, would ever touch his woman. No other men would lay claim to her attention or take liberties with her pride, her conscience, her sensibility ever again. No woman either. No baronets and squires who would only pick her up to throw her down again. No Kate to call her over to Dessborough and make a "favorite aunt" of her, if she had a demanding home of her own.

And Mrs. Garron Keith would be well provided for.

Food, shelter, protection. Possession. The basic offerings, surely, down long ages, of a man to his mate, to which only the niceties of "Society," of "Civilization," had given the names of "a house in Lydwick"—or Dessborough—"money in the bank," "duty" and "love." But he had not spoken of love. She did not suppose he had thought of it either, except in terms of hungers well satisfied, a primary need fulfilled, pride of possession and curiosity at rest.

A proposal which, if one could say nothing else for it, was not deceitful.

The door opened, bringing them a heavily laden tray of cold beef, game pies and pickles, a plum cake, a bottle of claret, the maids glancing at her as they hurried away, with the curiosity—she realized—of decent girls for a woman dining alone, at night, with a man to whom, they were all aware, she was not a wife.

Had he compromised her then? As Kate had compromised Francis?

"Mr. Keith, please tell me the truth. Is the road to Ullswater really impassable tonight?"

"Oh, as to that . . ." And he was smiling, quite unabashed. "I expect I could have got you there, had I cared to try."

"Then why—exactly—did you not?"

"Because I am a man who takes his opportunities. I told you that. And if I'd taken you to Ullswater you would have thanked me nicely and that would have been the end of it."

"As I shall thank you tomorrow morning."

"I dare say. But, by then, you will have spent the night with me."

"I beg your pardon . . ."

"My word," he said, looking very well pleased. "Such alarm. But there's no need—sadly, perhaps. But there it is. No need for panic, for the good reason that I've no need to lay a hand on you. No need at all. You've been here already, you see, for several hours, alone in the private parlor of an inn with me. And the inn knows what it thinks of that."

"The inn is mistaken."

"So it is. Yet I could take you now, Miss Blake, if I chose, and have your relatives begging me to marry you afterward to save your reputation. Couldn't I?"

"I couldn't recommend it, Mr. Keith. It would hardly be wise."

"I know. Because you'd hate me for it. So would I, bonny lass, in your place. And I don't want a wife who shudders every time I touch her. So all I've done is create a situation where people would be bound to wonder. A little measure of insurance, should the need arise."

Could her reputation stand it? he was suggesting. Or her mother's? The chin of Miss Oriel Blake rose to a sharp angle, her light eyes taking on the brilliance of ice.

"Mr. Keith, I am not open to persuasion by such methods. The people who know me would take my word and I care nothing for the rest . . ."

But Evangeline would care. She realized he knew that.

"Dear Miss Blake, have I said anything about persuasion? Surely I'm just giving you an example of my generosity—of what I could do if I had a mind . . . And an example of restraint to go with it—yes, Miss Blake—restraint, my admiration for you being such that I could so easily—well—succumb to the temptation . . ."

"Which—of course—you will not."

"Only if you—Miss Blake—should wish me to . . ."

Once again she was conscious of each sound around her, the crackling fire, the creaking of old boards overhead, the intake of her own shallow breath as he came toward her and, without speaking a word, removed a pin from her hair, and then another, watching each tress uncoil, his eyes narrowed with pleasure, until each one hung loose and smooth around her shoulders and the curve of her back. An act of possession to which she made no resistance, her stillness and silence absolute as he combed through the fine, pale mass with deft, pleasure-seeking, assertive fingers.

"Are we still speaking of marriage, Mr. Keith," she said at last, waiting until he had taken his hands away from her head.

"We are."

"Then there are certain—matters—of which you should be made aware." And even with him it would not be easy.

"What matters?"

"For instance—that I have no money."

His eyes on her hair again, he laughed at her. "So you say. But you'll have more money at the bottom of your handkerchief drawer without even noticing it, than Morag—my wife—managed to scrape together in wages in the six months before I married her. And as for the rest, I'm taking a wife, not buying a dog. I don't need a pedigree. So long as the breeding shows—and it does—then that's good enough for me. So rest easy. Come and have your supper in peace. You've got nothing to fear."

"Did I say," she murmured, walking slowly toward the table, taking her time as he had taken his, "that I was afraid?"

A silence fell, a moment of assessment, of measuring, that was almost acceptance on her part, almost a victory on his.

"You're a fine, strong woman, Oriel Blake." It was a tribute. Lifting her head, shaking her hair away from her face so he could see it, she looked at him. "So I am," she said.

Eight

Mr. Garron Keith's return to the Gore Valley, some five days later, was occasioned by an incident on a short stretch of the line just below his own site at the Merton Ridge Tunnel. A mishap by no means uncommon whereby the contractor, a smaller man in every direction than Mr. Keith, had found himself quite suddenly unable to pay either his suppliers of iron and bricks and wooden sleepers or, perhaps more drastically, his laborers' wages; thus turning loose upon the horrified villages of Dessborough and Merton a horde of angry, hungry men who, in need of sustenance before going on the tramp to look for work elsewhere, descended upon them like a plague of locusts.

Hen coops were raided, both eggs and chickens carried off and devoured over camp fires on Dessborough Moor. Farmers' wives found their kitchens invaded, not uncheerfully, by roving navvy gangs who, strolling casually inside, still resplendent in their moleskins and velveteen jackets and scarlet hat-bands, made off with anything that pleased them, hams and cheeses and home-brewed ale and, on occasions, the virtue of a not altogether unwilling dairymaid. And when the men of Dessborough and Merton felt obliged to make their protest, there were ugly confrontations, fisticuffs between farm-boys not noted for their murderous dispositions and young buck-navvies who knew of no time to stop a fight until the finish. A bloody finish, more often than not, with the pride and joy of several Dessborough mothers losing teeth, suffering broken noses and smashed knuckles, and with the owner of one particularly fine rabbit warren beaten within

156

what looked an inch or two of his life, when he lay in wait to protect his stock.

"Damned contractors," groaned the great engineer, Mr. Morgan de Hay, who happened to be in the neighborhood. "Damn the whole plaguey lot of them." Yet, nevertheless, it was to one of the "plaguey breed" that he addressed himself for help, Mr. Garron Keith in fact, who, at a price he felt entitled in the circumstances to name, agreed to take over the abandoned contract and as much of the workforce as suited him. Such members of it, that is, who had neither taken to the hills and fled, nor been detained at the pleasure of the local magistrates in Lydwick jail.

The remaining men were assembled by Mr. Keith who, having picked out a few he recognized, stated his terms and expectations in a language easily understood by the rest. He paid wages weekly, not monthly like some contractors, or not at all like others. And if that meant there was a "randy" every Friday night instead of just one Friday in four, then he had nothing to say to that so long as there was a full turn-out for work on the following Saturday morning. And Sunday too, if it came to that. No tommy-shop either. No food tickets. Cash. Paid out in small change from a hut on the site, not in a beer-shop—as some contractors did—in large notes that had to be changed across the bar counter, usually into ale, with the contractor taking his percentage of every pint of it.

"Fair's fair," said Garron Keith. "I pay on time. You get the job done in time. Or else you can all sod off." And having settled that small matter to his satisfaction, he paid a call on Mr. Matthew Stangway, in passing, to make known his intention of marrying the daughter of Mr. Stangway's wife. A statement—by no means a request—causing a degree of irritation which Matthew had converted, almost at once, to amusement, his very favorite emotion, which he had been more than pleased to demonstrate to Evangeline on her return from perhaps only a partial triumph in London.

"Impudent, of course," Matthew told her, counting upon her fury like a treat in store. "He sat there, my darling—just where you are sitting now—with his legs stretched out on the hearthrug, and even had the effrontery to tell me he wasn't bothered about getting any money with her. He'd take her with nothing but her petticoat, was the phrase he used. Crude but effective, of course, like the man himself. And one couldn't help but feel how much he was enjoying shrugging aside the issue of the dowry which one always finds to be so crucial with . . ."

"With gentlemen?"

"Indeed. So he was giving himself a high old time, one felt, by throwing it back at me—making sure I knew he didn't need it, that he could afford to support your daughter rather better, I do believe he implied, than the manner to which *I'd* accustomed her. I wonder if he can? Today, perhaps. But one wonders, with these speculators, about tomorrow. Really—one wonders."

"My darling," Evangeline sounded rather bored with all such wonderings. "I find the subject hardly stirs my curiosity one way or the other."

"You have confidence in him, then?"

"Dearest—I have never given the man a moment's thought. One would only need to do so—surely—had one any notion of accepting him? And since the possibility does not arise . . ."

"Dearest . . ." Matthew's voice rang with affection as it often did at his most malicious. "Your daughter *has* accepted him."

"Nonsense."

"I fear not, my love."

"And you have done nothing to stop her?"

"I? Ah—no. Let us say I hardly cared to spoil your pleasure in disposing of the matter yourself?"

"How kind. Then please arrange my journey to that backwater at once."

But having traveled north by uncomfortable winter stages to Miss Woodley's lakeside home, it was to meet a kind of resistance she had never encountered before in Oriel. A reserve of calm which seemed to extend for several yards around her, coupled with an infuriating disposition to agree politely with everything her mother said to her, while committing herself to nothing at all.

"The man is impossible, Oriel."

"Yes, Mama."

"A common laborer in a good suit. Heavens—one even had qualms about inviting him to dinner." *One*—she well remembered—had even judged him to be not quite good enough for Susannah and had said so, both to Maud and Letty. Even to Quentin, who would be sure to remember.

"He seems to be rather rich, Mama."

But what could the new-made fortune of a railway contractor mean to Evangeline now that she had tasted the splendors of Merton Abbey and Merton House in London's Grosvenor Square, or the Elizabethan manor in Kent where the elegant, if not truly honorable brother of Lady Merton, held his bachelor court? What could a solid residence, without either nobility or history to recommend it, purchased by Mr. Keith in the solid little market town of Lydwick mean to her when, with a little contriving, a little patience, her lovely Oriel might have a Mayfair salon, or become the mistress of *inherited* acres and privileges in Kent? And because these dreams, although difficult, were not entirely out of the question, she felt justified in employing every weapon she could think of to restore Oriel to her senses. Even a little cruelty.

"It will cause talk, Oriel. People might well say it had something to do with wanting to be married before Kate and Francis come home."

"Mama," said Oriel quietly. "It has something to do with that."

"Heavens, my darling—I know, I know. None better. But in such circumstances, one marries a king . . ."

"Well—I dare say—but there seems to be none available. Do you see any, Mama?"

"*Oriel.* They come in many guises—very many. There are kings of all shapes and sizes if one looks with an informed eye. And, while waiting for one to come along, one wears a brave face, my love—as you know so well how to do. I can forbid this foolish match, of course."

But, even so, Oriel was almost twenty-one, Mr. Keith, at thirty-four, amply possessed of both the means to elope with her and a disregard of the social niceties which might well incline him to do so. Not a prospect in any way to be relished, particularly with the Scottish border so near and Miss Woodley far too concerned with searching for the first celandines along the lake's edge even to notice an elopement, much less put a stop to it.

"Mama, the very last thing in the world I wish to do is quarrel, or offend you."

"Oh—why trouble about little things like that, dear, when you are setting about breaking my heart? You are throwing yourself away, Oriel, and I don't even want to get over it."

Yet no help, as she well knew, was to be expected from

Matthew who chose, rather, to aggravate the situation by writing not only to congratulate Oriel on what he presumed to be her engagement, but to mention—oh so artlessly—that Kate and Francis were now expected home in May.

"Then it would be best, Mama," said Oriel very frankly, "for me to be married in April."

"Well—yes, indeed." Evangeline had decided to try out her charm. "Unless, of course, you might care for a trip abroad instead? I expect I can persuade dear Matthew to foot the bill. Some elegant little watering-place, I thought, in the south of France—where one is hardly likely to be troubled by men with all this *new* money in their pocket . . ."

"Mama, one has to come home, you know, from holidays. And I *have* accepted him."

It had been decided, irrevocably in Oriel's opinion, two days after the rioting in Penrith when he had come to Miss Woodley's house, by arrangement, not so much to learn her final answer as to claim it. She had endured a restless night, and, waking to a light covering of snow beneath clear blue skies and cool February sunshine, she had stood for a long time in Miss Woodley's garden, quiet fragment of cultivation among the wild northern fells, the lake a mirror of pure silver beneath her, its encircling hills outlined, that crystal morning, in sharp frost, giving her, as always in this place, an impression of no one stirring, that the nearest gathering of so often intrusive humanity must be at least a hundred miles away. Pure solitude, an undramatic blending of herself with the bare heights and wooded hollows of the land, the eternity of deep, still water, in no way disturbed by her quite accurate knowledge of the hidden but nonetheless thriving communities around her; of the hill-farms and cottages and the even more astonishingly isolated "great" houses one discovered, always suddenly, among the fells and dales; of the lakeside bay of Howtown, only half a mile away from her, with its low, slate-gray inn and obliging landlord who had never yet refused Miss Woodley the use of his dog-cart and sensible old mare; of the lovely, almost secret bay of Sharrow on her other side, with the village of Pooley Bridge a mile or so behind it, standing a tidy sentinel at the northern tip of the lake; of the scattered communities of Glenridding and Patterdale across the water, dominated by the grandeur of Helvellyn and the perilous way to its summit along the aptly named Striding Edge.

She had heard both of huntsmen and shepherds who, combing that Edge after foxes or high-grazing sheep, had never been seen again, the fox-hounds taking to the wild, one supposed, only the faithful sheep-dogs turning up again, eventually—having guarded the human corpse until its decay, she'd been told—to claim their canine reward of being pensioned off by the late master's fire.

But that morning, with no room in her mind for tales of local disaster, she had set out to climb the pathway along Hallin Fell, the lake disappearing behind her, and then, between high-sweeping expanses of bare, empty land, to the almost invisible village of Martindale and its old church, the small, stone building which seemed, in its sheer simplicity and complete lack of adornment, to be a natural part of the wind and weather, to have grown there, from the Lakeland earth, with the same sure ripening, season by season, as the giant yew tree which had grown beside it. Two ancient pilgrims, church and tree together, surrounded by a low stone wall and, on that day, a carpet of snowdrops.

She had opened the gate and walked carefully among the flowers, feeling slight and solitary and happy to be so, as she had always felt in this hidden place, and then, tasting fresh snow in the air, had taken shelter against the hollow trunk of the yew tree, the vast spread of its branches touching the ground to make a dark, sharp-scented cavern around her.

She had come here many times before to contemplate the pains and pleasures of her childhood and girlhood, leaning, either in joy or sorrow or an uneasy blending of them both, against the antique trunk, impossibly old, six hundred years and more, Miss Woodley had told her, her fingers tracing with wonder and a strange feeling of pity the gnarled, dry wood, the scars and veins of it and—she felt oddly certain— the raw patches, the aches and regrets of anything which had lived so long.

And it was there, in the secret melancholy cavern of the yew tree where she had hidden, in days past, from other figures of unease and authority, that Garron Keith had found her, having walked up the fell path—in accordance with Miss Woodley's instructions—and down the bare sweep of the dale with the long, impatient stride of a man on urgent business, scarcely noticing the frost on the grass or the shrinking flowers, but simply intent on *getting there*, as fast and as directly as he could.

And as he bent his head to enter her cavern, his feet heavy on the fast-thawing ground, his presence had been an intrusion only because he had seemed to fill the space she had claimed so long ago as her own, giving her a brief illusion of hiding and discovery. Of capture.

"So here you are."

"Yes."

"Waiting for me, Miss Blake, are you? Or playing hide and seek? I'm away down to Yorkshire again, very likely in the morning. And I want an answer from you before I go. If it's yes then I can see your father . . ."

"My mother's husband." The correction had been instinctive. It even worried her that she had felt compelled to make it.

"All right, then. The man in your mother's house. That covers everything. Shall I go and see him?"

"Yes."

"So you'll marry me, then, Oriel Blake?"

"Yes." She heard her own voice speak the word. "I will."

"I'd like to hear you say more about it than that."

She had closed her eyes and then, opening them very wide, looked at him carefully, seriously, ready to pledge herself in the words she had been considering for two silent days, walking in Miss Woodley's garden or among the first snowdrops at the margins of the lake. Days in which she had contemplated her situation deeply at times, clinically at others, showing herself no mercy, stripping away any clinging shred of hope—as a few shreds still *had* clung to her—of another Francis Ashington or the same one, in some miraculous fashion which did not require the demise of Kate—restored to her again.

It would not happen. He would come back from his honeymoon and live with his wife, bring up his children, at Dessborough, five miles away from her uneasy home with her mother. And although one did not marry one man to escape paying morning-calls as a single woman on another—of course one did not do that—she was in no doubt that in order to have a life of one's own, in order to exist in the world she knew, it was absolutely essential to marry somebody. And she could think of no man less likely than Garron Keith to remind her of Francis.

Not a good reason, perhaps, but if she could come to think of him as a refuge, then she believed it would suffice.

"I will do everything I can to be a good wife to you," she had said.

"And what might that be?"

What indeed? "Whatever you want in a wife," she had told him, with instinctive sincerity. "Will you tell me what it is?"

"Aye. I'll tell you. As we go along—as it occurs to me. When something doesn't suit me, you'll know about it. When it does you'll know that too. I'm not devious. And I'm generous. I've no plan to be the richest corpse in the graveyard. What I earn I enjoy, which means you'll enjoy it too. Royally, if this railway boom goes on. And when there's no more space for another yard of track in England there's the rest of the world to go at. Enough to last my time out, I reckon, and leave you a wealthy widow. And my bairns provided for."

"When should I meet them?"

"When I'm sure of you. When I've had my ten minutes with your mother's husband, and when your mother's had her try at convincing you not to throw yourself away on an upstart like me. Will you change your mind?"

"No. I won't do that."

"Can you stand up to her?"

"Mr. Keith, when I am sure of doing the right thing I believe I can stand up to anybody."

"Even to me?" He was broadly smiling. "We'll see about that."

What happened next she had known to be inevitable, the tree bark biting into her back as he leaned against her, his body hard and heavy and making a direct demand for which, those two days past, she had been preparing herself; not yet responding but not resisting a kiss which, even with her limited experience, she knew to be without hesitation or complexity, performed for the sole and simple reason that it gave him pleasure. And, from the start, they were both of the opinion that his pleasures must be her very first concern.

"I'm not prepared to wait," he had said. "Don't come to me with any tales of long engagements—or any engagement at all. The house is ready and so am I—the sooner the better. How long can it take to buy a white dress and a wedding veil?"

Until—according to Evangeline—her daughter should be restored to a proper sense of her own worth. An attitude not much softened by the house in Lydwick which, although large and solid and set in a garden extensive enough to be called "grounds," Evangeline found too new, too reminiscent of the upstart industrial classes among whom Kate, herself a wool-merchant's grand-daughter, would surely have been more at ease than Oriel, a true descendant albeit on the wrong side of the blanket, of gentlemen. While as for the diamond ring Mr. Keith had given her daughter to wear—with Matthew's permission, it pained her to add—she felt no inclination whatsoever to compare it with the pearl and amethyst cluster given by Francis to Kate.

The diamond was large, without flaw, without history, and very expensive. The amethyst cluster, no matter how insignificant it *might* appear, had belonged to Celestine Ashington who had been Celestine Merton, to Grizelda Ashington before her, to Barbara Ashington who had been *Lady* Barbara Goreham before that. A contrast between a noble inheritance and an "asset" purchased with sordid pounds sterling which—felt Evangeline—spoke for itself.

Yet a number of events suddenly occurred to alter her strategy, not least among them the extraction from Matthew of a substantial dowry for Oriel which, whether the bridegroom wanted it or not, was a vital matter of pride to Evangeline.

Not that she felt in any way disposed to thank him for it. "She *is* your daughter, Matthew, after all. And if you are determined to throw her away I suppose you might as well do it in style."

"My love," he looked dangerously innocent. "The man is making a fortune. It occurs to me that, really, instead of creating all this fuss, we would do better to snap him up. For if he goes on at this rate—who knows?—even the Mertons, who are often short of ready money, might find him a useful proposition. Young Dora Merton is often in debt, one hears, and never quite likes to tell her father—particularly whenever he happens to have been gambling himself. So is it beyond the bounds of her imagination, do you think, to sell her noble self to somebody like our Mr. Keith, who might not be dazzled by nobility but will know—one feels quite certain—just what it is worth? The opening of just about every door he might wish to enter, right up to a seat in Parliament, should he have the fancy. Especially since the Merton cousin, young Timothy, who is going to marry Adela, has no talent in that direction. You *have* heard, I take it, about the Merton engagement?"

Yes. She had heard, in a letter from Monte Carlo, how Lord Merton's nephew and legal heir to the title had announced his engagement to the elder and therefore correct Merton daughter, Adela, thus ensuring that the estate and title would remain in the family but dashing all hopes of it for Oriel. She had also heard, in the same chatty letter, of the unfortunate entanglement into which Lady Merton's brother had fallen with a fairly well-known actress, a mature and scheming woman who, having managed to move into his Kent manor, would "give him the devil's own job" as Lord Merton put it, to get her out again.

Certainly not in time for a spring wedding before Mr. and Mrs. Ashington came home again.

Yet it was the stricken appearance of Susannah Saint-Charles—so badly, so comically enamoured of Mr. Garron Keith herself—which showed Evangeline how best to change course. Only a matter of weeks ago she had warned Letty to keep a sharp eye on the plain and so awkwardly passionate Susannah, describing the object of her attentions as both dangerous and impossible. What better way, now, of saving face than by pretending it had all been part of her ploy to snatch him up for Oriel?

"The man is so obscenely rich," she purred to a hostile assembly of Maud and Letty, "that really—after a while— one rather loses sight of the few odd little things one may not have quite liked about him to begin with. One's eyes are dazzled, I suppose, by such a mountain of gold . . . And such a powerful nature—so tempestuous—I rather fear he has swept Oriel off her feet."

It was done.

"And it will be so delightful," she murmured, "to have my daughter established so close to me in Lydwick. A pleasant town, I have always thought. So much more—well—the sort of place to which one is accustomed than Hepplefield."

Thus giving Letty an extra scratch of the claws since Quentin, on the excuse that he found the daily journey between the vicarage and his offices in Hepplefield too long, but—as Letty believed correctly—because he could not tolerate the disruption of another baby in his parental home, had moved into "rooms," in Hepplefield's premier thoroughfare of Bishop Blaize Street, to be looked after by a landlady who, although competent and clean, was not his mother. A handsome woman too, one heard, with a calmness of manner one might even describe as dignified; thus making a pleasant change—Evangeline had been heard to murmur—from Letty.

"Yes. I am so pleased my daughter and her future husband have decided to settle in Lydwick."

It was a much smaller town than Hepplefield, untroubled by the industrial expansion which, with the touch of its demon wand, had doubled Hepplefield's population, and then trebled it, overnight. New factories were springing up in Hepplefield, they said, like toadstools, each one surrounded by rings of lesser toadstools that were the cottages to house its workers, the gin-shops and pawn-shops for their convenience, so that the same industrialists who had sown and harvested the ugly crop were now eagerly awaiting the coming of the railway in order to escape it, having realized at once that, although a man with a horse and a carriage is obliged to live within a mile or two of his factory gates, no such limits are imposed upon a man in a train.

But Lydwick, on its snug bend of the River Gore where the water ran too slow and shallow to turn a mill-wheel or power a steam-engine, had escaped industrial splendors and squalors alike, remaining the country town it had always been, a few quiet streets of bow-windowed shops selling good quality leather boots and saddles, choice tobaccos and rare, scented teas from China to suit the tastes of the neighboring "gentry"; a wine merchant to satisfy the palates of the discerning; a book-binder to cater to those who believed "intellect" to be still in fashion; a portrait painter who found much employment in producing the "likeness" in oils of a daughter on her wedding day, a son in uniform, a father taking up his appointment as a magistrate, a wife with a newborn heir.

Gentle, slow-moving Lydwick, therefore, surrounded not by the coarse, bare moorland of Hepplefield but by fresh, green meadows and wide-armed groves of chestnut trees, the peaceful refuge of well-to-do widows, retired academics, gentlemen's families of small distinction but ample private means, and of Mr. Garron Keith whose lavish appointment of the house he had lately purchased on Lydwick Green was, at once, the focus of many, not altogether admiring eyes.

Two houses faced each other across the "Green," the small, gray vicarage hidden by overgrown hedges which no vicar had ever thought to trim, and the "new house," the first to be built in Lydwick for fifty years and more, begun and then abandoned by a Leeds manufacturer who had left Mr. Keith to finish off the elaborate façade, the stone fruit and flowers and vine-leaves clustering above the front door which Lydwick, accustomed to the simple, elegant lines of the previous century had thought too overdone, too modern, too much in keeping with the overblown sentimentality of Queen Victoria and her prim and proper Albert.

The shopkeepers of Lydwick, having made their money in the days of the poor morals but excellent taste of the Prince Regent and his bucks and rakes and dandies, did not altogether approve of the good husband, good father, too-good-to-be-true Prince Albert, finding his virtues of small encouragement to the luxury and sporting trades. Nor did they approve of Mr. Keith either, finding *him*, at a glance, too common; although the young person who was to be his wife was someone with whom they could feel perfectly comfortable. A lady. No one in Lydwick could fail to recognize the breed, nor disagree with the general opinion that it would be a pleasure, as soon as Miss Blake became installed as Mrs. Keith in the ostentatious, high-ceilinged, overornamental splendors of the "new house," to take tea with her.

She would have a very fine drawing-room, after all, with a Grecian-columned marble fireplace, a ceiling across which plaster Cupids flew in pairs between garlands of plaster flowers picked out in gold, and with long windows opening to a terrace and a prospect of velvet lawns, clipped box-hedges, and a sufficiency of nymphs and more Cupids—stone ones this time—for a miniature Versailles.

Oriel had chosen nothing in the house herself, nor had she expected to do so, accepting it as a ready-made part of Garron Keith as she accepted his children, to whom she was presented, just a few days before the wedding, as "your new mother." It was not a phrase she relished. Yet it was another accepted formula, the "right thing to say" on these occasions which, considering the rate at which "real mothers" faded and died, were by no means uncommon. And although it sounded a decidedly false note in her ears, she did not think she would care to be addressed either as "Mrs. Keith" or "stepmama."

The children were a surprise to her.

"They'll need some polishing," the man she still hesitated to call "Garron" had warned her. "Their mother's family are mainly fisherfolk from the far north of Scotland, and that's where they've been for most of their lives. I've had them with me whenever I could. But it's not in *me* to polish them. I know I can depend on your mother's agreement to that. And maybe whenever I chose a governess I picked the pleasant ones who could put up with the traveling life, instead of the old dragons who might have taught the bairns their manners. So you'll have your work to do.''

But it was neither their roughness nor the awkwardness of their posture which took her aback. She had simply not expected them to be so blond. A girl of ten and one of eleven, with hair as silver-pale as her own, and a boy with the same deep tan as his nut-brown father but with hair the strong, rich gold of honey. Elspeth, the younger girl, tongue-tied and ready to be tearful with shyness, her wide blue eyes awestruck as they fastened on the flowing lines of Oriel's cream silk gown, the elegance of the brown velvet roses at the waist which had scattered their rose-buds, in the same brown velvet, all around the hem. Jamie, the honey-gold boy, sturdy and shrewd, with no living memories of his real mother to trouble him. And Morag, the eldest, named for the woman who had died, tall and reed-slender, her eyes pale enough to be called gray, their glance passing over and through her fashionable, expensive, high-bred "new mother" with unmixed hostility.

"She's the eldest and the strongest," Garron said when they had made their curtsies, given their stilted answers to Oriel's very correct questions, and then gone outside, on their father's orders, to play. "They've had a roving life. Here and there with me. Back to Scotland whenever I was away somewhere that wouldn't suit them—which was a lot of the time— to be looked after by this aunt, or that aunt—rarely the same one. So I reckon Morag has looked after the other two. In her own mind maybe she thinks she's their mother, which can't be good for her. Nor for them, either. From now on I can see to the boy. But I want those girls to grow up looking like you, and sounding like you. You'll know how to handle it.''

"Yes, Garron.''

She would do her best. For Morag, whose pale hostile eyes seemed, from that day on, to follow her everywhere; for Evangeline, still sharp and critical and so deeply disappointed; for Kate toward whom her feelings, in spite of everything, remained both warm and responsible; for Susannah Saint-Charles whose excessive weeping at the wedding was quickly explained away by Quentin—who else?—as being due to the miscarriage, the night before, from which his other sister, Constantia, had almost lost her life. No happy omen for a wedding, although Oriel herself had passed into a state beyond anxiety, wishing, quite simply, to get on and lead the life she had agreed to lead, to do the things she had promised to do, to look after her home and her husband to the best of her abilities in Lydwick or anywhere else he might require her to follow him.

To keep her word.

Money had been spent on the wedding ceremony, both Evangeline and Garron Keith having required, absolutely, that it should. The bridal dress of white satin, cut to resemble an arum lily and stitched, here and there, with seed pearls, announced its own value, while the diamond on the long, pale hand of the bride, the diamonds in her ears, the triple strand of pearls at her throat were sufficient explanation, in themselves, as to why the marriage was taking place. The church was full of flowers which, being still in the month of March, had obviously been procured at great expense, the wedding-breakfast at High Grange Park being costly too in terms of game pies and galantines and champagne, although rather restrained, due—it was said—to Constantia's sad "accident," to Letty's nervous collapse on hearing of it which seemed likely to bring on a similar "accident" of her own, to the fact that the Mertons were still in Monte Carlo, and that the bridegroom himself was impatient to get away. Not on honeymoon but on business in North Wales, to put in a tender against serious competition for a proposed railway which, at this vital stage of estimating costs and completion, absolutely required his personal attention.

"I have to get it right first time," he explained to Oriel. "If I go on the safe side and ask too much I won't get the job. If I ask too little then I'll bankrupt myself getting it done. So *I* have to go myself, not send one of my agents, to work out how many men I'll need and what they'll cost me, how many cubic yards of earth they can move in a shift depending on what sort of earth it is; how many bricks they can lay in an hour when it comes to lining tunnels and building stations and how much I have to pay locally for bricks. So if it works out wrong then I've only got myself to blame. And then, when I've got the figures right and can see my profit

I've got to go along to my bank and raise the capital. They won't listen to anybody but me.''

Nor could he take her with him, much of his journey being by coach on narrow mountain roads, some of it on horseback, all of it in rough company to which he would not expose any wife of his. Any wife? She had been wondering, lately, about that other wife, Morag the fisherman's daughter from the Western Isles. A tall, fair woman—like herself—she supposed, if those tall, fair children were anything to go by. Yet, although she might allow herself to wonder, she did not visualize the possibility of asking him whether or not he had loved her. Indeed, it might be better—far more comfortable—never to know.

"I'll make it up to you," he said. "I'll take you to France. I have some business there about the Paris to Rouen line. Maybe in September—which gives you time to get the house in order."

And so she spent her wedding night in her husband's new house at Lydwick, his children sleeping in the nursery wing on the floor above her, in charge of the governess he had chosen for her placid disposition but who, already, had found no favor with Oriel. It would be among her first tasks tomorrow, when he had gone to Wales, to tackle the woman about her haphazard teaching of deportment and pronunciation, the piano lessons not yet begun, the water-colors and the needlework samplers barely started, giving her the option to change either her methods or her situation. And then, when that sharp little interview should be over, there would be one or two matters to clarify with cook, congratulations to be offered to the butler, a man she felt certain of winning to her side, a personal maid for herself to be looked for, and a good, exceptionally patient tutor for the still very nearly illiterate Jamie.

Her husband had given her work to do, after all, and she planned to begin it in the only way which seemed fair and honorable to her: as she meant to go on. But there was the night to be got through, or over with, first. She was, and from the start had been, deeply aware of that.

The bedroom was high and ornate, chilly with new plaster, the huge bay windows slightly open because of the new paint, a heavily gilded ceiling bearing down upon her, the damask-covered walls closing in as she sat, rather more bolt-upright than seemed appropriate, in what she had claimed as *her* side of the bed, her territory, her long hair brushed loose and flowing, her pin-tucked, cambric nightgown fastened in a high frill around her neck, waiting for the completion of the ceremony at which, despite all the promptings of commonsense and caution, her role—it seemed to her—might well have been the sacrificial victim.

With more tact than she had expected, he had allowed her to undress alone, and even then did not touch her at once, although the mere sliding of his quite naked body between the same sheets which covered hers, its weight on the same mattress, was something from which she needed a moment—even two, if he would permit it—to recover.

"Don't think," he said, "that I don't know how innocent you are. Did your mother tell you nothing—about this?"

Evangeline, in fact, had said: "I dare say you will find it unpleasant. Perhaps one is even meant to. But what matters, dearest, is that *he* will like it. And when you see how much, then you will understand the power it can give you over him. Which seems only right and proper when one considers the power the law gives *him* over you. So make your own laws, my darling, when it comes to this little matter of—well, is there a decent name for it? Lust? And guard against too much generosity. Remember—in fact, never forget—that what a man gets easily he does not appreciate. Ideally you should make him beg for his privileges but—at the very least—you must see to it that he earns them."

"No," she said quickly. "My mother told me nothing."

She heard him sigh, although not, she thought, with impatience. "And you've asked no questions?"

"Of course not." He could not know, she realized, that this whole matter of "intimate relations" could not be considered fit, in polite circles, for any kind of direct discussion. And as for questions, to whom could they reasonably be asked? Certainly not to Evangeline who, in common with every other woman Oriel had ever met, upheld with a religious fervor the creed that a sin had not really been committed unless one talked about it. How else, after all, could one contrive to lose one's virtue and, at the same time, keep one's reputation? A feat which Evangeline had performed so brilliantly for over twenty years while managing, nevertheless, to raise her daughter in the state of total innocence so essential to the correct marketing of any young lady.

Innocence. Or was it ignorance? Not entirely. Yet, although Oriel knew and accepted with a sophistication far in advance of that magical status of "young lady," that her own, always strict mother had been the mistress of Matthew Stangway, and some others, she did *not* know, and, having never seen a nude, male body, could not altogether imagine the exact mechanics of the act of love. She knew that it would give her certain pain and possible power. Her own, short-lived response to Francis Ashington had caused her to suspect that it might even, in certain circumstances, be pleasurable. But *these*—this marriage, this bed, this husband, this stranger—were surely not the circumstances for joy. She felt no such response to this man. Nothing but a sudden rush of panic, telling her very plainly that the eggshells on which she had walked so delicately all her life were finally cracking; and her nerve with them.

She had closed her mind to the details of this act in order to live with her fear of it, as one closed one's mind to death. She had promised to perform it calmly enough in the church, not only tonight but whenever, and just as often, as her husband should require it. And if now his hands upon her seemed truly an invasion not only of the very parts of her body she had been taught to keep covered and secret, but of her whole nature, she knew she had no choice but to keep her word.

Sliding down on her back she lay completely still, her body cold as marble and clammy, she thought, where he touched it, her breathing shallow with the effort to stem the apprehension she knew she must not allow to become disgust.

Once again she heard him sigh. "I could leave you alone tonight, I suppose. Maybe that's what I ought to do. I know you're tired and scared—and no wonder. I understand that. But its not my fault, bonny lass, that they've kept you so ignorant. If you'd been brought up in a two-roomed house with half a dozen brothers and a stepfather or two—like some of us were—then at least ignorance wouldn't have been a problem. I see it is, with you. But, with me away in the morning, unless I enlighten you now you'll get to dreading the thought of it—and the thought of me coming back. So I'm going to do it now, Oriel, as carefully as I can. Then you'll know the worst—eh—and not make more of it, in your head, than need be. All right?"

Slowly—her tongue frozen, it seemed, far beyond the possibility of speech, as her limbs were frozen equally beyond pleasure—she nodded her head.

"There'll be pain to begin with. It doesn't last."

She nodded again.

Again he sighed.

"I reckon you're telling me to get it over and done with. And be quick about it. Come then . . ."

And so it was done, a physical joining together she had half-suspected but had not really believed until her bare legs were parted by a hot, male hand, hard fingers preparing a passage for that other male member for which she knew no name; his body pressing hard upon hers and then shaking suddenly in what looked like a fit but which she knew must be pleasure, ending in a long groan—of agony? did it hurt him too?—as he withdrew from her.

"I feel I should apologize," he said, "though I'm damned if I will."

Perspiration, she noticed, stood in large drops along his forehead, his mouth tightening, at the corners, with strain as if this equally famous and infamous act had cost him great effort, and some regret. Yet, at least, it *had been done*. It was over. She had submitted to it without crying out, without recoiling, without nausea, and genuinely believing submission to be all any man could require, to be as much, in fact, as any woman could give, she was unprepared for the faintly mocking air of dissatisfaction she could sense in him.

Was there something more? Something of which she honestly and truly had no notion? It must be shocking indeed. But even as the dread of it threaded uneasily through her limbs, still aching and throbbing from the use—she could only think of it as that—he had made of them, he fell asleep, leaving her alone in the dark, to think of Letty and Constantia and the stickiness now oozing from her body which may already have done its work and made her pregnant like them. How many times? She was twenty-one, like Constantia. Letty was forty-seven. How long did it go on? As long, she supposed, as he desired it, which, now that she had witnessed his explosive pleasure, she supposed would be very long indeed.

And to escape the disgrace of being an "old maid," to escape the ambitions her mother had for her, and her own fears, she had consented to it. To escape from Francis too, although she could not afford just now—she firmly decided—to think of that. She slept very little, disturbed at a very profound level by the bulk, the body heat, the deep breathing of the man beside her, although when he woke with the dawn and took her in his arms again, she summoned every last drop of her not inconsiderable resolution to fight off the taut protest of her nerves and muscles, to make her body as soft and supple as she possibly could so that she might appear, this time, to yield rather than submit.

"That's better," he said. And so it was. Better, surely— or so she had decided during the long night—not merely to endure what could not be avoided but to do her best to understand it. Better to *adapt* herself to his desire so that she might satisfy it fully, recognizing it as a vital part of the task she had undertaken and therefore—since it *had* to be performed—performing it well.

Better for herself too, although in fact she had felt nothing more pleasurable, this second time, than an absence of pain, a lessening of shock, an encouragement to believe that hopefully, quite soon, she would at least get used to it. And if not, then, in the interests of domestic harmony, for *his* peace of mind which must from now on be her greatest care, she would have to pretend.

"You made me feel a mite rough and ready last night, girl."

"I didn't mean to."

Leaning over her, supporting his weight on one elbow, he grinned. "I know that very well. And lucky for you I did, or else I may not have been so well mannered. Because I was well mannered, believe it or not. I had a little scared bird in my hands—which makes a change, I'm bound to admit—and I didn't mean to break its wings. Did I break them?"

Conscious of the sting of tears behind her eyes, she shook her head.

"Of course I didn't. You're a fine, strong woman, when you want to be. I've told you that. You won't break now."

"No." For who would trouble to mend her if she did? Not Garron Keith, she suspected, who, despite what she recognized as his present consideration, had chosen her, nevertheless, for specific qualities which did not include frailty, either of mind or body, among their number.

He smiled again, his broad fingertips brushing a moment against her breasts, his skin very dark and rough—they both noticed it—against hers.

"Good. So get up now and see your man on his way to work—as a woman should. It's half past four and I've ordered the carriage for five o'clock. I'll be dressed in ten minutes and then you'll walk to the gate with me—surely? Leave your hair loose, as it is, and put a shawl over your nightgown.''

She was half-amused, half-shocked, not knowing quite what to make of a request she would have suspected, in any other man, to be romantic. "I can't go outside like this.''

"If I say so then you can.''

"Garron—it's not decent.''

"Oriel—it's what I want.''

"Oh Lord . . .''

"Precisely. Down the garden path and to the gate. No one will see.''

The garden was full of shadows and silence, the house not yet stirring, the path bordered by chestnut trees so wide and standing so close together that it was still midnight beneath them. The air was cold and sharp, her shawl comfortably large, covering her from shoulder to ankle until he took her in a sudden embrace to which she responded bravely, her arms around his neck, her mouth opening to his kiss as he had taught her, her body making not the slightest movement of recoil when he pushed her shawl further aside and pressed her body, in only its thin covering of frilled cambric, against him.

"Be here when I come back," he said into her ear.

"When will that be?" And because he was crushing her so hard she sounded breathless and, quite possibly, eager.

"How can I know? When the job's done. I won't stay longer than I have to. And when I come . . ." He too sounded suddenly out of breath, his teeth biting sharply into her ear-lobe, startling her, making him laugh. "When I come make sure you have your hair down. I'll let you know." She heard the gate clang shut behind him, his sharp command to the coachman, the sounds of hooves and wheels diminishing with distance. He had not said how far, nor how long. A week? A month? Three months? He would let her know. And then, whenever his business demanded it, he would leave in this same headlong rush, over and over again. Would the years teach her to be sorry to see him go, or glad?

She turned to walk back over the ground he had led her, her eyes, the very pores of her skin, still full of him, his heavy, high-colored presence still there, dominating the path between the trees, until the shadows parted and she found herself abruptly, alarmingly face to face with another presence, a tall, silver-haired, cold-eyed girl staring not merely with hostility but with disdain at the loose frill at Oriel's neck, the thin cambric clinging to her damp body, the shawl which, having been thrown so lecherously aside, barely covered it. The shawl which *he* had disarranged with a desire no daughter ought surely to witness in a father. Particularly if the woman so desired was not her mother.

"Morag. What are you doing here at this hour?"

She knew it to be a foolish question yet could think of no other.

The girl, fully dressed to the neatly tied ribbons in her ringlets, lifted thin shoulders in a shrug, her smile bitter with a love and hate and jealousy which were all too big for her, too much, too terrible.

Dear child, don't suffer like this. I won't take him away from you. I'm not your enemy, whatever you might do. And, if you'll let me, I'll be a friend.

Yet even had she dared to speak the words she knew the girl would not listen. Not yet.

"Morag . . . ?"

"I knew he was away early. I came to see him off."

"Is that what you usually do? Would he have been expecting you?" *And has he forgotten you already, neglected you for the fancy new wife?*

Once again the childish shoulders moved in their thin shrug, the mouth into its bitter smile.

"Well, he didn't see me, at any rate."

And Oriel was in no doubt that Morag was really telling her, warning her perhaps "He didn't see me, because he was looking at *you.*"

Nine

It was the end of June before the young squire of Dessborough brought his lady home to her manor, her village, her parish, the many and various and no doubt in her view trifling duties which accompanied her position. The wedding journey, which had taken them from the old, elegant civilizations of Paris and Monte Carlo to the eternal Maytime of Madeira and the wilder shores of Lanzarote, had lasted ten months, as was quite normal among the leisured, landed classes to which they both belonged, although on their return they were both equally aware—Francis with deep sadness, Kate with a dumb bewilderment she carried like a weight of lead against her chest—that not only the honeymoon but the marriage itself was effectively over. Or that part of it, at least, which had seemed valid to them, the wild fires of honeymoon nights which had burned and bound them together, the languorous, amorous days when love, to Kate, had seemed glorious, all-consuming, eternal, and to Francis at least *possible*, sometimes barely a step away.

A time of total concentration, one upon the other, when her demand for his emotion had been satisfied by passion, unleashing in her a frenzy which had overwhelmed him by night and kept him in a constant heat of excitement by day, the call of her thin, frantic body tightening his nerves, heightening his senses to a summit of pain from which the only relief had been to possess her over and over again in every mood and every manner his acute sexual imagination could devise, to have her scorch him and scour him, to make him do penance for the raw pleasure her body gave him, to make

177

him marvel at, and occasionally almost to fear, the pitch of her sensuality, the fierce needs enflaming her, the wild clamor, a dozen times a day, of her body seeking his, nailing herself against him as if all that could ever content her would be to get inside his skin.

There had been no reticence. He had received a virgin bride from the England of a prudish queen where even tables were shrouded in heavy plush cloths to conceal their legs, a girl who had been taught nothing of sex other than that it was dangerous and dirty, yet who had stepped out of her wedding-dress like a naked, reveling Bacchante with flowers far stranger and wilder than English orange blossom in her hair. Scarlet flowers, vibrant and tropical and musky, such had been the color and texture of their early days together, all burned now, by their own heat, to cool ashes, leaving only the drab shades of duties not to be shirked, promises not to be broken, property for him to maintain, a child already two months in the womb for her to bear.

She did not want the child. Nor did he. Only the land and manor of Dessborough desired and claimed it, and it was therefore to Dessborough that they returned, a place where neither of them wished to be, alien territory to him, a familiar cage to her, although she did not, at first, understand the extent of her new captivity. Not, that is, until she found Letty and Constantia waiting one morning in Dessborough's low-ceilinged, deep-shadowed drawing-room, both of them pretending not to notice that she had only just got out of bed, each one bringing a child to show her, Constantia compensating for the one she had lost just before Oriel's wedding with a replacement due "quite soon," Letty with her newborn, hopefully last born, son. "Very pretty," Kate said.

"Yes, indeed—adorable—adorable," they echoed, going on to advise her, in whispers, about the care she must now take of her body since it had become the receptacle—no more and no less—of a human life, apparently of far greater importance, of far greater humanity in fact, than her own. No riding—it went without saying, of course, although they both said it—from now on. No strenuous walking. No sitting in drafts or sitting up late. No venturing outdoors any more than strictly necessary and running the risk of seeing something unpleasant which would expose the unborn infant to the terrible effects of shock. And, naturally—well—no *contact*— Heavens, how could one phrase it?—no *closeness*, at such

times, with one's husband. Goodness—absolutely not. No—
no, it could not be considered a failure of one's conjugal
duties. On the contrary—in Constantia's informed opinion—
one ought to welcome it as a rest.

"I see," Kate said.

And then there was Maud, talking of the advice only her
cousin Quentin was uniquely qualified to give on Dessborough's management and of how Kate must do her duty—no
more and no less—by persuading her husband to entrust all
such matters only, and implicitly, to him. And then Evangeline, with talk of responsibility to one's own position as first
lady of a perfectly adequate manor and all it represented,
and—rather more to the point—of the advisability of beginning, as one ought to go on, by "warming up" one's relationship with the Mertons, for the sake of one's husband, of
course, so that they might invite him to do the things ambitious men appeared so fond of, like sitting on committees,
becoming members of all the "right" clubs, meeting the
"right" people, so that, in due course, dear, clever, *ambitious* Francis might become a member of Parliament, the
governor of a colony, a baronet.

"Francis is not ambitious," said Kate.

"My dear," Evangeline looked faintly amused, "are you
quite certain?"

"Yes. I am."

"You astonish me. One would have thought a man of his
energies could hardly wish to be confined . . . However, you
know best, of course you do. But, just the same, it might be
as well to give a few dinners, a little dance, a garden-party
even, should the weather hold, here in these lovely grounds.
I dare say Oriel will be glad to help you. She is in London,
at present, with her husband. But when she returns—next
week, I think—we will all put our heads together."

"Is Oriel—well?"

"My dear." Evangeline made an airy gesture expressing
bliss. "*Well* is not the word to describe it. In her seventh
heaven, I should call it. Such a generous husband, who thinks
nothing quite good enough for her and so tends to give her
absolutely everything she asks for in double measure. One
rarely sees such adoration."

"And his children?"

Evangeline looked, for a moment, as if the word was un-
familiar to her, and then gave a brilliant smile. "Yes, indeed.

The little girls are charming. There is a boy, too. You will be bound to meet them.''

''Oriel herself is not expecting, is she?''

''Good Heavens, certainly not. She is in no hurry.''

''As I have been.''

''Never mind, dear. A good nanny, a good governess, a good school, will all help to take the pain away. And the world is full of them. Now then, Kate, how was Monte Carlo? So kind of the Mertons to lend you their villa. When can we expect to see them back at the Abbey?''

''I have no idea.''

In Kate's place Evangeline would have known the Mertons' movements *exactly*. ''Ah well—not long, one supposes, since there is Adela's wedding to prepare for. In September isn't it? A truly momentous occasion.''

And one, moreover, to which the Ashingtons, who were related to both bride and groom, would take precedence over the Stangways, and to which the Keiths might not be invited at all. An oversight which Evangeline did not intend to allow.

''Someone should give a party for Adela Merton, Kate,'' she now said. ''Just a friendly little gathering to introduce her to the ladies of the neighborhood. I believe her mother has kept her too remote from us, with the very best of intentions, one feels certain. But, just the same, the times are changing—broadening—and one hardly feels Adela, and her sister Dora, or Lady Merton herself, could come to any harm through the closer acquaintance of—well—of Oriel, for instance. Kate, dear, I believe you are the one to arrange it. Shall we say that Oriel is rather depending on you?''

Kate's next visitor was the vicar of Dessborough, a reverend gentleman with an arid, quite military manner who had called, not to explain her parish duties since, it was assumed, as a squire's daughter herself she must be well aware of them, but to draw her attention, rather, to the list of responsibilities she must, undoubtedly, wish to make her own.

''Undoubtedly,'' said Kate.

The village school, for instance, where the vicar himself spent an hour every morning explaining to his infant parishioners their good fortune in a God who, by arranging for them all to be born into the exact station in life which best suited them and in which He therefore wished them to remain, had eliminated the sin of Envy. The last Mrs. Ashington had often accompanied him to inspect the needlework of

the little girls and speak a few words of encouragement to
the schoolmistress. The new Mrs. Ashington must wish to
do likewise. Tuesdays and Thursdays, perhaps? The last Mrs.
Ashington had also been in the habit of presenting a layette
stitched by herself to every mother-to-be in the village whose
circumstances were thought to require it. Nothing extravagant, of course, nothing to turn the head. Assuredly not that.
Just the necessary linen, a shawl, a little cap, in hardwearing,
humble materials which owed their value in village eyes, to
the fact that they had been made by the squire's lady herself.
A kindly gesture which Kate would wish to continue, he knew
full well. He would provide the names and dates, as became
appropriate, along with the list of the elderly who had thrived,
every winter, on the late Mrs. Ashington's rose-hip jelly and
her hyssop cordial. He assumed the recipe could be located?

"Do feel free to assume," agreed Kate.

The good gentleman promised that he would. And then
there were the manorial tea-parties. The schoolchildren, of
course, twice annually and in the kitchen quarter of the house;
the village ladies perhaps four times, in the garden or drawing-room as weather permitted; the village *women* on May
Day and at Harvest Festival, usually in the Hall. The late
Mrs. Ashington had also made a point of attending all parish
weddings and legitimate christenings, and of visiting the cottages in strict rotation so that every housewife in the village
could be certain of the benefit of Ashington advice and supervision at least once a month. And, it being now eighteen
months since the late Mrs. Ashington had been called to rest,
the reverend gentleman supposed that Kate must desire to
take up the parish reins and grasp all parish nettles the good
lady had left behind her, at once. Would she also, perhaps,
be so kind as to convey his respects to her aunt, Miss Maud
Stangway, a lady whose energy and excellent judgment he
had long admired and could wish for nothing better than to
see it reflected in her niece. Dare he hope that Miss Maud
Stangway would now become a regular visitor to Dessborough?

"I expect so," Kate said.

Sitting that evening alone with Francis in the house that so
resembled her father's, she asked him, "Do you want me to
start giving dinners and dances?"

He was reading, in Arabic, a life of Mohammed the Law-
giver, wondering whether to pass a drop of the ocean of time

now confronting him, in translating it. But, as soon as she spoke to him, he put the book down and leaned toward her, believing she had a right to his attention.

"Yes. If you would like to, that is?"

"And would you like me to knit shawls for all the village babies born in wedlock, and brew hyssop cordial for the old men . . . ?"

Sitting beside the only lamp, the rest of the room in evening shadow, he could not see her face, only the outline of her thin, eager body, dressed up in one of the Paris gowns he had bought her; sitting, it suddenly struck him, like a child with empty hands, waiting to be told what to do. Had she been watching him, this hour or more, while he had been wandering, only through the pages of a book, perhaps, but very far away, nevertheless? He supposed she had. Watching and waiting for him to tell her which road to take, what to do next, when her road had been decided for her now, irrevocably it seemed, and each and every road *he* cared to take had been closed to him, probably forever.

Yet, because he had known how it would be from the start and she had not, because he had been aware, even in the white heat of their passion, of this fireside, this armchair, this dim room, biding its time to claim and diminish them, and she had not, he could not blame her. The time of diminishing was now. It had happened. Here was the room, the house, the tedious domestic hearth neither of them had wanted. And since his was the fault, the weakness, the folly which had condemned them to share it, then he must put down his book now—his one remaining salvation—and talk to her of knitting shawls and brewing hyssop tea.

"Would you care to do that?" he asked her uncertainly, knowing it would be far, far better for her if she *could* conceive a sudden passion for such things, but rather doubting that she ever would.

And it was her laugh, sharp and scornful and broken off almost painfully at its ending, which gave him his answer. "Francis, I have not the least idea in which part of the garden hyssop might be found. Nor even what it looks like. Although when the gardener asked me today if I wanted it for the house I said yes—lots of it—as much as he likes. And *he* seemed happy. I'll ask Oriel what to do with it. She'll know."

Yes. He supposed she would. But that was a direction in which he did not allow his thoughts ever to stray. A pointless, painful direction with no good in it anywhere, for anybody. He had married Kate, who had thought her love for him would thrill and burn and exalt her forever, so that to be alone with him in a wasteland would turn desolation into paradise. Except that this was not the wasteland she had bargained for. Was she beginning to understand that now, as he had understood it all along? Was she looking at him now and seeing nothing but a well-meaning, restless, ordinary man? A man out of step with himself who, although driven into the wrong corner, had made up his mind that, rather than fester there, he would set himself to fill the roles that corner offered, to teach himself—whatever it did to him—the patient, tedious job of being a village squire, the good landlord, the fair-minded Justice of the Peace, local upholder of law and order, careful farmer, father of his parish and watchful husband to his wife. He did not think any part of the job would suit him but he was determined to perform the whole of it, nevertheless. Faithfully. As he would be faithful, if only in his body, to her.

"Don't worry about the hyssop," he said. "The villagers can live without it."

"Ah—so you don't want me to be the Lady Bountiful, then?"

"Kate—I want you to do what pleases you . . ."

"Then find me a camel to ride on, Francis—or an elephant."

He got up and, kneeling by her chair, laid a hand gently against her stomach, his mouth close to her ear, playing the lover as the only sure means he knew of pleasing her.

"Would a camel-ride be wise just now?"

Had it ever been wise? Or even possible? Had she ever done more than confuse true freedom with the wild needs of her body and the clamorous triumph with which she had expressed them? Kate who, by stripping her body bare and sinking it into his, believed she had won eternal liberty, total emancipation, supreme power over her own destiny, only to find herself struggling now in the trap to which her overpowering sensuality had really led her; the trap of childbirth. Trapping him too, although he did not think she knew that.

He hoped—kneeling now beside her—that she never would.

"Do you want a *great* many children, Francis?" she said, her voice thin and, once again, ending very abruptly.

"Shall we have this one, first, and see how we go on? We may find one to be quite enough . . ."

"So you don't want me to be a fruitful mother, either."

"Kate?"

"It had better be the dinner-parties, then. Would you like *that*?"

"Rather better, I think, than the hyssop tea."

"Very well," she said.

It would, after all, be a kind of freedom, to poise, pen in hand, over those precious invitation lists, crossing out the names which did not please her. Aunt Maud. Aunt Letty. Constantia who could talk of nothing but babies. Quentin, perhaps. Or perhaps not, since he seemed far more amusing now that he no longer threatened her and had taken up residence in Hepplefield well away from his mother. Dare she even invite the Mertons, the whole pack of them, and "forget" to send a card to Evangeline? For the space of an idle, faintly malicious morning—the one on which Francis had agreed to sit as a magistrate on the same bench as her father and had spent an hour, in her presence, discussing with him the proper hand-rearing of pheasants and the new detonating guns to shoot them with—she believed she could. Until she heard that Oriel had come home again and remembered she was Evangeline's daughter.

She wrote a note at once and received an immediate reply. "Dear Kate, do come and see me." "Dear Oriel, I have so much to tell you, and to ask. Please come and see *me*."

But the first day of Oriel's return to Lydwick was taken over entirely by domestic crisis, due largely to the presence of Susannah Saint-Charles who, having offered to come and help with the children while Oriel was away, had spent her time quarreling with the new governess on the subject of her failure either to curb the vanity of Elspeth, the prettier of the girls, or to do something—quite urgently, Susannah thought— about the coarse language of the boy, Jamie, who had spent *his* time repeating, for the sheer pleasure of setting Susannah in a flutter, every bad word and vulgar expression he had ever heard. A varied selection, it seemed, culled from the vocabulary of Scottish fishermen, Irish bricklayers, the colorful ribaldry of Tyneside which came all too easily to his father's tongue, chanted with a high-pitched relish which had given Susannah a headache and caused her to speak sharply to the governess again.

Miss Moorhouse, therefore, was waiting, tight-lipped, in the hall as Oriel, tired from her journey, came through the door, wishing to be the first to state her case.

"Mrs. Keith, it may not be my place to say so, but Miss Saint-Charles—although one must assume her to have the best intentions—knows so little of children that—really—I am forced to say she does less good than she probably intends . . ."

"Oriel—oh dear—what a time we have had." Susannah had positioned herself on the upstairs landing by Oriel's bedroom door. "Such a time. I have hardly slept all night, worrying about whether I ought to tell you. But really, there is no shirking it. I am so sorry, Oriel, but your Miss Moorhouse cannot control those children. And in fairness to Mr. Keith—since one wishes to do one's best for him—you will have to speak to her. Is he not with you?"

Oriel shook her head which, she noticed, was just starting to ache.

"Oh—I assumed he was seeing to the horses—or the baggage?"

"No, Susannah. He has continued on to Glasgow." And in order to avoid Susannah's uncontrollable disappointment, quickly added, "I think I will just take off my hat and gloves and wash my hands before speaking to anyone."

In the eight weeks of her marriage she had spent only three of them with her husband, the other five alone in this house with his children, carefully, quietly approaching them as one approaches shy woodland creatures, making no sudden movement to startle them, no unexplained demands, taking one considered step at a time and learning, assessing, as she went; not expecting them to love her, since they had not chosen her, after all, not expecting to love them—at least not yet, possibly not at all—aiming rather for acceptance, liking, for contentment rather than happiness, presenting herself as the friend she wished to be, rather than the mother they all knew she was not.

Only Morag of the cold, watchful eyes had truly resisted her, just as only Morag—and Oriel herself—seemed capable of tolerating the awkwardly passionate, possibly well-meaning, certainly far from happy Susannah.

"I hate her," said Elspeth to whom both love and hate came easily, bursting through Oriel's door before she had removed the first hat-pin. "She watches and fusses—that Su-

sannah—and says I'm vain and quotes words at me from the
Bible that sound cruel and make me dream. And then she
talks about cholera in the navvy huts . . .''

"Cholera? Has Jamie been up there? Susannah . . ." she
went to the door, knowing Susannah would not be far away,
"*is* there cholera on Merton Ridge?"

"Oh, it appears not. According to Dr. Merewith. Although—according to the Reverand Field, our curate—it is
only a matter of time. And I am bound to agree with him."

"There was cholera once before," said Jamie, gleefully
appearing from nowhere. "Bad cholera. At a place like Merton Ridge. So many dying that the contractors ordered a stock
of empty coffins. And when the navvies saw them being carried up the hill to camp they all took fright and ran away—
to places like Lydwick and Hepplefield, where all the people
ran away from them. My dad told me."

"Good heavens," breathed Susannah.

"Ah well . . ." said Oriel. "I will just wash my hands.
Oh—Morag. There you are."

"When is my father coming home?" said Morag, her eyes
ever watchful, her tone implying "What have you done with
him?"

He had galloped off to Wales the morning after the wedding, returning ten days later to spend a week with her, his
presence filling every room, dispelling the cool good order
she had been maintaining with his demands for food and
drink whenever he happened to be hungry or thirsty—very
often indeed, it seemed—filling every ash-tray with his cigars, forever opening windows and ordering the carriage at
all hours, interrupting the girls' speech and deportment lessons, the process of "polishing" them he still required, with
sudden picnics, pony rides, visits to the best shops, and only
the best shops, in town.

Making love to her, too, every night and every morning
and sometimes in the afternoons, causing her considerable
embarrassment on two occasions when Susannah, having
called to voice some complaint about conditions at Merton
Ridge, had stayed on to press flowers in the nursery albums
with Morag, showing not the least suspicion of anything amiss
when Mr. Keith suddenly called his wife away. Susannah
judging the act of sex, no doubt, by the manner in which it
was practiced at the vicarage, strictly in the dark when all the
rest of the family had retired to bed, although Oriel—feeling

as if she had been committing adultery rather than lying obediently in a conjugal embrace—had felt less certain, on returning downstairs, of Morag.

He had gone away again after that, first to Carlisle, then
rushing down the length of the land to Cornwall, back again
to Wales, and then to London where they had just spent a
week together. Seven days of luxury and open-handed spending, gold bracelets on her arms, new gowns and hats, long,
sumptuous dinners, magnums of champagne, theaters, her
body aching and feeling bruised by his, although there was
nothing to show on the surface, her compartment on the train
back to Leeds full of parcels tied up in gold ribbon for the
children.

"I'm going on to Glasgow," he told her in Leeds, the first
she had heard of it. And so she had traveled to Lydwick alone
by road with all her luggage, a "fine, strong woman" who
could find her own way home and then set to rights—before
she had even taken off her hat—any little difficulties or dilem-
mas she might find waiting there.

"Oh—I forgot to tell you, Oriel. Cook would like a word
with you. She says her stove has become impossible, which
I told her seemed strange to me since it is brand new. However, she was most insistent and seemed not to realize I was
only trying to help. She says *you* will understand."

"Thank you, Susannah."

Well, at least she had washed her hands now and made
herself decent, even freshened her skin with a lotion she made
herself and had been teaching Elspeth how to make—of lemon
balm, chamomile, and marigold.

"Oh, and by the way, Oriel, there is a letter from your
mother. Her coachman brought it over quite early and seemed
to think it urgent. It is on the hall table with all the visiting
cards. I'll show you."

"Thank you once again, Susannah."

Evangeline had written explicit instructions that Kate
should not only be encouraged to pursue the Mertons but
guided as to the most effective means of so doing. "She has
become their cousin-by-marriage, after all, and must behave
accordingly. Lady Merton, I admit to be somewhat vague and
the girls are quite foolish but their generally weak intelligence
and lack of any ideas of their own makes them so vulnerable
to persuasion—does it not? If one can get close enough to

persuade, that is. Kate has that opportunity. Do take it for her, darling.''

And although she had not written ''It should have been yours in any case,'' Oriel understood.

But Susannah was hovering. ''Should you wish to send an answer at once I had better tell them to get the horses out again. Shall I? There is a note from Kate, too.''

So there was. A tight, impatient scrawl climbing up the page, corner to corner, which Aunt Maud would never have allowed to pass her scrutiny in the ''old days.'' Ten months ago.

Sitting down at her rosewood desk in the drawing-room window overlooking an acre of smooth lawn and young, carefully spaced rose-buds, she took out her own light blue notepaper—Susannah still hovering—and in quick, perfectly straight lines, penned her replies. She would drive over to High Grange and see her mother tomorrow afternoon, which would also give her the opportunity of taking Susannah back home to the vicarage. Kate would be welcome to come and see her as soon as she chose.

She came the next morning, straight after breakfast, alone and riding a black mare which caused considerable consternation to Susannah who, although unable, as an unmarried lady, to mention the subject of pregnancy, nevertheless felt it her duty to warn Kate of the dangers of horseback riding at such times.

But Kate, who had barely tolerated Susannah in the past, ignored her now, entirely dispelling the faint hesitation, the moment of distance Oriel had felt by throwing thin but surprisingly determined arms around her neck and hugging her tight.

''Oriel—you look more like a swan than ever.''

''And you—*Kate*, you are looking very smart . . .''

''Oh, Paris did that, I suppose . . .''

Then it had done well, the severely tailored black riding-habit, the white stock, the polished top hat which had certainly been made for a man with an audacious drift of wholly feminine white gauze trailing around it, the crimson rose on her lapel, all giving her a sharp-cornered, highly colored elegance, somewhere between male and female which both disturbed and held the eye. Not a pretty girl, of course. But who else looked like her, who else, with that schoolboy's stride and those abrupt, bony shoulders, could nevertheless appear so *female*—an altogether different quality from feminine— that even Susannah, who secretly wished very much to look like Oriel, was puzzled by her.

Kate, beginning now to create her own illusion, from a red rose, a length of white tulle, another of dark, dramatically cut cloth, as Oriel had once created it for her with a scarlet sash, and Francis, quite by accident, with a gold sari.

"Is that a *man's* hat?" asked Susannah.

"Yes. And the riding-habit was made by a man's tailor. What of it? Come, Oriel, show me your house, and all your lovely new furniture—Heavens, I've never seen anything newer—that nobody but you has ever sat on. Such fun that must be—isn't it?—when we were both brought up sitting on whatever our great-great-greater grandmothers could be bothered to leave us."

"Kate," said Susannah, much shocked. "How can you say that? Dessborough is so positively antique . . ."

"That *is*," Kate murmured, "rather what I said . . ."

The house was displayed, room by room, the children called to be presented to Mrs. Ashington of Dessborough, whose severe and very personal smartness did not appeal to Elspeth—the pretty one—who also wished to look like Oriel, and found no favor either with Morag—the watchful one— who knew, by acute instinct, that the lady in the top hat and veil was not much interested in children. Only Jamie, ready to be interested in anybody who had something he wanted, shook her hand cheerfully and peppered her with questions about her horse until, not concealing how much he irritated her, she told him, "It's a horse, for Heaven's sake. It bites at one end and kicks at the other. Go and have a look at it and see which end gets you first."

Susannah was shocked yet again. Oriel smiled and, the sun being hot, suggested a glass of lemon cordial under the chestnut trees, where Kate, once refreshed, could tell them about her travels.

"Oh—are you coming too, Susannah?" Kate asked.

The cool drinks were brought, Susannah sipping nervously, Kate draining her glass like a huntsman in an innyard and setting it down on the table with a clatter.

"Oriel?" she inquired, her eyes narrowing almost dreamily, fixed somewhere at the far edge of the lawn among the brave young lupins just bursting into flower. "Oriel, do you know what hyssop is?"

"Yes."

"Oh good, I thought you would. Do tell me."

"A plant," Susannah put in quickly, wishing to impress, and knowing, as the member of a large family, that unless she spoke at once she would not be heard at all.

Kate stared at her coldly. "I don't remember asking you."

"A herb," said Oriel, quite quietly, making a point of noticing neither Kate's hostility nor Susannah's clumsy bid for notice. "It grows in long spikes about two feet tall, with blue or pink flowers."

"And it has uses?"

"Oh yes. You can dry the flowers for pot-pourri because they smell so sweet. Or you can put the leaves in salad."

"Is that all?"

"No. You can make cough medicine out of it. Hyssop tea is good for catarrh and colds on the chest."

Kate wrinkled her nose. "Yes. That must be it. It would have to be."

"Kate—what *are* you talking about?"

"Oh—the last squire's lady, boring old Mrs. Ashington that she was—my predecessor. She kept the village alive all winter with hyssop tea, according to the vicar. How do you know about such things, Oriel?"

"My friend, Miss Woodley, in Ullswater, has a herb garden."

"And you see the sense to it? I mean—it pleases you? It gives you interest—and occupation?"

"Yes."

"Ah well." She refilled her glass from the tall jug of lemon juice and drained it briskly again. "I think I will do better with the dances and dinners."

"Kate . . ."

"Yes—I have quite made up my mind to it. Oh—by the way, Susannah, I met your brother Quentin on my way here, on *his* way to Merton Abbey. On very important business, of course. What else does Quentin concern himself with? But he says he will call here for you, nevertheless—in about an hour from now—and take you back to High Grange, to save Oriel the trouble. So you will want to go and get yourself ready, won't you, Susannah. Don't worry about leaving Oriel and me alone together. We'll just sit here, while you do your packing, and talk about 'married' matters, I expect—such as why I really shouldn't be riding that horse."

Remembering both her manners and her Christian principles, reminding herself that women in Kate's condition were
permitted to be strange, Susannah made her excuses and went
off as if it had been her own idea, pretending as she walked
up the garden path, that she had neither heard Kate's unkind
burst of laughter nor seen Oriel's smile.

"That was very rude of you, Kate."

"Yes. I know." Was this too a kind of freedom? "Why
do you put up with her, Oriel? You don't have to. I won't—
ever again."

"Well, maybe that's why I do it. Because nobody else
will." In spite of herself Oriel was laughing, seeing Kate and
only Kate, without the shadow of Francis—as she had
feared—hovering at the edge of her vision. Her lover who did
not seem to be the same man as Kate's husband, who, at the
moment of his engagement to Kate, had changed identity so
completely that it had become possible to think of *her* Francis as dead. Possible, far more merciful, a blessing even, if
it meant she could welcome Kate into her life again. Did it
even mean, she wondered, that all the time she had loved
Kate more than she had loved him? Truly, she hoped so.

"Kate—what *is* this talk about dinner and dances?"

"Oh—" Kate shrugged. "How best to pass the time, I
suppose. If Francis is to become the perfect country squire,
then—since I think hyssop tea quite out of the question—I
had better be a social success."

"And is that what—Francis—means to do?"

Beneath her daring hat Kate's smile looked almost painful.
"So it would seem. He can't leave me, you see, at present.
He says he doesn't want to leave me . . ."

"You should be glad—surely—of that?"

"So I should. He says Mecca will wait."

"Well—since it has been there such a long time already—
I suppose it will."

Her chin on her hand, Kate stared for another long moment
at the lupins, unblinking in the strong sunlight, deep in her
thoughts—of Mecca, perhaps, which, in the sense Francis
wanted it, would wait for no man—until she suddenly shook
herself out of her contemplations and said, "Now then, before Susannah comes back again, tell me why you married
that man. The truth. It matters."

"Yes." Oriel saw that it did. "Well then—because he is
very clever, and very generous. Because he asked me. Be-

cause I wanted to be married.'' She was smiling, making light of it in the expert manner of Evangeline who had always laughed anything too serious or dangerous or too likely to make trouble clean away.

"Are you in love with him?" Kate very bluntly said.

"Kate—Kate—*of course* I am."

"That means not. I didn't think you were. And he? Can we have a *real* conversation, Oriel? Can we stop talking in fairytales about everybody living happy ever after—like they taught us—and look at life as it is—in the eye . . . ?"

"Better not," said Oriel.

"Does he love you?" snapped Kate.

"Ah well . . ." But suddenly her imitation of Evangeline no longer sufficed. "He wanted very much to marry me. And now he would go to any lengths, I think, to provide for me, and protect me . . ."

"And you understand it all, don't you? You know what to expect from him, and what he expects from you?"

"Yes. I know."

"I don't."

"Kate—how is that?"

"Because I don't, that's all. Because something—some-where—has never been right with me. Never. And it's not right now. There's a false note that I can hear—oh yes, I hear it—but I don't know which note it is, or what I have to do to put it right. All my life there's been something ringing false about me—something off-key. As if I'd got into the wrong skin, somehow. As if I wasn't really who they said I was. I used to hope they'd found me, when I was a baby, on the doorstep in a basket."

And now? Suddenly, to Oriel, the lupins and the tidy rose-beds seemed very far away, all the color and vitality of the garden bleached and absorbed by Kate's bewildered anguish, and her own horrified response to it. For, if Kate was telling her that her marriage to Francis had turned out to be another "wrong identity," not love at all but just another attempt at self-discovery which had already foundered, then how could she—who had truly wanted to be his wife—possibly bear it?

"I suppose it is Dessborough," Kate said, biting her lip, twisting her riding-gloves together as if she planned to use them as a sling for casting stones. "And all the village talk and the farming talk and sitting up straight in the Ashington pew twice every Sunday. And then the hunting talk—dear

God! Yes—yes, I know I've heard it all before at High Grange. Except that I never listened. And I didn't expect that—*now*—I just didn't think it could be . . ."

What? The same? Her jaw clenched so tight that the muscles in her cheeks and her neck began to tremble, she clearly could not go on. Nor could Oriel break the taut and dangerous silence without a struggle.

"Kate," she said at last, very quietly. "You married a country squire."

"Yes." Kate's eyes were fixed, unblinking, on the lupins again, her hands abandoning her twisted gloves and falling empty, palms down, on the table. "Yes, I know. Except that I didn't see him like that."

Silence again, Kate's stare fastened, still painfully unblinking, on the flowers, one hand clenching now into a tight little fist until Oriel's hand, so much longer and cooler, came down and covered it.

"Then you were not looking at him very closely, were you?" she said.

Little sister, did you break my heart by mistake, then? Just another basket at the wrong doorstep? Except that this time it has to be final, and forever. If I can accept that—and cope with it—then so must you.

"When is your baby due, Kate?" she said. And, under the impact of the question, Kate's entire body gave a violent shudder.

"They say in December. Poor mite, what a time to be born—although that will be the least of its troubles . . ."

"Kate—don't say that."

But, freeing herself from Oriel's grasp, Kate twisted both her hands together and then brought them down as savage, anguished fists striking once, and then twice, against the garden table, setting the jug and glasses rattling.

"Oriel, I can't be a mother, don't you understand that? I don't even know what a mother is. Well—tell me then? What is it? Letty? Or Maud, taking her revenge? I won't revenge my slights and disappointments on a child. Or will I? *Could* I—if those disappointments went on long enough? Or is it my own mother, Oriel? Is that what's troubling me?"

And, speaking of Eva Kessler, Kate's voice sank to a whisper which sent a chill through Oriel's bones.

"I didn't know her, Kate."

"Of course you didn't." Kate's eyes had gone into the far

distance again. "She would have hated you on sight and told you so. Oh yes, even if you hadn't been—Evangeline's daughter—she would still have hated you because you were pretty . . . No. Not even that. She'd have hated you because you were *female*. Her jealousy had gone as far as that. One man. One love. Nothing else in the universe. I've seen her on her knees to him, Oriel, screaming and clutching him, and him standing there looking as if—yes, as if nothing was happening at all, as if he hadn't noticed her, even though she was nearly knocking him over. She once cut her wrists and bled all over him and all he did was ask Maud to get his jacket cleaned. And I—well—nobody seemed to be doing anything about bandaging her wrists and I *knew* it ought to be done—but I ran outside and hid. Because I thought if I went near her she'd turn her knife on me . . ."

"*No*, Kate . . ."

"Oriel—even suspecting she might was too much for me to bear. Even suspecting *I* might be capable of doing something like that—gets to be more than I can almost bear now. And don't shake your head, because you don't know what happens in me, what comes to the boil sometimes—or very nearly. You don't know how—people like me—can be swept away. No, you don't. Oriel, have you ever seen the pictures in the attic? My mother's pictures? No. I thought not. Portraits—of him, and herself, and a few of Evangeline. Terrible pictures. Don't ever be tempted to look. I don't know why my father keeps them. Unless—yes, unless he's afraid to burn them—unless he thinks all the hate and jealousy might come out in the smoke and *get* him at last. I understand that."

Oriel, with nothing she could bear to say, shook her head in a denial Kate would not allow.

"Oh yes, Oriel. You can take my word for it, because I understand jealousy and the fear that goes with it. I'm her daughter, Oriel. I'd be bound to know. Just as I know she'd have skinned me alive and served me up to my father on a platter if she'd thought it the way to his attention . . ."

"*Kate.*"

"Oh yes she would. Yes—yes—*I* know that very well—too well—because I have enough of her in me to . . . Yes—to frighten me. So that's my notion of motherhood—frightening and vengeful. Or just foolish like Letty. I don't want to be any of those things."

"You won't be. If it's there at all then it can be overcome."

"Stop saying the right thing, Oriel. Stop soothing me."

"No, I can't. Because you have to face this—and fight it. You were the one who wanted to be honest. You'll have your baby and then . . ."

"Yes. A good governess, a good school, will help to take the pain away. *Your* mother told me that. Poor mite, I shall just be its receptacle—like Letty says—and then leave the rest to other people who know what they are and what to do about it. I expect Francis will be a perfect father."

"Yes, Kate. I expect he will."

Silence fell between them. And then, suddenly shaking her head as if something had struck her between the eyes, causing her pain, Kate cried out, "She hurt me, Oriel. My mother. That's the memory I have of her. That's what 'mother' really means to me. Hurt. Always has. And what strikes me now—the really terrible thing that's just occurred to me—the real tragedy . . . Yes. This is it. I've just understood she probably didn't mean it—didn't even know she was doing it. She didn't *know*. And in that case—since I seem to be like her—I could do the same—couldn't I? Spread chaos and havoc and hurt—and never know it. And I don't want to do that—no, I don't. Oriel—have you ever seen me hurting people? Have I ever hurt you? Have I, Oriel . . . ? Please tell me . . ."

Silence again.

"Oriel . . . ?"

Holding Kate's hands and Kate's eyes firmly in her own, Oriel leaned toward her. "No," she said.

"Thank God," Kate answered, her breath escaping in a long sigh. "Thank God at least for that."

"Exactly. So now shall we get back to the real world—without any unnoticed damage—where we lead our real lives?"

For a long time, or so it seemed to both of them, they looked at one another, Kate's tight-clenched misery dissolving gradually into a tendency, by no means new, to laugh herself to scorn.

"So you see what I meant about the dinners and dances. I have to do something to earn my keep at Dessborough, after all. Do I not?"

For a moment more they continued to look, one at the other, both of them unblinking now, each one wholly intent upon the other, a contact from which they were dragged unwillingly by the sound of footsteps on the path, someone approaching them through the lupins, an intruder on whom they turned dazed, puzzled eyes, until a release of nervous energy crackled abruptly through Kate, propelling her to her feet with a cry of far too enthusiastic welcome.

"Quentin—the very man I wished for."

He did not, of course, believe her, although her outflung arms, her enormous smile, the wide-open gleam of her eyes, were all vibrant enough, all ardent enough, to have deceived anyone else.

"Why is that, Kate?"

"So that you can drive me home. I have done enough riding for one day."

"Certainly."

"And we can talk about the Mertons, since I have decided to captivate them, and you have just come from there. On *very important business,* I know."

He bowed very slightly. "Not really. Only a little matter of boundaries. Nothing to shake the nation."

"And is her ladyship perching on the edge of her chair, as if it were a cage with the door open, worrying if the weather is fit enough for her to fly?"

Most unusually for Quentin Saint-Charles he smiled quite broadly. "I believe one could say that."

"Oh dear." Kate made another new, very flamboyant gesture, trying it out, perhaps, on her clever cousin. "She was so all the time in Monte Carlo. Wondering, all morning, whether or not to go out and then wondering what to do when she got there. Not an idea in her head, poor soul. And Adela is much the same. Whereas Dora *does* have a thought occasionally, if only of mischief. You will like Dora the best, Oriel—when we have made them our dearest friends and are forever running in and out of their Abbey."

"Is that what we mean to do?" asked Oriel, standing up, her legs unsteady.

"Oh yes, darling. I told you. I have made up my mind to do it. Dinners and dances instead of that old hyssop tea. *Your* mother will be delighted."

Slowly, with no apparent purpose, Quentin placed himself between them, in such a way that Oriel could not be seen from the house.

"Should you care to plan your campaign with our Aunt Evangeline, Kate," he said lightly, "she drove in just behind me and is waiting in the drawing-room, I believe."

"My mother . . ." said Oriel.

"No time like the present," said Kate. They both moved forward but Kate was quicker, Oriel still behind the table, still, to her chagrin, feeling lamentably—*foolishly*—weak and unsteady, so that by the time she had freed her skirts from the barrier of wrought-iron garden furniture and her own unaccustomed clumsiness, Kate was already striding away across the grass.

"Give yourself a moment, Oriel," murmured Quentin so softly that, had she wished, she could have pretended not to hear him. But she could not insult his intelligence, quite possibly his kindness, by doing that.

"Oh—I am quite all right."

He smiled. "I know you will be. But there is no great rush. Kate and your mother will have plenty to talk about. So you may take your time."

He did not ask why she needed it, nor did he show the faintest alarm when she suddenly heard herself say to him, "I do beg your pardon but I think I am about to burst into tears." He merely continued to stand between her and the drawing-room windows, shielding her, less with his quite slender body than an aura of assurance and calm. Qualities she well understood.

"Do so," he said. "And at the same time bend over the table a little . . . Could there be some problem with the glasses? Perhaps you have noticed a very fine crack and we are looking for others?"

A moment passed.

"Thank you, Quentin," she said.

And still he did not ask her for an explanation.

"Do you wish to go in now?"

Where? Her husband's home, full to its brim, at this moment, with voices raised in demands for her to satisfy, hurt feelings for her to smooth over, with grasping hands waiting to claim as much as they could of her time, her energy, her notice, with faces turned hopefully, querulously, fretfully, in her direction? Was that where she wished to go?

"I think I must," she said.

Ten

Five months later, on a harsh, gray morning in November, Kate Ashington gave birth, in a great rush, to a daughter, a tiny, premature creature whose survival lay for some days in the balance, the anxiety thus caused being sufficient to explain—or to excuse—the young mother's apparent inability to touch or even to look at her baby.

The doctor had met such an attitude before. Or so he told the young father, Squire Ashington, into whose arms the newborn child had been hurriedly placed when the squire's lady had recoiled from it in what had certainly looked like horror. Not that there was any real need to worry. Squire Ashington was at once assured, by both doctor and midwife, of that. It would pass. And if not—well—one saw much the same with cows and sheep and bitches, and whenever one came across a rejected lamb one had only to find another ewe to suckle it. A good wet-nurse, therefore, would solve the problem, and would have been needed in any case, since the doctor did not suppose a lady of Mrs. Ashington's standing could wish to sacrifice either the firmness of her breasts or the number of her social engagements to the very frequent feeding required by so small an infant.

Particularly when all one had to do was employ a good, placid countrywoman with milk preferably from a recent confinement, who would be happy to sit all day and all night if necessary, rocking the cradle and putting the child to the breast every hour or two. Under the supervision—naturally— of a competent nanny. Nothing could be simpler. No need at all for Mr. Ashington to worry. Unless, of course, he might feel inclined to have the child baptized—fairly soon? A precaution, merely—no more—and often taken in cases of premature arrival. And with Dessborough church just a step away and the vicar entirely at his squire's disposal . . . ? No doubt the names had already been chosen?

Names? No. With Kate becoming increasingly morose as the autumn passed, there had been no cozy, fireside, hand-in-hand talk of names. Very far from that. And, glancing at the mottled scrap of humanity in his arms, remembering that it was female and ought therefore to be called after its mother, Francis nevertheless retreated instantly from Kate's sudden and far too frenzied refusal to permit the name "Katharine" to be used, even in second or third position.

"Ondine. Roxane. Berengaria," she said, her voice breaking on a high-pitched, jarring laugh which caused him to say quickly, "Anything you like—anything at all."

"Anything," she told him, sinking back again into her pillows and her blank-eyed torpor. "Not Kate."

But very soon Francis knew that what he had believed to be a private matter was slipping out of his hands. For Kate had given birth, he was quickly made aware, to an important child who, if she lived and had no brothers or sisters, would eventually inherit both Dessborough and High Grange. Thus giving several others—at least in their own opinion—certain rights and privileges over her. The "family" therefore descended *en masse* and at once, to let it be known that these fanciful Ondines and pagan Roxanes—reminding them so uneasily of the Kessler grandmother, so mercifully deceased—must be set aside at once. There were plenty of "family" names to choose from, after all. Sitting around Kate's bed, the "family council" lost no time in enumerating them. Grizelda, Celestine, and Barbara for the Ashingtons. Letitia, Maud, Clarissa, for the Stangways, as well as the very popular Katharine which, as Letty pointed out, she had chosen for her own eldest daughter who, so sadly, had been born too soon, just like this poor little soul, and had died a week later.

"She was so pretty too—such a little love," murmured Letty, ready to be tearful with memory, although, in fact, she had never been able to distinguish one baby from another, except Quentin who, if Kate had done as she ought and married him, would have been only too pleased, she felt, to fall in with his mother's wish for another Katharine. Suddenly, with the stubbornness of those who are neither very strong nor very highly regarded, it became of tremendous importance to her, almost as if it would give her *her* Katharine—of whom she had barely thought for twenty years—back again.

"Katharine would be very—*fitting*," she said.

"Suitable," declared Maud. "And it would please Matthew, since it was our mother's name too."

But the figure lying in the bed as if she were a million miles away lifted her head from the pillows just long enough to croak out the two words "Not Katharine."

"I believe we have decided," murmured Francis, "that it will not be Katharine."

The Stangway ladies raised their shoulders and exchanged pained glances, as if he had been an intruder. Evangeline, in the unusual position, for her, of having no ax to grind in this particular issue, smiled. Celestine, she suggested lazily, might be worthy of consideration as an Ashington name with Merton connections. Celestine, then; with—after some further discussion—Clarissa to follow, with the name of one of the godmothers after that.

Celestine Clarissa . . . ? Yes, indeed. But who were the godmothers to be?

"Maud and Susannah," said Letty.

"Susannah," snapped Maud, "and some connection of the Ashingtons."

"Oh—do you think so?" breathed Susannah. "Well—yes—I would be honored. I so love all children."

"I do feel one should approach the Mertons," murmured Evangeline. "Perhaps Lady Merton herself would find it too energetic. And Adela has her wedding on her mind. But Dora might appreciate being singled out . . ."

Once again Kate's voice emerged from the pillows, raised this time in what might have been a cry for help.

"Oriel."

Francis, seeing the end of his own tether clearly in view, quickly moved to her side. "Darling, you know Oriel is abroad with her husband."

But the voice from the bed was beyond reason or comfort. "She said she'd come back for the christening."

"Yes, I know. But she was expecting the baby to be born at the end of December—as we all were."

"She said she'd come back and so she will. You can send for her. Can't you?"

"No," he said, because it was the truth and he could not change it.

"Yes you can." That was *her* truth, and since there was nothing else she wanted, she demanded it.

"No, darling. She is moving about from place to place, and even if we could contact her, her husband may not see the sense in her traveling back alone just to attend a christening. In fact, I would not care, myself, to put her to the trouble . . ."

Kate's pillows were abruptly scattered as she sat up, skinny and sallow and unkempt in her lace bedgown, both hands clutching her disordered hair, her face flushed with what could have been temper or fever, or both.

"Oriel would not think it troublesome, Francis."

"I dare say. But, just the same, it would be a great inconvenience . . ."

"Indeed it would," Oriel's mother put in. "A Channel crossing, alone, in winter. I cannot think my son-in-law would allow it."

"Then we'll wait for her: I don't care how long," Kate said, her flush deepening to a damp and—in her condition—dangerous scarlet.

Too long, perhaps—was the thought in every mind—for the frailty of that tiny and so very quiet child. But how, without running the risk of fretting her into milk-fever, did one remind a newly delivered and decidedly hysterical mother of that?

"Nonsense, Kate," said Maud. "We have been advised to have the christening tomorrow, as you know very well. And it is hardly the moment, I would have thought, for extra complication . . ."

"I don't care what you think," shouted Kate, turning purple. "Oriel is going to be godmother. That's what *I* want. And I'm going to have it. So either we'll wait, or . . . Or—yes—somebody can stand proxy for her. Well—can't they? You can get married by proxy, so it stands to reason you can be a godmother the same way. Can't you? Francis?"

He had no idea whether one could or not. "Yes—absolutely," he said.

"All right then. So let Susannah stand proxy for her. She's used to that."

Deeply offended, Susannah gathered up her skirts and fled the room, followed by Letty who returned, some ten minutes later, with the information that Susannah could not speak for tears. Letty, therefore, would speak on her daughter's behalf and did so, ably supported by Maud, until Francis—apologizing for his wife who had retired beneath her pillows again—went himself to woo Susannah into a calmer frame of mind where she eventually consented—for *his* sake, she made it clear—to be godmother in her own right after all.

"And perhaps," he suggested, "one of Oriel's stepdaughters could stand proxy for her?"

Stepdaughters! Evangeline was seen to wince at the word, finding it aging. "Ah yes," she said, as if just recollecting them. "There is one who smiles and one who does not. Perhaps we could have the smiling one."

Elspeth? Susannah, having won her own battle, now moved swiftly to the defense of Morag—her own great favorite—the elder and far more responsible of the little Keiths who ought not to have her younger, and somewhat frivolous sister set above her.

"Morag, then," said Evangeline, wrinkling her nose as though pronouncing the name of a patent cough medicine.

"Perhaps," suggested Francis once again, "we might leave Kate, now, to sleep?"

He saw them all to the door, staying a moment longer at her bedside and then, understanding she had nothing to say to him—nor he, in fact, to her—going downstairs himself to find the house no more his own than the naming of his child had been. In the small book-room where he had hoped to sit for a while in total silence and smoke a cigar he found Matthew Stangway installed, for the same reasons, before him. In the parlor Letty was drinking a herbal tea to restore the ravages of her emotions, still talking of her own lost Katharine to Susannah. Evangeline, in the drawing-room, was writing graceful notes to the Mertons, on his behalf he supposed, inviting them to the christening. Maud had gone to the housekeeper's room with the openly expressed intention of remedying—for *his* sake, once again—six months of total domestic neglect by Kate.

"You will allow me, Francis dear boy, to speak a word to the good woman in your kitchen as well—while I am about it . . ."

He considered for a moment asking her how she dared even to suggest such gross interference, but the flow of energy, the spark necessary to ignite his temper utterly failed him. He was defeated by these people, appalled by them, *diminished* by them. That most of all.

"Miss Stangway—just as you please."

She walked away from him, sure of her purpose, while he, with no purpose at all beyond the desire to escape, to *run*— now, not a moment to lose—into breathable air, untainted space, hesitated in the hall, feeling that he might very likely choke to death where he stood. And not much caring.

Ought he to go upstairs again to Kate, lying torpid and stifled in her bed? But Kate did not want him. He was sure of that. In which case, might he not just slip off, take a horse, lose himself somewhere for an hour or two, a day, ride on to some place beyond the sound of Dessborough church bells, ringing for his daughter's christening, or her funeral? He knew the doctor did not think she would live. Nor—he regretted— did it seem to matter to him one way or the other. He had not even looked closely at her. Only at Kate, struggling in the final trap of her maternity like a fly in syrup, her lungs clogged with it, her body still rigid with shock. And he knew that whether the child lived or died there would be no other, that even if he had to live with her as a sister he would never make her pregnant again. Neither of them could stand it, and no child, surely, ought to be brought into the world so tragically unwanted.

Including this one—this new Celestine Ashington—for whom no place either in her mother's or her father's heart existed. Poor little mite, indeed. But there were many such and—if she lived—a great many plain, sexually timid women like Susannah who reserved their passions for "motherless" children, a great many "ladies in reduced circumstances" who would take employment as governesses, a great many schools for the finishing and polishing of young ladies whose mothers had no taste or time for such things.

And—eventually—he might even manage to get away again. Even to Mecca.

Hearing Maud's brisk step in the lower hall, coming no doubt to suggest more household improvements, he ran upstairs and strode along the corridor, finding himself outside the nursery door which he opened and then, as an entirely logical process, went in.

"Oh—Mr. Ashington." He saw, at once, that the stiff, starch-and-vinegar nanny newly arrived from Manchester, did not think it the business of fathers to invade any nursery of hers. "May I do something for you?"

He doubted it. And what a dismal room this was, low and dark with bars across the window and that farm woman sitting with her pendulous, swollen breasts and her vacant expression in the old rocking chair, knitting what appeared to be a sock with fat, noticeably dirty fingers. Were her breasts likely to be cleaner? Inwardly shuddering, he realized, with astonishment and considerable distress, that he did not want his daughter to be fed at *that* breast, to cling there in her total helplessness, at the mercy of *this* woman's ignorance and superstitions.

And this other woman's acid chill.

His daughter. Bending over the cradle, his nostrils twitching at the wet-nurse's raw, ripe odors, he saw her clearly for the first time, one creased, dark cheek on the lace pillow, a wisp of black hair straying from a lace bonnet, a mottled little fist as powerless as a leaf in an autumn storm, a tiny mouth pouting a huge indignation; an angry little air of hoping that all her requirements in life's adventure, just starting, were going to be met.

And met by him, of course. "By you, Papa . . ." Would she really call him that? Of course. "By you, Papa, since no one else seems likely to make much effort on my account. And *I* have done nothing wrong. Not yet, at any rate."

Suddenly a terrible, a well-nigh insupportable alarm bit through him.

"Nanny," he said tersely. "This room is far too cold. Have them build up the fire at once. And I would like a private word with you—outside—please . . . Now tell me—do you have confidence in that woman in there? Well, if you think it unwise to replace her just now you will have to keep a close eye on her. She is not to be left alone with the child at any time. And please oblige me by supplying her with plenty of soap and water. Well, yes, nanny. So that she can *wash*. You will further oblige me by making absolutely certain that she does."

Celestine Clarissa *Oriel* Ashington was duly christened the next morning and continued, thereafter, slowly but surely, to gain weight and confidence enough to make a great deal of racket whenever "life's adventure" happened to displease her, and to gurgle her approval when it did not. A pretty child, although it was some time before the godmother for whom she had been named had an opportunity to say so, Mrs. Oriel Keith being detained in France rather longer than expected by her husband.

It was not a journey she had wanted to make, a spur-of-the-moment decision of Garron's which, with Kate's confinement so near and her mood so unstable, had caused her an immediate pang of dismay.

"Garron, I can't be ready by morning."

"Yes, you can, bonny lass. No doubt about it."

His final word, which no consideration of leaving his own children, let alone Kate's, would sway. Nor would he specify the date of their return. When it suited him, she supposed. Yet his intention was certainly to please her, she knew that. And, understanding by now both his massive physical desire for her and the weight of his jealousy, his refusal to share so much as a particle of her attention with anyone—male or female—whenever he was there to enjoy it himself, she had gone off to pack her bags, to make arrangements with the governess and Jamie's harassed tutor, to write a note to her mother explaining her absence, and one to Susannah whose feelings would have been hurt otherwise and who replied, at once, that she would come over to Lydwick and stay with the children as often as she could.

And indeed, had it not been for her anxiety about Kate, the pressing need she felt to be there, *with her*, when labor began, she would have thoroughly enjoyed traveling with a man so careful of his personal comforts, so ready to heap every luxury upon himself, and therefore upon her, as Garron.

"There's business, of course, to be attended to . . ."

"Of course."

"But plenty of time, in and among, for French food and wine, *and* French gowns and hats."

"Thank you, darling."

"And French perfumes. Heavy ones, to last the night . . ."

They would not sleep much, she supposed, nor did it trouble her any longer, a "fine, strong woman" who could arch herself into his embrace and inspire such ardor that the heat of it blinded him—she hoped—to her own still uncertain response to pleasure. Whispers of it, merely, growing so pale by comparison with his huge joys that they invariably evaporated, half felt, just strong enough to tantalize her.

Not that she worried about it overmuch. Nor Garron either,

she supposed, so long as she remained cheerful, passive, absolutely and always to hand whenever his hand was there to take her. And when it was not? She did not question his fidelity. She simply knew that there could be no question whatsoever about her own.

"All right, bonny lass. I'll build a few French railways and buy you a diamond for every one. How's that? And then there's Russia . . ."

"Is there really?"

"Oh yes. A place that could do with some opening up, I reckon. What can I buy you from there? Don't be shy to ask, because when the Russian contracts start to come in they'll be enormous."

"Furs," she said. "Sables."

He nodded. "That's what I thought you'd want. Maybe next year. Now then, I have to be busy all day so take a walk around the town and buy *yourself* something—anything you fancy."

In any town, too. London. Brussels. Rouen. The Paris of Louis Philippe the Citizen King, son of the great class-betrayer, the Duke of Orleans, who, joining France's first revolution had voted for the execution of his own near relation, King Louis XIV, only to go to the guillotine himself soon afterward; thus escaping the rise and fall of Napoleon, followed by the resuscitation of the French monarchy by English dukes and Russian and German princes, and the reign of his own, now elderly son who had been put on the throne—largely because no one else had been available—by another revolution, not of the people this time, but by a consortium of bankers and businessmen.

A well-meaning but boring old gentleman, King Louis Philippe, it seemed to Oriel who met him on one of his famous strolls as she was shopping in the rue Saint-Honoré, recognizing him by the revolutionary tricolor in his hat, his umbrella, and the affable manner in which he would stop to shake hands and explain—if the person so honored happened to be a pretty English lady—that he had been a close friend—a very close friend indeed—of Queen Victoria's father, the unlucky Duke of Kent. The very same duke who, after twenty-seven years of domestic bliss with his "dear friend" Madame de Saint Laurent, had pensioned her off in order to marry a German princess and breed an heir to the English throne. Victoria.

"And how do you like our city?" this Monarch of the People asked Oriel.

"Very much indeed, sir." She had never spoken to a king before, finding him so exactly like any other self-important old gentleman—apart, that is, from the guards who were pretending not to guard him—that it took her a few moments to realize how deeply her mother would be impressed.

She wrote a note to High Grange, receiving in Evangeline's enthusiastic reply the news of the Ashington baby and how ably little Miss Morag Keith had represented Oriel at the christening.

"Well done," said Garron, pleased that "they," the leisured classes, old money instead of new, had singled out his daughter.

"Yes, indeed." She did not want to spoil his pleasure with her alarm, or irritate him with it either. "But if they had the christening so soon, then perhaps the baby is not very well . . . ?"

He shrugged and glanced at the date on Evangeline's letter. "Still alive when this was posted, at any rate. And I know you wouldn't be wanting to cut and run home again, would you? Before we're ready?"

Of course not. This was *his* time, he was saying. And by no means over yet. There was the theater tonight, a play which *she* had particularly asked to see, and dinner, in the Bois de Boulogne tomorrow with a pair of real Russian noblemen with money to burn and therefore plenty to invest in threading Russia with as complex a network of railways—if he had his way—as England. She had been looking forward to meeting them. She knew, without another spoken word, that he did not expect her enthusiasm to wane.

She could not, in all honesty, blame him for that.

She met the Russians, sparkled for one of them, became spiritual and soulful for the other, while Garron, whose jealousy of her time and attention did not spill over into business matters, sat back and watched the skill for which—both in his opinion and in hers—he was paying her handsomely. And because she had done well for him, because those two particular gentlemen, should they ever happen to have a railway contract at their disposal, would remember the name of Garron Keith because they remembered his wife, he decided to reward her with a trip south as far as Cannes.

A week, he thought. Or two, since he'd had a letter from

a certain, influential German gentleman, spending the winter along the Corniche d'Or, who thought a railway connecting various commercial, possibly even military centers throughout the Germanic confederation, might prove convenient for his particular group of friends. And since no one at the moment knew very much about building railways except British engineers like Locke and Brunel and de Hay, and British contractors like Peto and Brassey and himself, it was essential—in his opinion—to get in, and *now*, before these other countries found out just how it was done.

And when Europe was exhausted there would be America—if he was quick enough—Africa, Australia, China, any place on earth where there were businessmen with goods to be moved to market, and generals with soldiers to be rushed into battle.

Two weeks, then, in Cannes, which would give them plenty of time to get home for Christmas. And, if not, then *his* children knew that business came before pleasure, and that if he missed one train he'd surely turn up on the next, bearing gifts the like of which they had not seen since the date of his last arrival.

She would enjoy Cannes. He'd even take her on to Monte Carlo and drive her past the Mertons' villa if she really wanted a tale to tell her mother. Although Cannes was the best place for *his* money, just a fishing village it had been, a few years ago, until one of England's more enterprising grandees, Lord Brougham, had been turned back at the border on his way to Italy because of some epidemic of fever or other, and had liked the little place called Cannes so much that he'd decided to build himself a villa here. Thus setting a fashion among the English aristocracy which had provided congenial summer employment for lads who knew how to lay bricks and dig foundations and had a taste for adventure to go with it, like the then very young Garron Keith. Yes. He'd seen Cannes for the first time with a bricklayer's trowel in his hand, and gone on the tramp through France afterward to save the fare home. And now . . . Well—someday, when all the railway building was done, he might just come down here again, if he'd managed to stand the pace, and think about building a villa of his own. As near to Lord Brougham's as he could get; which, if nothing else, would always make his wife's mother jump at the chance of a visit.

Oriel ignored that, allowing him to show her around the

effervescent, exceedingly fashionable town he seemed to
know so well, succumbing quickly enough to its charm to be
aware that, were it not for her nagging anxiety about Kate,
the prospect of spending Christmas here—without the Stangways, without Susannah, without Morag, even without her
mother—would not have dismayed her. A Christmas without
obligation, alone with a man who, because he was richly,
unashamedly self-indulgent, created circumstances of luxury
and pleasure which indulged her too.

How restful: and what an odd word to apply to Garron
Keith who never rested anywhere, whose explosive energies
carried him from one building site, one boardroom, one
country, one enormous, richly seasoned meal, one grand hotel, to the next without ever—so far as she could see—the
least sign of flagging. A demanding man too, and hard to
please, who, giving excellent service himself, expected it
from others, so that woe betide any cab driver who delivered
him a minute late at his destination, any waiter who brought
him a less than perfect and less than gigantic beefsteak, any
hotelier who failed to provide him with the best accommodation in the house, anybody anywhere who attempted to fob
him off with excuses as to why a thing could not be done
when he made it an iron rule never to accept and never to
offer any excuses at all.

Yet, nevertheless—compared to the ceaseless patter of small
irritations, trifling distresses, little nervous spites and vanities
and suppressions encountered day in, day out, at Lydwick
and High Grange—how restful.

She traveled back there two days before Christmas with at
least three times more luggage than she had taken away with
her, not quite certain, up to the last moment, whether or not
he might tell her, when they reached Leeds, that he was going on to Glasgow or Cardiff or Land's End even, and send
her on the complicated road to Lydwick alone. But he came
with her, the cosseted atmosphere of fur rugs, footwarmers,
silver-topped flasks of brandy and coffee, reserved compart-
ments, private rooms at wayside inns where the landlords saw
every reason to treat a former, very generous bricklayer like
a king—which was *his* idea of winter travel—still wrapped
around her until the instant she crossed her own threshold.
To be greeted by a committee of Morag and Susannah with
the information that Jamie had a serious chill, the Christmas
Day turkey had not been delivered, while the Boxing Day

goose was certainly too small, her mother had expected her home at least two weeks ago and was "most surprised" at the delay, the tunnel at Merton Ridge was flooded with rainwater, and her friend Miss Woodley, from Ullswater, had died.

"Christ," said Garron Keith, ramming on his hat again and striding out of the door which had not even had time to close behind him, only one item of the catalog of errors appearing relevant to him.

"Two navvies have drowned," shouted Jamie, appearing at the head of the stairs in his nightshirt. "Two little ones who couldn't keep their heads above water. The tall ones got out all right." And since he was certainly going to be tall himself, Oriel could see him wondering how much, if at all, the small men really mattered.

"Get back to bed," she said.

"He has given us rather a lot of anxiety," murmured Susannah.

"Oh—I expect he'll live, by the look of him." As Miss Woodley had not. But Miss Woodley had been old and at peace with herself, her life fulfilled and satisfied. And over. How much—how terribly—she would miss her. How dreadful that she would never see that living garden, that silent house by the lake again.

"Jamie has been coughing all night for a week," said Morag, her body taut with accusation, meaning, Oriel supposed, "While *you* have been flaunting yourself before my father in foreign hotels, spending his money and keeping him away from *us;* at Christmas, and when we needed him."

"We have brought lots and lots of presents," she said.

"My father," said Morag, her accent, Oriel noticed, so much improved that it could have been mistaken for Susannah's, "always does."

The presents were unpacked and set out on the hall table, the excitement effecting a miracle cure on Jamie and on Elspeth too who had been sinking, these last few weeks, into a lethargy which Susannah had feared as the beginning of a "decline"; although the gold-wrapped, beribboned package had little effect on Morag who appeared to regard all this extravagance—perhaps correctly, thought Oriel—as a bribe.

Other matters were also settled, the goose and turkey, the right amount of holly and mistletoe for the house and where to place it, whether to follow the new fashion for Christmas trees, brought over from Germany by Victoria's Prince Albert.

"Yes," chorused Jamie and Elspeth.

"In the Western Isles of Scotland where we always go for Christmas . . ." began Morag.

"We eat herring and oatmeal," scoffed Jamie, "and sleep in wooden boxes like coffins built into the wall."

"And we have to help with the housework," said Elspeth disdainfully, being well on the way to forgetting that she had not always had a maid to make her bed and do her hair.

"*And* help fillet the fish." This was Jamie again. "Outside on the beach in the early morning when it's freezing—biting—bitter cold."

"And it smells," said Elspeth, looking as if she might faint at the memory.

"It's healthy—better . . ." muttered Morag as, most unusually for her, she turned and, quite definitely, fled away.

In tears?

"What's *she* crying for?" asked Jamie, who did not care.

"For Aunt Flora and Grannie Macleod, I expect," said Elspeth, her nonchalance letting it be known that she could no longer feel these people to be very closely related to *her*.

"For Aunt Flora?" echoed Jamie, looking puzzled about it.

For her mother, perhaps? Oriel had wondered how Garron Keith, town-dweller, far more at ease with the smokes and steams of industry than the mist of a moorland sunrise, had met and married a fisherman's daughter from those remote Scottish islands. She knew now—the wine having turned him sentimental on one or two occasions—that Morag Macleod had been a parlormaid in a doctor's house in Newcastle, a respectable girl who, when the strapping young foreman of a navvy gang had made her pregnant, had assumed rather than expected that he would marry her. And now, twelve years later, here was her daughter, another Morag, pampered with gifts from Paris and Cannes which had failed to impress her; and her daughter Elspeth queening it—rather too readily—over housemaids such as her own mother had once been.

"I'd better go after her," Oriel said. But Susannah had already done so, her skirts swishing up the stairs, her voice reaching them on a breathless note as she called out, "Morag—what is it, dear? Now *do* open the door. You can tell *me*."

And it was not until Susannah returned, keeping silent about what, if anything, she had been told, that Oriel, having gone through her letters and invitations, sent off a note to her mother, and snatched a moment or two to think of Miss Woodley, had any chance of asking for news of Kate. And, of course, her child.

"Oh yes—*our* little goddaughter," beamed Susannah, meaning, of course, hers and Morag's, since Oriel—she felt certain—had understood straightaway that all the nonsense about proxy had been—well—just nonsense really. Just a whim of Kate's, best forgotten, particularly since Morag had behaved so beautifully at the christening and was taking the responsibilities of godmother so much to heart. Oriel would not wish to deprive her of that.

Oriel did not suppose so, although, in fact, she made no definite answer.

"So your goddaughter is doing well, Susannah? And Kate? I wrote to her several times and have had no answer."

Susannah shook her head, assuming an expression Oriel supposed to be pity. Poor Kate. But Susannah, virgin daughter of the vicarage, felt obliged to speak so guardedly of all matters relating to the intimate processes of marriage and motherhood that even Oriel, with direct experience of sensuality, could hardly understand her.

The birth had been difficult, of course, but then, somehow, one had always expected that of Kate, with whom nothing had ever been simple. Was that Maud's voice, Oriel wondered, talking through Susannah? And if she did not care to nurse the child herself had there been any need to make such a fuss about it, when so many ladies, these days, felt they had done more than enough simply by bringing an infant into the world and saw no cause for high drama in leaving it, thereafter, to others? Surely *that* was a hint of Evangeline? But Kate *had* made a fuss, *had* been highly dramatic. Or else she had said nothing at all, for days—and days—on end, huddled in bed with her face in the pillows and her eyes open just staring at the wall, refusing to wash or let them brush her hair or change her linen, pushing away all food, all advice, all sympathy, picking up one of her pillows and hurling it—simply hurling it—at anyone who went on too long trying to be kind.

A shocking performance, the whole household walking on tiptoe and poor Francis haggard and quite gray with worry, looking older every time one saw him; which had been very often, of course, since one had felt in honor bound to do what one could, no matter how loudly Kate howled at one to leave her alone, and spilled the hyssop tea one had specially brewed for her, all over her valuable antique counterpane.

"I felt sure I had heard her talking about hyssop tea," said Susannah, looking hurt. "And I assumed it was a favorite . . ."

"Yes," said Oriel. 'I do see that you would, Susannah. Well—I don't suppose I can manage to see her today but I will drive over—somehow—tomorrow."

"Oh no, Oriel. There would be no point to that. The Mertons have taken her."

"I beg your pardon."

"You didn't know?" Susannah appeared surprised that the doings of the Mertons had not been published in the Paris press. "Oh yes—your mother seems to think they have made a great mistake. In inviting Kate and Francis to the Abbey for Christmas, I mean, and then up to their castle in Scotland until the end of February, when they are all to come back here for Dora Merton's birthday dance. So we shall none of us see Kate until then. Oh yes—we are all invited to the dance. Your mother says it is to compensate us for having Adela's wedding in London. She thinks *that* was a great mistake too."

Evangeline drove over an hour later to express her opinions herself, showing cool displeasure at finding Susannah still in residence in her daughter's house, and Oriel herself busy in her larder, checking over the Christmas plum cakes and puddings, the stand pies and port-jellies and chestnut stuffings, the mince pies and oyster patties her husband had told her to provide with a lavish hand.

"Susannah, my dear, how is it you have not yet gone back to the vicarage? Run along now and pack your belongings and I will take you home in my carriage. Your place is with your mother, surely, with Christmas almost upon us. Especially since she has lost Quentin."

Susannah, brought up very strictly to obey her elders, at once retreated.

"Lost Quentin, Mama? What do you mean?"

"Oh—nothing, dearest. I am only making mischief. He has established himself so comfortably in his rooms in Hepplefield and misses his family so little that he can spend no

more than Christmas Day with them. Letty is quite dis-
traught—as you would imagine. Does it really matter?''

Not to Evangeline, certainly, who was still incensed not
only by the Mertons' sudden appropriation of Kate, but by
the manner in which she had learned of it, not from the Mertons themselves but from her own coachman whose
"cousin"—for want of a better word—was a parlormaid at
the Abbey. Obviously they were doing it for Francis. Obviously one's heart bled for the poor man, tied to a wife in the
grip of a melancholy which could very well prove fatal, and
with the girl he ought to have married tied—so hurriedly—to
somebody else . . .

"Please, Mama . . .''

"Nonsense, Oriel. I am speaking the truth. Occasionally I
find it refreshing. The Mertons pity him. We all do. And
when they have spent a Christmas with Kate in her present
mood we shall very likely pity the Mertons. She is a specter
I should not like to see sitting at my festive table, I do assure
you—with her hair unbrushed and her nails dirty and her skin
like damp clay. And her *eyes* just boring holes in the wall,
or the carpet. And all, my dear, for the very common-or-
garden reason that she has had a baby. Good Heavens, Lady
Merton is so very particular she cannot sleep twice between
the same sheets, and his lordship cannot bear silence. He is
positively uneasy unless one constantly chatters to him—about
this and that . . .''

Usually about himself, of course. Flattery? What—Evangeline wished to know—was so wrong with that? A social device, a tool, which she had always employed to advantage in
much the same way as the Mertons' other guests, sophisticated, attractive people, would also do, encouraging Francis—soulful and sorrowful and interesting as he currently
was—to join their company and ignoring the nuisance Kate,
who, for all they cared, could sink into the melancholy pit
she seemed so intent on digging, and drown.

And both the Merton girls had been "fast." Yes, of course
they had. "High-spirited" one had officially called it. But
"fast"—and often furiously so—would have been nearer the
mark. Dora—who had never concealed her partiality for her
Cousin Francis—still was. Fast and rich and over twenty-one,
an age at which, if she took it into her head to elope with the
squire of Dessborough, as her Aunt Celestine had done with
his father, one could hardly stop her.

"Aren't you looking rather far into the future, Mama?"

"My dear, if you had seen Kate as recently as I have, you would realize that Francis might be a widower any day now."

And since, by the look of Garron Keith, it seemed unlikely that Oriel could manage, at the appropriate moment, to be free herself, Evangeline felt fully entitled to be aggrieved about it.

"Well, I suppose I had better be off. At least I can take that ninny Susannah off your hands and back to that even greater ninny her mother. Poor Letty, she doesn't know—really she doesn't know—that what ails her at present is jealousy—pure and simple—of her darling Quentin's handsome landlady."

"I dare say. But if she doesn't know, then I don't think you ought to tell her, Mama."

"My dear, why waste my breath? She would never believe it. Goodbye then, I will see you on Christmas morning. You will come to High Grange church with me, of course—won't you?—to defend me from my dear friends and relations. And luncheon afterward—naturally. Your husband can spare you to me for that."

But when Garron returned home that night, very late, very cold, considerably mud-stained and soaked to the skin by the rain which, yet again, had flooded through the clay of Merton Ridge, he was in no mood to make concessions of any kind to anyone. A tub of hot water, clean clothes, hot food and plenty of it eaten from a tray in the armchair by the parlor fire, his wife's total attention. These were his requirements. After which he would glance at the correspondence which had accumulated in his absence, smoke a cigar or two over a glass or two of brandy, and take his wife to bed.

Yes, two navvies had been killed. Short men, as Jamie had said, who had failed to keep their heads above the floodwater. But one had to bear in mind that after six months of digging and blasting, these two were the only fatalities. Due in part—as he believed the whole site to be aware—to his insistence on using dynamite instead of gunpowder, even though it cost him five times as much.

"Did those men leave families?"

"Of a sort."

"What sort?"

"Oh—wives they never got round to taking to the altar. And a few children I expect. They'll be provided for."

"By whom?"

"By their mates. They'll all put a penny or two in the foreman's hat."

"Will you give them something?"

"I might. But not with anybody else looking on. Do you know how many men fall into cuttings, on pay-night, and don't even know which bones they've broken until morning? Or how many lay down dead drunk on top of Merton Moor where the rain never stops and then, about ten minutes before the pneumonia kills them, start wondering what caused it? Or how many blow themselves up through carrying dynamite about in their pockets to keep it warm? Your Cousin Susannah says there's a death to every mile of track and thirty to a tunnel. So when it comes to compensation, I'd rather pick and choose . . ."

"Yes—of course . . ." But she was thinking, as she had been thinking to some extent all day, about Miss Woodley, and had not really heard him.

"So I'm going to be busy, Oriel, this next day or two— devilish busy. The tunnel's a mess. That clever bastard de Hay was out by a bloody mile in his findings. Mainly rock, he said, to blast clean through, and that's what I allowed for. And that's bad enough. But clay's different. Clay can be hell. Once you open it up and the light gets to it, and the bloody rain, there's no holding it. It expands. It can get so lively that even when you've lined it twice and three times over with good bricks you've paid good money for, it can squeeze the mortar out between them. Christ—I hate clay. So I'm going to be up at the tunnel now until it's drained and sorted out, or it's going to cost me a fortune. It's not de Hay they'll come looking for if it's not ready on time. And it's not de Hay who'll lose his penalty money either. You'll manage all right—with the kids? Won't you?"

"Yes, Garron. I will." Once again she was barely listening, although she was, nevertheless, perfectly well aware that he had asked her to serve up the spirit of Christmas single-handed on the most ornate platter she could contrive, to these children who were still quite strange to her.

"I want their bedrooms to look like Aladdin's Cave on Christmas morning. We got enough presents, didn't we?"

"Oh—enough for a school, I think. Or two. Yes—yes, we did. Garron—listen—do you remember the cottage by Lake Ullswater where I was staying last winter?"

"Yes. Yes, I do," he said and then, as if remembering exactly how and why, reached out to the piled up correspondence on his desk. "I have a letter about it from a solicitor in Penrith."

"About Miss Woodley? She died—while we were away."

"Yes, that's what the letter tells me. It seems she left her house to you, and her lawyer is asking what I want done with it."

Asking *him*? Of course. For she understood quite well that as a married woman, the law allowed her no separate identity apart from her husband, her body belonging to him so irrevocably that, so far as the law was concerned, she *was* him. Mrs. Garron Keith, the shadow of Mr. Garron Keith, whose guardianship of her was as absolute as the control he exercised over his children. More absolute, in fact, since his authority over his children would end when they reached twenty-one, whereas she remained his for life.

Quentin Saint-Charles had explained it all to her in his precise, legal fashion on the day he had drawn up her marriage contract. "You do understand, Oriel, that on marriage a woman relinquishes all her legal and financial rights to her husband? That is to say that such property as she brings into marriage becomes his property, to be administered or disposed of as he thinks fit, with or without her consent. Likewise in the matter of inheritance, all legacies to her becoming his, absolutely and without any obligation on his part even to inform her as to what he does with them. Nor can she sue him at any time, or take any kind of legal action against him whatsover, since in law they are the same person. And one can hardly sue oneself."

"Yes, Quentin, I understand." And, at that moment, since she had no property and no prospect, that she could see, of acquiring any, it had seemed irrelevant.

No longer.

"Garron . . . ?"

He shrugged, the letter still in his hand, but not weighing very heavily there.

"Yes. A ramshackle old place, as I remember. Better get rid of it, I suppose, before it falls down. Although it won't be looking its best in this cold weather . . ."

It seemed to her that her own body was being menaced. "Garron"—and her mouth seemed drier than she had ever known it before—"couldn't we keep it?"

"Why?"

It meant nothing to him, she knew that. She did not even dare to contemplate, at this vulnerable moment, how much it meant to her.

"I could take the children there in the summer." She knew, although he did not, that she was pleading with him. "The fresh air would do them good. And Jamie would love it."

He shrugged again. "I can think of places he'd like better. A bit on the quiet side for our Jamie, I should have thought. And lonely for the girls. I doubt we'd get our money's worth out of it, Oriel. The money I'd have to spend, that is, to make it fit to live in and keep it that way."

She saw his hand begin the movement of tossing the letter back on to his desk to be answered, whenever he happened to remember it, with a brief request to sell, and said quickly, "Will you reconsider?"

"What?" He had given the matter as much consideration already as it seemed worth. And then, his eyes which were always shrewd and keen growing quickly suspicious, he rapped out "Why?", the tone of his voice warning her that she had alarmed his sense of possession and would have to tread warily.

And how could she say to him "Because only there have I ever been at peace. Only there have I felt truly undisturbed, unmolested, free from other people's schemes and maneuvers. It is the only home I have ever known"? She knew she could not. Yet if he took that home away from her, those few memories of childhood content, that prospect of one calm acre of her own where she could breathe unencumbered air, she also knew she would be unable to forgive him. The wound would fester and spread to everything around her. For all their sakes she must not allow that.

And since she could not browbeat him, was in no position to make demands, not even, with any guarantee of success, to ask outright, she would have to use such weapons as came to hand. She had never flirted with him before, nor with any other man for that matter, but, having all her life watched Evangeline strewing dainty little promises of delights which might, or might not, be forthcoming, she knew very well how it was done.

"It's so lovely there, Garron. The garden is so beautiful."

"You have a garden here, three times as big . . ."

"I know. I know." She knew, too, that the warmth in her

voice, the hint of laughter, had caused him to look at her *very* keenly now. "But there is the lake and the high fells, which always makes me feel so energetic. And the track up to Martindale and the old churchyard—do you remember—with the enormous yew tree . . . It must be the most romantic place on earth. I feel romantic there, in any case. You must remember how—well—invigorating—it is?"

"Yes," he said. "What of it?"

"Do I take it you've forgotten already?"

He shook his head. "No—no. I've not forgotten. Do *I* take it you want to build a little shrine where I proposed to you?"

She made a wide, airy gesture, giving him her permission to take whatever view—and, just possibly, whatever liberties—he pleased.

"I don't believe you, Oriel." Yet she saw the corners of his mouth twitch slightly with amusement, his eyes narrowing no longer in scrutiny but the acknowledgment of his readily aroused desire, and the advantages her present mood gave him. And it was not in his nature—as she had gambled—to neglect an advantage.

"No, bonny lass, I don't believe you." But he was smiling openly now, enjoying both the pretty game she was playing and the prospect of his own generosity. No doubt she was "handling" him, as women did, but, equally without doubt, he could afford to be "handled," when it suited him, if it made her more than usually accommodating. It was a situation with which he was both comfortable and familiar. A lakeland cottage then, if that was what it took to make her eager and happy and glad—on the whole—that she had accepted the proposal he'd made to her under that yew tree. Why not? It would cost him far less in time and trouble and hard cash than the Merton Ridge Tunnel. He was even—although secretly—delighted to have found something she wanted badly enough to ask.

"All right," he said, tossing the letter from Miss Woodley's lawyer into her lap. "Write to this Mr. Braymore and tell him whatever you want to tell him. I'll sign it."

"Thank you, Garron."

"Happy to be of service, ma'am. I presume there is a reward?"

She went upstairs with him in a glow which carried her through the next few, often difficult days, the strains and stresses of being a "family at Christmas" when the father was away from early morning to late at night, shouting curses and instructions through the sleet storms lashing down on Merton Ridge, and the natural mother gone beyond recall of anything but the imagination of Morag, her eldest daughter, who set about inventing memories in the unconcealed hope of annoying the "new wife."

Thinking of her cottage, her own calm acre, such memories did not annoy her, her glow warm and deep enough to survive every attempt the Festive Season made to snuff it out. The cool, dismissive manner, for instance, in which Morag unwrapped the books and shawls and fans and bonnets, the beautiful porcelain dolls dressed up like queens, the exquisitely sad clown, the musical boxes, the water-colors, the flower prints, the coral earrings and beads, the gold locket, the angel cameo, all of them chosen by Oriel, leaving them extravagantly neglected all day, ostentatiously underfoot, until the cameo was broken, the earrings missing, the head of one porcelain lady cracked open, while Morag spent her time gazing—whenever Oriel was looking—at a religious picture sent by Susannah.

The perhaps equally cool manner in which Evangeline received the information that Oriel could only spend half an hour on Christmas morning at High Grange. The half-hour itself, with Maud serving port wine and Madeira as if it were hemlock, Matthew locked away in his book-room, Morag and Susannah whispering together, Letty waiting in visible agony for Quentin who had promised to come early, terrified that he might not come at all and then speaking to him sharply the very moment he did, unable to stop herself from asking him every one of the questions she had vowed never to ask at all, about his rooms in Hepplefield which she could not bring herself to visit, his landlady whom she could not bear to see, his friends of whom he ought surely to have no need, and dropping hints which only she imagined to be veiled as to why he had so callously turned his back on his family and broken his mother's heart.

The drive back to Lydwick and the violent quarrel halfway when Morag finally noticed her missing coral earrings boldly swinging in her sister Elspeth's ears. The grand Christmas dinner to follow, the turkey and oyster patties, the roast lamb and caper sauce, the mince pies and plum pudding all kept waiting until Morag could be brought to admit that her father would not come. Her refusal, afterward, to join her brother and sister in the games of Hunt the Slipper and Blind Man's Buff, or the Charades bravely organized by Oriel, who did not care for games herself. The gnawing fatigue in her bones long before the children had gone to bed, her cheeks aching with the effort of constant, usually false smiles, her throat sore with constant words of encouragement, approval—usually false, too—and good cheer, her eyes smarting with the strain of watching them, checking their needs and their humors, what else—what next—what now, ready to pour oil on their troubled waters before—if possible—the trouble had begun. Her assurances—very false these—that their father would run straight upstairs to see them the very minute he came back from the Tunnel, when she knew very well that his immediate needs would be of an altogether different variety.

None of this dimmed her glow. He came to her in the middle of the night straight from Merton Ridge, wet and filthy, foul-tempered and often still foul-mouthed with the vocabulary of the site. She brought him hot water herself to spare the sensibilities of the servants, washed his hair and scrubbed his back like any miner's wife in his home village, gave him food and sex in lavish, often double helpings, and sent him off to his work again before going to wake and feed and entertain his children.

"You're a good woman, Oriel."

She smiled and nodded, knowing he meant "strong," strength being more to his liking any day than virtue.

"And you'll be telling me I'm a good man, I reckon?"

She nodded again. "*And* modest."

Good too, she freely admitted, according to the estimation of the world he lived in; and, increasingly, in her own. A man of iron nerve and muscle, capable of gigantic labor, hearty and demanding in all his appetites, open-handed, unsentimental. A hard man, blinkered by his own forceful needs and ambitions, seeing first and foremost what he wanted himself and making sure he got it, giving to others what he believed they ought to have, or the things he had wanted himself at their age, or in their situation.

He had given her a gold chain set with diamonds for Christmas and diamond earrings of which he fully appreciated the value, and her quiet, lakeland acre which had little value for him but was beyond price to her. She was grateful, hopeful. Had it not been for the hovering phantom she knew to be Kate, never far from the edge of her vision, she may even have been happy. And, even as things were, she was often very much amused.

In the middle of February—Kate still locked away, so far as she knew, in the custody of the Mertons—she went up to Penrith to lay claim to her inheritance, traveling for the first time with her husband and children all together, and, when she and Garron had separately assessed what the cottage required to make it habitable—very little in her opinion, a great deal in his—returning home to deep snow and the still, clear magic of a midwinter night. The town of Lydwick was made of cut crystal, their own house silver with moonlight, the garden a pure carpet of snow, its surface unblemished until Jamie, with a wild whoop of glee, plunged knee high, then breast high, across it.

"That's far enough," called Oriel, entirely without conviction. "Silly boy," murmured Elspeth, the pretty one, the vain one, who had been complaining all day about the cold and the mud on her shoes, her face slightly bemused now as *something*— she really didn't know what—drew her into the snowdrift after her brother.

"She's younger than she thought," said Garron, ducking the first snowball his son hurled at him, receiving the second full in his chest, and then, suddenly bareheaded as Elspeth's haphazard handful struck his hat, wading in among them, firing missiles of his own, hard and accurate ones it seemed, playing even this game, gleefully perhaps, but nevertheless to win.

"Father . . ." said Morag reprovingly, picking up his hat. Oriel took it away from her. "He may need your help, Morag. Look—it's two to one."

"Oh . . ." The snowballs were flying now, thick and fast.

"Come on, Morag," shouted Garron. "Where's my girl . . . ?"

Shaking herself, as if released from a spring, she bounded away. "I'm here—watch out—Jamie, you *beast* —take *that* one—from me . . ."

Such fun. Standing on the path, her ankles tingling in the snow, tasting the crisp air, her eyes full of sharp little winter stars and a few stray tears, Oriel knew a moment of equal joy and sorrow that would, in a moment more she thought, blend into a wholly acceptable compromise. Not the life she would have chosen. Nor the man she would have chosen either. But a life, nevertheless. A man who valued her, who often made her laugh, who was, in fact, even handsome. Children who needed many things she could give. Perhaps a child of her own one day.

And it was as the thought of children released the thought of Kate—who had been destroyed, it seemed, by the strange wounds of getting the man she loved and bearing his child—that she heard horses, and running footsteps; an excitement which, at this hour, surely meant disaster, something too urgent, too fatal to be left until morning. An accident? Or worse?

Kate. Had her self-torment led to self-destruction, to the ending of a life she no longer knew how to live? Kate? Oriel knew she could not bear it.

And there Kate was, although it took even Oriel a moment to recognize the woman in the dark red ball-gown and black velvet cloak who was suddenly *there* in the snow, splashing it about like sea-foam in the faces of the two men who accompanied her, the third man—Quentin Saint-Charles—striding along the path to Oriel, telling her succinctly and at once everything she wished to know.

"Yes, it *is* Kate, Oriel. I do apologize. She arrived at Merton Abbey a few hours ago, I don't quite know from where, and insisted on driving over to see you. No, Francis is not with her. I believe he is still in Scotland, with the child. Those two are Merton cousins who have taken rather more than a drop too much, as I expect your husband will realize, and are both in love with Kate. Or so they were telling her on the way over. You will see that she is looking much better."

But Oriel was too stunned even to reply as she watched poor, broken Kate skimming the snow like a wild bird, a crown of dark red feathers doubling her height, her black cloak thrown back like giant wings revealing bare shoulders, a red dress which clung to her waist and bared somewhat more than half her breast, the skirt molded by the snow against a body which seemed to ripple and quiver with her own delight in the power she had suddenly acquired over these men—any men—who desired her, who could see and taste and smell in her a glorious unleashing of what *they*, at least, understood as sensuality.

"What fun," she kept on calling out, still skimming the snow. "What an absolute lark."

Look at me; she was really saying—Oriel heard it loud and

clear—*Look at me. Here I am. Kate who was dead and is alive again, although perhaps she still doesn't know what for. Come and teach me, if you can. Kate, who has left her husband and child in Scotland, and drives out in the middle of the night with rich young men who say they love her. And why shouldn't they? Why shouldn't she? Better, at any rate, than hiding unwashed and terrified in her bed.*

"I suppose when one is sufficiently desperate one will be likely to try anything. Perhaps one is fortunate, Oriel, never to feel *quite* that degree of desperation." It was Quentin who had spoken, and then Garron, appearing suddenly at her other side, and murmuring what she understood to be his version of the same judgment in her ear.

"You'll do no good fretting over that one, bonny lass, because there'll be no helping her. She'll cause a stir while her flame goes on burning, I don't doubt it. But once it burns down then—well, I've seen it before and there'll be no lighting it again. I'm sorry, lass, believe me—I'm sorry for *her*—but there it is. All it amounts to, by the way she's carrying on right now, is a matter of time."

Eleven

A matter of time? Garron Keith was not the only one to think so throughout that hectic winter and the very nearly frenzied spring and summer to follow, nor the only pair of eyes to watch with speculation as Kate—who had been in turn the nuisance, the rebel, embarrassing in her passion, limp in her despair—acquired the surface dazzle and allure of a diamond; with a fire beneath it at which there seemed no lack, at any time, of men both young and old, waiting to be burned.

Biding their time. Which would not be long in coming, according to an increasingly bitter Aunt Maud, for whom it could not come soon enough; to Evangeline who, as part of her game with Matthew, was more than ready to hasten it along; to Lady Merton who, as a woman of fashion, had become very virtuous since the accession of the prude Victoria; and to Lady Merton's younger daughter, affectionately known from childhood as "Madcap Dora," who apart from cherishing a certain fondness for her Cousin Francis, did not care to see her own reputation for wildness and waywardness suddenly eclipsed by his wife.

Not that Kate was beautiful, of course. No amount of diamond sparkle could achieve that, as Dora Merton well knew, her own attraction depending entirely on such things as her recklessness on horseback, her unpredictable "fits and starts," her enthusiasm for organizing elaborate games of "hide and seek" at which couples who wished to be alone were never found, and the simple fact—much talked of in Merton circles—that one really never knew what that Madcap Dora might get up to next.

And the suspicion that she was beginning to look little more than eccentric beside the flame and dazzle of this new Kate did not please her at all.

At Dora's birthday dance that February Kate wore a scarlet satin dress which, toward the end of the evening, "fell off" her shoulders, a mishap serious enough to send any other woman scuttling for cover but of which Kate seemed so oblivious that one felt bound to conclude she had done it on purpose. Thin shoulders, too, with nothing that ought to have been enticing about them, nothing that *ought* to have caused so many gentlemen—Timothy Merton, Adela Merton's new husband, and the young aristocrat with whom Dora herself was contemplating marriage prominently among them—to have behaved so foolishly.

"Bees round a honeypot," Dora had muttered contemptuously, wondering how it was that the honey—from such a source—should not be sour.

"The girl has turned out quite wanton. Who would have thought it?" murmured Evangeline, highly delighted. Although Matthew Stangway, for whom all honey had lost its sweetness, merely nodded his head.

"So it would seem."

"You have another daughter, Matthew. *My* daughter."

He smiled, perfectly reading her mind. "Ah yes. But I have a granddaughter too, my darling—an entirely legitimate and, one supposes, wholly innocent Miss Celestine Ashington. Whatever happens to Kate I am in honor bound, surely, to provide for my grandchild? In fact, with regard to certain, and I fear exceedingly substantial portions of family property, I would have no choice."

Miss Celestine Ashington. An heiress for High Grange, then, as well as Dessborough, six months and then rapidly approaching twelve months old, a pretty, sturdy child, a black-eyed amber-skinned Ashington in appearance, who could hardly be aware that the highly scented, highly elated creature who occasionally, never more than briefly, flew across her path was no scarlet and ebony bird of paradise, no flash of jeweled lightning, no vivid and quite possibly dangerous whirlwind, but her mother.

"Wanton," repeated Evangeline at every opportunity, adding, for Matthew's ears only, "A legacy, one supposes, my darling, from the Kesslers." Since Eva Kessler, as he must surely remember, had taken strangely to motherhood too.

"A quite natural rising of high spirits," Quentin Saint-Charles kept on repeating with Oriel's full agreement. "Spirits, which, having sunk so low after the birth of her child, have really nowhere else to go now—wouldn't you think?—but up?"

Neither Evangeline, nor Madcap Dora Merton, nor little Celestine's nanny who, like Dora, was slightly in love with Francis, seemed inclined to agree.

"And I am not aware," persisted Quentin, "of any one name which has been linked in any truly damaging circumstances with hers. That she flirts and fascinates, yes—perhaps surprisingly—so she does. Yet if she has allowed anyone to compromise her to an extent that her husband might feel *really* threatened, then I—as her family lawyer—have not heard of it. Have any of you?"

"No," said Oriel, firmly and loudly. "Absolutely not. Thank you, Quentin, for bringing the matter up."

But Kate, after all—as Evangeline was quick to imply—had managed to get herself well and truly compromised once before, when it had suited her. And now, despite Oriel's and Quentin's assertions that it was no more than an attack of "high spirits," just a perfectly harmless excess of dancing and flirting, letting her ball-gowns slide off her shoulders and her riding-habits show far too much ankle, giggling in corners with Adela Merton's new husband and Dora Merton's new fiancé, getting lost in the old ruins at Merton Abbey with no less a person than Lady Merton's bachelor brother, the wicked, worldly, yet so very wealthy baronet Evangeline had once dreamed of for Oriel—! Very well. Oriel out of loyalty, and Quentin for reasons no one could fathom, might talk of these "high spirits" as much as they pleased, but to Evangline and Madcap Dora, as well as to Lady Merton's worldly-wise brother, and those two hopeful young gentlemen, Adela Merton's husband and Dora's not totally beloved fiancé, it remained a much more realistic matter of time. And time only.

"She may be your friend and maybe something more," Garron Keith told his wife on the eve of his departure to inspect his sites abroad, "and I'm not saying I don't feel sorry for her and understand something of what drives her. But she's no fit companion, the way she is right now, for any wife of mine, I'm telling you. I don't want you gadding about with her while I'm away. I'm sorry, but that's that. You can be sure I'll know about it if you do.''

Susannah, she supposed, would tell him. Or Morag. Yet his ship could not have reached Calais before the crisis, which had been on the simmer for some time at Susannah's own home of High Grange Vicarage, blew up into proportions which brought Susannah to Lydwick, not to take note of Oriel's behavior, but in tears.

"It is Quentin. He will not come home, you see. And Mother is falling ill with missing him . . .''

So much so, in fact, that Letty's entire household, which had never been particularly stable or efficient, had fallen into a chaos which her reverend husband, as he closed his study door on it, had termed absolute; the housemaids unsupervised and therefore doing as they pleased, which had never been much in any case; the younger boys playing truant from the excellent school their brother Quentin had found for them; Letty herself huddled blank-eyed in her parlor-chair all day long. A disaster for which Quentin, from his handsome rooms in Hepplefield, showed no proper sense of responsibility. No more, that is, than to continue the payment of school fees for those brothers still in need of them, the maintenance of another at Cambridge and of the brightest of his sisters at an establishment for young ladies in Carlisle, which, as he informed his reverend father rather coldly, appeared quite enough to him.

He would come to see his mother every Sunday morning and spend a conciliatory, hopefully pleasant hour with her. That much at least had been obtained.

"Why have you turned against me?" shrieked Letty every Sunday the very moment she saw him. "What have I done to deserve it? Am I not good enough for you—now . . . ?'' And, for the rest of the week, she would write frantic notes to Hepplefield, begging his pardon, excusing herself, blaming herself on Mondays and Tuesdays, blaming him by midweek, accusing him of heartlessness and callousness and promiscuity by Friday evening, lying prostrate with nervous exhaustion all day Saturday. Going slowly mad—who could doubt it?—and driving her vague, petulant husband and her far from naturally robust children mad with her.

It could not continue. And since all hope that Quentin might do the decent thing and return had faded it became a matter of urgency—particularly to Letty's reverend husband—that some other, stronger, more capable woman must take over the roles of housekeeper and mother in Letty's place. A procedure considered perfectly normal in the case of widowers and husbands, like Mr. Saint-Charles, whose wives, for one reason or another, had failed them.

Yet only two candidates could be made to come forward, both unwillingly. Maud, the elder, unmarried sister of the "sick" wife, and Susannah, her eldest unmarried daughter, either or both of whom could be asked very much as a simple matter of family duty to give up whatever private affairs a spinster lady might be supposed to possess, and devote themselves exclusively and with a tender heart to the household of their suffering male relation, Mr. Rupert Saint-Charles.

"Maud," murmured Evangeline. "It will be a great wrench, of course, but I know I must let you go. Letty needs you, it seems, far more at her vicarage, than I—and *my* husband—in our home."

"It is Susannah's place," declared Susannah's sister, Constantia, who, already expecting another child saw no reason why Susannah should escape her own share of drudgery. And what, after all, would Susannah—with not even a prospective husband in tow—have to sacrifice except her visits to Oriel at Lydwick, her strange friendship with Oriel's stepdaughter Morag, her peculiar obsession about bringing Christian principles and some basic notions of hygiene to the navvy camps which she kept on visiting in the company of the High Grange curate, the weak-eyed and—in Constantia's opinion—the weak-headed Mr. Field?

"My mother needs Susannah," she said.

"No," assured Evangeline, seizing her opportunity to reign alone at High Grange. "It must be Maud. An older woman with more authority—more endurance. *Maud.*"

Much acrimony ensued. Constantia, with something of her brother Quentin's cleverness, applied at once to her father—who did not really care which woman looked after him so long as one of them did—obtaining his agreement, because it was easier to say yes than no, that he would feel more comfortable with Susannah, would feel more of a sense of *rightness* about it himself.

"His own daughter, you see, his own flesh and blood . . ." Whereupon that daughter, in a state of near hysteria, flew at once to Oriel begging her to make it absolutely clear that the entire Keith household needed her, relied on her, far too often for her to commit herself elsewhere; an opinion enthusiastically backed by Evangeline who, in her desire to be rid of Maud, believed herself entitled to Oriel's support in full measure.

"This is my golden opportunity, Oriel my love. So you will come with me now to their family council—won't you, darling?—and put in your own bid for Susannah . . ."

"Mama, I have been doing my very best for the past year and more to discourage her . . ."

"I know, dear. But your time will come. Only think how long I have been sharing my home with Maud? I rather feared it to be a case of until death us do part—*hers* if at all possible. But now—well, dearest, such a chance is not likely to come again. I really can't miss it. So, if Susannah annoys you, as I know she must, then compensate by making good use of her. Put her to work, my darling, at least until I have got Maud properly out of her splendid bay-windowed front bedroom in *my* house, and safely installed, somewhere or other, in Letty's. She can have Quentin's room, I suppose, unless his mother insists on keeping it untouched, just as it used to be when he was her precious virgin boy and her heart's darling. A long time ago, I imagine. Longer than she likes to think."

"Poor Quentin."

"My dear, what *do* you mean? You must know he is earning himself a tidy little fortune from railway business and Merton business. *Such* a tangle those Merton affairs are always in—not just his lordship's either—they must be more than glad of all Quentin's famous discretion. And have you seen that handsome housekeeper of his? Thirty-five at the most and moves like one imagines a Spanish empress ought to move. She undulates, dearest, and smolders. Your husband would understand what I mean."

"*I* understand, Mama."

"Of course. So—having grown so worldy-wise—you will help me to rid myself of Maud, I know. You have only to tell the famous 'family council' how much you rely on Susannah, your husband being so much away, and I should then find it fairly easy to prove that no one relies—nowadays—on Maud. Yes?"

"Yes, Mama." Where her mother was concerned she allowed herself no choice.

"Thank you, my very best love. And please don't look in

such despair about it. You know very well that as soon as I have disposed of Maud we can turn our attention to Susannah who will be 'got-rid-of'' double quick—you have my promise.''

She accepted it, bore with it, even though the often hysterical presence of Susannah, throughout the summer and autumn while the domestic issues of the vicarage were still being decided, not only kept her away from Ullswater—the calm acre she did not mean, in any circumstances whatsoever, to share with Susannah—but distracted her rather from Kate, who, for her part, had no pity to spare for her vicarage cousin.

"The solution is simple,'' she told Susannah one sparkling Lydwick morning, tapping her riding-whip with sheer impatience against her high, black boots, the man's top hat on her head garlanded now with scarlet. "Stop moaning and wringing your hands, for Heaven's sake, Susannah, and pestering us with problems which might sound positively boring—for all you know—compared to our own. Just run away, Susannah. Disappear and be yourself somewhere—if you know what that is—where they can't find you. That's what I'd do . . .'' And as the inevitable young men who had ridden over to Lydwick with her began to chorus "Oh no, Kate—we'd search to the ends of the earth . . .'' she suddenly struck her boot one sharp, final blow and, calling out, "All right then—I'm off—let's see who finds me. *Now*,'' ran off down the garden to her horse and galloped away. "Wait for me, Kate.'' "And me.'' The men who hoped to be her lovers were after her.

"To Arabia on a camel,'' murmured Oriel, suddenly close to tears which—happily, she thought—Susannah was in no mood even to notice just then,

"What? Arabia? Francis used to live there, didn't he?''

"Yes.'' She had seen no more of him, this long year, than had been strictly necessary, offering him the exact degree of courtesy—no more. How could it be more?—than he gave to her. Quite enough.

"Do you mean they're going back there . . . ?'' demanded Susannah, briefly alarmed about it. With Celestine, *her* goddaughter, she was really saying.

"No. How could they? How could *he*?''

Yet how, on the other hand, could he continue to endure the life he was leading here? How—not a few of his acquaintances wondered—could he bear to live with Kate? Surely her fast behavior, her constant junketings at Merton Abbey and elsewhere, her neglect of her own home and child must be a bitter grief to him? Brave, noble, *handsome* Francis, going so quietly and so very competently, it was said, about the business of his estate, with never a complaint, the shadow of anxiety everyone could see hovering about him disappearing the very moment he knew himself to be observed. A man to be admired and pitied. Yet when Madcap Dora Merton, who was not precisely passionate about her fiancé, offered her Cousin Francis a most direct form of consolation one summer evening after a champagne picnic lunch and a good claret at dinner, he had rejected her so gently, with such exquisite consideration and wry good-humor as to transform that very rejection, although quite positive, into one of the most romantic moments of Dora's life. Causing her, even, to discard her current fiancé and take another who, ultimately, suited her no better.

She continued to be romantically in love with Francis. So too did his daughter's nanny who turned out to be far less stiff and starchy than she had seemed. So too did most of the young maidservants at Dessborough and one or two of the daughters, and wives, of his tenants. So too—perhaps—did Mrs. Oriel Keith, although she managed never, or at least only very rarely, to think of it; whereas it simply did not occur to Francis, who had never been aware of her love in the first place, to look for signs of it now.

He would have considered it to be presumptuous, pointless, holding to the view that "Miss Blake," who had married a richer, far more ambitious man than himself, was far better off—as it had turned out—without him. And to regret her now, to indulge himself by wondering how different his life, his child, his peace of mind, possibly his honor, might have been in her calm hands, could only be hurtful and unsettling and wasteful of his energy at a time when he needed all the strength and patience he could muster.

He was in love with no one and did not envisage the possibility of ever being so. Although, since he had first looked closely at his daughter, emotion had not been lacking in his life. *Present* emotion in the black-eyed, beguiling scrap of humanity produced by his own inability to control his passions. *Remembered* emotion in the black-eyed woman—not Kate—who had been his wife. And then emotion of another kind—he shrank from calling it pity—for Kate herself who did not know how to be a wife any more than a mother and was terrified—he knew it—by her own lack of understanding. Emotion, of a sort, was there too.

But he could not teach her. She had asked him for miracles he had known, from the start, he could never perform. She had asked him not only for total love but for total freedom which the love itself had inevitably canceled out. She had seen him as a liberator, yet it had been her own passion for liberation confused so tragically with her passion for him, that had led her even deeper into the very trap from which he—and he alone, she believed—had come to rescue her.

She believed it no longer. All her fine faith and hopeful excitements had gone. And, watching love itself die in her, he had felt only pity which, knowing how much it would insult her, he had concealed by pretending to notice nothing amiss.

Indeed, what could be amiss that either of them dared admit? She was his wife and he her husband. He had never truly wanted it. She did not want it now. Rather than fall in love they had simply taken each other prisoner. He had known that from the start. She had learned it in slow agony. And if, having recognized in advance the extent of his own sacrifices—the journey to Mecca not least among them—*his* regrets must be more specific, he accepted her fear and confusion to be the greater.

He might suffer—indeed, he did suffer—the crushing of his true self into the false identities of husband and country squire. But at least he knew exactly what that true self had been. Whereas Kate, still wandering in her own dark places, her own deserts, had never found herself at all. She had found him instead, had attempted desperately to *be* him and, in her inevitable failure, had imprisoned them both.

It was not in him to blame her. On the night she had thrown herself into his arms he had been a man of more than adequate experience, she a child who ought not to have been beyond his control, who could have been stopped—by him— had he retained the good sense to do it. He had not stopped her. During their short engagement he had submitted, without the least struggle, to the role she had allotted to him in her intensely woven romance, playing the lover to her precise instructions, encouraging her fantasies, stopping short only at the act of physical possession which she had freely offered. And afterward he had taken her away to the "abroad" she had always thirsted for and made love to her all night and all day, infected perhaps only by *her* fever but doing nothing to cure himself, only too glad, in fact, to remain delirious until she fell victim—he knew she saw it as that—to the fatal disease of pregnancy.

He had done nothing to prevent it. She had spoken, during those honeymoon nights, of wanting his child and had even appeared to do so, until the feel of it stirring not in her erotic imagination but in her own belly, had thrown up into her mind, suddenly and undeniably like nausea, the word she had proved unable to stand. Mother.

"I can't do this," she had told him then. "I can't do it, Francis. I can't *be* it." But, like everything else, it had already happened and, with mystical Arabia still firing her imagination, with flight, escape, liberty—always liberty—filling her mind, he had brought her back to Dessborough and had watched, with helpless distress, what had seemed to him the process of one child giving birth to another.

Had she died in that process he would have felt, for the rest of his life, that he had murdered her. Yet it had been largely to stop himself from contemplating what her death might mean to him—his own liberty, in fact—that he had first gone to look at his child and had realized—before that first look had been over—that liberty of the kind he had once known and still longed for, could exist no longer. There had been Arshad, the woman whose mind and heart and most intimate nature he had known as well as he knew his own. The woman to whom love and knowledge had bound him. Now there was Celestine, unknown to him as yet but who, no matter what the turn of her mind or the balance of her nature might be, would always hold him. The woman he had loved because of her qualities. The child he would love with any qualities or with none at all, for the frighteningly simple reason that she was his daughter.

He had not expected to care for her. Had the choice been his he may not have done so, recognizing too well the implications of lifelong commitment. There had been no choice. Arshad and Celestine. Two deep, lasting loves in his life. None in Kate's. And it was for this reason—guilt, he supposed—that he had shown patience, and demanded it of others, throughout those nightmare weeks of her depression when, uncombed, unwashed, she had tried to reject life and had ended only by rejecting her child; and himself.

He knew she feared her baby. He even knew the fear to be involved with feelings of her own inadequacy and her tortured relationship with her own mother whose memory, even now, caused her to shudder. Yet, since the child had to be fed and protected, he knew of nothing to do but take it away from her to the care of the wet-nurse who disgusted him and the nanny whose starch, somewhat to his regret, had melted so soon away, leaving Kate—since no one else knew how to heal her—to heal herself.

He had taken her to Merton Abbey that first Christmas because it appeared to make no difference to her where she went, and he had been desperate to escape the gloom of Dessborough. For three days she had remained in her room, still silent, still fixing her blank gaze on the wall, and although, on the fourth morning, he had gone down on his knees at her bedside—in another fit of guilt, he supposed—and vowed, like a man administering medicine, although he prayed she would never know it, that he loved and needed her, he nevertheless suspected that it had been Lady Merton's desire to keep her upstairs, safely hidden from such fastidious souls as herself who could not bear the sight of suffering, which had eventually persuaded Kate to sit up and call out, none too pleasantly, for combs and mirrors and hot water.

A new Kate, of course. Another desperate experiment, perhaps, as doomed as all the others, to failure. And just as his guilt had inspired his patience in her sickness so too did it become the source of his tolerance, his willingness to turn what many considered to be a blind eye, when she was sick no more. Or, at least, when her symptoms had changed drastically enough to make it seem a different disease.

She had asked him for freedom. And although this new life of hers, this constant carnival, this hungry lapping up of anything that passed for pleasure, was neither freedom as he understood it nor the pure, precious liberty she had once craved for, it was the best he could give her. It was all he could give her.

He gave it.

"Dora thinks I am making you miserable, Francis."

"No, Kate, I'm not miserable."

"Are you not? Nor jealous either?"

"Do I have any true cause for jealousy?"

"No—as it happens—none whatsoever."

He may have been the only one to believe her, except Oriel

perhaps and that cold, clever man Quentin Saint-Charles, yet believe her he did, for, in her sudden emergence as an exciting woman, a desirable woman, it was power not promiscuity, it seemed to him, that Kate had really discovered. The power—at last—to win notice, admiration, attention, whenever she needed it. And her need of such things he acknowledged to be very great indeed. Power to attract and to subdue, power to tempt and then the even more delicious power to disappoint, power above all to still her lifelong hunger for affection by arousing, all around her and completely, often cruelly at random, its substitute; lust. The power to make people care for her now, at the very moment when her own ability for caring seemed to have gone off-key, astray, sadly missing.

So that when she wandered off into the woods with Lady Merton's disreputable brother or the newly married Timothy Merton, taking good care that everyone should see them go, neither the young bridegroom nor the old roué looked particularly triumphant on their return, Kate's being the only eyes to sparkle, *her* smile the only one with anything in it approaching mischief or satisfaction.

Wanton? So she appeared to be, but only in promises made so very openly that no man could aspire to win her unless he was ready to do it practically in the public eye. "Follow me." She could speak the words with her body, leaning across a dinner table with her face and bare shoulders in full lamplight, or with the challenge of her smile, the provocative raising of an eyebrow across a ballroom floor, directed always at a man who was dancing with another woman. Very often these men left their partners and came to her. Too often, bringing her their hopeful lusts, their adolescent dreams, their aging fantasies, the enmity of the women they had—at her glance—abandoned. She had acquired the power not only to make men desire her but to make them suffer.

"Come now, Timothy, let us have no more nonsense. For one thing, you are married to Adela. So trot along and make love to her. I expect she likes it."

This, spoken in the great, fan-vaulted cloister of Merton Abbey, her voice echoing with such force and arrogance that Adela Merton, a few yards away, saw no alternative but to stride over to Kate and slap her hard across the face.

"Tut—tut," said Kate. "Such a fuss." Over a totally unremarkable, ten-a-penny young man like Timothy? No doubt that was her meaning, although she made no explanation to Francis as he drove her home, other than to say, "I expect I ought to be sorry."

"I expect so."

"Why didn't *you* hit me?"

"I saw no reason."

"There was none—not really. Only in his mind—which I suppose is what hurt Adela. He will be unfaithful to her eventually. Probably just as soon as he can. Although not with me. You do know that?"

He knew. How could he, of all men, doubt her word when he—of all men—had experienced the terror which, quite independently of anything in her mind, had seized her limbs, causing them to shake and quiver and her skin to crawl with the force of a silent scream the first time he had tried to make love to her, a full four months after the birth of Celestine? Tried and failed utterly, defeated by her body's blind fear that he might make her pregnant again. And even when he had explained, carefully, skillfully, the methods to ensure that he did not, and she had understood them, she had trembled so violently at his touch that he had merely caressed her, almost companionably, for a while and turned away.

"In time . . ." she said, "just a little time . . ."

"Of course. As much as you need."

But time had gone by.

"Francis—listen to me. I know I'm useless—useless and strange and a burden . . . Everyone says so. So if you should need some other woman—a mistress, I mean—then I don't think I ought to complain about it . . ."

"I would prefer to have you, Kate." The right answer, although untrue of course, since thoughts of a mistress had already occurred to him and been rejected only because of the complications. And because, in some odd way, he knew it would hurt Kate. He had had mistresses before in any case. Now he had a daughter and a wife who seemed to him every bit as newborn and fragile and horrendously breakable as her child.

"Would you really prefer me?" she said, honestly frowning. "I don't know why. I wouldn't want to live with me, in your place. I'd want to murder me, I think, like Adela does—and Dora. I suppose you've heard that Dora's new fiancé was seen at my bedroom door, last Wednesday—when I stayed overnight at the Abbey?"

"Oh yes. Someone told me.'

"And you replied 'Ah well—so long as it was only at the door, we need hardly worry,' or something similar . . . ?"

"I believe I did.''

He also believed that she had invited Dora's new fiancé—who bore a remarkable resemblance to her last one—up to her room in order to be found there, giggling and gossiping in her doorway, a champagne glass in hand, well after midnight. While he—her husband—as all the Mertons must have reminded each other over breakfast the next morning—had been busy at Dessborough with the care of her home and her child.

"Kate, my love," Evangeline, also a guest that night at the Abbey, had told her, "I believe you are a force for destruction. Which is something I hardly suspected, even when you used to amuse yourself by leaving scissors around for me to sit on when I first became your stepmama."

Was it true, wondered the Gore Valley? Was she really malicious, callous, hateful, wanton, as the Mertons said?

"Of course I am," she told the ever-growing, ever-changing band of men who were not, or at least not physically, her lovers; even though some of them, quite a few of them in fact, were apt to boast of more favors than they had ever received. And when they obediently chorused "No, Kate. We won't have that. You're splendid. Glorious," she laughed at them, tossed her head in its tall, shiny hat, thrashed her boots with her riding-whip, and reduced them to a quick, and altogether predictable, ecstasy.

"Poor things—my lovers," she would sometimes say to Francis, or to Oriel. "It doesn't really matter what I do to them, does it, since they're not even real—poor things. Not real at all. Do you know that?"

Possibly Francis—and Oriel—and Quentin Saint-Charles did. Although it all seemed real enough to Adela Merton—married, of course, for her title and her money—who, when her husband finally succumbed to the temptation of a woman she had thought of as her friend, blamed Kate most bitterly as being the one who had first given him the inclination. Real enough to Dora Merton whose new fiancé soon went the way of the one before him, and the one before that; and to Lady Merton who, although refusing to admit even the possibility of sin in her own family, rather thought it should be punishable by hanging or flogging or banishment to a penal colony—for life, of course—in others. Real enough too to Evangeline who issued regular bulletins on Kate's behavior or lack of it, after every visit to Merton Abbey where she had succeeded in becoming a regular guest; and to Maud who had need, these days, of any scrap of consolation to come in her increasingly weary direction.

Malicious, promiscuous Kate, defended only by Oriel who had evidently been brought up—said Dora Merton—to find an excuse for everything; by Quentin Saint-Charles who most likely thought up some way of making money for himself out of it; and by Francis who—supposed Dora—was putting such a brave face on it for the sake of his child. That delightful little creature, that adorable, black-eyed little angel whose first birthday party her own malicious, promiscuous mother had not attended.

Yet even the Mertons, who so hated her, could not bear to keep away from her for long, needing her constantly under their eyes to see for themselves the mischief she was up to, the better—it seemed—to defend themselves against it. And the better, of course, to let her know how much she was detested.

Another Christmas passed, bringing a New Year in which the whole world the Mertons recognized as civilized seemed, all of a sudden, to be exploding around them so violently that Lady Merton took to her bed and, following the collapse— yet again—of the French monarchy, thought it highly likely she would stay there. Not that the Orleans family meant very much to the Mertons who had preferred the Bourbon Kings of France—any one of them—to this Orleanist *Citizen* King Louis Philippe. Although it still shocked them badly to hear the news, that February, of this new revolution, which had sent him scuttling for safety through the Tuileries Gardens calling out to the mob, as he went, that he was abdicating. A precaution considered quite necessary by Lord Merton when one remembered that other French Louis, not too long ago, who, through not abdicating in time, had gone to the guillotine, thus losing both his crown and his head.

Yet, although Lord Merton did not really like the man, it seemed quite natural to him that the exiled Louis Philippe should take refuge in England with Queen Victoria who, having set aside a spare palace at Claremont for his accommodation, could not really be held to blame when, as a result of lead being found in the drinking water, his French Majesty was obliged to move out, with his Queen and various royal duchesses, and take up residence—temporary one hoped—at the Star and Garter at nearby Richmond.

It could not happen *here*, of course, insisted Lord Merton, meaning revolution, it seemed, rather than lead-poisoning which, of course, could happen anywhere. The English throne could never fall, although even Lord Merton felt obliged to admit that they had started to topple just about everywhere else. What was the world coming to?

"Long live the Revolution," murmured Kate, with the clear intention of hoping to shock the Mertons who, at that particular moment, were not aware that in their own city of London, men called Chartists—and many thousands of them, at that—were celebrating the overthrow of Louis Philippe and professing themselves quite ready, unless she granted them their civil liberties, to do the same to Victoria. As men—it abruptly seemed at the start of that unfortunate New Year— were doing all over Europe, the citizens of Milan suddenly rising in ferment against their Austrian garrison, the Sicilians clashing at Palermo with their Neapolitan rulers, Vienna ridding itself of Prince Metternich, barricades erected and bullets flying in Berlin, violence rearing its ugly head in the streets of Rome, the Irish rushing into the fray to parade their banners, beneath English noses, proclaiming "Ireland for the Irish," the Prussians finding themselves so unpopular after the massacre they had wrought in Berlin that Queen Victoria was obliged to withdraw her invitation to their ruling Prince William to come over and be godfather to Princess Louise, her new baby daughter.

A whole storm of assorted trouble, powerful enough to keep frail, fastidious spirits like Lady Merton in her bed from which she trusted the peasants of Hepplefield, should they also heed the call to rebellion, would not care to drag her, but which fired other, younger spirits with a disturbing restlessness. The world, very evidently, was changing. France was to be a Republic again. The peoples of Europe were rising as one, it seemed, to claim their liberty. And there were those, like Kate and Dora Merton's newest fiancé— rather different from the others—who wished them well of it.

"Liberty, Equality, and Fraternity," chanted the newest fiancé, a wild young man, the son of an earl with an elder brother between him and the title, which would have made him a poor proposition for Dora, had the brother's mode of life not made it extremely unlikely that he would ever marry and produce an heir.

"Yes," said Kate. "That's right. Liberty and all the rest of it. Let's wear a revolutionary tricolor on our hats and go galloping all over the estate shouting *Vive la France. Vive la Révolution.* That ought to stir them up a bit."

So much, in fact, that Kate, returning in a high state of elation, due not only to fresh air and frolic but to the brandy the newest fiancé always kept in his pocket, was slapped again, this time by Dora, who—with *this* fiancé—was rather more than usually in love.

"Tut—tut. Such a fuss," Kate said, riding off at a gallop to Lydwick, the first place she came to, having remembered that Oriel's husband, as so often, was away. Nor, to her surprise, was she obliged to suffer the irritating presence of Susannah who—Oriel told her calmly—had taken herself off, not long ago, in a considerable state of disarray.

"You mean you've quarreled with her, Oriel? I can't believe it."

"Well, it wasn't easy. But I have."

"And sent her packing?"

Hopefully. Although it was by no means certain, considering Susannah's awkward position at the vicarage where Maud, who had been installed there now for some months, kept insisting, nevertheless, on her right to Susannah's time and services, finding the vicarage family with its burden of sick wife and boisterous children somewhat too much for her, not to mention the vicar himself who, although so endearingly absent-minded, could be more than specific enough where his creature comforts were concerned. Susannah's assistance was clearly needed. A young, single woman in good health and strength who ought to be doing her duty by her own family instead of running around navvy encampments and devoting herself to the stepchildren of a woman who was not even related to her in any way one could decently mention. Evangeline's daughter, in fact, who was only copying her mother by unloading on to other people's far more respectable shoulders the work for which she was accepting the benefit, but did not care to do.

"Oriel has no need of you, Susannah," snapped Maud, several times daily. "I must insist that you stop running over to Lydwick at the drop of her hat and stay here in your own home to do what is no more, after all, than your duty. Your sister, Constantia, has told you the same, over and over.''

Opposing forces were mustered once again, Oriel, who had been scaling down Susannah's visits lately with great tact but equal firmness, finding herself caught up once more in domestic hysteria, involving not only the Stangways and the Saint-Charleses but both her stepdaughters, Morag insisting she should at once invite Susannah to come not just on long visits but to live with them, Elspeth threatening to run away from home if she did, both girls, having said their respective pieces, turning on each other so fiercely that Oriel's apparently endless patience had snapped. And she had barely separated them and sent them off in disgrace to sulk in their bedrooms, when Susannah arrived, demanding Oriel's instant presence at another ''family conference'' at High Grange. Constantia would be there, Maud and Evangeline, and her father, the vicar. Even Quentin had promised to come over which meant—since brother Quentin did not make journeys for nothing—that her fate was to be irrevocably decided. Oriel must hurry, therefore, and make it plain that she could not handle her husband's large house and his rapidly growing children in his frequent absences without the help of her cousin—if only by marriage—Susannah.

''Which is no more than the truth,'' ended Susannah unwisely. ''You do need me, I know.'' And receiving no immediate reassurance, she added sharply, ''Well, you do, don't you?''

Standing, looking carefully at each other, they both heard a voice from the upstairs landing calling out what, without catching the words, they understood to be ''Is that Susannah?'' But before Susannah could spring forward to confirm her presence, Oriel raised her hand in a gesture which very coolly stated ''You had better stay where you are,'' and went herself to send Morag, rather curtly, back to bed.

She had been mother to these children for less than two years and, for most of that time, to oblige her own mother, had allowed Susannah to usurp her place. Or try to. And although her own sentiments toward the children were practical rather than romantic and, unlike Susannah, she felt no urgent need to make them love her, they were nevertheless her responsibility, as much as this was her house, its absent master her husband. The whole adding up to *her* life which not even her mother ought to ask her to share with Susannah.

Yet, although Evangeline had asked, and Oriel still felt unable to refuse her, she could at least make her feelings clear.

Returning to the drawing-room, she gave Susannah another cool stare.

"You asked me just now if I needed you, Susannah. And the answer is no I do not, not in the very least. Although, in view of your awkward situation at home, and to oblige my mother, I am quite prepared to come over and tell your relations that I do . . ."

Chaos had ensued, tears, reproaches, accusations of ingratitude and jealousy and, as Susannah calmed herself enough to take her leave, a hint of real dislike which warned Oriel she had made—or had perhaps long had—an enemy.

"What on earth can she do to you?" asked Kate. "So let her hate you. If she enjoys it as much as Dora it can only do her good."

And it was in this mood of mild defiance that she accepted, largely at Kate's insistence, an invitation to dinner at the Mertons, knowing quite well that Garron would not approve of it, although—as Kate was quick to remind her—by the time he found out about it, if ever, it would be far too late for him to forbid her to go.

The invitation had come from Dora, Lord Merton being in London, Lady Merton still in bed quite speechless with anguish at the thought of so many continental thrones already toppled, the dread of how many more to come, and so the gathering was young and informal; just plain, mousy Adela and her already unfaithful husband, Madcap Dora and her newest fiancé, Oriel herself, a nondescript young man to make up the numbers, Kate, and—taking Oriel by surprise—Francis.

"It is just to prove that my husband and I do occasionally dine together," Kate said, her voice hard and bright, her eyes even harder and full of a positive, quite unnerving venom whenever Madcap Dora came into view.

Had they quarreled again? So it seemed. Yet, in the half hour before dinner, Oriel was too diverted, too enchanted—although she certainly did not call it that—by Francis to take much notice, listening with nothing to spare for anyone else as he told her the unremarkable tales young fathers tell about their probably quite unremarkable daughters.

It was their first real conversation since the day he had not, after all, asked her to marry him, and although that could not and ought not to matter now, the simple pleasure of breaking through the stilted barriers of politeness and truly meeting again continued to fill her mind so that the splendid, impersonal meal surrounded by footmen with the manners of archbishops, was half over before she became aware of the increasing tensions between Dora and Kate; between Dora and her newest fiancé who had worn the tricolor and shouted *Vive la Révolution* with Kate; between Kate and Adela who always supported her sister and had her own ax to grind in any case, preferably in Kate's ebony, beribboned head; between Kate and Francis whose efforts to restrain her, as everyone could see, were merely making her worse; between Francis and Dora whose wish to offer him sympathy and draw him into her fold seemed to give him none of the pleasure to which she rather felt herself entitled.

Only Oriel, sitting on the edge of their conflict, could really see it, so that she—if no one else—remembered—afterward—that as they had lounged uneasily about the drawing-room after dinner the idea of playing the foolish, dangerous game of Snapdragon had come from Kate.

"Let's do something, for God's sake, before we all die of despair . . ."

And because it had seemed better, after all, than listening to Kate and Dora taking verbal pot-shots at one another, the wild young fiancé had gone off to find the ingredients any good Snapdragon required, a large, shallow pewter dish, enough inflammable spirit to fill it, matches to set it alight, several pounds of currants to throw into the flame and then snatch out again bare-handed and swallow, still burning, until he—or she—who swallowed most had won.

It was the popular, very nearly traditional game which Oriel had refused to allow the Keith children to play over Christmas although it seemed to be played at all the other houses they visited, her aversion to it so strong that she had even stood out against Garron when he had grumbled that, with proper supervision, it did no harm. He had never played it himself as a child, he readily admitted, since no one, where he came from, had been able to afford the currants, much less the spirit to burn them in, but could Oriel deny that it was as popular with children everywhere, at Christmas, as Hunt the Slipper and Blind Man's Bluff?

"No Snapdragon here," she had said.

But now, as the bowl was set down in the center of what she assumed to be a priceless Persian rug, currants and spirits flung in together and hilariously, carelessly ignited, the matter was beyond her control.

"Not for me," said Francis. "And not for Oriel, I rather think."

Not for Adela's husband, either, who thought too highly of his performance on the piano to risk casual damage to his hands. Nor for Adela herself, who, although she had taken part as a young girl when she had felt the need to impress someone or other with her daring, saw no need for that now. Only Kate, then, and Dora's wild, revolutionary fiancé who would be an earl, one day, if he managed to outlive his brother. And Dora herself? That she did not want to play was clear to one and all; that she—Madcap by reputation—was terrified of the sudden lake of blue fire even clearer.

Had Kate known, perhaps, that she would be?

"What childish nonsense," she said, shrugging her shoulders, trying to dismiss and belittle it.

"Oh Dora," murmured Kate almost caressingly. "Are you scared stiff, poor thing . . . ?" And sinking down on her knees, the revolutionary earl-to-be beside her, she thrust quick excited fingers through the flames without even turning back her sleeves, retrieving one currant after another, still burning, and extinguishing their fire in her mouth.

"Come, Dora, if you're quick enough you'll feel no pain. And brave enough, of course. There *is* that to it. Come and beat me."

Dora, her face pale, her mouth set, shook her head with a movement she hoped would be read as disdain. But her fiancé, her wild earl, was now taking his turn, squatting on his knees beside Kate, six currants to her eight, ten to her round dozen, fourteen—yes—fourteen . . . "Come on, Kate—beat me . . ." She did. "Sixteen. Come on now, let's try again. Beat *me* this time. You'll enjoy that. Poor Dora—she doesn't know what she's missing."

And exploding with laughter they fell against each other, heads together, hands together, drunk on sheer recklessness, expecting nothing from Dora but her disapproval, her jealousy, which, in their present mad enjoyment they had ceased to notice, this fiancé already slipping through her grasp, it seemed, like all the others, poor Dora who was afraid of heights and fire and loneliness and who, because she *was* afraid, had won her nickname of "Madcap" by climbing tall trees, riding tall horses, falling in and out of love with every change in the season, collecting all those fiancés. Poor Dora, standing now rigid as a maypole, with no intention in the world of joining in, as everyone could see, so that when she suddenly flopped down on the carpet beside that scandalously giddy couple, it was as much a shock to them as to Oriel, who had certainly not expected it, causing them a great deal more giggling and falling about and tomfoolery, a great swishing around of light silk skirts and trailing sleeves, a sudden awareness, stabbing through the onlookers, of danger.

A children's game? Who, in their right minds, thought Oriel . . . ? "Be careful," she called out.

"I think that's enough," said Francis.

It was too late. And, in the first sick horror, they could not see who was burning until the fiancé had pulled Kate clear and the bowl, with its tongues of blue fire, had started to make a torch of Dora, fed by her own wide skirts, her dozen petticoats, the voluminous shoulder-to-ankle drapery of her silk shawl.

Oriel heard the room echoing with screams, her own perhaps, certainly Adela's, as clearly as she saw the young fiancé, who had flung his arms around Kate, squeeze his eyes tight shut, while Adela's husband—she could see from the corner of her eye—was wringing his hands and backing away, bent almost double as if someone had crashed a fist into his middle.

She and Adela—she very accurately remembered—moved forward together, not knowing what to do except that it must be something, until Francis leaped before them, his arms going around Dora as she started to run in a panic which would have fanned the flames, falling to the ground with her and then, the sleeves of his own jacket burning, seizing another priceless rug and wrapping her in it, rolling her in it, himself on top of her, holding her down until the fire was out, and Dora . . . ?

Dead? Oriel, for a sick moment, could not look and then, the terrible odors of charred fabric and flesh clogging her nostrils, smoke clawing her eyes, she ran to them—to him, really—and bent over, her hands under his armpits, helping him gently, as a matter of stark necessity, to rise, dismissing as irrelevant, beside his need and Dora's, the plight of Adela's husband who was vomiting now in a corner, of the fiancé who was standing with his face to the wall, of Kate who had not meant to cause this but who would know, nevertheless, by now, that she had.

No one else, in those first moments, could function in any way at all except Oriel, and so she functioned, knowing that Dora must be kept warm and still until the doctor came, that Francis' arms and hands must also have immediate attention although he, being fully conscious, did not appear to think so; knowing, when these vital emergencies had been attended to, that the servants must be kept calm and prevented from running upstairs to Lady Merton with the news that her younger daughter had very nearly been burned to death; knowing that the husband and fiancé must be taken into another room and given cigars and a great deal of brandy; and that something—although she was not sure just what—must be done about Kate and Adela Merton who remained rooted to the spot, white and rigid and clenched so tightly in shock that Oriel's own body could feel the unbearable tension of their muscles, the crashing and thundering of their hearts.

It occurred to her that they should be kept apart.

"Adela, the doctor says Dora is conscious and you may see her now." He had said nothing of the kind, although in fact she was conscious, her face and the upper part of her body relatively untouched so that the sight of her would at least cause no additional shock to her sister.

Without replying, Adela moved away.

"Kate, the doctor is going to give Francis something to make him sleep. Won't you go up and see him first?"

Kate shook her head. And so she was still there, immobile, chained to the scene of what Oriel supposed must now seem to be her crime, when Adela came back, already aware that her sister, although in great pain and the prospect of far more to come, was not visibly disfigured and would live.

"Kate," she said, her voice a whisper with something almost greedy in it, as if now—at last—she had found the means to assuage both her grief and her vast hunger to be avenged, to strike a blow—lethal if she could—in the defense of her sister; and of herself. "How are you, Kate? Well enough, I expect. You haven't quite managed to kill Dora, I know, but near enough . . . ?" Her voice was rising now.

"Answer me, then. Don't stare. What's the matter, Kate?

Are you grieving because you're not a widow yet? Is that it?''

"Adela." It was Oriel who broke in with an attempted remonstration, Kate remaining quite still, taking this punishment as she had once taken Maud's, in silence.

"So—Kate Ashington—you haven't managed to kill your husband either, although he might even be glad if you did— the grief you cause him—the humiliation . . ."

"Adela," said Oriel very sharply this time, because it *had* to stop. "I know why you are saying this. So does Kate. But not now."

"Shut up!" shrieked Adela Merton, the sound ripping through all of them, although Kate gave no sign that she had even heard it. "Keep out of this. Who are you to tell me what to do? And who is she? A devil, that's what she is. A destructive devil, who takes pleasure in tearing us apart. A *monster*, who crucifies her husband every day of his life for her amusement—and for other people to laugh at. Didn't you see her, taunting my sister, taunting and trapping her, getting her own back because she heard Dora telling somebody today that women like her aren't fit to have children . . . ?"

A quick gesture of protest from Oriel. No movement of any kind from Kate.

"And they're not," thundered Adela, her voice, strident at any time, vibrating now, hurting her throat, no doubt, as much as it hurt Oriel's ears. "*She's* not. God help that child. God help it. Everybody is saying so. Will you try to burn *her*—your daughter, Kate—one day when she's grown up and you take a fancy to her man . . . ? It wouldn't surprise me— no, no—nor anybody else . . ."

The great voice catching in her throat at last, she burst into tears, her whole body heaving with them as Oriel took her by the arm and led her away upstairs to her maid, her own sleeping draft, her quiet bed, not to her husband who was still overcoming his shock with brandy in her father's library.

Downstairs again she found Kate exactly as she had left her.

Dear sister. My sister. What now? Can you get over this? Can you bear it? How can I help you? You must know that I will. Probably forever.

But nothing in Kate was listening.

"Go to bed now," she said gently, receiving in reply a sharp nod of the head as Kate walked quickly away.

She returned to Lydwick a half hour later since no one at Merton Abbey had thought to ask if she cared to stay the night, and, waking early the next morning, she had already ordered the carriage to take her back to Kate and Francis, no matter how much the Mertons might resent it, when Kate's letter was delivered. And, remembering afterward, that she had gone out into the chilly garden, the unopened envelope in her hands, and sat for rather a long time under the chestnut tree, it always seemed to her that she had known in advance what Kate had to tell her.

Dear Oriel. It's no use, you see. I know that. Adela is not famous for being right but last night, in her way, I suppose she was. And since hers is the way of the world, what can I really do now except the decent thing? They will be better off without me, you know. Of course you know. And Francis knows. And, as we once told each other sitting in your garden, he is a wonderful father. It was what she said about that part of it really—you know, about turning on my daughter like she thought I'd turned on Dora. Can't have that now, can we? So I'm off to fight my revolutions somewhere else, in a warmer climate, perhaps. No, no, not hell—or not yet—so don't worry. France, I think. Or one of those little foreign states where absolutely everybody one comes across is fighting for freedom. I love you, Oriel. Keep well and beautiful. Kate.

And in the following pandemonium it was not realized until quite a late hour of the afternoon that she had left with the newest and certainly wildest of Dora's fiancés.

Twelve

It was a clear summer morning, some three years and the half of another later, that Quentin Saint-Charles, having walked from the village of Pooley Bridge at the northern tip of Lake Ullswater to the serene isolation of its shore between the bays of Howtown and Sharrow, entered the garden gate of a long, low cottage set on the fellside looking out through pale blue air, across pale silk water; and, continuing along a path edged with a profusion of lavender and clove-scented gilliflowers, encountered, without any surprise whatsoever, a number of disdainful, well-nourished but decidedly stray cats.

Not that the highly acclaimed legal gentleman, Mr. Quentin Saint-Charles of Hepplefield, was in any way famous for his interest in nonpedigree animals, mountain scenery, or even in respectable women, although as Mrs. Oriel Keith came around the corner of the house to greet him, a basket of rose petals for pot pourri over her arm, her garden hat swinging from its ribbon around her neck, leaving her bareheaded yet still elegant in the sun, no one could have faulted the greeting exchanged between them for either its warmth or its ease.

"Quentin—such a surprise."

"Not an inconvenient one, I hope?"

"How could it be that? The girls are here—and Jamie somewhere or other on the fells—but they all seem happy enough with their own company. I am glad to see you."

"And I. I happened to be in Pooley Bridge, on Merton business—his lordship being a guest at Lowther Castle. And I thought it a pity not to step over . . ."

"It would have been."

He smiled. "I had a sudden wish to know how your lemon balm and chamomile and all your rosemary and marjoram and whatever else are growing."

"Oh—very well. In some abundance even, I'm glad to say."

He bowed his head in swift acknowledgment. "Of course. I never doubted it."

He was no gardener, she knew that, with even less ability or interest than Garron, her pit-bred, city-bred husband, to tell one plant from another or hazard a guess as to its uses. To Quentin— and to Garron too—herb teas and remedies came in neat jars or packets from the shelves of an apothecary, just as naturally as shirts came from a tailor, not from the patient earth where she, whenever she could snatch a day, a week, a blessed month these past three years, had been planting them with thought and affection; chamomile with its daisy flowers to make a rinse for fair hair—like hers and Elspeth's and Morag's—or a healing lotion for sore eyes; sweet lemon balm to cure headaches and attract the honey-bees; spicy wild marjoram for the kitchen and blue rosemary which, sadly, did not seem to improve the memory as the country people said; blue and white spikes of comfrey to lay upon open wounds—Jamie's, more often than not, after his fell-climbing—and to ease sore, winter chests; red bergamot to soothe frayed nerves; tall, tangy hyssop for the tea she had never made for Kate.

And because she thought it likely he had come with news of Kate, having lately returned from abroad where he usually managed to meet his errant cousin—Oriel did not know how or where—she said quickly, "I have planted valerian too, which is supposed to make a sleeping draft, although it means the garden is always full of cats. They seem to love it."

"Do you sleep badly, Oriel?"

"Oh—sometimes." She smiled. Not here, of course. Unless the moon spread enough silver across the lake to draw her out, enchanted, into the garden to stand quite still and look at it, feeling herself happily alone in an unpeopled world, nothing stirring around her but thin, pure air, no sound but the faint lapping of water, a quick rustling in the grass as a rabbit scampered home, a long-drawn breath of wind along the fells.

Sleepless nights such as that she felt to be a privilege. Although elsewhere . . . ? Yes, perhaps at Lydwick, almost certainly at High Grange whenever she went to stay with her mother, a good hot cup of valerian tea would not go amiss; might even see her through until morning. Nor had she the slightest objection to the cats who came, day and night, to sniff daintily at her pale valerian flowers, even feeding a few of them on what Morag, who did not care for cats, considered a far too regular basis; the persistent ones, the timid ones, the ones who, from a proud yet nervous distance stared at her with wide eyes, half expecting, from her too, the kick, the well-aimed stone the rest of the world had given, hoping it would not come, supposing that it very likely would.

Reminding her of Kate.

"Quentin . . . ?"

"Yes," he said, his eyes too on the cats. "I have just come back from France, as you know—settling one of the more fragile of Lord Merton's affairs. And having settled it—yes, I managed to see Kate."

In another garden, three years and four, or was it five months ago, sitting with Kate's letter in her hand, Quentin's name had been the first to enter Oriel's mind. If anything *could* be done, then Quentin would know. She had been quite sure of that. And, going back into the house, taking her own pale blue note-paper, she had watched, as if from a great height, her own long, very steady hand precisely penning the words, "Dear Quentin—as a matter of some urgency may I ask you to come at once . . ."

He came: very evidently between two serious appointments which meant—*of course*—that he could not spare her very much of his time. Ten minutes, perhaps?

"I suppose," he had said, "it is about Susannah?"

"What about her?"

"Why—this foolish engagement she has just entered into with the curate . . ."

"Has she?"

His eyes had sharpened. "Have you really not heard? High Grange is talking—I gather—of nothing else."

"Oh. Then their voices have not yet carried to me."

He looked impatient still, but rather surprised. "Indeed? Then why am I here, Oriel? I assumed you wished to put your side of the story to me?"

"Why should I have a side to put?"

He had shrugged. "Because the engagement is quite foolish and since it seems to have happened as a result of a quarrel my sister had with you, then you are being held partly to blame.''

Somewhat to her own surprise she had shrugged her shoulders, rather flippantly too. ''Oh, that. She has only engaged herself to the poor man to get out of the housework at the vicarage. It doesn't mean she will ever really marry him.''

''Yes, Oriel.'' The slight, rather supercilious lift of his eyebrow had warned her of a coming reprimand. ''I dare say. But it has caused a great deal of distress to my mother and Aunt Maud who realize—as clearly as Susannah—that one cannot claim anywhere near as much domestic assistance from a fiancée as from an unattached daughter in residence. And for some reason, you—Oriel—appear to have made an enemy of Susannah . . . I supposed you wanted my help in bringing about a reconciliation?''

Very brusquely, she remembered, she had shaken her head. ''That would be quite pointless, Quentin—a *real* waste of your valuable time.''

''Oh.'' He had never seen her even mildly angry before and, although possibly only faintly, she had seen that it interested him. ''May I ask why?''

''Why not? Susannah hates me because . . . Well, I'm not sure if she wants to be Garron's wife in any other way than running his home and having the use of his income, but I do know she wants to be Morag's mother. Which means—doesn't it—that I'm in her way?''

Had it been her calm voice speaking those words, *her* fastidious mind which had released them? She feared so.

''Oriel . . .'' She had never forgotten how intently he had looked at her, with something in his keen face that could have been pity; although not for her. ''I would appreciate it—very much, Oriel—if you would never say anything at all like that to Susannah.''

''Oh Good Heavens, Quentin, you ought to know that I never would.''

And it was then, in silence, that she had given him Kate's letter.

''Yes,'' he had said after a moment. ''I see.'' And then. ''Tell me what you can, Oriel.'' Calmly—since what other way had there been to go about it?—she had told him, everything she knew, or guessed, or suspected, and in neat chronological order at that, about the events leading up to Kate's flight from Merton Abbey. Terrible, sorrowful things, some of them, about which—

just then—there had been no time to break her heart, and to which he had listened without a tremor.

"Do you suppose," he had said, "in the circumstances, that she has left a letter for her husband? Taking into account his injuries and possible sedation . . . ?"

"Not with me."

"Which may mean, I fear, that she has left no letter for him at all."

She had looked at him, very steadily. "Which means—I think—that, in your opinion, I should be the one to tell him."

"I fear so. When his doctor considers the time appropriate, that is."

So had it been. She had gone at once to Merton Abbey and had waited there—rather a long time—for an interview with Francis' doctor, enduring the cool stares of Adela Merton—the only member of the family as yet in any way functioning—who, although not going so far as to turn her out, quite clearly could not imagine what business she thought all this might be of hers. What a pity, Dora's sister had even suggested, that Kate, whose business it surely was, did not seem much concerned since no one had even seen her, as yet. Still slouching in her bed, very likely, judged Adela. Or off on one of her wild escapades, having forgotten all about Dora's agony, the whole family's bitter despair. Did Mrs. Keith happen to know where she was? Oriel had shaken her head, smiled, looked vague, and had continued to wait, not only for Francis to recover but giving Quentin time—before the whole family pack descended—to put the wheels in motion by which Kate might at least be found.

Not brought back, of course—unless she wished it, or her husband chose to exercise his legal right to compel her home, which seemed unlikely—but just to prevent her, somehow, from vanishing into thin air so that no one could help her, no one would ever know what had befallen her, which, no matter how bad it turned out to be, would be better, surely—Oriel had insisted—than the flights of a worried imagination.

"She knows where you are, Oriel," Quentin had said. "She could always get in touch with you."

Yet, just the same, he had hurried off back to Hepplefield and the electric telegraph, the post office, the agents a clever lawyer like himself often employed in his work of uncovering or of seeing that others did not uncover his clients' secrets, knowing, as she had known, that by servants' gossip alone, the news of the accident to Dora and Francis, the rumors of other strange goings-on at Merton Abbey, would spread, drawing like a magnet all those who, under the guise of offering consolation, would feel fully entitled to ask a pertinent question or two. Not the least of which would concern the whereabouts of Kate, making it imperative that before that question began to echo all along the fan-vaulted passages of Merton Abbey she must have had her half hour alone with Francis.

"Mrs. Keith—I believe you are waiting to have a word with me?" Even now, in unguarded moments, the doctor's soft, courteous voice sometimes slipped into her head, reminding her of the stab of raw panic it had brought her that day. Yes—a word. She had been waiting for his permission to tell the man with whom she had once been very much in love that the woman he had jilted her to marry had now jilted him, and their baby daughter, for reasons it would be difficult indeed even to imply. Would her legs even carry her to the impersonal splendors of the Merton bedroom where he was now lying? Would her tongue move when she got there?

"Mrs. Keith . . . ?"

"Yes, doctor."

And perhaps because it had seemed so impossible it had happened, not easily, but far more naturally than she could ever have supposed. He had looked pale, his arms awkward with bandages but, this not being his first encounter with pain, showing no resentment, no shock, having come to terms long ago with his body's susceptibility to breakage and damage; its sorry lack of anything approaching immortality.

"Francis, you did a wonderful thing last night."

"Oh—yes. You may say that once, Oriel, but please not again."

And, incredibly, there had been a moment of laughter.

"How are you feeling?"

"Strong enough, Oriel. Which is perhaps a good thing—is it not?"

No reason, then, to delay. No possible excuse for waiting any longer, for committing the crime—she realized it would be that—of allowing Adela Merton, or Maud Stangway, or her own mother, or anyone but herself to rush in and tell him *their* version of Kate's flight. And so she had given him Kate's letter and, his hands being bandaged, had held it out for him—steadily—at what she judged the best distance for him to read.

"Thank you, Oriel."

And then, sitting down beside him, she had given him the only gift she could even imagine, the truth, telling him, slowly and quietly, what had happened between Adela and Kate and what was happening now, at Dessborough, where she had stopped a moment on her way over to check the well-being of his child and calm the panic she had found already rife among his household staff.

"Let me drive over with you," the child's nanny had pleaded, much shaken, "to help him home." But she had refused her permission and, receiving his nod of approval, had gone on—once again, very slowly—to tell him of conditions at the Abbey, where Dora had started to improve and Lady Merton, unaware of her daughter's accident, had collapsed afresh at the loss of her Persian rugs; and in Hepplefield where Quentin had already commenced his inquiries.

"I am sorry, Oriel," he had said. *"Sorry."*

For Kate? Yes. They had both understood that. And for others too.

"Yes, Francis. So am I."

He had wished to get out of bed, then, to return at once to his own home, and while he had bullied the doctor into helping him to dress, Oriel had gone downstairs to make his decision known to the Mertons.

"Nonsense," had declared Adela, who would be *Lady* Merton one day if her husband lived long enough to inherit the title and who felt altogether within her rights, therefore, to be as imperious as she pleased. Suspicious too, knowing that something was afoot, some new conspiracy of the "petty gentry" against her own ancient and extremely noble name. And if she thought the Stangways and Ashingtons somewhat beneath her she had expected to make short work of the wife of a common railwayman. But Oriel had merely smiled, agreed most pleasantly with every one of Adela's objections and then, when Francis was ready, had just as pleasantly walked out of the house with him and taken him back to Dessborough in her carriage.

And it was there, late in the afternoon, that Adela had ridden over to confront them, both together, with the treachery of her injured sister's newest fiancé which, considering her condition, had so far been kept from her, but which had sent Adela into a shaking, freezing rage through which she refused, absolutely, to accept her own husband's explanations as to why he could not seal off the ports, block the roads, and drag Kate home, preferably to her execution.

"Men," Adela Merton had snarled. *"Husbands,"* spitting venom at both her own and Kate's who—the shock of his burns, no doubt, turning his brain—had said in a voice which she, at any rate, had found unnatural: "At least it means she is not alone. Not for the moment, at any rate."

And he had sounded glad of it. *Glad.*

So too had Quentin Saint-Charles, knowing—although he had refrained from pointing this out to Adela—that a woman alone would have been far more difficult to trace than the wild young son of an earl who, if he wished his allowance to be paid on time, could not keep himself anonymous.

He had not done so, although just where Quentin had found him and what had transpired Oriel was uncertain, beyond the fact that the romance—if such it had ever been—had not lasted long, the young man returning home to marry, very quickly, a lady of awesome good breeding whose powerful father, at least, would know how to deal with him; Kate continuing abroad in circumstances which the Mertons, and some others, hoped—understandably, even Oriel admitted—to be of abject destitution.

Yet only a day or two after the elopement, long before there had been news of any kind, Garron Keith, returning from his extensive trip abroad, had called his wife back abruptly—brutally, it had seemed to her—to the confines of her own home and the concerns proper to her situation as his wife, which did not include any consultations about fallen women in the Hepplefield offices of Quentin Saint-Charles or—*most certainly not*—any running over to Dessborough Manor to see how the deserted husband was getting along and to lavish affection upon his motherless child.

"It's not your business," he'd said quite harshly. *"I'm* your business. And you have children . . . Well, enough of them, I should have thought . . ."

And realizing he had been about to say "children of your own" and then avoided it, since they were not hers and he had not wished to say *"my* children," had been unable, with any honesty, to say "ours," she had asked rather coolly, "Are you suggesting I neglect them?"

"No. Not yet. What I'm telling you is not to start. Particularly not for *that* child."

And it had been then—precisely then—that something tense

and ugly had inserted itself in the air between them, hovering like a silent snarl of warning. Jealousy?

"I beg your pardon, Garron." She knew she could not let it pass. "What is wrong with that child?"

"Nothing I know of," he had answered, speaking through the tension, the ugliness, with a clenched jaw, and keen, hard eyes. "Except that her father meant something to you once, didn't he?"

"Yes," she had answered steadily, knowing she could not afford the risk of trying to lie. "I have always thought him a fine man . . ."

"So it must have upset your apple-cart when he married Kate."

And outwardly cool, inwardly terrified that he might forbid her to visit Dessborough Manor again, she had assumed, as always in times of crisis, her mother's crisp sophistication of manner, shrugging her shoulders and saying with Evangeline's worldly-wise composure, "Good heavens, Garron, one could quite see the reason for it. Kate is worth a fortune."

"Aye," he said, heavily sarcastic, not quite liking to see so much of her mother in her, she thought, but resigned to it, even reassured, since such women were too careful of their comfort and their reputation to throw good homes—like his—away. "And I suppose *one* also sees—Oriel—that she can't take her fortune away with her, either. Which means her husband has now got the lot. Which further means he can afford to buy the very best care and attention for his daughter, and doesn't need you."

Yet no express command had been given, the strength of her wedding vow of absolute obedience to her husband had not, after all, been put to the test, and, having done everything in her power to please him during the month he had remained at home, playing her role of wife-mistress-mother to the full satisfaction of all his domestic appetites, she had proceeded, as soon as he went off again, to make careful, discreet arrangements how best to please herself.

He had been away a great deal that year too, traveling thousands of difficult miles, driving himself every bit as hard as he drove others, racing always ahead of the demon "Time" which, this year, next year, certainly too soon, would bring the railway boom to an end; sleeping too little—what fool could spare more than an hour or two, here and there, for sleep in a world full of amateurs and opportunists waiting to steal a march on him?—

eating and drinking too much, to *fuel* himself, as engines were fueled, to stay the uphill course that would make him enough millions—and it would take more than one or two—so that, whatever happened, he would be secure. And it seemed, after all, that so long as his wife was always there, in his house, in his bed whenever he too happened to be in it, his children healthy and smiling and happy with the sackfuls of presents he brought them—Christmas coming a dozen times a year to the house on Lydwick Green—then he was satisfied. Or at least he saw no pressing need to complain.

"I should hope," she told him, "that you can trust me." And, although deeply offended, as, shaking his head with a wry grin, he answered, without the least hesitation, "No, Oriel. One of the first things a man on the make learns is to trust nobody," she nevertheless consoled herself with the simple fact that she *knew*, absolutely for certain, that she was doing nothing wrong. For even had she been tempted to wrong-doing, her concern for her reputation, her old uncertainties about her place in the world, her need to think well of herself, would have prevented it. Indeed, she *was* to be trusted and it was soon clear to her that only because Garron knew this did he allow her—albeit grudgingly—her measure of freedom.

It was a life and by no means a poor one, by no means without its joys and compensations, by no means without its friends among whom she now counted Francis Ashington— since she could apply no other word to him—and Quentin Saint-Charles to whom she applied it with an open heart, even though he was often far from open himself, telling her only what he wished to tell her, in the full knowledge that it was not always what she wished to hear. And, as Kate had left this usually pleasant life of hers, Susannah had joined it again, her engagement to the curate, Mr. Field, dragging on with little hope, on his part, of ever being able to afford marriage, and no wish on her part, it seemed, of ever being married at all, contenting herself with her missionary work on the local building sites and with correcting the turmoils and tribulations of every family she could—except her own, that is, at High Grange vicarage.

Kate's disappearance had not affected, nor even much interested Susannah. Nor had Maud, still painfully adapting to her new life of thankless drudgery at the vicarage, felt more than a self-righteous moment of "I told you so" where Kate's behavior was concerned. But Evangeline had seized upon it in all its aspects of shame and glory and wrung the last drop out of every one, making it clear to Matthew that unless he now took sensible legal steps—long overdue in any case—to ensure her own future, she would set about poisoning his by making every revelation about Kate and her mother as loudly and publicly as she could.

There was nothing to be done about the estate of High Grange, of course, which on Matthew's death—"and you are not a *young* man anymore, my darling"—would pass, through Kate, to Francis. So too would the Kessler money on the very day Kate became twenty-five, a husband—as the law stood—retaining his right to take possession of all his wife's property and future inheritances whether she lived with him or not. Making it essential, therefore, in Evangeline's view—"Since I am younger than you, dearest, and women who have avoided turning themselves into brood animals like Letty tend to live longer in any case"—that a house be purchased, furnished, and made over to her entirely, possibly in Lydwick, so that "dear Matthew" might have the comfort of knowing her to be secure when he passed away.

Quentin, she supposed, would know how to manage the legal formalities to ensure that Francis—who seemed to be getting everything else—could not snatch her new little house from her, Quentin being very clever at such things, having already tracked Kate down, it seemed, and—although Evangeline was not prepared to say how she knew this—arranged for Francis to make her an allowance. Or talked him into it, for devious reasons of his own, perhaps. Unless, of course, Francis—by sending his mad wife those few unnecessary pounds every month or so—wished to ease his conscience about the Kessler fortune he would be getting in five years from now.

Yes. Five years. And before that day dawned Evangeline—she kept on declaring—must have a house of her own, all right and tight, although, of course, she would not dream of living in it until Matthew had been carried out of High Grange in his coffin and Francis had put the whole estate in dust-covers until Celestine should be old enough to possess it.

It became an obsession with her.

"Who knows how things may turn out?" she told Oriel, over and over. "It makes no difference whether Kate lives or dies or who she decides to live with, for that matter. Her husband still gets the Kessler money, the estate, the coal—

everything. And with no strings attached, no obligation to give any of us—*me*, in fact—a penny. Good Heavens—I used to feel sorry for him but he is really coming out of this very nicely. No wonder he is making her a small allowance. A token of gratitude to her, I expect, for going off and leaving him in peace, so that when he does come into her inheritance he can actually enjoy it.''

"I imagine, Mama," Oriel murmured, "that the small allowance is as much as he can manage."

"Indeed." Evangeline was not at all moved to sympathize. "We all know *that* will change. She was twenty, wasn't she, when she ran off? And she gets the Kessler money at twenty-five. He hasn't long to wait. And, in the meantime, every penny piece he gives her is an affront to the Mertons."

"I don't think they know about it, Mama, unless . . ."

She did not like to add "unless you have told them" although Evangeline, of course, readily understood.

"Oh no," she said, "no, no. I would not dream of adding to their burdens by even hinting at it. Francis is their cousin, after all, and they would be bound to see it as the blackest disloyalty. No, poor things. They have had more than enough to bear."

A situation of which Evangeline had taken full advantage, realizing at once that with Dora still frail and fretful, with Adela now living apart from her husband, with Lady Merton still waiting in a state of panic for the revolution, and Lord Merton at the end of his never particularly resourceful wits, a great deal of sympathy and practical understanding was surely needed. A golden opportunity, in fact, which Evangeline seized so thoroughly that although each one of the Mertons still thought of her—or *thought* they did so—as the "pushy" wife of a gentleman of only middling fortune and local importance, it was Evangeline in whom Adela Merton confided her wish to be separated from her husband and all the anxieties it had created; Evangeline who persuaded Dora to dance and ride again and look about her for another fiancé; Evangeline who skillfully fed Lady Merton's terrors so that her ladyship soon felt uncomfortable about going either to her castle in Scotland or her mansion in London unless Evangeline went with her.

There were those, of course, who believed Lord Merton to be Evangeline's lover. Maud, for instance, and the housekeeper at Merton Abbey, the entire household staff in the Scottish castle where gossip was hard to come by, a parlormaid or two in London and in Monte Carlo where she had already spent a triumphant, exceedingly well-dressed summer.

Matthew Stangway had no comment to make about it whatsoever, just as he had never made any comment about the disappearance of Kate, although Oriel was at all times very quick—very nearly cutting as a knife—to defend her mother, and had even spoken sharply to Maud, around whom one usually trod warily, about certain comments of hers when Evangeline had gone alone with Lord Merton to the opening, by no less a pillar of virtue than Queen Victoria, of the Great Exhibition at the miraculous Crystal Palace specially erected to house it in Hyde Park.

Oriel had visited Hyde Park herself a few weeks later, traveling to London by train with Morag and Elspeth and Jamie in a reserved compartment from which, at every station, she had had an excellent view of the working people who, ten years ago, would have been lucky to get ten miles beyond the places in which they had been born, coming now, every day, in their tens of thousands, to see the wonders of the industrial world on display for them, from May to October, at the Crystal Palace.

Just how many people could have got here by stage-coach, Garron Keith, railway builder, wanted to know as he escorted his wife and children beneath that mighty crystal dome, over a hundred feet high. Certainly not the 68,000 a day they were packing in now. Certainly not these northern millworkers and those farm hands from Dorset and Suffolk, taking advantage of the cheap excursion rates on the trains some of them had never even seen before. And which now, moreover, they might well be thinking far more wonderful than the Exhibition itself, all these mechanical inventions for doing one thing or another and the raw materials with which to do it, all these silks from Bombay and worsted cloth from Hepplefield and Bradford, these Bowie knives from Sheffield for use—one supposed—in the far west of America, all these French tapestries and rugs, these Indian pearls and Spanish lace mantillas. Even the Koh-i-Noor diamond itself. Although, in the civil engineering section, both Garron and Jamie were more than a little taken by the model of Liverpool docks complete with more than a thousand rigged ships.

Jamie, deciding then and there to be a civil engineer, set himself to count them and had to be lured away by the offers of fresh strawberry ices at the audacious price of one shilling a glass which, as Jamie demolished his fourth, Elspeth and Morag their second, caused Garron to remark that the confectioner who had paid £5,500 for the exclusive right to sell refreshments must already be considering it money well spent.

Not—as Oriel knew very well—that he would have grudged them a dozen ices apiece and would, she thought, have been only too pleased to buy that model of Liverpool for Jamie, had it been for sale, as well as any pearl or diamond to which she had taken a fancy, right up to the Koh-i-Noor itself.

"Now there's a diamond," he'd said, impressed mainly by what it represented and the thought of what *he* could do with assets such as that; and laughing, shaking her head, she had answered, as if they had been standing at a shop-counter, "No—no. Not today. I'm more in the mood this morning for something to match my eyes."

They had spent a pleasantly tiring week of sight-seeing, shopping, expensive meals, excursions on the river to stop, at likely looking places, for more expensive food and wine and general merrymaking, after which Garron had gone off to inspect his various sites up and down the country and she had made the journey to Ullswater and that one precious site of her own.

She had not expected to see Quentin here. But then, one did not *expect* so subtle and self-contained a man. One accepted, rather, that he would come when it seemed right to him and that every visit of his would have a definite purpose. Yet, since the purpose would only be declared at what he judged to be the right moment, Oriel spent a few moments of her own offering him cool drinks, inquiring about his journey, taking him out into the garden again to show him the pale, perhaps sinister valerian flowers, the cats dancing, languorous and bemused, around them, and the two daughters of Garron Keith who had no interest, just then, either in feline ballet or the odd obsessions of their stepmother for herbs and spices. Not too much interest either, perhaps, for one another.

"Good morning, Mr. Saint-Charles. Isn't it a lovely morning?" Elspeth, at least, could always be relied on to make herself pleasant if only because, having few ideas in her head just then beyond the fine, fair hair which grew upon it, the blue of her own eyes, the "peaches and cream" of her complexion which had started to win her admiring glances whenever she went to Penrith, she liked to know what impression she was creating.

A poor one, it seemed, on Quentin who, with no time to spare for flirtatious young ladies of fourteen, merely and very coolly replied, "Good morning, Miss Elspeth. Yes—very fine."

Nor was he any more affable to Morag who, although far less flirtatious and certainly more intelligent than her sister, knew enough—too much, thought Oriel—about Quentin's disagreements with *his* sister, Susannah, to make her rather stiff with him.

"Good morning, Miss Keith."

And the manner in which she replied "Good morning" plainly conveyed her own absolute support for Susannah, her own pained surprise that, having objected to his sister's engagement to the curate Mr. Field three years ago when she had wanted to be engaged, he would not help her to break it now when she did not.

"I do believe that young lady dislikes me," he said as they moved on to the garden's edge and then, across a narrow, steeply sloping field to the very margin of the lake.

"Oh—at fifteen I suppose we are all prone to foolish dislikes. And even sillier 'likes,' I'm afraid. She is not fond of me at the moment, either."

"Does that worry you?"

"Well—I shall be glad when it comes to an end—if it ever does. But she would have resented any woman Garron had married, wouldn't she? I can't blame her for that. And I suppose there is nothing even personal in it."

That was the way she chose to look at it, in any case, the compromise for which she had settled. And, apart from Morag's need to criticize, there had been few dramas or upheavals, Oriel seeing to it, in the main, that no matter how carefully Morag looked for trouble, there was rarely very much for her to find. She felt no more emotion for these children, or only rarely, than she supposed they felt for her, yet, nevertheless, she had built a home around them so much in accord with their needs and natures that not even her exacting husband had found cause to complain. The boy Jamie was being brought up to be a man and showing great enthusiasm for it, the girls to be ladies who, once married to the wealthy husbands Garron had in mind for them, would disappoint no one in the arts she had carefully, and even with good-humor, taught them, the flower arrangements and fine embroidery, the copperplate handwriting and painting in water-colors or on china, how to play a few romantic pieces on the drawing-room piano and pronounce a few selected lines of Shakespeare or Keats or Wordsworth by heart, how to get the best out of servants, how, above all, to prove, by one's own luxurious lack of any useful occupation, the ability of one's husband to pay lesser females to do the work.

It was what Garron wanted for his daughters and she had set herself to achieve it, finding a willing pupil in pretty, flirtatious, happily "luxurious" Elspeth who would be snapped up, Oriel estimated, in a year or two and who, the moment she became mistress of her own house, her own carriage, her own pin-money and calling-cards, her own account with her own dressmaker, her *own* easy life would promptly forget about any other. While Morag, perhaps, might learn more, resist more, might even be worth more—*would*, for certain, have been worthier, deeper, so much better had Susannah not interfered with her—but, in the end, helped along by the dowry her father could give her, would probably marry a man of his choosing and become what he saw as a good wife.

And, in the meantime, before those gilded wedding-bells started ringing, they learned their lessons, took what Oriel offered, *made use of her* as their father, perhaps without realizing it, had implied they should, accompanying her, eagerly in the case of Elspeth, at least willingly on Morag's part, to Hepplefield and Leeds and London, or to her lakeside cottage where, even in that isolated spot, they had soon made "useful" acquaintances, spending a great deal of time with the daughters of a solicitor in Penrith or with a large, interestingly well-to-do family on the other side of the lake at Watermillock who were forever giving parties or dashing off to look at waterfalls or Roman ruins or stone circles, allowing Oriel—more often than she thought Garron realized—the luxury of being alone.

"Playing Marie Antoinette again, are we?" Garron usually inquired when he appeared, heavily sarcastic and always somewhat out of the blue, to take her home, frowning as he stooped to enter her low doorway, looking around him, never with much enjoyment, at the herbs hanging in bunches from the kitchen rafters, and at the kitchen itself, the well-scoured stone floor, the well-used wooden table at which the very kind of chopping and peeling and scraping of raw fruit and vegetables his first wife would have done a great deal to avoid seemed always to be going on, the inevitable basket of kittens by the hearth, the insultingly small, old-fashioned cooking-range, black-leaded to perfection by a "daily woman" from Howtown who probably despised it as much as he did. As much as his first, overworked, overfertile wife would have done.

"Yes," he invariably said ten minutes after his arrival and then once or twice more while she hurriedly took her leave of her plants and her stray kittens, arranging for them to be watered and fed until she could come back again. "Marie Antoinette. You might call it fun, Oriel, but any woman who *had* to do it would call it drudgery. And she'd be right."

Yet he did not forbid her to return, as he could have done, nor even to interest herself in news of the girl to whom her true instincts of maternity, her feelings of unconditional love and responsibility, were still directed. Kate.

"How was your journey, Quentin?" she now said, referring not to his walk from Pooley Bridge but to his recent trip to France, on family business, it seemed, since Kate would deal with no one else, even Oriel's letters, which Francis passed on, returning unopened. All Oriel knew of her, therefore, were the dry details Quentin had given. Dora Merton's fiancé had taken her to Paris and, very quickly, left her there. She had gone next to Germany where, very luckily as it turned out, *someone*—Quentin had not said who, although Oriel believed he had had more than a little to do with it himself—had put her in touch with a branch of her Kessler relations. After that she had "traveled," had returned to France, had been ill and recovered, had handed back to him, again unopened, the latest letter Oriel had asked him to deliver.

Now, as they stood quietly by the lakeside, he returned it to her, smiling as, holding it a moment in her hand, she bent down and let it slide gently into the water, an obliging breeze rippling across the surface to take it away.

"She answers my letters, and even meets me, because I mean nothing to her," he said, his voice and manner cool without altogether concealing his offer of consolation. "I impose no stress on her because she doesn't care . . . "

"I don't believe that, Quentin. She must know all you have done for her."

He smiled. "Ah yes. But, you see, she doesn't know why. And since my motives have always been suspect and have usu-

ally turned out to have my own best interests at heart . . . Well—
she can allow herself to believe the worst. And I have done
nothing more heroic, you know, than arrange for the transfer of
another man's money—and not too much of it either—to her
account. Is there anything particularly worthy about that?''

Smiling, she ignored the question and asked another.

''Has she been wise with it?''

''The money? Of course not.''

''Is she in debt?''

''Frequently.''

''Oh dear . . .''

''Quite so. But really, before giving way to alarm, one
should bear in mind that debt and disgrace are very much the
fashion among some of her new acquaintances.''

''I dare say.'' She was by no means reassured. ''But people go to prison, don't they, Quentin—surely—for debt?''

''Oh yes.'' He seemed happy to agree. ''But only people
of no account, or not very much. People who have no rich
relations. Or none that are willing to buy them out. Which is
hardly the case with Kate's present charmed circle of friends.
Half of them could be locked up for debt and the other half as
revolutionaries, I suppose, if their fathers were not government
ministers or bankers or heirs to some title or other . . .''

''I see.'' The ''golden youth'' of the privileged classes, doing
their frantic best to acquire a little tarnish. Was it any stranger
than the satisfaction she often found herself in dirtying her own
pampered hands with potato peelings or black lead?

''At least try not to worry,'' he said.

''Will she be staying in France?''

''Possibly. I believe she is waiting for the new Republic to
fall.''

''And will it?''

''Very likely. Particularly since one of the leading new
republicans is Prince Louis Napoleon Bonaparte . . .''

''Who is—exactly . . . ?''

''The Emperor Napoleon's nephew. The only one of the
Bonapartes to mean anything since Waterloo.''

And, walking back across the field to her garden gate, he
lectured her, very precisely, as to Prince Louis Napoleon's
attempts to convert the new Republic into a dictatorship, disguised as a monarchy, with himself—of course—at its head.
Very much as his famous Uncle Napoleon had done. Some
of Kate's friends were pledged to support him, others just as

determined to tear up the paving stones of Paris for barricades and resist to the death. While Kate, Oriel may be relieved to know, had merely pledged herself not to miss the fun.

"Will you stay to luncheon, Quentin? Beef broth and dumplings."

"Herb dumplings?"

"Of course—full of lovage and parsley from my own garden. With an elderflower sorbet to follow."

"That sounds almost like witchcraft, Oriel."

"Possibly." Garron had often said the same thing. "But it *is* delicious."

"I believe you. Sadly I am expected elsewhere. In fact I think I had better set off at once."

He shook her hand, rather formally, in farewell and went off as calmly as if he had simply stepped across a well-paved street to pass the time of day with her, instead of hazarding his visibly expensive shoes over three uneven lakeside miles, an absolute composure about him which would have been quite chilling had she not been aware of many things in his life which, she now believed, had forced him to adopt that air of distance and authority. His mother—for instance—still repeating, ever more shrilly, that he had ruined her life; his father unloading upon him, with malicious pleasure, the full responsibility of his young brothers and sisters who, for their part, had been brought up to use him in full measure; his sister Constantia forever at his throat to find better employment for her husband, his sister Susannah pestering him as ardently to ensure that her fiancé, the penniless curate, would never be promoted high enough to afford marriage; the sorry situation of Maud who held him entirely to blame for her miserable frustrations; his own, much-talked-of relationship with his handsome housekeeper who had left him recently to be replaced, at once, by another, every bit as handsome.

Walking slowly back into her garden, she wondered how much he really cared for Kate, how much more, perhaps, than anyone—certainly Kate herself—had ever realized, her own mood lightening instantly as she remembered that both Elspeth and Morag were going over to Watermillock that afternoon, leaving her blissfully free of them until whatever time their practical, good-natured hostess, Mrs. Landon, brought them back again. Late, she hoped. Tomorrow with any luck. But it was not to be, the arrival of their father immediately after luncheon—ten days before she had ex-

pected him—putting an end to the visit altogether, obliging
her to send her "daily woman's" son with a letter of explanation to the Landons of Watermillock and then to fetch Jamie who was out somewhere on the fells helping—or
hindering, perhaps—a local farmer to train his sheepdog; to
make her usual swift arrangements for her garden and her
cats; to pack her bags and the children's bags, as quickly as
she could, while Garron, looking tanned and fit as a whole
orchestra of fiddles, sat in the sun with his daughters, receiving their welcome and dispensing his presents.

His good-humor set as fair as the weather, it seemed, until
something ended it, bringing him to her bedroom—where he
had never spent the night, putting up always at the George at
Penrith, even the Buck Inn at Howtown—and keeping him
there, in the doorway, staring at her as she folded the last of
her chemises, with a familiar menace.

"There was a man here this morning," he said, speaking
a blunt accusation; and laying down her armful of linen, she
knew she would be well advised to answer at once.

"Yes. Quentin Saint-Charles."

"Which you forgot to mention."

"No, Garron." And from her past experience of his possessive rages she made her voice tart and steady. "You've
only been here half an hour, and either you want me to be
ready for the four o'clock train or you want me to sit down
and have a conversation. When have I had time to tell you
who called—who didn't . . . ?"

"Tell me now," he said, still hard and wary and, although
she never cared to admit it, quite dangerous.

"Tell you what?"

"Why he should be in this godforsaken area, for one
thing?"

"Oh good Heavens." That much was easy. "He has two
sisters at school in Carlisle, so I suppose he has to come up
occasionally to settle their bills. And today he had business
with Lord Merton who is staying at Lowther Castle. I think
Quentin was having lunch there, although he didn't like to
admit it. My mother would be speechless if she knew. *She's*
never been invited there."

But even the thought of Evangeline at a loss for words did
not divert him.

"That tells me why he's in the district, not why he came
to see you."

"He is my cousin, you know—if only by marriage . . ."

But he shook his head, still sharp and alert, telling her that a man did not walk over six rough miles on a hot summer morning to see a distant cousin.

"Are you suggesting, Garron, that my behavior has been in some way . . . ?"

"Oh for God's sake," he snapped, "just tell me the truth—if you know it when you see it . . ."

But hearing somewhere behind the threat, the insult, just a whisper of something else which asked not so much for the truth as to be put out of this possessive misery, she said quickly: "I gave him a letter for Kate when he went to France. She sent it back and he returned it. That's *all*. What else could there be?" And when the hardness, the razor edge of his tension persisted, she said sharply, "Garron, this is all so unnecessary. Don't you know, by now, that I would never have a lover—never!"

"Why not?"

Because her mother had had at least a dozen that she had been aware of throughout her childhood, and almost certainly had one now, unless his puny, weak-eyed lordship retained only the desire for such things and had lost his capacity for the performance. But nothing, not even this direct physical menace, could ever make her admit it.

"I gave him a letter for Kate," she said, gritting her teeth and waiting, knowing, as she had known once or twice before, that unless he believed her now, unless his tension eased, his offended muscles relaxed, he would be more than likely to strike her.

"So it *was* Quentin Saint-Charles," he said, speaking quickly. "You'll swear to that?"

"Ask your daughters," she threw back at him. "They saw him. Call them up here now, both together, and ask them?"

Had either of them told him otherwise? She could not believe it. Far more likely no name had been given at all, some joke made, perhaps, about "stepmama's visitor," so that, without listening to more, his mind had leaped—for reasons they both knew of—very likely to Francis Ashington.

"It *was* Quentin," she said.

No other name had been spoken. No acknowledgment of any one man who troubled him more than the hundred others who might have designs on his territory, his possession, his woman, had been made. And, as fast and furiously as his temper flared, so now it flickered and was gone.

"Listen," he said, tension ebbing out of him with a speed that made him shake his head as if emerging from water. "That sounds like Jamie in the garden—doesn't it?"

Picking up her linen and beginning to fold it again, she agreed that it did.

"Let's get home, then," he called out.

He had just signed a contract, he told her, that could make him a million or break him, of course, although he didn't believe for a moment, waking or sleeping, that it would. And he was off, before the month end, to sign another. Congratulations were in order, champagne and plenty of it the very moment they got to Lydwick, with whatever took her fancy, the next morning, from that jeweler in Leeds her mother was always mentioning. And anything else, within reason—except this damned little house—that she wanted.

"Lowther Castle," she said, adapting, as always, to his humor.

"Maybe next year."

Her sins, supposed or otherwise, were not merely forgiven but forgotten, swept so thoroughly away by his return to good humor that he would have been considerably put out had she done other than forget all about them too. He had come home not to be cruel but to be indulged, not to accuse his wife but to cosset her, a blunt, clear-sighted realist who did not expect her to love him or long for him but who thought it only right and proper—considering all the advantages he gave her—that she should behave as if she did.

How refreshing, it suddenly seemed to her, almost how wonderful, that he knew the difference.

Thirteen

She believed she had found the formula by which she could live with a fair measure of content. She knew Garron did not love her in anything approaching the deep, emotional—in his view, no doubt, sloppy and sentimental—manner in which she had been prepared to give love herself; although not to him. A totality of feeling, perhaps even a dangerous excess which now, reaching the mature age of twenty-five, then twenty-six, she thought best to put away with all her other dreams of adolescence. She believed her husband's affection to depend entirely on her own good behavior, that, in his own blunt terminology, he expected to get exactly what he was paying for, and, in the case of any discrepancy, that it should be more rather than less. But, no matter how unromantic, how downright unflattering his attitude might seem, at least she knew where she stood with it, knew the mark beyond which she must not step, knew not only his rules but exactly what her reward would be if she obeyed them, her punishment if she did not.

He was exacting, of course, demanding in the extreme, the center of his own, made-to-his-exact-measure universe with herself as his chief satellite, the entire household on Lydwick Green coming to a standstill whenever he entered it, the better to regroup around him, yet, for all that, he was not capricious, his demands remaining the same, the rules he formulated to ensure his pleasures always clearly stated, easy to understand. Her prompt unflagging attention to each and every one ensuring her a beautiful home, a staff of well-trained servants, accounts with the best shops in Hepplefield and Leeds where she might replace her furniture and restock her wardrobe as often as she chose, a surfeit of leisure and luxury with no questions asked about her bills for the simple reason that, in his view, she had earned it.

She knew him to be intolerant and not the least inclined to anything even resembling self-sacrifice. She did not suppose for one moment that he would show much sympathy should she suddenly collapse into physical frailty, and none whatsoever should she take refuge in nervous hypochondria, like Letty. She knew, for certain, that he would tolerate no social-climbing nonsense from her in the manner of Evangeline, no caprice, no criticism of the least of his actions, nor even very much in the way of Christian charity which, in his opinion, began and ended at home. She knew he desired her and was fond of her, that he would defend her with the single-minded ferocity of a lion and, should circumstances ever require it, would go hungry himself to ensure she was fed. Yet she also knew how quickly and completely these sentiments would evaporate should she ever deliberately cease to fulfill what he saw, most precisely, as her part of their bargain.

Why not keep that bargain, therefore? Not just to the letter but beyond, employing her sensitivity, her powers of invention, her good-will, to give him more than he had even thought to ask for, thus gaining not the romantic love of which she did not think him capable, but his warm appreciation, his generous approval, a strong, personal friendship which—if it lasted—she believed she might come to value more than anything else in her life.

And when he was pleased with her—and he *was* pleased, she knew that—his generosity could extend even to giving her things, or permitting things, he would really have preferred her not to have. Her lakeland cottage, for instance. Her constant gleaning of news of Kate through Quentin Saint-Charles. Her visits, even, to the Ashingtons, father and daughter, at Dessborough Manor, although these visits, by unspoken agreement, were never returned to Lydwick Green. Her long patience with the tantrums and miseries of Susannah, which he would have preferred her to reserve entirely for his children, who had tantrums enough. Most of all her visits to Merton Abbey, disapproving strongly—as he did— of the goings-on of the aristocracy in general and of her mother very much in particular, although—she noted with some appreciation—he had always stopped short of actually saying so.

Just as she, even when pressed, had stopped short of admitting that she found his daughter Elspeth shallow, his daughter Morag deep and difficult, his son Jamie a boy like any other, since only had she loved these children would she have felt free to criticize. And not loving them, liking two of them well enough, sometimes pitying, sometimes putting up with the third, she learned—during the years when, quite placidly, her beauty undimmed, she reached her midtwenties—to compromise, to value exactly what she had without yearning unrealistically for something more or something else; to accept, without plaguing herself as to the reasons why, that she liked her husband rather more than she liked his children and had even learned to desire him, not so passionately as to cause her any embarrassing restlessness when he was away, but quite enough to send her happily to bed on his return and to keep early nights, late mornings, several very private afternoons, for several weeks thereafter.

No sign of pregnancy had ever shown itself and neither of them had ever mentioned it. If a child came then he could afford to give it a royal welcome, but if not, then he had children enough, particularly the boy, Jamie, big-boned, loud-mouthed, pig-headed—a real *boy*, thank God—who would stand well over six feet tall like his father, and who, when he left Hepplefield Grammar School in a year or two would be apprenticed, whether he liked it or not—although he appeared to like it well enough—to the hard, hectic, risky, yet while it lasted supremely lucrative trade of the railway contractor.

Oriel would see little of him then, the Gore Valley line being already finished and officially opened with an elaborate ceremony in Hepplefield Station with banners and speeches, in the presence of every imaginable species of local grandee, civic dignitary, and railway director, as well as quite half a dozen Lord Mayors; Oriel in black fur and velvet with a white osprey feather in her hat and a great many diamonds; Elspeth and Morag in blue with rather more gold chains and pearls than she—although not their father—had thought appropriate; Evangeline a marvel of sophistication in dove gray with a diamond on her finger which, by the way she displayed it, might well have been the Koh-i-Noor itself; Lord Merton—and Oriel refused to discuss with anyone the possibility that he might have given that scandalous diamond to her mother—barely reached Evangeline's shoulder; Matthew Stangway standing remote and immaculate at her other side, taking absolutely no notice; Garron's army of navvies drawn up in quite military formations, resplendent in scarlet velveteens and pale, well-brushed moleskins, sporting their gold charms and chains and earrings like medals as they waited to be congratulated.

A great day, bringing to the Gore Valley what it had asked for and believed it wanted, ending in an unwise bonus of barrels of ale for the navvies, the more distinguished guests adjourning to a banquet at Hepplefield's Assembly Rooms which Garron Keith had been obliged to leave in something of a hurry to do what he could—not much—to calm his now drunken and therefore riotous labor-force in the streets outside.

Every ale-house and gin-shop in Hepplefield's lower quarters had been smashed that night, windows put through just to hear the music of breaking glass, benches and tables thrown out into the alleyways and—because what else could one do with rotten wood?—set alight, Hepplefield's whores, of whom, since industrialization, there was a notable multitude and variety, relieving so many scarlet velveteen or moleskin pockets of their final wages that Garron Keith had little trouble the next morning in finding enough bankrupt, still far from sober men to complete the work-force at a contract he was undertaking in a particularly remote and therefore, from the navvying point of view, particularly unpopular part of Scotland.

Oriel's own position in Lydwick had suffered quite severely during the months the railway line had been going through, few of her neighbors caring to include her in their invitations when the main topic of conversation could only be the devastation her husband's laborers were bringing to their quiet, and above all dignified little town; Oriel receiving only the coolest of nods, the most pained of smiles from anyone who had failed to see her approaching in time to cross the street and avoid recognizing her altogether. A bleak time for Morag who suffered it in tight-lipped silence, and for Elspeth who, at fourteen, believed her prospects for a good marriage irrevocably dimmed, a hey-day for Jamie whose black eyes, skinned knuckles, cut lips, and burst noses had become facts of everyday life to Oriel.

But the navvies had moved on, the plight of the tobacconist's parlormaid and the young wife of the admittedly elderly cobbler who had moved on with them gradually forgotten, Oriel's connection with the Mertons and the Ashingtons remembered as Lydwick returned to normal, despite the brand-new railway station which, on the whole, was seen as an advantage, if one could make allowances—that is—for the rather coarse-grained men from Hepplefield who kept emerging from it with their stonemasons and architects to talk, in loud city voices, about getting away from their own mill-yards and building themselves houses on pleasant tracts of good, arable land.

Oriel felt in no way responsible for that, being very pleased to make the acquaintance of a French milliner who—to a certain clicking of reproachful tongues among the wine merchants and saddlers—soon opened a shop in Lydwick's High Street, Oriel buying a great many hats and spending pleasant afternoons in the pretty bow-windowed little shop sipping white wine and nibbling ratafia biscuits and learning as much from her hostess as she learned from Quentin Saint-Charles himself about events in France. Predictable events, in fact, involving the transformation of Prince Louis Napoleon Bonaparte, with a certain amount of bloodshed, from President to the new Republic, to a fully fledged emperor, Napoleon the Third.

There could be no doubt that *this* Napoleon knew how to get the most out of his chances, Oriel's milliner showing great enthusiasm, not only for the man himself, but for his plans to rebuild Paris, to construct wide boulevards, grand squares, splendid hotels which would make her native city—which was quite lovely enough already—the wonder of the civilized world.

Was Kate still there, Oriel wondered? Yes, indeed, Quentin told her, and finding much to interest her in this new regime, these opportunists with every intention of turning themselves into multimillionaires, these clever men—and women—intent on profit, clustering around this latest majesty who had a very precise understanding of such things. As men who had spent most of their lives in exile often had. Yes, Kate had seemed rather taken by the atmosphere of high risk and high fashion Napoleon the Third was creating, not a particularly moral climate, of course, since one could hardly expect a man who had survived so long in exile and then climbed to power in just about the only way he could—that is, over the aims, the best interests, and, alas, the bodies of others—to set much store by saintliness.

"And those friends of hers you told me about, Quentin, who were going to man the barricades . . . ?"

"Ah yes. I believe they did so. She has other—rather older—friends now."

They had died, then, some of those young people in their revolutionary efforts to achieve—what? Oriel had no idea. She only hoped they had been quite clear about it themselves.

"Quentin, would there be any point, do you think, in me giving you another letter for Kate the next time you go over?"

"Oriel—if you do then I will certainly deliver it."

It did not occur to her, at any time, that he would do less than he had promised. Nor that he would ever mislead her or maneuver her in any way. Although she did not always take his advice, particularly when it concerned Susannah of whom she once again fell foul.

The living of Dessborough church became vacant that year. Susannah's fiancé was a curate in search of a living. Francis—as Squire of Dessborough—now had a living to bestow.

"Quentin," suggested Oriel, "why don't you ask Francis to give it to Mr. Field and your sister Susannah?"

"Because," he answered promptly, "my sister Susannah does not want to be Mrs. Field."

"Oh—surely . . ."

"Yes. Surely. She wants to be a missionary. Not to darkest Africa, I hasten to add. The navvy sites are quite enough for her. And so long as Mr. Field remains a curate he can escort her to any camp she takes it into her head to visit with her Bible. But if she becomes a vicar's wife she will have her husband's church and congregation to attend to on Sundays. And her vicarage and, one can hardly doubt, her offspring, every other day of the week . . ."

She saw his lip curl slightly at the word "offspring," the likelihood of Susannah proving as fertile as her mother and Constantia causing him such evident distaste that, wondering if the memory of so many mismanaged babies, so much inefficient, downright messy maternity throughout his own childhood had caused him—since Kate—to avoid marriage, she rather forgot about Susannah, thinking Quentin far worthier of her consideration until later that same afternoon when, in an unguarded moment, she repeated what he had said about the Dessborough living to her mother. Whereupon Evangeline, in a spirit of pure mischief, promptly drove over to Dessborough and asked Francis to oblige her by offering his church at once to Mr. Field.

"Why not?" she said, in answer to Oriel's reproaches. "They have been so appallingly droopy of late, at Letty's. It can do no harm to stir them up."

As indeed it did, to such an extent that Oriel, in the manner of one taking flight, had herself gone to Dessborough where Francis, with wry good humor, had agreed just as readily, to cancel the offer on any pretext they could muster.

"Perhaps," she said, thinking as Evangeline had taught her, "an old friend of yours could turn up? Or better still, a distant cousin with a better claim . . . ?"

He was instantly, and with the same wry humor, willing to oblige. "Yes—of course. Although I don't know where I am to get him from."

But she, as Evangeline's daughter, could not be dismayed by a mere detail such as that. "Oh—from nowhere at all. He could just write to you—from China, perhaps?—saying he is coming back and asking you to keep the living open. Couldn't he?"

He bowed, smiling to her ingenuity. "He could. If that is what you would like him to do. And China seems most suitable."

"Yes." She knew of no one who would be likely to go there unless Garron, of course, had any plans about building Chinese railways. "And then, in a little while, it will blow over and you can take someone else."

"Poor Mr. Field," he said.

She had not thought of that. "Oh dear—yes. I see what you mean."

He smiled again, quizzically, quite warmly. "Yes, indeed. I am quite ready to do it, of course, but I thought I ought to mention that we are sacrificing Mr. Field rather—aren't we?—for Susannah."

And was she worth it? Of course not. But what was Mr. Field worth? She had no idea and did not believe, moreover, that she had any right to judge. Not on that cool, pale January morning, at any rate, with another lavish Christmas just behind her, another year just starting to unroll itself through the sun and storm of three hundred and sixty-five more days, most of them pleasant and steady and soon over, colored by her own subtle tints of harmony and compromise, of a sense of purpose and a job well done; one of them—toward the year's end—her twenty-seventh birthday, another of them Kate's twenty-fifth.

What more would the year contain than that? She had never spoken of Kate to Francis, preferring to wait discreetly, courteously, until he mentioned her himself. And, until he did so—if ever—she was happy to talk of Celestine, of the garden, of life's pastel-tinted, well-mannered surface, of good humor and good order, of the everyday tasks which, in their dozens, came always so obligingly to hand, ignoring the folly of "what might have been" so thoroughly, so mercifully, as to banish all restraint between them. Enabling them, in a manner they both found delightful, to talk freely, lightly, easily about anyone but Kate and each other.

About Dora Merton and "nanny" to whom Francis remained Sir Lancelot incarnate, about his tenants to whom he was a distant but responsible squire, about his neighbors with whom he shot and hunted and chatted freely—as she did—without really saying much at all, even about the ladies of fashion who, coming season by season as guests to Merton Abbey, were quick to offer him brief, extremely fashionable consolation which—as she knew from Evangeline—he did not always turn aside. And now here she was inviting him to conspire with her, just as fashionably, about the replacement of a vicar so that his fiancée might avoid becoming a bride and remain a missionary.

He smiled at her again, and then, his eyes amused, smiled at his housekeeper who had positioned herself in the parlor window to keep watch as they strolled through the sleeping, January garden, at "nanny" mounting *her* guard from the nursery window above, while Miss Elspeth Keith, who rarely noticed anything but herself, sat fur-wrapped and a hundred miles away on the garden swing, apparently unaware of her position, in that house, that garden, as her stepmother's chaperon.

"Ought this clerical Chinese cousin of mine to have a name, do you think?"

"It will make no difference," Evangeline told her a few days later. "Susannah has already put us on trial, my love, and found us both quite guilty. Of trying to get her married, that is, when *she* is trying so hard to have all the advantages of marriage with none of the obligations. And, my goodness—one look at her Mr. Field is enough to tell me that obligations there would certainly be. Timid as a rabbit, the poor little man, and just as fertile—one ought not to doubt it. Susannah would be overrun. Just like her mother. Such a crime we tried to commit—you and I—by *almost* securing him the income on which to do it. And since she cannot punish us, she will never forgive.''

"Thank you, Mama."

And it was, therefore, with more than usual reluctance that she gave in to her mother's request to accompany her, that evening, to Merton Abbey.

"For Heaven's sake, Oriel, why not? Your husband is abroad—very much as usual. And please restrain yourself from moaning to me about his children. You have a house-keeper and a governess as well as a houseful of other ser-vants, all eating their heads off, no doubt, who can take care of them. A position in society is what you ought to be think-ing of, Oriel—as I do.''

"Yes, Mama."

Yet, if Oriel did not like the social position Evangeline was carving for herself it was her place, she believed, not to crit-icize but to defend, and hotly sometimes, having retaliated sharply even to Garron's comments about the number of ban-quets, balls, theaters, race-meetings, shooting-parties, polo-matches, coaching meets, regattas, both in England and abroad to which Lord Merton—his wife's "nerves" making her un-available—had, this last year or two, escorted Evangeline.

"My mother's husband does not complain," she had in-formed her own husband, quite coldly.

"So I've noticed. He watches and smiles, which strikes me—being a simple man—as an odd way for any woman's husband to behave. In your place I'd ask your mother—in your own ob-scure fashion, of course—what she thinks she's doing."

Evangeline, when most discreetly asked, had been in no doubt. "I'm feathering my nest," she had said, very cool and bright. "What else? And, good Heavens, Oriel, since husbands have this tendency—as all the world knows—to pass on and leave us widows, you ought to do the same. I have no intention, I do assure you, of finding myself with nothing but my memories to live on when Matthew goes, and Kate's husband arrives the day after to turn me out of High Grange. Be sensible, Oriel. Your husband is older than you, and what position will you have here when he burns himself out with overwork, or overindulgence—or both, more likely? Just bear in mind, my love, that his coffin will not have passed over the threshold before that boy of his rushes in to claim the house and the business, with his sisters a step behind him to make sure of the rest. What of you? Nothing, dearest—do think about it—except what his will allows you. And unless you push him now, *hard*, while you can, it may not be much. The widow's mite, Oriel. And I have no intention—*ever*—of living on that.''

She had herself pushed Matthew, *very hard*, already into buying her one of the new houses shooting up everywhere, these days, around Lydwick which, although still apparently unfurnished was, in fact, an Aladdin's Cave of sofas, rugs, lacquer cabinets, inlaid tables, crystal and china, all quietly removed from High Grange and kept under covers. The nest, already duly feathered, for her widowhood. While, as for her association with the Mertons, just why—she asked Oriel with even a touch of indignation—did it follow that if Matthew had reached the end of his ambitions she had done the same?

She had not. Her life, by her own efforts alone, was growing rich and full. She had—at last—the very things she had always desired, friends who were not only rich—since Garron Keith was that—but in high places. Friends, moreover, who were acquainted with those even higher than themselves, with Queen Victoria, for instance, and her Prince Albert, although no one much cared for *him*, since, after fourteen years of wedded bliss he still had not learned to dress or shake hands or ride his horse quite like a Englishman.

"He is German, Mama."

"So he is." So too was the Queen's mother, the Duchess of Kent, from whom she may have inherited her strict sense— by no means English either, in Lord Merton's view—of morality, which still disinclined her to welcome, at her court, a gentleman of Lord Merton's lineage for the odd reasons that his elder daughter had separated from her husband, his younger daughter had more than earned the nickname of "Madcap," his wife had long since taken to dosing her "nerves" with brandy, while the gentleman himself—and was it any wonder?—had found consolation in the *friendship*, no more, of an intelligent woman.

"He never seems very intelligent himself, Mama," Oriel said tartly, setting off most unwillingly that January evening to spend a few hours in his company.

"Dearest." Evangeline was mildly amused. "Never mind

his intelligence. He is *devoted*. What more could one possibly need?''

"To be perfectly frank, Mama," and Oriel was rarely that, "I wonder why you need to bother with any of the Mertons at all."

"My dear, what a question." Evangeline's voice, reaching her daughter from the darkened corner of the Stangway carriage, trilled with laughter. "For exactly the same reason as I have *bothered* with all the other Mertons we have come across on our travels, you and I. Such as those—for instance—who happen to call themselves 'Stangway.' Whereas—surely you see that, my darling—they are just Mertons, all together."

"I dare say." In fact, yes, she took her mother's meaning perfectly well. Yet—thinking with her mother's mind—she wondered, having got the Stangways very much where she wanted them, if it could be worth the trouble, if—at Evangeline's age—it was even wise to embark on this elaborate, and surely very tiring, conquest of the Mertons?

"Mother—what are you really after?"

"My own darling." And once again Evangeline trilled and sparkled with laughter. "Who knows? Lady Merton might be carried off one day, by one of her so very many nervous spasms. And if it just so happens that I am a widow by then, living in my pretty little house in Lydwick Park with all my glass and china and my lacquer cabinets . . . Well, his daughters would not like him to make me into the new Lady Merton, of course. I hardly blame them. But young ladies cannot always have just what they want."

"Mother, that wife of his will live forever."

"I dare say. I dare say." She did not sound particularly dismayed about it. "But you can't be *sure* of that, Oriel. Matthew will probably live forever too, but that has not stopped me from getting my own house and furniture together, just in case. One has to keep as many doors half-open as one possibly can. And—as it happens—I am fond of Matthew."

"Are you?"

"Oriel. I have known him—well—for over thirty years. And—yes—shall I tell you something shocking?"

"Perhaps not."

"But I will. And you must allow me to indulge myself, since I couldn't possibly say this to anyone else but you. The truth is I would love to be Lady Merton. I would be marvelous at it too—Lord yes, a definite cut above magnificent. No doubt of that. But if I ever managed it, if I actually got the title and the money and the family jewels, and the villa in Monte Carlo all to myself . . . Well, the first thing I should want to do about it, the thing that would please me absolutely the most, would be running to Matthew and telling him just how I'd done it—just how much it was worth—just how I was going to keep the best of it, the jewels and the social position and the house in London for instance, away from those silly girls of his even when his even sillier old lordship was dead. And since my poor darling Matthew would have to be dead himself before I could start it . . . You see? How shocking."

"Yes, Mama. I see."

They made the rest of the short journey to Merton Abbey in silence, Lord Merton himself coming to meet them in his vast but never very well lit hall, a weak-eyed, weak-chinned, fussy little man who owed the fact that no one noticed him at all—thought Oriel—with anything sharper than mild irritation or warmer than pity, to his power and property, his ownership of enough land and the houses and shops, the villages and market towns standing upon it, to enable him to appoint, as his fancy dictated, the vicars of several village churches and, even in these new days of electoral reform, at least one member of the House of Commons.

"I don't hold with that," often declared Garron Keith who would have exploited such privileges to the full had *he* been born with them. Nor would Lord Merton have entertained, even to a light family supper, the wife of a self-made rail-wayman had she not been the daughter of his Muse, his Inspiration, his Evangeline, who, the moment she entered his presence, transformed him, by her unfailing magic, into a glorious male creature, as hard-muscled and virile as the common railwayman himself, yet with all the pure authority of noble birth.

Therefore he needed the presence of Evangeline, basking in it, frisking in it, in the opinion of Evangeline's daughter, like a foolish puppy, performing tricks for her applause which were rarely either pretty or comical, and sulking, *very* comically this time, whenever anyone else dared to claim her attention. His wife, for instance, whose nerves required a great deal of Evangeline's sympathetic conversation; his daughter Adela who, although still refusing to live with her husband, seemed consumed by her jealousy of the woman now doing so; his daughter Madcap Dora, still drifting from one romantic attachment to the next and needing Evangeline to explain why none of them was really suitable.

"My one remaining pleasure in life," Oriel had often heard Matthew Stangway tell her mother, "is watching you at work—Evangeline my love. For wages, of course. One merely hopes they will be adequate."

The only other member of the party that night was Quentin Saint-Charles, appearing after supper on a matter of business—something to do with the allowance paid to Adela's husband, it seemed, which Adela was resisting—and then, to Oriel's great relief, joining the ladies in the vast, tapestry-hung chamber which Lady Merton used as a family parlor.

The room itself was always cold, the chairs always too far apart, the conversation—when Lady Merton and Adela were present—always stilted, Dora curling up, her feet on a priceless sofa, and nodding off to sleep while her father, strutting up and down before Evangeline, explained the likelihood of British intervention in the war just starting between Turkey and Russia, now that the Russians had shown their hand by sailing out of Sebastopol right into the Black Sea harbor of Sinope and sinking the Turkish fleet at anchor there. A bad business. Particularly since one had known all along that the Russians were just making excuses about wanting to protect the Christian Holy Places in Jerusalem and Nazareth. Convenient excuses, at that, when one remembered that Jerusalem and Nazareth and the rest of Palestine as well were all in the shaky possession of the Turkish Empire. Poor Turkey. About to fall to pieces and shed its ancient, so very *sizable* empire to the four winds, according to the Tsar of Russia who seemed determined—if it did—to grab a chunk of it for himself. Couldn't be allowed, of course.

"Of course not," murmured Evangeline.

No, by God. Absolutely not. If the Turkish Empire—in the interests of fair play—needed propping up, then England, with some help, it seemed, from this new Napoleon's France, would just have to get along to the Crimea and do it. Not that anybody expected it to take long. Quite a picnic, they had been saying the other day at his club. A fine sight which not a few of his friends were already thinking it a pity to miss. So much so that there was already talk of going out there, to this Crimea wherever it was, with a good pair of field glasses

and a decent hamper of claret and cold game, on purpose to
observe the Russians get their beating.

"How about it, then, my dear, dear Mrs. Stangway? Shall
we organize a little trip of our own out there? How about it—
Dora, Adela—? Why not? A glimpse of decent men in honorable action can only do you both a power of good?" And
so excited, so demanding of attention did he become that no
one, in that huge, chilly apartment, noticed the snow until,
with seasonal, entirely silent rapidity, it had covered the hard
snow already on the ground, drifted to a depth far beyond the
safe performance of any horse-drawn carriage, and effectively
cut off Merton Abbey, by no means for the first time, from
its village.

There was nothing to do but stay the night, unwillingly on
the part of Oriel, and of Quentin who had appointments in
Hepplefield the next morning, but with a great show of fun
and frolic by Evangeline whose task as Muse and Inspiration—despite any personal fatigue—must be to transform
every little inconvenience into a treat, so that when she drove
away tomorrow every one of the Mertons would be saying
"Whatever would we have done without her?" And even
Lady Merton, often capricious and not always pleased to share
her various homes with anyone to whom she was not closely
blood-related, would be eager to invite her to London and to
Monte Carlo again.

*My one remaining pleasure in life is watching you at work—
Evangeline my love. For wages, of course.*

Hard work it seemed to Oriel and, lying in the by no means
luxurious bedroom allocated to her on the third floor of the
house, she hoped, like Matthew Stangway, that the wages
would be adequate. Invitations to London and Monte Carlo,
she supposed, at the very least, where Evangeline might meet
other men richer and more powerful, far more to her taste
than this present bemused and besotted little lordship. This
much she knew her mother to be aiming for, motivated by a
need to escape the fate and the malice of women like Maud,
a need to arrange matters by her own light-handed, cool-
hearted expertise so that when High Grange did become the
property of Francis, or another, she would be in a position
to laugh as she took her leave, driving off in her own carriage
to pleasures of her own choosing, in her own home.

No mean achievement—thought her daughter—for a woman
who had had nothing to begin with but her own wit and charm.

Working for wages. Always that. Taking the chance as it came, whether it happened to be to her taste or not, doing whatever a woman, in this world designed by men, saw the need to do, no matter how little she cared for it, sometimes just to survive among them. Fascinating whoever could be fascinated, for as long as fascination itself could endure; for wages. *One merely hopes they will be adequate.* These words, of Matthew Stangway's, were in her mind when she fell asleep, and then, very quickly it seemed, woke again, chilled to the bone, stiff from the discomfort of a hard mattress and the alarm of finding herself in a strange place. A dark place, too, until her eyes adjusted to the gloom, and a silent one until her ears picked up the sounds she did not afterward ever hope to forget. The sounds which she recognized at once, by some deep instinct, as tragedy.

Once before, when she had dined in this house, one woman had almost burned to death, another scarred by the guilt of it into taking flight. What now? She did not remember lighting her bedside candles, although later, she found them lit, a beam of winter moonlight pouring through her window and through a window at the end of the corridor too, so that when she flung open her door she had no difficulty in seeing the drunken, disheveled figures staggering toward her, an old woman in a crumpled nightdress and a man half her size, in a gaudy dressing-gown who, because she could not stand up alone, was dragging her—painfully dragging her—bumping her and shaking her, with no thought of gentleness or care or of anything else but his own expediency, along the passage. A human, female bundle, causing him evident embarrassment, to be got rid of as quickly as he could.

Her mother.

She was aware neither of the speed with which she traveled toward them nor of the violence hissing through each word she threw at this ridiculous, besotted little man—besotted no longer? "What have you done to her?" A demand he was too breathless, too near the end of his always feeble tether to answer, so that it seemed to her, long afterward, that somehow, by the sheer force of her anguish, she had gathered them up and swept them both along the passage, through the door she had left open, into the dismal little bedroom where she shoved the man away from her as she would have freed herself from a clinging, overheated dog, and laid her mother down on the hard, narrow bed.

Evangeline who had been eternal, and who now . . . Suddenly she was aware of her own body shaking, her own breath laboring to match the scraping agony that was her mother's breath, Evangeline's lips thinly drawn in a snarl not of temper but of raw pain, one hand, which had been young and supple only that evening, taut and ancient now, clamped like a claw over the source of it, within her chest.

"Mother—"

But it was the gasping, gangling little lord, all in a rush, who answered. "She was taken ill . . . in my room, you see. Dreadful—dreadful. Couldn't leave her there. Couldn't have it known—servants and all that—and my wife in the house. You understand?"

Yes. Pausing a moment, in the chill half-dark, somehow to right herself, to find stillness and, through it, the calm she needed, she understood far too well. He had taken her mother into his bed that night, whether as a lover or a kind of doting nursery governess she could not tell, but certainly wanting her there, enjoying her, using her, putting her through her paces, whatever they were—for wages—until, like a bolt of thunder, the teasing, the titillation, the laughter, had become torment for her, shock and then embarrassment for him, the dread of servants' gossip and a wife who would not stand the humiliation, the reminder of neighbors who would snigger behind his back, and of a prim and proper queen who would never allow him—or his wife—in her presence again should his valet draw back his bed curtains, in the morning, to reveal a dying woman.

She understood. As she understood how, in the grip of blind panic, he had dragged that woman *out*, over his threshold, down one corridor and then another, up two short but quite likely fatal flights of stairs, along this final, dingy, third-floor passage to her daughter, in whose scanty, spare-room bed she might be found dead or alive, and no questions.

Yes. With a cold, bitter, utterly still part of her mind, she understood.

"Bring someone to help me," she said. And when he began to mutter about the need for absolute discretion—how servants talk—his wife—how *he* must not in any way be involved—therefore how could *he* go for help without letting it be seen he was "in the know" and thus giving the game away—she leaped to her feet and almost fell upon him, appearing twice his height herself as her mother had always done, and, seizing both his wrists like twigs in her savage hands, shook him to silence before hissing at him again, her mouth very close to his ear this time, her teeth bared—or so he might suppose—as if to bite: "Bring someone to help me. *Now*. And if you're not back in five minutes I'll go out into that passage and scream your house down. I warn you. *Do it*."

A thought struck her, like a lifeline in raging floodwater. "Quentin," she said. "He's in the house. Don't come back yourself. Send him. Five minutes." And, her hands still tight around his wrists, more than ready to break them, she dragged him to the door and pushed him hard in the direction she supposed Quentin to be, somewhere—not far, please God—on this shabby third floor reserved, by Lady Merton, for her lesser guests.

"Be quick about it." With one last hiss, one final shove between his brittle shoulder blades she sent him on his way, leaving the door open for light and for identification before dropping down on her knees again beside her mother, performing such small acts of caring and healing as she could, undoing the cambric frills around Evangeline's neck, propping up her heaving, grieving shoulders on those damnable, thin, insulting pillows, easing her mother's body on the scratchy mattress she would not have inflicted on a kitchenmaid. What wages were these? The very ones, she supposed, that women like Evangeline—and herself—had always dreaded.

"Mother." It was a time for love. Only that. If anything else could follow it, then very well. But love first. For who else did she have of her own in the world? Who else—in her fashion—had always protected, defended, kept both their heads above water, schemed never for one but always for two? Evangeline, a woman adrift in a world where women had never been a favored species. Yet—nevertheless—Evangeline who had been eternal.

"Mother—don't be afraid. I'm here. I won't leave you."

That was Oriel's love which, in Evangeline, emerged as strong, but differently, a hand, older now than even a moment before, groping forward to clutch and compel, a frantic, wheezing whisper rushing out the words that had to be said, *had* to be heard, that she knew her hoarse, failing voice could not repeat. "Oriel—the diamond . . ."

"What . . . ?"

"My ring—*take*. Take it. Yours. Say nothing."

"Mother."

"Here—on my hand. *Oriel.* I have asked him—Matthew—to give you my jewels. But one never knows. Take it. *Now.*"

She took it, slipped it for safekeeping on her own finger, tears pouring now, her own chest torn apart again with her mother's agony as, impelled by the urgently groping claw that was Evangeline's hand, she leaned forward, took her mother in her arms and held her, their wet, cold cheeks pressed together, Evangeline's hoarse, insistent whisper directly in her ear.

"There's a blue velvet bag . . ."

"Yes, Mama." How often—how often—had she murmured that answer?

"*Oriel.* Here—downstairs. In *his* room. Blue velvet. I always have it with me—always . . ."

"Yes, Mama."

"Get it, Oriel. *Take* it. And say nothing . . . Nothing to Matthew. Nothing to your husband either . . ."

"Mother?"

"Blue velvet—remember."

Her breathing now was a torment, the killing effort of speech shrinking her, draining her to an empty shadow within Oriel's embrace.

"Three hundred pounds, Oriel. Enough to live on—for a year at least—whatever happens . . . You see? Time to get something else started. I never let it fall below three hundred. Neither must you. Take it now—keep it. Hide it. *Say nothing to your husband.* Oriel . . ."

But there was no more, her last word—Oriel—spoken on the tip of a knife thrust which turned her to a column of rigid steel and then collapsed her, dispersed her, although Oriel held what remained a moment longer, before laying it gently and with infinite care back among the shabby, lodging-house pillows, smoothing the damp hair, doing up the cambric frills of the nightdress, replacing the Merton diamond on the still hand, before turning to the presence in the doorway of which she had been aware for some moments now. She was uncertain how long.

It was Quentin who stood there, she recognized him, it seemed, not by sight but by some other hidden sense which would have rejected anyone but him.

"I have sent a groom to fetch the doctor," he said.

"Yes." She felt, with a spasm of pure horror, that her body was turning to cold, cumbersome marble. "Thank you, Quentin."

He had also brought a maid to light the bedroom fire, a footman with lamps and candles, smelling salts, fresh water, brandy. Remedies no longer needed by Evangeline for whom the final gift—in this house—could only be a closed door, the decency of solitude. It was what Oriel needed too, although, muffled within her cold, stone casing, she could not, somehow, force her voice to speak.

Take me somewhere to be alone before the stone cracks and I get out of it. I don't want these people—these of all people—to see me grieve.

"Come," he said.

She did not know how he had found a shawl but there it was, warm cashmere wrapping her from ankle to shoulder as she walked, still cold and solid, through corridors she neither saw nor wished to remember, to a room she knew, at any other time, she would have called pleasant, in which a fire was already burning.

"The housekeeper's room," he said. "As the family lawyer I am more of a servant here than a guest. So I know my way around the back stairs."

She felt her mouth move in a smile, her head nod at him, mechanical acts of politeness too deeply rooted to fail even now, through this frozen cage which still held her body. Although the ice would crack, of course, was doing so already in places, fine hairlines appearing which the grief and rage in her would soon force wider.

"Come and stand by the fire, Oriel, and drink a glass of brandy."

She did so, although it did not seem to warm her, her most coherent feeling being gratitude, not for the shawl or the brandy or all the efficient management of death and disposal she knew would follow, but for his silence, because he had not pronounced the obvious phrases of consolation, had not said "You have had a shock. You will get over it. I do not think she felt much pain."

But what did that matter? She was dead when she had wanted to be alive. She was helpless now, defenseless, at *their* mercy instead of they at hers, an empty body on a cheap mattress with only that extravagant diamond solitaire on her finger to show that she had been Evangeline.

Her wages.

"Quentin," she said, the ice having thawed now to a transparent screen through which she wanted, simply, to know that he, alert and silent and accustomed to cold himself, could hear.

"Yes, Oriel?"

"You may have found my mother vain and self-seeking . . ."

"Yes," he said quietly. "I may have done."

It was not, of course, the right answer, not at all the thing he ought to have said, or that anyone else she could think of would have been likely to say to her—only to each other. Yet it was the one answer she could tolerate. The only thing she could possibly bear. The truth.

"You didn't like her, Quentin?" And inwardly she was pleading for that whiplash of truth again, for the honesty which—being so rare—would finally shatter the ice and allow her, as she knew she must, to grieve and rage free.

"No. But what does that matter? Your opinion of *my* mother will not be high. Which does nothing to alter the sense of responsibility I feel for her."

For a whining hysteric like Letty? Letty who dared to be alive when Evangeline was dead? Letty and Maud. And Lady Merton, to whom life seemed nothing but a burden. These miserable, worthless, ugly women, all alive, all strong enough to moan and complain and issue their own petty decrees for their own comfort, while Evangeline lay upstairs on that soiled mattress.

She heard, as if disembodied, the growl, rising louder and louder, in her throat, saw her hands clench into fists and start raining blows first on one another then on the red flock wallpaper of the housekeeper's room, striking hard and haphazard until she could actually feel the pain and, with it, the start of tears, drowning—as he may have known they would—her need for violence.

Had he reminded her of Letty in order to bring this about? She thought so. And now, standing quite still, he allowed her to weep unhindered by any sign of pity, waiting, as a man might wait for a woman to do her hair, until the first storm was over.

There came a discreet knocking on the door, a prudent voice calling, "Mr. Saint-Charles, the doctor is here."

"Thank you, Mrs. Mountjoy." He sounded as cool and noncommittal as if she had merely announced the arrival of the postman with the morning's mail. "Please show him upstairs. I will be there very shortly."

There was a moment of careful silence.

"Oriel, will you stay here now for a while?" Evidently he had judged her strong enough. "There are things to be done, certain people to be informed, which need not concern you. I will send a maid to help you dress."

"Thank you."

"And then, when the road is clear enough, I will take you home."

She thanked him for that too, sat down in the armchair by the fire, the cashmere shawl still around her, her feet on a stool as he directed, and closed her eyes, not on tears but simply to free him from the concern she knew he felt for her, so that he might go and take what care remained of Evangeline.

But then . . . "Oh, Quentin," and her voice was very steady, "one thing I must tell you. My mother is wearing a diamond ring—quite a large one."

"Yes." *His* voice was crisp. "So I noticed."

"Should anyone suggest removing it, would you please ask them not to. It was her wish that it should be buried with her. She told me."

Wages, she thought grimly. *Wages*, of which her daughter would not have her deprived. A pittance, no more, and little enough to give, when one remembered that she had died for it.

Once again Quentin seemed to read her mind.

"Oriel—I must tell you . . ."

"Tell me, then."

"I know exactly what occurred. Just as I know—of course exactly what Lord Merton expects me to do about it."

Briefly, crisply, she nodded.

"I am sure you will do it very well, Quentin."

She did not intend to criticize, simply to acknowledge the way he made a good part of his living, as she had always acknowledged Evangeline's methods, and Garron's, and her own. And there were others, beside the Mertons, to be considered.

"You are going to hush it up."

But, shrugging slightly, he shook his head. "If I can. But this is a large house, you see, full of the kind of people his lordship tends not to notice . . ."

"Servants."

"Yes, indeed. And since his lordship is not popular, one can expect them to talk rather loudly, should they find anything to talk about . . ."

"You mean if any of them happened to be about when Lord Merton was murdering my mother?"

She had spoken the words clearly, each one a separate, sharpheaded icicle aimed not wildly but with skill, and, smiling at her rather gently she thought, he said, "Do you know, I would have expected Kate to say something like that. Although she, of course, would have marched straight into Lady Merton's bedroom and shouted it through the bed-curtains.''

She found it possible to smile, as Evangeline, at every crisis, every disaster, every defeat in her life, had always done. "Yes, Kate would. Whereas I don't suppose I shall say it to anyone but you.''

"I suppose not.''

He bowed, completely impassive, and left her, a maid appearing soon afterward with her clothes and hairbrushes, jugs of hot water and the kind of plain, household soap she—and Evangeline—had never used even in childhood, so that when Quentin returned with her cloak to tell her the road was open as far as Lydwick she was not only dressed but rested, having slept for two full hours in the armchair.

A bad mistake, the waking memory of Evangeline striking her a body blow which, as the pain coursed through her, translated into the plain, inner cry of *Mother, please don't leave me.* For whatever else Evangeline may have done, it had never been that.

"Put on your cloak,'' Quentin said and when she stared at him, for just a moment, quite blankly, her eyes saying *Cloak? What cloak? I want my mother,* he took the garment and wrapped it around her with distant but careful hands.

"Come now. There is no reason for you to stay here. Uncle Matthew has arrived and you may not care to see him just yet. Later this afternoon, I thought.''

But Adela Merton was waiting for her in the hall, a woman who, feeling herself much sinned against, was growing ever more zealous as to the punishment of sinners. Or, if they themselves, for any reason, were not to hand, then at least their offspring upon whom, with the full permission of the Bible, their sins might be transferred.

"Mrs. Keith is just leaving,'' said Quentin, placing himself quietly between them, but Adela, to whom he was only the family solicitor, stridently brushed him aside.

"Indeed—Mrs. Keith *is* leaving. I expect you know, Mrs. Keith, that this sorry business has caused my mother an enormous amount of distress?''

"Indeed?'' said Oriel, speaking, moving, smiling—and very graciously—as Evangeline. "I cannot suppose it has caused *my* mother much pleasure, either.''

And, still as Evangeline, as an act of love, a fitting memorial, she swept across the wide hall and *out*, away, her skirts swaying, her cloak sweeping royally behind her as Evangeline's used to do, her head tilted—for as long as she could endure it—at Evangeline's provocative, quizzical, always elegant angle.

Quentin gave her his arm across the snow and helped her into his carriage, nothing in his face or manner to indicate that he was doing anything other than escorting a lady home after an evening spent, more or less pleasantly, with friends.

"Bravo," he said. "Except, of course, that Evangeline would not have left all her secret rainy-day money behind."

She had forgotten it entirely. Not that it mattered. Not that she wanted a penny. Except that it had been Evangeline's final, anguished effort, her gift of love as she most deeply understood it, to the daughter she had always feared to be not quite hard enough, not ruthless enough; thus obliging her to be hard and ruthless for two.

"No," she said, her voice throbbing with affection. "My mother would not have forgotten her money."

He smiled. "I must confess that neither would I. You may think money easier to give than some other things you value. But for those of us who need it so acutely we could not do without it, then—well, yes, Oriel, I think you ought to receive it gladly."

And raising her hand very briefly to his lips he then placed into it, slowly and carefully, a small but bulging blue velvet bag.

"Banknotes," he said quietly, as if in the habit of making such remarks to her every day of the week. "Lighter than gold, of course, although less reliable. Your mother will have exchanged them, quite regularly I think, for new ones. A sensible precaution. Should you find the least difficulty in doing so I will, of course, be only too glad . . . If, that is, you feel able to trust me?"

Closing her eyes very quickly now, she wondered why he thought it necessary to ask.

Fourteen

The Merton servants were extremely quick to gossip, a certain footman on his clandestine way to visit a certain parlormaid having not only glimpsed his lordship and what he had at first assumed to be his drunken lady-love in the upper passage but had followed them—an easy enough matter on that poorly lit third floor—very nearly to their destination, thus being in a position not only to know in how rough a manner the poor lady had been dragged there but to overhear the shriek with which her daughter had accused Lord Merton of murder.

Those had been Mrs. Keith's exact words, declared the footman with relish, "You have murdered my mother," and although no one in the servants' hall doubted the official verdict of heart failure, it was generally held by all that had his lordship left the poor lady in peace to get on with her attack in his bed then she may—who knew?—have survived it. So they said from the start in the servants' hall. So, by the afternoon of the same day, were they saying in Merton Village, then Dessborough, then Lydwick and High Grange, and the better areas—growing fewer in number—of Hepplefield itself.

Not, of course, that the blame directed at his lordship in any way excused Mrs. Evangeline Stangway's presence in his bed to begin with. By no means. Which rather made it the most wickedly diverting scandal to have struck the Gore Valley for years.

The Merton servants, contrary to their master's expectations, had known from the start, of course, about his relations with Evangeline. So, very likely, thought Oriel, had Lady

Merton and her daughters who, although perfectly happy to ignore it so long as it was never mentioned and Evangeline never forgot her "place" as a social inferior among them, took violent exception to the first whisper of scandal, Lady Merton going off post-haste to lock herself in her Scottish castle the moment the word "murder" was mentioned; her daughter Adela, who thought adultery rather worse than murder since her own husband had started committing it, going herself to join a friend of a religious persuasion in Cheltenham; his lordship himself bolting, perhaps wisely, to Monte Carlo, his panic containing elements of bewilderment and distress which—although he did not openly admit it—had even touched the heart of his astute lawyer, Mr. Quentin Saint-Charles.

Only Dora Merton rode over to Lydwick Green, badly startling Oriel who, seeing her striding across the lawn in riding-boots and habit with a crop in her hand, thought for a terrible moment that she had come to whip her. Madcap Dora, capable of anything, who had almost died by fire rather than admit her fear of it, an excitable young girl no longer but a thin, nervous woman approaching thirty, still unwed, unloved, although she had tried "love" in many and various of its guises; and "jealousy" too, both of Kate and Oriel, but who now held out an abrupt hand which squeezed hard and said, "Look here—I'm sorry. This must be damnably difficult for you. No—no. I won't come in. Just wanted you to know that when all's said and done, one couldn't in all honesty blame you. *I* can't, at any rate."

Although Dora's mother, and her sister Adela, of course, seemed ready to blame anyone who did not bear the name of Merton, having stated clearly before their separate departures that although a certain sympathy was due to their neighbor, Mr. Matthew Stangway, one would do well to bear in mind, where Mrs. Oriel Keith was concerned, that old piece of wisdom which stated, quite clearly *Like mother like daughter.*

An attitude which, even in the few days before the funeral, had spread to Lydwick, a town of strict manners which was owned, in the main, by Lord Merton's cousin, thus causing considerable anxiety to Morag and Elspeth, young ladies now every bit as polished and proper as their father had intended, who thought it a black injustice that their reputations, and consequently their "chances" should suffer for the follies of the mother of their father's second wife. They had not even liked Evangeline, and with fair reason since she had never treated them with anything warmer than indifference and had known far too well, in their early, uncertain days, how to make them feel awkward and overdressed, how to raise pained eyebrows at what she had called the "regional quality" of their speech, and wrinkle her nose as if still detecting the odor of Scottish herring upon them.

And although they showed more sympathy for Oriel, to start with, than she had expected—having once lost a mother of their own—it dried up, rather, when their invitations around Lydwick began to be canceled and it transpired that even their friends the Landons from Watermillock by Ullswater, had heard of Evangeline's scandalous end from certain local grandees who were acquainted with the Mertons.

"We shall never be able to show our faces there again," wailed Elspeth who, these three years past, had been falling in love with the eldest Landon boy for a week or two every summer, gaining nothing in the way of consolation from Oriel but a sharply spoken "If your face is worth looking at there's no need to hide it": which sounded, to both Elspeth and Morag, like something Evangeline herself might have said.

Nor would Oriel make any kind of public denial of her supposed accusation of Lord Merton, an easy enough matter, since her word would naturally carry more weight than that of a night-prowling footman, her silence encouraging the rumors which, as Letty and Maud and Susannah pointed out to her, it was her duty—for Matthew's sake—to stifle.

"I have no debts to pay to anyone," she said coldly, knowing full well that Matthew Stangway's difficult position had brought nothing but satisfaction to his sister Maud who, the moment she heard of it, had packed up and left the vicarage, installing herself with some personal triumph in her own, old room at High Grange, letting it be known to one and all that she was needed, once again, to look after Matthew. As he had always needed her, of course; except that this time there would be no unwanted child to worry him, as Kate had done, no predatory, scheming mistress—like Evangeline—hovering on the fringes, waiting her chance to break in. Only Matthew and herself, or so it would be, as soon as the short "lying-in-state" should be over.

Not long.

For Matthew's sake the funeral would certainly be well-attended, the opportunity taken by all decent-minded men

and women to close ranks around the bereaved husband—as
Maud was not slow to point out—although the dead woman's
daughter, having first talked too wildly and then gone into a
sulk and refused to talk at all, had not yet had the grace to
visit her mother's coffin, now on display, just as it ought to
be—in spite of everything—in the South parlor at High
Grange.

Maud herself had seen to the funeral arrangements, the
flowers and candles, the black armbands for the servants,
black borders on Matthew's notepaper, even though—of
course—no one really supposed him to be precisely heart-
broken. Such was not her brother Matthew's way in any case,
and one could hardly be accused of telling secrets if one said
that this second marriage of his, a mistake to begin with, had
grown steadily worse. The truth was—and Maud Stangway
had never been shy of the truth—he would be better off without her. A fact of which he was himself quite sufficiently
aware, needing little more to set him right again than what
Maud firmly called a "return to normality"; the house looking as it used to look, running as it used to run; everything
back again in its old good order. Including all the glass and
china and the good lacquer furniture his late wife had smug-
gled out and hidden in the house she'd made him buy for her
in Lydwick Park. Maud had already made her arrangements
to deal with that.

And although Letty, of course, would miss her at the vicarage, everyone was called on from time to time to make
some little sacrifice or other, and it was Matthew now who
must be considered. Letty understood that. Everybody understood it. Except Evangeline's daughter, need it be said,
who—with her mother still lying in the South parlor between
Maud's flowers and candles—had announced, very curtly, that
the question of who was to help Letty at the vicarage was of
no concern—and no interest either, by the sound of it—to
her.

Oriel saw Matthew Stangway only once before the funeral,
in her own home where Quentin, at her request, had accompanied him on a mission merely of good manners, it seemed
to her, rather than any of the things which a bereaved and so
scandalously betrayed husband might have felt the need to
express.

She gave him tea. He drank it, answering each one of her
polite formulas with another to match, saying what anyone

who might have been eavesdropping would have expected to hear. She knew perfectly well that he was her father. So, she supposed, did Quentin. But it was far too late for that.

"I presume," he said on leaving, "that you will wish to *attend*—is that the word?—your mother before the funeral. To sit with her, as Maud is doing?"

"No, thank you. I would rather not."

"As you wish—naturally. There will be some small, legal matters, of course, which you might prefer Quentin to explain to you."

Thinking of the blue velvet bag, she smiled.

"Yes. I am sure that would be best."

"Very well. Is there anything I can do for you?"

"No, thank you."

He went away.

"Is there anything *I* can do?" asked Quentin.

"I don't think so."

"Are you telling me to go away and leave you to suffer in peace?"

She smiled at him, rather palely. "I am really quite all right, Quentin, you know."

"Are you? You look very much to me like a woman at bay. A lovely lady fox—yes?—with the hounds not far off."

She smiled again. "Well—yes. Perhaps. But there is nothing very new to me, you know, Quentin, in that."

Yet, for the whole of her remembered life, she had courted the favor of those "hounds" with all the care and delicacy of one who does not think herself quite worthy, earning her place among them often very tediously, in strict obedience to the rules these "respectable people" had made to suit themselves, putting their interests always before her own, since they had the rights of birth and wedlock, the whole weight of traditional morality on their side, and she did not. As a child she had felt the need to be better behaved than other children—who had mothers *and* fathers—in order to be considered half as good. As she grew older she had modeled herself, with great determination, on Society's view of a perfect woman, a perfect wife, a perfect mother, choosing perfection because it did not seem to her that she, with her far from perfect background, could afford anything less.

Yet now, when the dreaded blow had fallen, when she, who had so feared scandal found herself at its very center, she could not manage—and she *had* tried—to care so much as a fig for it.

Only for Evangeline.

Yes. Behind her cool eyes, her cool voice making the polite remarks she had always made to those she called her friends, giving the polite instructions—never commands—she had always given to her servants, she could hear distinctly a new voice quite ready to admit, if only to herself, the many things Evangeline had been. Many things to which ugly names could easily be given, especially by those to whom security seemed as natural as drawing breath. But there had been no security, at any time in her life, for Evangeline. None whatsoever. And it seemed now, to Oriel, that her mother had shown the same skill and shrewdness, the same hard-headed, hard-working, gritty determination merely to keep a roof over her head as Garron had employed in the pursuit of his vast rewards and powers. The same personal risk, day in day out, as he took, in order to gain for herself no more than the privileges which other women were able to take for granted. A home of her own and no problems about paying the bills. A "place" in society for herself and one for her daughter who had been spared the life of mistress, kept woman, whore, only because her mother had been all these things for her.

A whore? Very well, if it made the Mertons feel better to say so. A mistress? Certainly. But since lovers came in pairs this new voice in Oriel saw no reason why her mother should take all the blame for that. A kept woman? Very obviously, since how—this new, sharp voice inquired?—could any woman of these so-called upper classes possibly keep herself unless, failing the requisite supply of male relations willing to keep her, she chose to settle for the genteel drudgery of a governess or a paid companion? A wife? Never entirely, having lived far too long, before her marriage, in a world where men were not only the prey but the enemy. Nevertheless—always a mother.

She went several times before the funeral to stand outside the house in Lydwick Park—all locked and shuttered now—which Evangeline had worked so hard to make Matthew buy, knowing full well that should anyone see her there it would be rumored, and probably reported to Maud, that she had been assessing the property with a view to somehow getting it for herself. An intention she knew Maud would believe since there had already been some talk, between her and

Letty, of what an excellent home it would make for the ever-growing family of Letty's daughter, Maud's favorite niece, Constantia.

Oriel had no idea what Matthew intended to do with her mother's house, and did not care. If it came to her, then Garron, she supposed, would either sell it or keep it—as seemed best for *him*—as a possible wedding-present for Elspeth who, at almost sixteen, had marriage very much in mind. It was not the house itself which drew her and kept her standing there in the sharp, January wind, but her mother's light, by no means extinguished voice reminding her of vigorous scheming, vigorous living, vigorous satisfaction, not only in the house itself, but in every item of purloined furniture it contained.

"Look, Oriel my darling, I have got this wondrous pair of vases—Sèvres don't you see, and quite, quite valuable. Yes, I know they have been in the South parlor at High Grange for a generation or two, but never mind that. They were broken, my dear, quite shattered—such a dreadful accident—when the mirror above the mantelshelf became unhinged and fell on top of them. I picked up the pieces myself—so as not to upset the parlormaid—and buried them deep in the dustbin. In secret, of course. How's that? Maud does not believe me, needless to say. Nor Letty, who says her late mother once promised them to her. And she was not terribly pleased when I said that if she'd ever managed to get them to the vicarage they'd have been smashed to smithereens long ago. Well—here they are now, my love. All mine. I'm just on my way to pop them in my private Lydwick Park treasure chest."

The light voice echoed in Oriel's head each time she entered the empty garden and stood by the locked door. Who had the key? Matthew, she supposed. Or Maud, who would be here, soon enough, to pack up the Sèvres vases, the Chinese cloisonné, the Crown Derby, and take it all back to High Grange, congratulating herself, no doubt, on having turned out to be more eternal than Evangeline.

Who would have thought it? Certainly not Evangeline herself who had handled Maud and all the other Stangways with such expert calculation, and—as it had turned out—to no avail. They were all back now in their rightful places, like the Sèvres vases, pretending that Evangeline had never moved them an inch. But it seemed to Oriel, on those bleak pilgrimages, that for her no "rightful place" existed. Without

Evangeline she was, quite simply, alone, with nothing to truly call her own but a few hundred pounds in a blue velvet bag and a terrifying compassion, a burning fury at the waste of the woman who had given them to her.

Only to each other had they ever really belonged. And it was with her eyes on the barred door of the house her mother would never live in, that Oriel came to terms with her personal solitude. For who else, with any respect for reality, could she now call her own? Not Garron, whose need to possess his woman was certainly not followed by any corresponding need to be possessed. Not Elspeth and Morag for whom she had done no more, she knew, than carry out their father's instructions to polish and perfect them and who remained strictly his daughters, never hers. Not the boy Jamie with whom her relationship was easier but whose gaze was fixed firmly now—and quite properly—on the wide, exciting world outside his home. Only Kate, for a while, had aroused that special closeness, that sense—through thick and thin—of belonging; the affection which did not depend on her good behavior, or Kate's, as it had never depended on Evangeline's, but was simply *there*.

No longer. And it was the emptiness, the sense of alienation from this world her mother—and Kate—no longer inhabited, which troubled her the most.

Garron would not be home for the funeral. In fact—very much as usual—she did not even know where Garron was, other than that it was somewhere in the Balkans. Slovakia? Herzegovina? Croatia? Rumania? Any, or each of them in turn. *"En route"* was the expression used by his various agents and offices who had all made cheerful attempts to contact him while warning her, just as cheerfully, that even if their messages arrived on the right day at the right hotel, he could hardly cover such distances and be back in England on time. Not for a funeral, at any rate, which rather fell into the category of things not to be delayed.

She did not think he would even try. Indeed, she was fairly certain that his agents knew exactly where to send their messages, allowing him the freedom to choose whether or not to receive them. And why, she reasoned quite calmly, would he feel inclined to put himself out for Evangeline who had never even pretended to like him? No, he would stay in Budapest or wherever he happened to be, returning home when he had done as much or more—never less—than he had intended, his baggage full of any luxuries for which Budapest, or any of its neighbors, might be famous, his concern for Evangeline extending no further than a walk to the office of Quentin Saint-Charles to find out if any of her property had escaped her husband's jurisdiction and, if so, to make sure his wife got her share of it.

Yet, on the morning of the funeral, she would have been glad of his presence, his tendency to dismiss the Stangways as feeble and irrelevant now that his riches outweighed theirs. He served to reduce them to far more manageable proportions in her eyes, his broad and, in Stangway opinion, overdressed figure beside her acting as a sure barrier against Letty, who was frankly alarmed by him, and even against Maud who, despite her assertions that one could always smell whiskey on his breath, rarely came close enough to sample the odor herself.

But, predictably, he had not chosen to be found and, not wishing to inflict her private tragedy on Morag, who offered to accompany her, or on Elspeth who did not, she set out alone through a cold wind which seemed entirely appropriate. She looked very cold and self-contained herself, her mourning-veil drawn back over her hat—as Evangeline would have worn it—so that everyone could see her dry eyes, her faint, somewhat superior smile of greeting as she walked into High Grange's South parlor where, to the consternation of all present, she declined, most politely, to look at her mother.

Everyone else had done so, Maud positioning herself by the coffin where, at each new arrival, she removed a heart-shaped piece of white satin from Evangeline's face, allowing the newcomer to peep and murmur whatever seemed right to them—"How peaceful. Oh dear—how sad. What a pretty coffin—such a rich lining . . ."—before she neatly replaced it again.

Letty had already gazed at the dead features several times, feeling it her duty, for Matthew's sake, to set an example, followed—also for Matthew's sake—by a halting procession of ancient spinster great-aunts and second cousins always brought out of hibernation, it seemed, on such occasions. While the Saint-Charles' children had been lined up and obliged, even forced in one or two cases, to do the same. "One must try to forgive, you see—always—anything," said Letty, once again in the hope of consoling dear Matthew, although she shot a vicious glance, nevertheless, at her son

Quentin who happened to enter the room just then, his appearance reminding her that he had failed to visit her, as promised, the previous Sunday.

He too glanced down into the coffin and then, before Maud had had time to complete her trick with the white satin cover, walked away with an air of one who has "arrangements" in hand.

"The flowers," murmured Letty, on a note of agony. "Such a profusion which—under the circumstances . . . So kind."

"You will want to look at them, Oriel—and read the cards," said Maud, wishing it to be known by one and all, even by Oriel, that the sympathy these cards and other tributes contained was addressed exclusively to Matthew, regretting the humiliation he had suffered—since what else could it be but that?—on the death of his wife.

"No thank you. I would rather not," said Oriel, very politely, moving into a corner of the room where Francis Ashington quickly joined her, cutting her off most adroitly, she noticed, from the rest.

Francis had been kind to her. She saw that he wished to be kind now and found herself wondering how best to give him the opportunity. Already he had ridden over to Lydwick and spent time with her, a commodity of which she understood the value, talking of very little, never once of Evangeline but simply being there, his presence in her home which he had never before visited, not only giving her comfort but making a declaration that he, a cousin of Lord Merton and a relative, to some extent, of every sizable landowner in the Gore Valley, had no intention of withdrawing his acquaintance from Mrs. Oriel Keith. He had even met her, one day, in Lydwick High Street, probably not at all by chance, and, dismounting from his very noticeable black mare, had engaged her in a lengthy conversation of which Lydwick's elite had been acutely aware.

Several people had sent cards of sympathy after that, improving her status at least with Elspeth, and now he was beside her once again, in this hostile South parlor which would, one day, belong to him, guarding her—she thought with a smile—from her mother's enemies who might well transfer to her, at any moment, the pent-up grudges they had been nourishing for years against Evangeline.

The gallant Squire of Dessborough, his sword at her ser-

vice, letting it be known that in his view Mrs. Oriel Keith
was in no way responsible for her mother's sins. His defense
of her causing him some embarrassment, she quickly realized, from several of these old Stangway ladies—Letty among
them—who thought him heroic to have come to the funeral
at all when Evangeline's betrayal of Matthew could only remind him of all that Kate had done—appeared still to be
doing, alas—to him.

"Thank you, Francis," she said, knowing how easily, almost how naturally, she could have added "my dear friend."

Men in black frock coats and tall hats swathed in black
crêpe came in to close the coffin and remove it, piling the
polished mahogany lid with a display of floral tributes more
magnificent than several of the spinster great-aunts believed
they had ever seen.

"How kind," murmured Letty, signaling to her daughters,
by taking out her own handkerchief, that it was time for tears.
"How truly generous everyone has been. There is even a
posy from Dora Merton. One hardly knows *what* to say."

"Perhaps nothing would be best?" suggested the voice of
Evangeline, speaking crisply through Oriel.

The coffin was carried through the door and in the direction of the waiting carriages, the church of High Grange parish being a tidy step away. And, realizing she must go with
it, Oriel was suddenly aware of Matthew Stangway standing
before her, looking no more remote and weary than usual:
although that, of course, was very remote indeed.

"I think you will have to take my arm," he said, and,
surprised that he could sense her reluctance to do so, she
nodded, put her hand on his immaculate sleeve, and went
with him to the leading carriage where Maud and Letty joined
them, taking their places as the "nearest and dearest" of the
deceased.

The last time Oriel had entered High Grange church with
Matthew Stangway had been on her wedding morning. The
time before that it had been as a bridesmaid to Kate. The
time before—the first time—had been his marriage to Evangeline. And now, as on those other occasions, the church was
full, the Stangway tenants and employees crowding on the
hard wooden benches at the back, the Stangway "friends and
neighbors" taking up the upholstered pews at the front in
numbers upon which both Maud and Letty remarked in grat-

ifying whispers as they kicked their prayer cushions into place
and arranged their skirts.

Oriel did not exchange a word nor even a glance with anyone, remembering nothing of the service which, delivered in
Rupert Saint-Charles' weak, nasal voice was perhaps meant
to be assumed rather than heard, her senses tuned to the very
lowest key she could manage so that neither the fussy weeping of Letty nor the elegant, empty presence of Matthew
Stangway—closer than she would normally have found easy—
meant anything to her.

But once outside in the cold churchyard, standing at the
very edge of the newly dug grave, the crowd of "friends and
neighbors" behind her became oppressive, their very pity for
Matthew excluding her, consigning her to the ranks of his
enemies, as she had seen clearly enough in the way they had
all shaken his hand just now at the church door—not hers—
inviting him to dinner the very moment he could manage it,
reminding him that he was, after all, "one of them," as,
most regrettably, his wife and—by the small, embarrassed
smiles they kept on giving him—his wife's daughter too, had
never been.

"How kind," he had said, several dozen times over, without paying anything that could be called attention to anyone.
"How kind," he said again as, the ceremony completed, he
led Oriel, closely followed by Maud and Letty, back to his
carriage, wishing, she supposed, to reach High Grange before the congregation, who were all coming back to drink tea
or Madeira and to remind Matthew, all over again, that he
was not alone, having good friends in plenty, a loving sister
in Letty whose children would surely be a consolation for the
sorry end of his own, and, above all, a sister like Maud to
look after him.

"I shall do my best," Oriel had heard Maud say at least
twenty times that morning, lowering her voice whenever she
noticed Oriel, to whisper, "I don't expect it to be easy, after
all he has had to put up with. Heavens—if you knew the
half."

They would all know far more than that by the end of the
afternoon, thought Oriel, shivering as she reached the carriage, dreading the hour—could she escape in less?—which
she must now spend at High Grange, enduring veiled hints
and glances or close scrutiny from those who hoped, by taking her unawares, to find out some detail, some snippet, of

Evangeline's immoral, yet—for all that—certainly entertaining past. An ordeal she would have to face alone, by the look of it, Francis being nowhere in sight and Quentin, when she finally caught a glimpse of him, engaged in what looked like a private conversation, very much on the fringes of the crowd, with a woman in a heavy mourning-veil.

She did not know who the woman was, nor, as she allowed Matthew to help her into the carriage, did she think it of any importance, an opinion not shared by Letty who, with her foot on the carriage-step, suddenly snapped, "Who's that? Over there with Quentin? Maud—who is it?"

Maud, who had rather washed her hands of Quentin, snapped just as crossly that through so much black veiling she could hardly be expected to tell.

It did not suffice for Letty. "Who? Is it his housekeeper? Would he bring that woman here today?"

"Hardly," said Maud.

"Letty," said Matthew, "do get in the carriage."

"So who is it then? Who is he carrying on with now? Some married woman, I expect. And not for the first time."

"Letty." Matthew did not sound patient. "Get in." She did, leaning out of the carriage as far as she could to give herself a platform and calling out, half appeal, half command, "Quentin," to which he merely replied with a nod of his lean head as she drove by, before turning back to his companion.

"There. Did you see the way he snubbed me? Have I deserved that? His own mother."

And she proceeded to enliven the drive to High Grange with an account of the dissipated life her son lived in Hepplefield, to which Maud did not listen, and which Matthew eventually cut short by a terse "Letty—I do believe I have heard enough."

No one spoke to Oriel. Walking once again into the South parlor she sat down, arranging her black silk skirts in the elegant lines Evangeline would have liked to see, removing her veil and then, as the room began to fill with those Stangway "friends and neighbors" to whom any sympathy shown to her would be an act of disloyalty to Matthew, waited until she could take her leave without appearing to run away. She did not expect to come here again and therefore wished to make her final departure with dignity, proving—when the moment came—to one and all that she was going not because their coldness or any feeling of shame on her part had chased her out, but because she was ready. Yet when Quentin approached her in his professional, family-lawyer manner and asked her, loudly enough to be overheard, if she would mind stepping into the book-room for a moment, she was glad to get up and follow him, walking straight-backed and graceful, through a cloud of speculation as to his motives. Money, of course. What else, where Mr. Saint-Charles was concerned. Money, or rather, in this case, the lack of it, none of the "friends and neighbors" expecting, for a moment, that she would be allowed very much, no matter what her mother's will—if she had made one—might have to say.

But at the book-room door he merely said, "There is someone to see you, Oriel," and giving her a little push across the threshold, disappeared, leaving her alone with the woman in the heavy mourning-veil—with whom, to his mother's chagrin, he had been caught in that churchyard conversation—the veil removed now to reveal a dark but not funereal traveling coat, a thin, elegant body suggesting the woman of fashion, a faintly Oriental head of black hair pulled back into a chignon that was startlingly severe yet just as startlingly effective, a face of high cheekbones, a nose imperious rather than heavy, slanting eyes very slightly crinkled at their corners, a long, quizzical mouth, its colors discreetly enhanced by paint as the sallow skin had been turned to amber by a bloom of powder. A woman of brittle but undoubted sophistication, several years too old to be Kate but who—nevertheless . . .

"Kate?" Five years of silence, of total absence, brought a question to Oriel's voice, but not to her arms as they reached out, nor to the rest of her body as Kate stepped forward and hugged her, bringing a musky, intentionally voluptuous scent of tropical flowers with her.

"Yes, it's me. Don't collapse with the shock." Even the voice was different, its tone much lower, its accent polished yet quite neutral like those who, belonging anywhere and everywhere, do not wish to be identified.

"How . . . ?" Oriel was still too overcome to put her own words together.

"Oh—Quentin got in touch with me . . ."

"You never answered my letters."

"Well, no. But this time Quentin said you needed me. Or,

at least, if not me and me alone, then somebody you'd be able to feel entirely on your side. I could see I filled the bill.''

Obvious questions, *little* questions, which had nothing to do with all she was really feeling, began to pour now from Oriel's tongue.

''And so you came all this way . . .''

''I did. You once sneaked into Hepplefield for me, didn't you, and spent every penny you had on that red sash and those firefly pins—do you remember? I still have them. I even wear the pins sometimes. And when people start oohing and aahing about the style, the originality, the *je ne sais quoi* of our clever little Kate, I tell them about Oriel, who first showed me the way.''

''Kate.'' She didn't want to think too much about that. ''Hepplefield is nearer than France . . .''

''But it's not how far you travel, my love, it's what you do when you get there. So don't thank me. Don't dare. Just take me for granted, as I probably used to take you.''

There were smiles at that, a flash of studied brilliance from Kate, a brave attempt from Oriel.

''Kate—how *are* you?''

''Very well. We'll come to that later.''

''When did you arrive?''

''Not a moment too soon. Quentin did all his clever things, of course, with tickets and timetables, but for all your husband's trains, there's still that awkward stretch of water to get over. Why doesn't your husband dig a tunnel under *that*? They'd make him a lord and give him a million. Quentin was quite peeved with me for arriving too late for the service. He was taking me to task for it when Aunt Letty spotted us—poor soul—and got rather the wrong impression. Not that she'll be better pleased when she finds out it wasn't one of his lady-loves, but me . . .''

As Maud would not be pleased. And others.

''Kate, who knows you're here?''

Kate smiled, by no means wildly, understanding the implications, it seemed, with great accuracy.

''My father knows. Quentin thought it best to get his permission for me to enter his house. And since no one has tried to throw me out I assume he got it. I also assume my father recognized me in the churchyard, even under these veils Quentin provided, although he hasn't been near me yet. And Francis knows. Quentin said it wasn't right to give him a shock. He said I'd done enough of that already. So he went over to Dessborough, even before he telephoned to me, and Francis said yes—absolutely—whatever Oriel needs she must have—and he'd even come to the funeral just the same and risk bumping into me so he could look after you himself in case my train broke down, or my ship sank . . . That was noble of him, I rather thought.''

"Yes. He is noble."

"And thoughtful of Quentin. He was *furious* with me for being late, although he must have known I couldn't help it. So there are those of us who do care for you, Oriel, some of us maybe even more than we should."

She paused, giving Oriel time to take in the warmth of that caring, the depth of anxiety felt on her account, the trouble gladly taken, and then, with a smile, went on, "Quentin said you felt alone and *at bay*. I know that feeling. Maybe Quentin knows it too. Even Francis. In fact—yes, I have to admit he must. And now that I see you I know why they were both so worried. You look like spun glass, Oriel, ready to shatter the moment those bitches in there screech one sour note too many."

But calm returned to Oriel now like the return of breath, and with it the clear knowledge of all that had been done for her. They had combined together—her friends, her sister—to show her that even if she remained "at bay" forever there would be somebody beside her, two backs, or three, or more, pressed up *together* against Society's wall. And she would not insult them now by any aloofness, any holding back, any mouthing of the trivial formulas Society claimed to be good manners. She would speak the truth now—to her friends, at any rate.

"These mothers," said Kate. "I have finally laid mine to rest. Can you?"

"Can they?" said Oriel, gesturing in the direction of the South parlor. "Although all they are saying about my mother, in there, is fairly accurate. She will have done everything they are thinking and then—on top of it—rather more than I expect they can imagine."

"I can imagine those things, Oriel."

"Yes. So can I." She felt her teeth to be chattering slightly. "And if I've been spared the need to do them myself it's only because she did them first, and well enough, to feed me and clothe me and raise me to be a marriageable commodity. I don't even know where I was born, Kate. Somewhere secret and uncomfortable, I expect, with no guarantees made to my mother about anything, and more than a faint possibility of her being abandoned—just left to get on with it as best she could. And then blamed because her 'best' was good enough, as it turned out, not only to survive but to do it in luxury. They'd have thought better of her, I suppose, those 'friends and neighbors' in there, if she'd left me on the doorstep of an institution in a basket and gone off to drown herself for shame.''

Kate smiled. "You know they would."

"Yes, I know. And I've been kow-towing to them all my life, courting their good opinion, walking on egg-shells everywhere I went . . .''

"For your mother's sake," said Kate.

"Yes, of course," said Oriel, without asking her how she could possibly know. "To protect her. To cover her tracks. To put myself in a position where I could look after her, if things went wrong again—as we always knew they might. Always. She never lost the dread—although she wouldn't have called it that. She just pretended to ignore it, and let it weaken her heart . . .''

What a relief it was to speak, to disperse in blessed words some of the brooding pain, the bitter resentment which had so nearly choked her.

"Which is why," said Kate, "she went after the Mertons, I suppose. Another and rather golden iron in the fire, just in case . . . ?''

"Of course. So she could spend her widowhood in London and Monte Carlo instead of here, with Letty and Maud."

Kate's new, brilliant smile flashed out again. "An understandable ambition. How much do you hate Lord Merton?"

"Do I hate him? He only did what my mother would have expected him to do. Put himself first. As she would have done herself, except that she wouldn't have panicked. She may even have asked him to drag her up those stairs to my room, to make it look right . . .''

"For his sake, you mean? To spare him embarrassment?"

"No, of course not. For her own sake. And mine. Even if she thought she was dying, she'd have done her level best to beat it, you see. So she couldn't take the risk of being found *half*-dead and likely to get better, in his bed—could she?—

which would have meant the end even of High Grange, let alone Monte Carlo. That's how she would have seen it.''

And pausing a moment as if for breath, she looked directly at Kate and slowly, carefully pronouncing every word, made full confession of her true burden. ''If that had happened— you see—then her husband would have felt obliged to disown her. My husband may have ordered me to do the same, and if I'd disobeyed him he might well have disowned me. Like mother like daughter, they say, and most men seem to believe it. So how would she, at her age, and me at mine, have lived then? Very poorly, unless I'd set about supporting her in the way she used to support me.''

''As you would have done, wouldn't you?''

''When it came to it—yes. Of course I would.''

''And she wouldn't have wanted that?''

''No. She wouldn't.''

''So you feel *you* helped to kill her?''

''I do. I feel she chose to die in a cheap maid's room to save me from scandal. I feel one of her reasons for being in bed with that poor little fool at all was to provide insurance for me—to equip herself to look after me if the man she'd never wanted me to marry suddenly lost all his money. That's what I feel. I wish I could feel something else.''

''Oh—well—let's see. Could you try feeling mildly pleased—do you think?—to see your sister.''

Through the stale air of the book-room, the odors of old tobacco and old leather, the word ''sister'' hung almost visibly between them, a small but shiny thing flecked hopefully with sunlight, until the sound of the door opening sent it scurrying away into hiding once again.

''I am intruding, of course,'' said Matthew Stangway, their father, his manner as elaborately courteous, his face as distant and faintly disdainful as they had always known it, his familiar, beautifully polished barriers raised most securely, it seemed, against these intrusions of female tragedy.

''Hello, Father,'' said Kate, a well-groomed, sophisticated woman of the wider world, who could easily have passed for thirty.

''Ah, Kate,'' he said, his voice, like hers, sounding as if they met every day. ''I trust you had a pleasant journey?''

''Delightful.''

''I am so glad. And so sorry to interrupt you now, in case your time should be limited. As mine seems to be. Which makes me think it wise, Oriel, to give you this now—before other matters arise . . . Your mother's jewelry. She was— most insistent—that you should have it.''

The box he put into Oriel's hands was large and ornate and very familiar, her mother's treasure chest to which other men, besides Matthew Stangway, had contributed, although he, having known her by far the longest, had given the most. Costly, fashionable pieces chosen by Evangeline for their re-sale value—just in case—Oriel remembering vividly and acutely now, her mother's triumph at the acquisition of every one.

''This ruby brooch would pay rent on a comfortable little apartment for six months, should anyone need to do so, Oriel. Just as these pretty, pretty pearls would treat us to a summer in Italy or the South of France—if it ever happens, that is, that no one rushes to invite us. And these gold bracelets— well, my darling, people *listen* to gold. Do remember.''

They were all here now, she supposed, a small fortune acquired with skills and energies which had had nothing small about them. Her mother's prizes which she knew Garron would forbid her to wear, wishing to see her only in the ''prizes'' she had herself won from him.

''These are not family jewels, Kate, as I'm sure you un-derstand,'' explained Matthew Stangway to his legitimate daughter. ''The Stangway pieces have been removed and placed in Quentin's care. These are personal effects which Oriel should have.''

He appeared, rather oddly, to be requesting her agreement. ''Of course,'' she said.

''Then perhaps, Oriel, if you would check over the contents it would avoid any possible misunderstanding— later . . . ?''

She nodded, and finding it easier to obey than to inquire his actual motives, she raised the lid, looking without really seeing until something struck out at her quite violently, caus-ing her to blink and look again and then to stare at the mag-nificent diamond solitaire her mother had thrust upon her in the moment of dying and which she had returned a moment after. Evangeline's wages; which she had wanted acutely and absolutely to put into the grave with her.

Blanched with shock, she flung out a rigid arm, pointing at the ring with horrified accusation. ''*That*. What is that?''

''My dear.'' Matthew Stangway sounded not in the least

disturbed about it. "It is a rather large diamond, given to your mother by Lord Merton. If *I* know that then so, I imagine, must you."

Nor did he show any other sign of agitation when she let the lid of the box fall shut and wheeled around upon him, in a white fury so ungovernable that she was alarmed by it herself.

"I particularly asked that this ring be buried with her. I told Quentin . . ."

"Ah yes." He smiled, rather as he might at a restive horse which it was the groom's business, surely, not his, to soothe. "Quentin did mention it. Several times, I seem to remember. But there were those who did not think it right to dispose, in that way, of so valuable a jewel. Whereas I—my dear—could not bring myself to believe that your mother would have wished it, in spite of everything Quentin said. Come on, Oriel—she did not wish it, did she?"

Fury ebbed out of her to be replaced by something far more complex. "No. She didn't wish it. I did."

"May I know why?"

"My reasons would not please you."

"Do you know me well enough, Oriel, to judge?"

She gave him a level stare. "No. Does anybody know you?"

"Your mother did."

She had nothing to say to that, although he waited a moment with his empty courtesy, before he went on, "And I knew her, of course—dare I suggest it?—even better than you did."

"You may have done, I expect."

Very slightly, a faint smile on his lips, he bowed to her. "Thank you, Oriel. I knew her better and for much longer, my dear. Ten years, or very nearly, before you were born. So I am quite certain she would never have asked you to put the Merton diamond in her coffin. My dear child, if she had, then you would have done it yourself, I think. Or tried to. But no, the diamond was meant for you along with all these other costly odds and ends which have the great virtue—as your mother must have told you—of being *small*. Portable, my dear, and easily concealed about the person so that should you ever feel the need, for instance, to run away from your husband, you would have a very fair chance of taking these with you. Which brings me to their other virtues. They are at once easily salable and easily hidden away. Thus making it far more difficult for your husband to claim them back, as he would be entitled to do, than household furnishings or a piece of land. Your mother—my wife—would think of that. Would she not?''

"Yes." There was no shame in admitting what had been the essence of Evangeline. "She would. She did.''

He smiled suddenly and broadly, which, since she was not accustomed to it, took her somewhat aback. "Thank you, Oriel.''

"I beg your pardon?'' And what startled her was that he had sounded genuinely grateful.

He smiled again. "Should it surprise you that I hoped she had remained—true to form, shall we say—up to the end? I understood her. It would have—disappointed me, rather—had I been proved wrong.''

"And you knew—how she was living?''

For a moment which seemed very long to her, a moment in which she was aware both of Kate's keen scrutiny and her careful silence—leaving this conflict, whatever it really was, to them—he did not answer. It even began to seem that he would not answer at all, but then, as if deciding that some kind of reply was due, he sighed. "Did I know about Merton? Yes, I fear so. Had she trusted me he would not have been necessary. But she was not a trusting woman. Whereas I—I do confess—gave her no reason to be so. There was a game we played—a contest, of sorts. It had gone on for years. She believed I had grown tired of it—given in. My lack of enthusiasm threatened her. I feel unable to tell you more than that. Except, perhaps, to express regret that I have found myself unable to help you during these difficult days. Not that I have tried, of course, since it would only have been a wasted effort. Perhaps you know that. But had the capacity existed I would have employed it gladly on your behalf. You are a beautiful woman and, I rather imagine, naturally virtuous. But we have never known each other. When you were a child it seemed unwise. Later there seemed no need for it. And sentimentality must surely be out of place now. Nevertheless, if there is something you would like done, or something you would like to have, and you think it within my power, please tell me—so that I can put the wheels in motion.''

"Nothing, thank you.'' In her amazement she could say

no more, by no means enough, she thought, although, nodding briefly, as if *that*, at least was settled, he turned to Kate.

"May I know how long you intend to stay?"

An expression of quiet amusement coming over her face, she met his eyes. "Not here, Father. There's no need for Aunt Maud to fret about that. I shall take a room in Hepplefield. Quentin will see to it."

"I dare say he will. But you mistake my meaning. Your twenty-fifth birthday is not too far away."

"You mean the Kessler money?"

"I do."

"That is not why I came back, Father."

He smiled, quite broadly again. "My dear, you may think it odd—or out of character—but I am quite ready to believe you came only for Oriel."

"Thank you. Although others may not, of course."

He shrugged, as if the Kessler inheritance did not really concern him. "So I imagine. It will seem far more likely to most people that you came to find out how much, if any, of your mother's money you can get for yourself. Or even to effect a reconciliation with your husband, now that he is to become a rich man. I suppose there is no possibility of that?"

Her face, her *mask* of mature, perceptive, wholly adult amusement did not falter. "No, Father. I think I have done him quite enough harm already."

"There is the child, of course . . . ?" He was merely throwing a suggestion into the air.

Neatly she caught it. "Ah—yes. But I have done her no harm, have I, other than leave her in peace, which some people—Aunt Maud, for instance, and all our dear Mertons—must consider a positive benefit. If that is the only good thing I have done I wouldn't want to spoil it. Would I?"

As he had bowed with his empty, disdainful courtesy to Oriel, so now he bowed to Kate. "My dear, it is a very long time since I hazarded even a guess as to what you might want to do. And all I feel in any way entitled to ask now is if you know yourself. You are under no obligation, of course, to answer."

She smiled beautifully, brilliantly, bestowing upon him a gala performance. "I'll answer gladly, Father. So far as Francis is concerned what I would really like—what I feel to be only right and proper—is to find some means of setting him free."

"You mean divorce?"

"I don't know. Quentin says it is atrociously expensive and only men can do it. So if Francis thinks it wrong to waste so much of the Kessler money which he sees—Quentin says—as really belonging to his daughter—which seems reasonable enough to me—then that will be the end of it. But one can feel free, you know, without getting a law passed to say so . . . I believe I do."

"You are not short of money yourself, then, Kate?"

Once more her brilliant, artful smile flashed out at him. "I eat. I pay my rent. I dress—rather well—sometimes I travel. Francis pays me a small allowance through Quentin— as much as he has been able to afford up to now. And, from time to time, I even *earn*—think of that. Not a fortune, of course. More of a pittance, in fact. But fun, sometimes, more or less. The Kesslers in Austria and Italy and France have helped, very kindly, to find me employment. Quentin put me in touch with them. But I think you know all this—don't you?"

"Through our excellent Quentin? Some of it—yes. Enough to know you have not suffered from starvation."

She did not ask him, although her clever, supple face conveyed the question with wit and sparkle, what he would have done about it if she had.

"Quite so. May I ask if your thoughts of freedom are in any way due to your having met some other man you would like to marry?"

She nodded, one swordsman to another. "You may ask, Father. And I expect you will be relieved to hear that no, I have not met some unscrupulous foreign adventurer who might turn up here any day now—or not a day later than my twenty-fifth birthday to grab what he can and then leave me coughing myself to death in a cheap lodging-house somewhere while he spends it on another woman . . ."

"Yes," he said calmly. "I am very relieved to hear that, Kate. Does it mean you are less romantic than you were?"

"I believe so. It also means that my acquaintance with cheap lodging-houses—and I do have such an acquaintance— is not one I should care to repeat. It has made me cautious."

"And clever, I think."

"Possibly. Like you, Father, perhaps."

"No—no. Your energy, my dear, your urgencies, the many things that drive you, exceed by far anything there has ever been in me. You are hungrier, Kate, than I am. So was your mother. And I am not speaking of bodily hunger. If you have found the right channel for your appetite then I wish you well, although I could not, at any time, have directed you."

He looked at them both for a moment in a silence neither of them attempted to fill and then, glancing through the window, he said, as if he had caught sight of a clock in the distance, "I must be off now."

They did not ask where, although his destination, on such a day, was hard to imagine.

"You do know, of course," he said from the doorway, "that you are sisters?"

"Yes, Father," said Kate.

He glanced inquiringly at Oriel. "Yes," she answered. "We *are* sisters. I am so glad."

The door closed behind him.

"Where can he be going?" she wondered. "It looks like rain out there."

"I don't know." Kate was frowning. "How odd—that is the first conversation I have ever had with him. The first one in my twenty-five years. And if he were not my father what I would be thinking now is what an interesting man."

Where was he going? A moment later they saw him, through the window, a heavy, caped greatcoat around his shoulders, walking in the direction of the orchard, bare now with January yet planted densely enough to provide a brief cover for anyone who did not wish to be seen, quite at once, from the house and called back again by Maud to bask in the pity of those "friends and neighbors" who, Maud having been generous with the sherry and the Madeira were beginning already to voice, if only in whispers, their grudges against Evangeline, and to take up all the misdemeanors of her past, real or invented, which *of course* they would never have dreamed of mentioning, except that now, perhaps, as things had turned out, it might make Matthew feel better to know.

Sitting on a pile of logs, it amused him to wonder what those "friends" would make of it if he told them he knew already, had always known, and that now—without her—there was nothing he cared to know any longer, about anything.

It was as simple as that. Love did not even seem to be involved in it. Although he had fallen in love with her, in his season, he well remembered it. Madly in love, until he had

grown, not tired of her, but used to her, occasionally en-
raged, often amused, but still bound to her as if—he understood it now—they had been members, he and she—he and
she only—of a slightly different species to the rest.

Her daughter, beyond the pale hair and eyes, the cool grace,
did not resemble her and even if she had he was too dry now,
too withered, to inflict himself upon her. A young Evangeline
would not have tolerated him in any case and he had no use
whatsoever for the pity he knew himself quite clever enough
to stir in the heart of *his* daughter, Oriel. While as for Kate,
no pity there, why should there be? Amusement, perhaps,
had he felt even faintly inclined for it. He did not.

Inclined for nothing, in fact, but to sit in the chill wind of
a January afternoon beneath naked trees which would bear
fruit six months from now, and again a year after that, bustling on from season to season with a sense of right and
purpose he found intolerable. They knew their place in the
world, these trees, like his daughters, one who was grieving
now but would recover, one who was growing surprisingly
strong and would probably—he feared—make a great deal of
noise about it. He did not feel inclined to tolerate that either.

The truth was that it did not really interest him, as nothing
else had interested him for a very long time that had not been
recounted to him by Evangeline, the world outside himself,
from which he preferred to keep his distance, being translated for him daily and exclusively by her. Evangeline, his
window on the world, his salvation—how she would have
laughed at that—his final source of whatever it was—he saw
no point in trying to name it—which made it worth his while
to separate one day from another.

They would all be the same now, those days, those years,
without her. Identical. Tedious. Quite intolerable. And sitting
there, in the cold wind, he grew angry with her, for a while,
because she had failed to be eternal, had not even managed—
at the very least—to live until he was gone.

He heard Maud call him from the house. His sister who
still wanted so much, preparing now to devote herself entirely to him, in order to serve, as he well knew, her own
best interests. Not that he blamed her. He was simply not
inclined to put up with it. And Letty, demanding patience he
did not possess. And Letty's children, from whom Evangeline had always screened him so effectively. He could not
bring himself to care, had never cared, whether Susannah

married her curate or not, whether Quentin remembered to visit his mother, whether or not Constantia had another baby for whom, if she did, he felt no wish whatsoever to prepare a future.

The word "future" itself deeply offended him.

"Matthew—where are you? People are leaving and want to say goodbye—naturally . . ."

As it was right and proper, Maud's voice implied, that they should.

"Here Maud," he called, standing up and waving a cheerful hand. "Just coming . . ." She waved back—or did she beckon?—and then, the wind disturbing her neat hair and skirts, disappeared inside. Evangeline had never liked the wind either, he thought as he took the pistol from his greatcoat pocket, looked at it for a while and then, realizing most accurately the havoc his death would cause, raised it to his head, smiled, and fired a shot.

Fifteen

A month later, on a sharp-textured February morning, Francis Ashington was considerably disconcerted to find Oriel alone in her Ullswater garden, a dark woolen shawl thrown gipsy-fashion around her shoulders, half a dozen kittens waltzing in time to the movement of her black skirts as she hurried through her acre of snowdrops and faint purple and gold hints of early crocus to meet him, her hands outstretched, her mouth smiling in a welcome that had a measure of surprise in it nevertheless.

He had come here by arrangement to meet Kate who, having so far avoided any discussion with him beyond the essential details of getting her father buried, had at last agreed to see him in private for an hour or two at Ullswater. She had expressed herself all eagerness to see Oriel's cottage. He was to be a guest at Lowther Castle. A simple matter, therefore, to walk over from Askham to Oriel's carefully nurtured acre of fellside, arriving in good time on the appointed morning to be told that Kate was not there.

"Francis, I am so sorry, but she has gone back to France quite urgently—for several days, I think. Surely she must have let you know?"

Smiling, although he felt very, very far from pleased, he shook his head. And then, his sense of fair play reasserting itself, he smiled again, ruefully but with more warmth.

"It occurs to me she may have done. I left Dessborough a day or so before I intended—ten days, in fact. And my housekeeper may not have remembered to send my letters on."

Or known, in fact, just where to send them, since having

told the good woman he was bound for Carlisle, he had only remained there overnight, spending the past ten days tramping the Roman Wall built by the Caesars in a time he could well imagine, to seal off their peaceful, profitable English colony from the marauding northern tribesmen they either could not, or did not think it worth their while to conquer. Ten days in which he had sought to exhaust himself, eating sparsely, drinking only natural running water, sleeping on the hard ground again as he had done so often in India, deliberately risking exposure to the biting north wind of the Picts and Scots, rushing toward him over those bare hillsides with the same snarling savagery, the same lethal intent to freeze his blood, or drink it, as the Scottish tribes had shown, year in year out, every fighting season, to the Romans.

How those Roman officers brought up in the sun and civilization of Italy, must have detested this barbaric northern posting. As British officers, in his day, had rarely seen cause for celebration on being sent to the Northwest Frontier of India. But he had survived that frontier in the same way, he supposed, that had he been a young Roman of good family doing his military service, he would have survived this one. Except that he would probably have fallen in love with some British girl who spoke only a few halting words of Latin or Greek, with a Druid for an uncle, a tribal chieftain for a father, her brothers in league with the Scots and ready to let them through the wall and cut *his* throat at the earliest opportunity.

Such a love, he felt—having come to terms long ago with his own restless nature—would have been an essential joyful torment in such a situation and he had still been contemplating it with wry amusement at the George in Penrith where he had gone to shave and scrub himself clean—having registered in a false name to avoid any explanations of his vagabond condition—before presenting himself to the civilized world again.

And now Kate's message to him canceling their meeting was probably in Carlisle, she was in France, and he in a garden full of snowdrops above Lake Ullswater with a woman he had once very definitely wished to make his wife.

It would not do, of course.

"Never mind," he said. "I'll just stroll back to Askham—such a pleasant morning." But the beautiful, desirable, enticingly solitary woman would not hear of it. Yes, she was

alone but seemed neither surprised nor alarmed about it. Her
husband, who had hurried home to claim her share of the
Stangway inheritance, had gone abroad again. Her husband's
son was away somewhere on a tour of her husband's construction sites. Her husband's daughters, who had indeed accompanied her to Ullswater, had been staying with friends for a
day or two on the other side of the lake at Watermillock and
would not be back until late that afternoon. Sometime after
tea she rather expected. But what on earth did any of that
matter?

"Do please come in, Francis, or I shall feel quite insulted." And bending his head slightly, he entered a room
fragrant with pot pourri and beeswax, a wooden floor black
with age and gleaming with polish covered by fringed, floral
rugs in subtle pinks and sharp apple greens, armchairs and
footstools in the same colors drawn up to a log fire admiring
its own reflection in the richly burnished copper of coal buckets and pokers, toasting fork and fender. Lamps, copper-
based and pink-shaded, were burning to dispel the February
gloom, one on a gate-legged table standing in a low alcove
papered with a design of water-lilies, the other beside a sofa
scattered with plump velvet cushions in rich colors, not one
of them matching yet all of them in pleasant accord, while
every available surface held its wide-brimmed china bowl—
each one of a different design, a different color, a different
nation, all of them in harmony—into which she had crumpled
the dried petals of roses and lavender, larkspur, jasmine,
clove-scented pinks, lily of the valley, and bound them together with orris root to make her pot pourri.

On the floor at one side of the hearth stood a vast copper
bowl of winter hyacinths and plants he could not name with
delicate, many-colored foliage; an oval basket at the other
side, containing, among bright blue cushions, a mother cat
and a further selection of much younger kittens.

"You seem to be much concerned," he said, smiling down
at them, "by things feline."

She smiled down at the basket too and shook her head.
"Yes, although not entirely by design. I grow valerian in my
herb garden which brings the cats here like magic. It goes to
their heads too—my goodness. So whenever one of them turns
up on my doorstep in *that* condition, I feel obliged to take
her in. After all, giving birth in my fireside basket must be

better than in a ditch or a haystack somewhere—wouldn't you think?''

He thought so. And if it occurred to him to wonder—as it did—whether or not she was disappointed, grieved, or even thankful at never having given birth herself, he betrayed no sign of it.

"What happens to them when you are away?" he said.

"Oh—they have excellent service. There is a kind lady from Howtown who comes every day to look after their house and feed them. And to distribute them, too—or as many as she can—among her acquaintances. As I do myself. There is a very handsome selection of Lakeland cats keeping down the mice in Lydwick. I feel quite proud whenever I meet one. And now, Francis, what may I give you?—it *is* a cold morning.''

Now in that warm, fragrant room where, having accepted a glass of Madeira and several slices of pale, lemon-scented cake to match, he found it easy to lean back and stretch out his legs on the hearthrug, almost glad to have been spared a high-strung interview with Kate. Glad, that is, just now when he was still feeling the strain of his Roman ramblings and had got up before dawn that morning to join a shooting-party of self-important city gentlemen who had found nothing endearing about his skill with a sporting gun.

Yet Kate, high-strung or not, would have to be faced sometime. And, in the middle of telling Oriel how his shooting companions had felt inclined to penalize him on finding out that he had been a soldier and something of an explorer—although no one remembered that very clearly now—he suddenly paused and said, "Was it really urgent, do you think—her trip to France?"

"It was urgent for her, Francis."

"Indeed. So is keeping out of my way. Could that be why she went, I wonder?"

Oriel smiled and shook her head. "No. Not this time."

"You sound rather more certain, I confess, Oriel, than I feel."

She smiled again, very pale, very slender in her heavy mourning dress yet by no means crushed by it, looking capable and serene, her elegant feet on firm ground, her hair tied up only by a black ribbon and hanging all the way down the long arch of her back to a waist so small he thought it likely he could encircle it with his hands. Realizing that he felt much inclined to do so, he looked at her even more closely, wondering how fiercely she would—or would not—repel him, and then concluding that it made no difference, since he would never make the attempt.

He had had a fair number of casual lovers these past five years, beautiful women some of them, all of them richly married and intending to remain so, the greatest attraction of each one in turn having been that he could desire her body, sometimes with real ardor, while the mind, the self, the identity within it meant nothing to him at all. And the last thing he wanted now—or at any other time, he rather suspected—was an involvement with a woman who might, who certainly *ought*, to mean a great deal.

No. He had made up his mind, a long time ago, that in a pure spirit of fairness to all concerned he must confine himself to physical excitements in the company of physical women, avoiding, no matter what it cost him—and, indeed, it did not cost him very much—all who showed even the slightest signs of wanting something else. Already, yesterday evening, on his arrival from Penrith, the wife of one of his shooting companions had indicated to him, very clearly, her willingness to relieve his natural tensions. Good enough, he thought. Ample. While, as for the rest, he had his daughter Celestine to unlock and absorb his powerful instincts to protect and cherish; the memory of his wife Arshad to cause him a kind of grief now that had its element of pleasure; his engaging fantasy—today—of the British tribal chieftain's daughter; another fantasy, just as engaging, tomorrow.

There was also Kate. And, having made up his mind, on his Roman ramblings, that the only way he could settle his conscience about the Kessler money would be to ask her to return to him and, furthermore, actually to take her back if she so chose—as wife, sister, lover, anything she pleased so long as she left him a certain freedom to please himself—he thought it time to make a start.

"I am sure she wrote to you," said Oriel. "She wrote to me, and since she has probably put the same things in your letter . . . Well, she has gone off to welcome a friend of hers out of prison. A political prisoner, of course. Somebody who opposed this new Emperor Napoleon who—quite understandably—locked him up and has now let him out again. Not so understandably. Kate was very surprised about it, and thrilled, and wanted very much to be there—with the man's wife and children and other people—to welcome him home.''

"Oriel," he said very gently. "It was kind of you to mention the wife and children, but quite unnecessary. The question of jealousy, or anything like it, does not arise, you know. Happily, I think. Would it help, in your opinion, if Kate knew that?''

He saw her hesitation and, leaning toward her, said with an urgency he knew would touch her, "Please, Oriel. We have known each other long enough and well enough to be frank. And you understand how important this is. I have already inherited High Grange with all its land and its very profitable colliery. In a few months' time I shall have the Kessler money falling on me like a snowstorm of pure gold. All because, and only because, I am Kate's husband. The law may call it mine—*does* call it mine—but the truth is that until I find out what *she* wants to call it, I really don't know what to do. We are talking of her family home, after all, not mine, and it can hardly stay in dust covers forever. I have no intention of ever living there. Kate may do so—if *that* would please her—with my blessing. Otherwise I shall have to put it up for sale. Unless Miss Maud Stangway should beat me to it, that is, and burn it down, as she threatened.''

It was quite true, remembered Oriel, very calmly now, that Maud, giving way for the first time in her life to hysteria at Matthew's funeral, had screamed out her intention of setting fire to her ancestral home, preferring to see it consumed by flames and herself with it rather than lived in by a stranger; even by the strumpet Kate for whom the "wages of sin" had turned out very profitable indeed. Just as they had for that other strumpet, Oriel Keith, daughter of the woman who, albeit from the grave, had murdered Maud's beloved brother.

A terrible day, that second funeral, neither Maud nor Letty, nor any of the "friends and neighbors" for that matter, being prepared to accept that Matthew Stangway had killed himself for anything even remotely approaching love, putting it down entirely to the shame with which his wife had covered him, the wounds inflicted by her on his sense of honor which, turning to gangrene, had been too much for him to bear.

Evangeline—Maud kept on repeating, to the accompaniment of Letty's tears—had murdered him. An opinion shared so fiercely by all but an approximate half-dozen at the funeral that few had felt any need to be even civil to the murderess's daughter, although rather more clemency had been shown to Kate who—should the Kessler money lure her back to her husband—might well, as the mistress of two noble estates, become a social force to be reckoned with.

But Kate had paid little attention to anyone, not even to Dora Merton who had come in person this time to deliver her own posy, along with an ornate wreath from her sister Adela—still in Cheltenham—and a letter from her mother's new secretary-companion—still in Scotland—expressing Lady Merton's regrets.

"I find your logic somewhat faulty," Kate had told her Aunt Maud, the Merton letter in her hand. "If my father's death was an inevitable result of his wife's adultery with Lord Merton then how is it that Lady Merton—who was made just as much a fool of—is doing so well?"

A remark which had caused Maud to aim a slap, expertly ducked by Kate, and to begin crying out, very loud, her hysterical threat of arson and the casting of her own person into the flames.

Yet she had packed her bags quietly enough a few days later and moved back to the vicarage, her services as caretaker having been declined by the new master of High Grange, who had dependants of his own, a surfeit of Ashington spinsters and retired gentlefolk all with a greater claim on his conscience than the Stangway relics, thus obliging Maud, like all the rest, to accept the authority of a new generation, her power at an end because no man of property now existed who either relied upon her services or respected her advice. And although her brother's will had set aside a house on the estate for her use during her lifetime and a sufficient income to maintain it she had remained, so far, at the vicarage, not only taking over Letty's domestic responsibilities once again but upholding the fiction that her sister was unfit to cope with them herself. An arrangement which enabled Letty to remain idle, and Maud important.

Oriel herself had inherited her mother's house at Lydwick Park which Garron had immediately put up for sale, along with a sum of money her mother would have called "reasonable"—enough to imply affection, too little to cause gossip—which she supposed had been paid into Garron's bank by now and would, she hoped, give him some satisfaction, since it meant nothing to her. Her mother's jewelry had been locked up in the safe at Lydwick Green to which only Garron had the key, with—as it happened—her permission although, re-membering his marked disinclination to see her wear it, she supposed he would have done it anyway.

Only the blue velvet bag had been kept from him.

Kate had inherited the bulk of everything else with more to come, free of all entail or any other encumbrance except, of course, that it belonged as completely to her husband as, in law, she belonged to him herself. A union *she* could only dissolve, it seemed, by dying although *he* could put an end to it should he be willing to pay out the small fortune such a rare and cumbersome procedure as divorce could cost. A decision no responsible friend or legal adviser could ever urge him to take, the woman having no right to claim so much as one penny from him, no right to see her child unless he chose to consent, no right to set foot in what had been her ancestral home without his express permission, no right to remain there the moment he told her to go. He could sell High Grange if he chose without her knowledge, much less her permission. Or he could live there in luxury with a bevy of expensive courtesans, while his wife starved outside at the gate. He could take the Kessler money and gamble it or squander it on other women in the comfortable knowledge that the law allowed his wife no room even to complain.

Yet it was not with legal wrongs and rights but with his own view of reality that Francis was now concerned.

"I have to settle it," he told Oriel. "And quickly. I don't care too much about the property. Money sits quietly enough in a bank. They seem to know what they're doing at the colliery. I can see to the running of the estate easily enough. I don't mind her taking her time there. But there's Celestine."

Yes. Oriel had known it would be that.

"I'd like to know her intentions for my own sake, Oriel, I can't deny it. But for my child's sake I *have* to know them. Everybody knows she's here. Everybody has their own version of why, and how, and for how long. And people gossip. My housekeeper and nanny and all the housemaids gossip. So do the tenants and the village people and the neighbors. So do the men I hunt with and shoot with and even my colleagues on the bench of magistrates. And they sympathize—with me—quite loudly whenever they get half a chance. Celestine is six now and I can't know what she overhears or what she makes of it. She asked me once—about a year ago—

where her mother was and I told her the truth. Abroad. She didn't ask me why. It didn't seem to matter. So I thought I'd take it at her pace, wait for the next question and deal with it as it came. But not now, with Kate flitting backward and forward between Paris and Hepplefield, and that damned Kessler fortune about to fall into my hands—making me seem a 'damned lucky fellow' to some people, branding me a fortune-hunter to others. And I don't want my daughter growing up with any suspicion in her mind that I married for money. Or that I did less than everything in my power to share it with the woman who brought it in.''

"Of course not." No one could deny him the right to be hard and angry in the defense of his child. Kate herself did not deny it.

"You've spent a lot of time with her, Oriel, these last few weeks," he said. "Do you think she wants to see Celestine?"

She paused, a long moment going by before she gathered her words into what she thought—hoped—might approach the truth. "I think"—and it was not at all easy to describe—"I think she *wants* to see her . . . Lord, that sounds . . ."

"I understand." Thankfully she saw that he did.

"To begin with she felt so unfit to be a mother. She felt she was doing Celestine a service by going away. And—yes— perhaps she was. She thinks if she'd stayed at Dessborough she'd have kept you so busy and so worried about *her* that neither of you would have had much time for Celestine. She knew she couldn't be a mother but she wanted to give her child something—something vital, just the same. So she gave her you.''

He smiled. "Are those Kate's words in direct quotation?"

"More or less."

"And now—having delivered me into the prison of fatherhood—what next?"

"Is it a prison?"

"What next, Oriel?" But he was still smiling.

"I think she's afraid of using Celestine."

"I see." She thought it quite likely that he did.

"Using her as a test, I mean, for herself. She's calmer now and much more than five years older. Much more. She seems to have come to terms with her own mother, and her father— and the rest. And she felt entitled to hurt herself in the process as much and as badly as it took. But she feels no entitlement to use Celestine as some kind of experiment, to see if she can get that side of herself sorted out as well. She sees the risk . . .''

''Yes. So do I. She must also see the need to discuss it with me. It *has* to be done, Oriel. And quickly. Can you tell me what is really holding her back?''

She shook her head and, leaning toward her, his pleasure both in the scented repose of his surroundings and the contemplation of this exquisite woman he thought too valuable to touch, giving way to the urgency which had driven him along the Roman Wall, he said sharply, ''Oriel, I am sorry to lay this burden on you, but if you could bring yourself to tell Kate . . . How can I phrase it? It occurs to me that she may have misjudged the degree of hurt—or the type of hurt—she did me.''

''How is that?''

The mellow chiming of a clock somewhere in the room gave him an irritating reminder of the luncheon his hosts had requested him not to miss, the time it would take him to walk back to Askham and change his clothes and manner to the correct degree of country-house elegance, with this unsettled business of his wife and child ever at the forefront of his mind. Goddammit, something would have to be done. Something immediate—*at once.* Something to shock Kate into seeing him, even if he had to shock this step-sister and friend of hers—his friend too—to do it.

''She assumed me to be in love with her,'' he said, like an officer issuing commands on parade. ''Romantically, I mean—when we married.''

''And you were not?''

''No. I was not. I am not proud of it. It is simply the truth. It also means that in meeting me Kate would have no excessive emotions or jealousies or recriminations of *mine* to deal with—if that should be troubling her. My aim is solely to discuss how best to arrange our lives and the fortune about to come crashing into them. In my view the most workable arrangement would be for her to come back to Dessborough. Terms of friendship only would be perfectly acceptable. Otherwise she must be properly established somewhere else, in a manner we all think safe and sound, and unlikely to shock Celestine when she finds out about it. You do see, Oriel—don't you?''

Silence. Long enough and deep enough for him to regret

his words, particularly when she got up and, crossing to the window, stood there with her back to him, looking fixedly across the lake, convincing him more than ever of the embarrassment he had caused her until, turning toward him with an expression which could not—thank God—be called hostile, she astonished him by asking, "Why were you not in love with her—and never have been, by the sound of it?"

He stood up too and went across to the window as if drawn there, remembering once again and far too clearly that this was the woman he had meant to marry, not Kate, wondering in spite of himself—since it could make no difference now—how much better or worse his life would have been if he had.

At least he could have gone to Mecca.

"You may tell me the truth, Francis. In fact, I rather think you should."

Her voice, coming through a smile in which he saw friendship and encouragement and a little sadness, told him of her need to know. Therefore he had no choice but to tell her. "She was very young, Oriel. Much younger than eighteen then, just as you say she is older than twenty-five now. She mistook my intentions . . ."

"Which were?"

"*Oriel.* You must know that I meant to marry you—if you would have had me, that is."

She smiled, almost lightly it seemed to him. "Oh yes, I would have had you, Francis. No doubt about that. What I would really like you to tell me is why you decided not to ask?"

How could she have failed to understand? It had been so obvious to him, so hysterically cut and dried, such a farce and a tragedy rolled into one, that he had believed it impossible to miss. And then, as the alternative struck him, he was horrified. "Oriel, you surely didn't think it was because of your mother—or your background . . . ?"

"Of course I did."

"*Oriel*—such things could never matter to me."

"So I thought—to begin with."

"And you were right . . ."

"I'm so very glad."

"You would have been so perfect . . ."

"Thank you, Francis."

"I came over to High Grange that night to propose to you . . ."

"So I *was* right."

"Yes. I expect you usually are."

"Oh—I try not to make it obvious."

"I was early, or you were late, having dinner. And Kate hadn't dined . . ."

"I remember."

"She met me. She thought I'd come for her. Oriel, please do believe me . . ."

"I do."

"I handled it so badly—lost my head—and then that foolish woman rushed in and started screaming rape . . ."

The word "rape" and the incredible amusement of her reaction to it steadied him, bringing to his notice how closely they were now standing together, his need to explain, to make amends, having been accompanied by a series of urgent steps toward her which had left her pressed up against the window, his body not an inch away from hers, his mouth, speaking directly to her mouth, even nearer.

Quickly he backed away.

"Did I hurt you?" he said.

Smiling, shaking out her skirts and moving gracefully, lightly, away from the window, she nodded.

"Badly?"

"Yes. Rather badly—at the time."

"I didn't expect to. I thought . . ."

"Yes, I know. That I was cool and sensible and much the best candidate for the situation on offer."

Watching her move through the small room full of furniture and bric-a-brac as gracefully and accurately as one of her cats, her wide skirts disarranging nothing, he was enchanted once again by the lightness, the ease, with which her manner beckoned him, inviting him into her life all over again, it seemed, not as a lover he thought—with some regret—but as rather more than a friend.

"Situation on offer? You must think me a monster of conceit, Oriel."

She smiled full at him, so much at ease, making him so easy that anything could now be said.

"Men are brought up to be conceited, Francis. So perhaps you can't help it. I also think you are generous and brave and responsible. And very interesting."

"I think you are quite wonderful, Oriel."

Her smile gave him gracious permission to think so, his

pleasure in her company marred only by another intrusion from the clock, telling him that he was late already and must—considerably against his inclination—make his excuses and go.

"Of course, Francis. I'll walk a little way with you. As far as Pooley Bridge if the wind has turned no colder."

It had not, although as they went out into the garden it came rushing greedily toward them, a loud-voiced predator grabbing Oriel's cloak and tugging it half off her shoulders, lifting her skirts so that a pair of terrified kittens, bolting for shelter beneath them, became wildly entangled with each other around her ankles, causing her to stumble against Francis who, having caught and steadied her, continued to hold her, one hand finding the magnificent curve of her back which had been in his vision all morning, the other going to the nape of her neck and into her hair, his mouth on her mouth, kissing her as if the world had but ten frenzied minutes to endure and then, remembering the true length of a day much less of eternity, releasing her.

Steadying herself now, one hand still on his shoulder, she held out the other toward him, palm upward and outward. "Francis—don't apologize. I know you think you should. But please don't."

She was smiling very gently, very steadily, very much—he clearly understood—his friend.

"Oriel, I can hardly apologize for what I don't regret."

"I don't regret it either, Francis—although . . ."

"Yes," he said, warmly, easily—returning her smile. "There's no need to tell me I can't be your lover. I know. I wouldn't worry you by asking. It wouldn't even be necessary—would it?"

Her hand still resting on his shoulder, she leaned forward, letting her palm take her weight, and very gently, with exquisite care and cherishing, placed a kiss on one corner of his closed mouth and then the other, a gift of affection which spoke to him delicately, sweetly, altogether freely, of friendship, of a kindred spirit even, in no way of sensuality. One of the most moving approaches, it seemed, that he had ever had in his life from a woman.

And as they walked arm-in-arm through her snowdrops and out of her garden gate to the lakeside, Swarth Fell standing tall and somber to one side of them, a cold expanse of water to the other, he found it possible, and then easy, to tell her of Arshad, the other woman whose approach had moved him, in a time which now could only be called "long ago."

"It just seems that my emotional courage has never recovered. I suppose only Celestine, so far, has really managed to slip through my guard."

"You will lose her too, you know," said Oriel gently. He smiled. "I know. Hopefully to a young man quite madly in love with her. I could hardly stand in the way of that."

"And what will you do then, Francis? Make your pilgrimage to Mecca?"

Smiling once more into the wind, he shook his head. "No, there's no point to that any longer. A former acquaintance of mine, one Captain Richard Burton—Ruffian Dick, we used to call him—has just got back from there, very much alive. And what mattered, you see, was to be first. He will be writing extensively about it, I expect, and lecturing to the Royal Geographical Society—and getting lots of encouragement to go off and be the first European to set foot somewhere else. All that."

How much did "all that" still mean to him? A great deal, she imagined, as, parting from him affectionately at Pooley Bridge, having promised to do everything in her power to make Kate talk to him, she walked back slowly along the lakeside, listening to the wind and the water, lengthening her stride for the sheer pleasure of exercising her own sure-footed strength, her ability to breathe even and deep and free, so many things lifted from her heart that felt light enough to rise—easily, pleasantly—from the ground and fly. And if her liberation was composed, in part, of the knowledge that her mother no longer depended upon her and that the man she had once so much wanted to love her had never done so, she seemed well on her way to coming to terms with it. Neither his kiss nor her own enjoyment of it had taken her by surprise. It had been pleasurable, exciting, and final, leading her not into his bed but into his affections where she meant, most decidedly, to stay. He was a man she cared for and who cared for her, but it did not follow—she saw that now—that he was a man for love.

She must talk carefully to Kate, who might not be a woman for love's real burdens either. Yet, walking back through her snowdrops, the fells rising from the lake, one upon the other, the high, solitary places where red deer might be seen wandering at this season, the air was so fresh, suddenly so still, this quiet center of the world so very much her own, that she was taken considerably aback to find Morag in the parlor, standing on the hearth-rug by the basket of kittens, her face set in a rigid expression which meant—as Oriel knew too well—that someone had offended her.

"Morag! What are *you* doing here?" She had not meant to speak so sharply but, having assumed herself to be alone, and—moreover—wanting to be alone, the shock was not pleasant.

"Why shouldn't I be?" Morag did not appear to be finding it pleasant either.

"Because you should be over at Watermillock with the Landons, and Elspeth. She's not here as well, is she?"

"Oh no. Don't worry about that. You're safe from her."

Oriel sighed, adjusting her mind and all her new exhilaration with it to this level of everyday. "Don't be foolish, Morag. I don't mean you're not welcome. You took me by surprise, that's all."

"Yes—didn't I? You changed color just now when you walked in."

Was she attempting to apologize? The sourness in her voice did not incline Oriel to think so.

"How long have you been here? Did the Landons bring you?"

"About half an hour. And no—I walked."

"I didn't see you?"

"Should you have?"

"Well, I've been down to Pooley Bridge and back—about half an hour each way. How did I miss you?"

Morag shrugged a peevish shoulder. "I came the other way, through Patterdale around the fell."

"That's a terribly *long* way, Morag." And rough too, in any weather.

She shrugged again. "Well, it's the way I came. I'd just had enough of watching Elspeth batting her eyelids at Tom Landon and him nearly going into a swoon every time she did it—making a fool of himself . . ."

Had Morag, plainer but finer than Elspeth, taken a fancy to Tom Landon herself? A handsome young man with startling violet-colored eyes and not too much behind them, in Oriel's estimation. It seemed quite likely and, remembering the pains of seventeen, she said, "Never mind. I just hope Mrs. Landon wasn't offended at your leaving like that."

"She doesn't know. She was out, so I just told Elspeth and set off . . ."

Evidently there had been a quarrel. But—as Morag ought to know—one did not break the rules of hospitality for a thing like that. Coolly, precisely, Oriel told her so; Morag standing tall and tight-clenched, one narrow hand nervously clasping and unclasping the other, her jaw set at a hard angle.

"Ah well," sighed Oriel, coming to an end. "I'll have to find the gardener's boy and send him around to Watermillock with a note letting her know you've arrived . . ."

"As you please," said Morag, spitting out the words with a bitterness which seemed—surely—out of all proportion?

"It doesn't please me, Morag."

"Don't worry." Suddenly Morag seemed altogether beside herself, as if some deep, long pent-up fury had finally spilled over. "I won't come here again—to displease you. I detest this place . . ."

"Really?"

"Yes—really—hate it . . ."

"Why is that?"

She hesitated, shook her head, rather as if the words rising in her throat were strangling her and then, evidently thinking better of them, snapped, "Elspeth has friends here. She's all right. So are you. I have nobody. You should let me invite a friend of my own, as I asked you—as I always ask you . . ."

But the friend in question having been Susannah, Oriel calmly shook her head.

"No, Morag."

"Next time, then?"

Oriel knew she was being challenged. "A friend of your own age, yes—certainly."

"You mean not Susannah."

"Yes, Morag. That is what I mean."

Morag, in a state of nervous irritation so strong that it seemed almost to bewilder her, tossed her head. "Well, it must be as you say, of course."

"Of course."

"But what I'd like you to admit is why you dislike her so much, when she's been such a great help to you . . ."

It was an old argument over which Oriel, in the interests of domestic harmony, had always skated lightly. But perhaps she had been discreet and compassionate for too long. Perhaps the time had come—at last—to tell the truth.

"Susannah has not been a help to me, Morag. I have been a help to her . . ."

"Really."

"Yes, Morag. Really. I have never needed her company—quite the contrary—but she has always been in great need of mine . . ."

"I won't hear this—not from *you* . . ."

". . . which I have given because I understood her need and felt sorry . . ."

"I'm going upstairs—to write to her, if you must know . . ."

"You will go when I tell you. I understood her need, Morag, and her fears."

"What fears?"

"Of the very things she wants most. She wants marriage but she lacks the courage to take on a husband. She wants a family but not every day, not three hundred and sixty-five days—and nights—a year, whether she feels up to it or not. She wants authority without responsibility. She only wants to get involved with the bits and pieces she fancies and leave the rest—which is most of it—to somebody else. And the only way she can do it is to impose on some other woman who is kind enough to put up with her . . ."

"That's disgusting . . ."

"Of me, I suppose you mean. Never mind."

"I do mind. And what amazes me is how *you* can bring yourself to criticize anybody."

Because of Evangeline? Oriel smiled. "With a perfectly clear conscience, Morag," she said.

The next few days passed uneasily, Elspeth returning from Watermillock of the opinion that Morag, by upsetting the Landons, had ruined her life, the only decision remaining to her now being whether to drown herself, or her sister, in the lake.

"Please do it when the gardener is here," Oriel warned her, "since I shall not rush to pull either of you out." But Mrs. Landon, a woman of an easy disposition, soon invited them to stay with her again, accepting with a tolerance in which Oriel noted a hint of relief, Morag's decision to spend a few days instead with an acquaintance in Penrith, a Miss Broderick, the only daughter of a local solicitor.

"It might even be a kindness," Mrs. Landon assured Oriel pleasantly, the Brodericks having just lost so much money, through no fault of their own, that they must surely be in need of someone to cheer them up. Had Oriel not heard, Mrs. Landon wondered, that the Milne, Morrissey Bank had failed to open its doors for business a day or two ago? A terrible shock for any poor widows who had trusted Messrs. Milne and Morrissey with their savings, or any men of business who now would be unable to draw their money out, even to pay their workers' wages. A most distressing affair, bank failures, bringing down so many perfectly good businesses with them, and giving rise on every occasion to a crop of suicides by those who, on the day before, had had so much to live for. Thank goodness Mr. Landon was not affected. She hoped one could say the same for Mr. Keith?

Oriel hoped so; although, enjoying her solitude, walking out every morning to the giant yew tree in Martindale and then beyond in search of the red deer, the sound of running water never leaving her ears, the feel of it always beneath her feet, any anxiety—which had not been much—about the Milne, Morrissey Bank receded until the afternoon when, coming down from the fells totally at ease with herself, feeling clear-sighted and sure-footed and only slightly out of breath, she found Garron waiting for her in the cottage as irritably and accusingly as Morag had done.

"Where the hell have you been?"

"Fell-walking."

"Yes. So the mud on your skirt tells me. You look like an Irish tinker."

"Thank you."

"No compliment intended. Get me something to drink, will you? Whiskey if you have it. And then go and make yourself look decent."

Pertly—knowing that it *might*, although not necessarily, make him smile—she dropped him a housemaid's curtsy.

"Straightaway, sir. As soon as I've sent off a note to Watermillock and one to Penrith, to let the girls know we're going back to Lydwick—if that's where we are going."

"I don't know. We might be. Just fetch the whiskey. And a decent crystal glass."

She brought it, went upstairs to wash and change into the plain black silk dress her mourning for her mother and the man she could not really think of as her father demanded, brushing her hair into a decent chignon, rinsing her hands in chamomile water to sweeten them, her face in a lotion of

elderflower to make herself pale again after her hour in the
cold, open air, putting long drops of jet through her ears, a
cameo at her throat, several rings on her fingers, banishing
the Irish tinker—or was it, she suspected, the Scottish fisherman's daughter he had first married?—and returning to him
as the "lady" his present position required.

He was sitting in the armchair by the fire, smoking a cigar,
a glass of whiskey, which did not seem to be his first, in his
hand, his long legs stretched out on the hearthrug, dominating the whole fireside area so that, the second armchair
pushed well away, she had no choice but to sit down, already
apprehensive, on the low stool rather too near his feet.

"Why is it, madam," he said, his eyes never once leaving
the brightly burning logs to look at her, "that you are never
to be found in your own home—as you ought to be—but in
this godforsaken place which brings me miles out of my direction . . . ?"

"Because," she murmured, "you told me you would not
be back until the second week in March, and as we are still
in February . . ."

"A man may change his mind."

"Of course."

For a long, uneasy moment they both continued to stare at
the fire, Oriel listening very carefully to the crackling of the
logs, the faint, pleasant scuffling of the cats, the occasional,
familiar creak of the elderly house as it settled around her,
the weather announcing itself outside the window, the sound
of her not particularly excellent whiskey—since she mainly
kept it for the gardener—splashing once more into his glass.
Which meant, of course, that he had filled it too full.

"You look tired," she said. "In fact you don't look well."

"I don't feel it."

"Then let me get you . . ."

"*No,*" he said. "There's no need to fly off on your broom-
stick to fetch those herbal teas of yours. The whiskey will
do."

"For what?"

He leaned forward, his eyes narrowed and keen, his mouth
tight-drawn. "To get up my courage, Oriel—to say a word to
you that has to be said . . ."

Courage? She could not believe he had ever lacked it. But,
just in case he did, then she—who had so often felt crushed
and defeated—thought it only right to help him along.

"Is it the bank? Milne, Morrissey?"

"Christ. What do you know about that?"

She told him and, leaning back again in his chair, he gave a heavy, echoing sigh, coming from a very deep and now very raw part of him, and briefly closed his eyes.

"So there we are," he said. "Milne bloody Morrissey. Three days ago I'm a rich man, getting richer by the hour. Every one of my contracts running full steam ahead for completion day, no viaducts falling down, no tunnels caving in, every mountain I meet on the way small enough to run the track over instead of blasting it through—which is cheaper—and safer. Every man who works for me getting his pay and his bonus the minute it falls due. And then, this Monday morning, my bank doesn't open its doors for business and won't, until it can settle its debts. Ten million it owes. Not bad, eh?"

Her throat had gone unbearably dry, yet, imagining *his* anguish, *his* turmoil, she knew she would have to speak at once.

"What does it mean?" For the moment it was the best she could do.

He smiled, rather, she thought, like a man going to the gallows or surveying a battlefield. And knowing it was for a crime he had not committed, a massacre of which he had not been the cause, she felt her throat grow parched and burning again, her heart beginning to pound, in jerky fits and starts, against her chest.

"It means," he said, staring into the fire again, "that I can't draw out my money through closed doors. And when they sort themselves out, if ever, they might pay me ten shillings or two shillings to the pound. Or nothing at all. Which is bad enough . . ."

"But there's worse?"

He gave his strange smile again and then glanced at her, relieved, she thought, that she had kept her voice so steady.

"I don't expect you to understand business. You weren't brought up to it."

"That's not to say I couldn't understand, if you wanted to tell me." Once again her voice was very steady.

"All right." He paused, choosing his words, and then, shaking his head sharply as if to dislodge a persistent, nagging pain, he turned to look at her. "All right. I gamble a little. I take risks that pay off a lot more—if they pay off at all—than other men's solid certainties. You'll have an idea how much it costs to build a railway—the iron and the wooden sleepers and the bricks I have to buy, *and* pay for, a hell of a long time before anybody pays me. And the men of course, who have to be recruited and housed and provided with picks and shovels and carts and heavy horses to pull them—all that—before they've even laid a yard of track. So I finance my contracts by taking something like half of my payment in shares from the railway company, at a discount and in advance. Just pieces of paper, at that stage, offered for sale at a pound apiece, shall we say, but not really worth a brass farthing until the railway gets built. All right?''

She nodded, her chin on her hands, giving him the only thing she could just then: her utmost attention.

''So then I deposit my shares in the bank as security for the money they graciously lend me—at a high rate of interest, I might add—month by month to pay my suppliers and meet my wages bill until I get the job done. At which point, if it's a *good* railway which happens to be going where people want to travel, those shares that I got for one pound each might be worth two pounds—or three. Or more. Enough for me to settle my debt with the bank and ample to spare.''

''All right,'' she said. Enough for her to live on, too, in the luxury he had always encouraged, the lavish daily spending, the expensive dallying in foreign hotels, the gold bracelets and silk dresses and extravagant hats which he—she realized—had needed to give her rather more than she had needed to possess.

''If I'm guilty of anything,'' he said, his voice ringing hollow, ''then it's overtrading. Taking on too much at once. Spreading myself too thin, if you like. But—goddammit—there's only so much railway track a country can stand and once it's in—then it's in—and we'll be reduced to laying down track that doesn't go anywhere, which is a mug's game. I set out to avoid that. To get in fast and furious and grab as much as I could. And it *worked*—until Monday morning. You know that.''

''Yes. I know.''

''So I'm in a vicious circle. I've taken contracts all over the place, some of them within a few months of completion. And I may not be able to complete even one. The money I borrowed to do it doesn't exist anymore. It's just scraps of paper called railway shares in Milne, Morrissey's vaults,

worthless until I finish the railway I *can't* finish because
Milne, Morrissey can't release the money to pay my suppliers, which means not only that they'll stop supplying me
but might well take me to court for what I've had from them
already.''

A vicious circle indeed.

''What can you do?''

He grinned, looking suddenly—although only for a moment—himself again. ''A 'gentleman' might shoot himself,
I reckon. So I won't do that.''

''I'm pleased to hear it. What, then?''

He drew very deeply on his cigar, refilled his glass, and
then, intercepting her glance which inquired, ''Is it necessary, or even wise, to drink so much?'', took a long, hard
swallow and raised the now half-empty glass to her.

''What I have to do is raise money—if I can. Talk to other
banks. Talk to the liquidators who've moved in now to Milne,
Morrissey's and persuade them to raise a loan elsewhere—if
they can—so that I can get a line or two finished and those
shares quoted on the open market.''

''Will they do that?''

He shrugged, the heavy movement of his shoulders telling
her how tired he was, weary to the bone already with talk
and travel, pursuing dead ends, treading broken promises underfoot, with how many tons of bricks waiting to be paid for
on the site of every tunnel, how many thousand navvies waiting, with their women and children, for their wages.

''I don't know,'' he said. ''Officialdom moves slow. And
there'll be a dozen other men besides me out to convince
whoever needs convincing that *their* business commitments
are the only ones worth supporting. Because there won't be
enough support to go round. And even if I get my share of
it, it could take months. I haven't got months, Oriel. And my
navvies only know how to live from one Friday pay night to
the next. It's Thursday now. Tomorrow I'll be paying them
out of the cash I keep in the safe at Lydwick Green and one
or two other cash-boxes elsewhere—for as long as I can.''

Some men, she suspected, would not have paid their navvies at all, hanging on to those cash-boxes, even disappearing
with them, safe and not too unsound, across the channel.

''Of course,'' she said. And then, ''Garron—when did you
last eat?''

He looked slightly puzzled. ''Christ, I don't know—somewhere in London yesterday. The kind of boiled beef you wouldn't give to the cats.''

"I'll make you something then, quickly."

"Later." Once again he stared into the fire, picking up the poker and expertly prising apart a pair of smoldering logs. "*Later.* Let me say what I came for. It might improve your appetite. Or not. I don't know."

Patiently, her chin still on her hand, she waited.

"You're a cool customer, aren't you, Oriel? Most women would have been sobbing or swooning by now, I reckon, or damning me to hell for ruining their lives for them."

"It doesn't sound to me, Garron, that you're to blame."

He took another quick, hard swallow of the gardener's spirit. "Thank you kindly, ma'am. But you might change your mind about that if I don't pull it off. And I have to say I'm not sure I can. I'm talking about three and a half million pounds to complete the work I have in hand. It made me a very comfortable man, on paper, until Monday morning. And by this time next year, it would have been . . ."

His voice stopped. She saw his eyes close tight shut and then open again, looking as if the pain behind them had not moved an inch.

"Christ," he said. "Just listen to me now and let me get this over. I don't know how much I can get together. These bankers feel easier lending to the men they went to Eton or Harrow with than to men like me. But I'll raise something. Then I'll divert my men and my resources to the lines nearest completion and get them finished so I can raise more. If I can hold it together long enough then—yes—maybe—But all it's going to take is one accident, one stretch of swamp that takes longer to fill than I'd bargained for, one tunnel that needs a second lining—trouble with the men—anything—all the things that happen every day of the week somewhere or other—and I'm finished."

"Through no fault of your own."

"That doesn't console me. It makes me feel worse. I won't take ruin well, Oriel. That's for certain. And I don't expect you to take it with me."

A long silence fell between them, broken by her calm, so steady voice. "I haven't always been rich, Garron."

He gave a snort of what she knew to be heartfelt derision. "You haven't been poor either. Your mother may have had to be careful at times but she could always pay her parlormaid and hire her carriage. That's not poverty. And you just play at it here, my lass, brewing your witch's lotions and potions and pottering about in your garden with somebody else to do the heavy work and a grand house full of servants to go back to whenever the mood takes you. Poverty is when you have to do the digging yourself, and the scrubbing, and the patching up and making do, not just when the fancy takes you but year in year out—*forever*. I didn't marry you to bring you down to that.''

Quietly she straightened her back and folded her hands smoothly, neatly, in her lap. ''But we are married, Garron, nevertheless.''

''Yes.'' And she knew that this was what he had really come to say to her. ''But that doesn't mean we have to live together. No—don't interrupt—just listen to me, woman, until I've done. I've thought it all out. I've had plenty of time, sitting on those damned trains, here and everywhere, this last day or two. When I asked you to marry me I offered you a rich life. If I hadn't been sure I could provide it I wouldn't have asked. Would I?''

She shook her head.

''And even if I had you wouldn't have taken me—would you?''

She shook her head again.

''All right. So let's admit the truth, Oriel. In a case like this I reckon it's always best.''

She thought so too. ''Yes, Garron. The money was important. I don't suppose we would have met without it.''

''That's right. So if the money runs out . . . Well—fair's fair, after all. We get what we pay for in this world, and if it looks as if I won't be able to go on paying . . .''

His voice stopped again abruptly and then, just as abruptly, went on. ''You're a rich man's wife, Oriel. And if it turns out I can't afford you then I won't break you either. You don't even understand hardship, so how can I ask you to endure it? I don't mean to ask you, anyway—and that's that. I'll keep Jamie with me. Wherever I end up I'll be able to forage for the two of us. I'll send the girls back to Scotland to their mother's kin. And I'll get you an income signed over to you— enough to live on. The money the Stangways left you never went to Milne, Morrissey. Your cousin Quentin couldn't see the point in moving it from one bank to another so I left it where it was. You could just about live on the interest. So

I'll get your clever cousin to place it, somehow, beyond the reach of any creditors of mine. The same with that little house of your mother's. That's what we'll do.''

Standing up, she walked over to the window, her point of refuge it seemed at times of emotion, although, as the day darkened and clouded over, she could see little beyond the wall of her own garden, only guessing at the somber, relentless aspect of the winter fells, the immense silence of the water. And, as she looked out, it seemed that the whole essence of herself was flowing inward, to the man behind her who thought himself to be worthless without his grand house, his wardrobe of London tailored clothes, his three and a half million.

She did not.

"No, Garron. *This* is what we'll do.''

He stood up too, just a shade unsteadily she thought, looking very big and strong in the small room with its low ceiling yet—for the first time in her experience of him—vulnerable, ready to bluster and shout perhaps that he would have his way but tired out and hungry, with a pain in his head and as much in need as a man could be of somebody—some woman—to hold his hand and murmur to him that she trusted him, believed in him, and that everything would be all right.

A strong woman, of course, and Oriel, smiling at him across the warm fragrant room, had never felt stronger.

"You can't send the girls back to Scotland, Garron. It's been too long. They wouldn't fit in there now. Morag would be terribly unhappy. And I daren't think what Elspeth would do.''

"Do you think I don't know that,'' he groaned, "but what else . . . ?''

"I'll tell you. Sell my mother's house in Lydwick Park. It must be worth a lot. And use the Stangway money as well. It might only be a drop in the ocean but surely every drop must count. And since this cottage isn't worth much at all— or so you keep on telling me—then I'll make a home here for the girls, and for you and Jamie. Oh yes—just listen to me, Garron, until I'm done. I listened to you. Jamie likes it here. Morag doesn't but she'd prefer it to gutting herring in Scotland, and if she understands it's to help you then I'm sure she'll do her best. It could be the making of her. And Elspeth has the Landons—Tom Landon in particular. And since you haven't lost money through incompetence—quite the reverse—nobody will have anything but sympathy for the girls, and enormous admiration for you if you put things right. As I have, Garron. Enormous admiration—whether you put things right or not.''

''You admire me?'' His voice came to her, rough-edged and sharp, through the gathering twilight.

''Well—yes. Even though you *have* just been trying to cast me off.''

Once more he shook his head with the restive movement of pain. ''Oriel—the trouble between us is that, half the time, I can't tell—you having been brought up so sheltered—if you even *know* what's what—or what you could be letting yourself in for.''

Tossing her own head, fine and steady and entirely free from pain, she laughed at him. ''Of course I know. You need a base, Garron. Somewhere to come home to. And you need that whatever happens—or fails to happen. Not just hotel rooms and all that goes with them. Beef I wouldn't give to my cats, and the company of certain women whose profession I ought not to know about, when you're feeling miserable—who won't make you feel much better. And won't set a good example to Jamie either. You'd really do much better to keep me on and get your money's worth out of me, darling—as I've had mine so often out of you.'' Had she made him smile? She thought so. ''You're not nineteen anymore, Garron, you know—with nobody to fight for but yourself. You have a family who ought to stay together. Elspeth and Morag would make very odd wives for Scottish fishermen after all you've had me teach them. And if you went on the wander somewhere in South America or Australia—which is what I expect you're thinking—you could lose Jamie out there and never see him again. You wouldn't like that. *I* wouldn't like it. And the girls need you. I think you need them. And money sent up to Scotland whenever you happen to have it, isn't the same as a father. So let's try and get through this together, shall we? That's what we ought to do.''

She felt rather than saw him cross the room to her, pressing her up against the window as someone else had pressed her not too long ago, his arms sliding around her, his aching forehead hot and heavy against hers. ''Oh God, Oriel. I feel terrible,'' he said.

''*And* you look it. Let me get you some dinner now.''

''I think I'd be sick.''

"Good Heavens, is my cooking so bad? Then come upstairs. I have a herb pillow and all sorts of dried flowers in my mattress that smell like paradise—or as one hopes it does."

He had never spent the night here before and now, her mouth to his ear, deliberately coquettish, her body already offering a direct comfort of its own, she whispered, "It's getting dark. Too late for the George at Penrith or the Queen's Head at Askham. And the Buck Inn at Howtown is full. I think you'll just have to sleep with me."

As he had been big and forceful and vulnerable in the small parlor so did he seem to fill her bedroom with its pale walls, its scents of violet and lemon, its window always slightly open to the moonlight, and the sounds of the high fells, as he lay on her bed for a while, exhausted, bemused even, while she placed her cool hands on his throbbing temples and then kissed them, kneeling beside him with only her long pale hair to cover her, each part of her body yielding to him as he reached out and touched it and then the whole, moon-silvered length of her falling over him, lightly, languorously taking him into herself and holding him there, exciting him almost to worship rather than possession and then fulfilling him, emptying him at the same time of his pain and his pleasure, so that he could rest.

Half-asleep, exhausted now beyond reason yet no longer aching, he muttered, "What happens to you in this place, Oriel?" And then, waking suddenly after what seemed to him ten minutes but, in reality, had been an hour, he called out, still from his dream, "I've never imagined such a woman."

She was sitting on the window seat, still naked, her hair around her shoulders, looking out at the moon on the water; and reaching her in one stride, he picked her up, as if he thought she might fly out through the tiny mullions away across the fells, and held her tight.

"What are you doing?"

Smiling, she leaned her head into his shoulder. "I was thinking, Garron . . ."

"What?"

"That this might be our wedding-night. Shall we say it is?" She knew he was going to carry her back to her herb-sweet mattress and make love to her again. Her body was already waiting. He did so, urgently, taking possession, reasserting his claim, his woman, truly now and irrevocably his own.

"I would have let you go," he said, considerably out of breath. "I meant what I said. You could have had the money and left me to do the best I could on my own. And I'd have wished you luck."

"I know."

"Not now, Oriel. Do you know that too?"

She could feel the whole length of his hard body trembling.

"Yes, Garron. I know."

"Then remember it. Because God help you if you try to leave me now. And God help anybody else—man, woman, or child—who tries to take you an inch away."

Sixteen

The next morning, on her advice, he sent for his daughters and explained to them his exact position; Morag, who had heard a great deal about bank failures from her friend in Penrith, springing at once to defend him, declaring she would help in any way possible, do his book-keeping if he could no longer afford a secretary, run errands, go out—if it came to it—and earn money herself as a governess. While Elspeth, who understood nothing of banks and did not think it the business of a young lady even to carry money in her pockets, much less earn it, threw her arms around him nevertheless and—quite forgetting how all this might damage her position with Tom Landon—offered her father the contents of her trinket box.

"Keep it for now," he told her gravely, realizing the sacrifice she believed herself to be making. "I'll come to you at need." And even Morag showed no temptation to point out to her the true worth of her few strands of pearl and coral compared to their father's need. Although both girls appeared somewhat chastened and thoughtful when he pointed out to them that had it not been for Oriel's intervention they might well have found themselves back in Scotland harvesting the herring.

"I couldn't have borne that," Elspeth kept on whispering to Oriel, sitting very close to her on the train journey home, holding her hand as they walked along the platform at Lydwick, following her around the house for several days to make sure she was still there, had not changed her mind, or had it changed for her by her relations who would surely advise her to take the money her husband had offered while it still existed and go away.

"I suppose it is even wrong of us to try to keep you," she said, once or twice, her scared eyes pleading with Oriel to say "No. Absolutely not. You have every right," and then squeezing her hand in a burst of gratitude when she did say, "Well, I don't know about that, but I'm staying anyway."

"Let me get you a cup of tea?" murmured Elspeth, still living in the world where all she meant was "Let me ring and order it, in your favorite china with a little posy of spring flowers on the tray."

Elspeth was scared, eager to please since she doubted her ability to do anything of a more practical nature, eager to let her father know how much she trusted him to restore her to a position where Tom Landon of Watermillock would feel safe to go on wooing her; or, failing that, how much she trusted her father's wife to teach her how to become a most enchanting Cinderella. And although Morag had far less to say about it and seemed uneasy, at times, in Oriel's company, experiencing some difficulty in meeting her eye, she placed herself, nevertheless, entirely at Oriel's service, working quietly beside her through long hours—some of them painful to Oriel—making an inventory of the valuables in both the Keith house and Evangeline's which, at need, she would be able to sell.

A pair of Meissen vases to settle a week's wages at the site of a Welsh or Scottish tunnel, a Crown Derby dinner service to do the same elsewhere, a Turkey carpet or two to settle the account of a local brickmaker and encourage him to take the risk of supplying more; a diamond solitaire for which Evangeline had paid a fatal price to Lord Merton to buy perhaps half a mile of iron track.

Listing each item with an estimated value beside it, Oriel knew, very well, that in her place her mother would have considered no alternative except to bolt as fast and as far as she could, taking her crystal and china, her child, certainly her diamonds very firmly with her.

"Why, I ask myself," and she could hear the cold and furious amazement in her mother's voice, ". . . Why, Oriel, are you giving away my prizes, my wages for which I worked and suffered, to that man you married against my wishes? Oh yes indeed, I know he could take them all by force, with the law on his side, since he is your husband. But such laws are to be evaded, my love—*got around*—as you know very well. So what is stopping you from hiding a good half of them away and selling them for yourself, later . . . ? Good Heavens, all you have to do—if he asks—is tell him my china is smashed, my pictures worthless, or that a thief broke in and stole the best . . . How do you think I got them in the first place? And I gave them to you, Oriel. Only to you. So that whatever happened to anybody else you would be safe—and free.''

''What is the matter?'' Morag asked suddenly, a silver statuette of Artemis the Huntress in her hands, a near-naked figure which Evangeline, suddenly declaring it to be an embarrassment to Letty who had grown most puritanical since she had stopped having babies, had decided to ''whisk it away to the attic where your sister will not have to look at it, dear Matthew,'' bringing it, instead, to Lydwick Park.

''What should be the matter?'' said Oriel.

''Something. You looked as if you were going to cry.''

''I was thinking of my mother.'' And, Evangeline having always been a delicate subject, she was surprised—and then pleased—when Morag, uncomfortable with her sympathy, muttered, ''Yes, I thought that must be it—these being her things. I'm sorry. I didn't like her but you did, so—I'm sorry.''

The girl was really saying, ''If I had a cat that scratched everybody but me then I expect *I'd* like it too. I'd be bound to wouldn't I—maybe very much.'' And had Oriel dared she would have reached out and drawn the thin, unyielding girl toward her in a comfortable, woman-to-woman embrace.

Yet, although such daring still seemed a shade premature, it was to Morag she turned for practical, always willing help as the household prepared itself for war, ready not only to withstand a siege but to provide a solid base of operations and creature comforts whenever their soldiers, their fighting-men—Garron, his agents and foremen, his irrepressible son Jamie—required them.

All social engagements were canceled, all accounts with local tradesmen settled so that there should be no embarrassment about milk or meat or eggs, all members of the household staff called together and informed—as Oriel thought only decent—that although she could pay their wages now and in the foreseeable future she would bear no grudge against any who chose to take up an advantageous situation elsewhere.

Evangeline's house in Lydwick Park was sold, its contents being stored away for the present, all separately wrapped and labeled in Morag's neat hand. The Keith house, in Lydwick Green, was mortgaged, to the hilt, of course, as everyone was rightly saying, only the lakeland cottage remaining free of debt because—it was generally assumed—no one would care to lend on it.

"How dreadful for you, Oriel dear," said Maud and Letty, driving over together. "Your poor mother would turn over in her grave."

"I'm here," said Kate, having returned by no means apologetically from France. "Use me. I don't know what for but whatever it is I'll do it. Remember."

Francis Ashington wrote a dignified letter of condolence to Garron whom he hardly knew, and, in a private moment with Oriel offered services which she—despite an untimely interruption by Susannah—understood to be those of a knight in immaculately shining armor, available the very moment she became a lady in distress.

Quentin Saint-Charles made some discreet murmurings which she interpreted as a request—should her husband go completely under—to allow him to employ his legal expertise on her behalf, thus salvaging as much as a clever lawyer could, for her personal use, from the wreckage. These various offers of support giving Oriel a deep pleasure hardly spoiled at all by Susannah's frequent, vaguely biblical mutterings about guilt or the bringing of the spiritually tainted to justice.

"What is the matter with *her*?" inquired Elspeth who rather hoped it might be something unpleasant.

"Old age and virginity," said Jamie to whom the latter word was, nowadays, of considerable interest.

"Nothing," said Morag sharply, so nervously, that it crossed Oriel's mind to wonder if Susannah had done something, or confided something, about which Morag was worried.

Surely not? For what else could it be but the old, old story of the curate Mr. Field who had been engaged to Susannah for almost five years? Poor man. Oriel had always felt sorry for him and rather guilty when, just before her mother died, she had persuaded Francis—entirely on Susannah's behalf—not to give Mr. Field the living of Dessborough's church. Susannah had wished to be a fiancée from whom no mother

could expect too much in the way of domestic assistance,
rather than a bride for whom domesticity would be inevitable
and, considering Mr. Field's earning power, lamentably single-handed. But Matthew Stangway's death, by releasing
Maud to take up permanent residence at the vicarage, had
also released Susannah from her remaining obligations. Mr.
Field, therefore, had been given his marching orders, whereupon Oriel, entirely in a spirit of making amends, had driven
over to Dessborough, only a week after Matthew's funeral,
and secured for him the post of Francis Ashington's vicar
which was still vacant. A good deed in her opinion, which
had caused both her and Francis a great deal of amusement.
An unpardonable interference, somehow or other, to Susannah, possibly—suggested Francis—because the living was
reasonably paid with not too much work attached to it, and
because, at the very beginning of his occupation, Mr. Field
had made the acquaintance of a healthy, solid, very cheerful
Dessborough girl, only nineteen years old and terribly flattered to have caught the new vicar's eye.

On the day Francis called at Lydwick to offer Oriel his
help, they had still found a moment to laugh about Mr. Field
and had been heard to do so by Susannah who, since she
ought not to have walked unannounced into Oriel's drawing-
room, had felt unable to complain—at least not to Oriel—of
what she found there. But she had complained to others, putting around a discreetly worded opinion that Mrs. Oriel
Keith's pleasure in her "friendships"—with those of both
sexes—had always diverted her so much that her sudden devotion to her husband in his time of trouble, although no
doubt just as "saintly" as people were saying, might also
have its share of guilt.

"Ask her exactly what she means by that," advised Kate,
who would certainly have tackled Susannah herself had she
not been fully ostracized by Gore Valley Society, thus making her intervention of no use at all.

Nevertheless. "You ought to have this out with Susannah," she said. "You ought to invite her to tea with at least
a dozen other people and ask her, straight out, in front of
everybody, just what she has against you. That's bound to
settle it."

But when Morag heard this suggestion she turned chalk-
white and, after a moment of strangled silence, gasped out,

"Oh no—I wouldn't do that. No—I wouldn't. She's been under a lot of stress lately . . ."

"Hardly more than we've been under, Morag," murmured Oriel.

"Oh—I know. But—you see—it may not be you she's annoyed with. It may be somebody else—really . . ."

"Morag." And, driven by the spirit of defense for those with whom one has labored in cheerful adversity, Oriel felt herself to be bristling. "If Susannah is bothering you—or bullying you—in any way, and I mean any way, then you have only to say so. And I'll sort her out double quick."

"No," said Morag, closing her eyes as if she were praying. "Please—absolutely not."

Was Susannah jealous, wondered Oriel, of the new rapport between Morag and herself, the natural ease with which—when it really mattered—one strong woman could recognize and turn to another? Or jealous, quite simply, because the Keith household, in its time of crisis, was pulling together without her help? Had it hurt her to discover that, when it came down to it, Morag's love and loyalty belonged exclusively to Garron and to those *he* trusted best to help him? It seemed highly likely, and so highly like Susannah that Oriel let it slip easily from her mind, taking no steps other than to keep Morag out of Susannah's way. "Morag is a tremendous help to me," she told everyone and it was true. Morag, the proud and loving daughter who, having coped with the realization that Oriel was on her father's side, Susannah only scheming for herself, had placed her own very useful energies entirely at Oriel's disposal, becoming a valuable part of the façade of calm and confidence Oriel was, day by day, creating.

She had never realized how much money Garron kept in the house, would never have slept easily if she had, but during those first taut weeks following the collapse of the Milne, Morrissey Bank—further complicated by the suicide of Mr. Morrissey, the bank's founder—she carried the keys of the strong-box all day in her pocket, concealing them all night under her pillow, ready to pay out, with a charming smile, any man who presented himself to her with Garron's authorization.

"My navvies have to have their wages," Garron had told her before setting off for London. "And it's not only because they might gang together and kill me if they don't. I have to keep them working, and since they work for money then, if it takes the last penny . . . You understand?''

She understood. And, taking her understanding beyond their need of this week's wages to some reasonable assurances about next week and the week after—when a man and his family would have an identical need to eat and drink—she received each one of the site managers Garron sent to her with half an hour's rational discussion, before settling his wages' bill, over an excellent pot of tea, demonstrating not only her confidence in her husband's ability to retrieve the situation but that she had enough intelligence to appreciate what ''the situation'' actually was.

''If the men take fright and run off,'' Garron had warned her, ''then we're finished.'' Therefore *she*—while he was busy with lawyers and bankers and railway officials—took it upon herself to see that they did not, presenting herself to the visiting site managers not as a drawing-room lady, the kind of ''contractor's luxury item'' they may well have been expecting, but a level-headed, competent, thoroughly decent woman who sent them back to their work-force looking cheerful, feeling, often in spite of themselves, that if Mrs. Keith thought the job was safe then perhaps it was.

''They all keep telling me about this wonderful Mrs. Keith,'' said Garron, home not even for a day but just long enough to collect some cash and eat a hastily prepared luncheon before setting off again to settle the temper of a difficult site in Lancashire. Then back to London and the negotiations which Mr. Morrissey's suicide had done nothing to bring forward, merely providing excuses—in Garron's opinion—for delay under the guise of shock, or sorrow, or respect.

He had no respect for Milne, Morrissey whatsoever, or no more than they would have had for him had he made rash investments—which he had not—or failed to meet his obligations which, although he could not meet them now, of course, was Milne, Morrissey's fault entirely, not his.

''Did you go to the funeral?'' she asked him.

''I did.'' And helping himself to another slice of apple-tart and half a jug of cream, he grinned at her. ''Mainly to make sure he was dead. And I wouldn't have been the only one ready to nail him back in his coffin if he'd tried to get out of it.''

But Mr. Morrissey's death had not been the only one, the irrevocable collapse of several businesses, the atrocious position of many private individuals who had not only lost their savings but could no longer draw money to pay their outstanding bills, having resulted in at least three cases of heart-failure Garron knew of, one sad end by drowning, the disappearance—presumably abroad—of several men who evidently could not face their families, and a great deal of hysteria, from both sexes, requiring both legal and medical attention.

"Which goes to prove what they say about an ill wind," said Garron. "Providing, of course, all those doctors and lawyers everybody is calling in can manage to get their fees."

He was looking tired and strained but, having expected that, she saw no reason to make it worse by telling him so, concluding that the tiredness could be put down to his journey while the strain might be noticeable to no one but herself.

"There's hot water," she said, "*very* hot, ready upstairs, and a clean shirt . . . And I've had that greatcoat of yours cleaned and brushed—the one with all the extravagant shoulder capes and the fur lining. I thought the navvies might appreciate seeing you look expensive and—well—quite handsome."

He laid down his spoon and fork, got to his feet, held out a hand to her, the fierce pressure of which she accepted almost without flinching.

"There isn't time," he said. "Not to make love, anyway. And I won't use you like a . . . You know what I mean."

Smiling—not wishing to remind him that he had used her in that way rather more than several times before—she slid her arms around his neck and, crushing her against him, he muttered into her ear, "When this is over I'll buy you a diamond twice the size of your mother's. Twice the size at least—I swear it."

She smiled once again, "Thank you, Garron," thinking it a pity she could not quite bring herself to tease him as to why her price had gone up.

She brought him his many-caped greatcoat instead, the early March day turning chilly, adjusted the pearl pin in his cravat, added a cream silk muffler, walked with him to the garden gate, her hair hanging down as she had done on her wedding morning, waving him goodbye and then, turning to find Morag behind her as she had also done on that distant day, throwing her arm—at last—around the girl's shoulders and walking companionably back to the house with her, their heads together.

She knew his first objective must be to recover his railway shares, lying worthless in a bank vault, there being no point in risking everything he still owned in bringing a railway line to completion and profitability unless those shares were in his possession. And since they could only be released to him on repayment of the loan for which they had acted as collateral, money already eaten up by both the raw and human materials of his trade, he must now seek to borrow elsewhere, and mainly on trust, enough to buy his collateral back again. At which point a hazardous race against time must be embarked upon to get his most profitable line finished, his completion money—in cash—in his hand, his shares floated on the stock exchange and, if they should double or triple their value, enabling him to finish the next good line, and the next, and the one after until—if he managed to stave off death by exhaustion or frustration or sheer bad temper, not always his own—he would be back on his feet in a few months again.

His first task—completed within the bleak week of the bank failure—had been to convince the railway companies that they would find it cheaper, in the long run, to give him their support, if only verbal, instead of turning him off his sites and making them over to another contractor. And it pleased Oriel that the famous engineer, Mr. Morgan de Hay, who had been her dinner partner on the night she met Garron, had consented to accompany him on his rounds of such banks with money still to lend, Mr. de Hay, who had become even more famous and more accustomed to being listened to, freely expressing his opinion that as contractors went, which at times could never be far enough, Mr. Keith was as good as any bank would be likely to get. Efficient above the average. Reliable, even. A hungry fighter who, now that his appetite had been whetted again, would be as likely to get his lines finished as anybody else Mr. de Hay could bring to mind just then. And far more likely than some.

"He's another one," said Garron, "who wished to be remembered to the lovely Mrs. Keith."

"I remember him," she said and wrote him a note to say so when she heard of the visit he had made with Garron to a line he had engineered and Garron was constructing, a hundred and twenty miles across the Midlands, to explain the likelihood of Garron completing it in the time he said he could, and the certain profitability if he did so, to representatives of Garron's new bank.

"Midland line agreed six months," he telegraphed to Oriel, sounding a note of triumph which he instantly dispersed by arriving three days later to inform her that although six months might seem reasonable to the bank and certainly to de Hay who was only interested in getting his own line done, it would be too long for Garron to hold his overall interests together. Six months would mean the collapse of other lines he valued every bit as much as the Midland crossing, since how long did she think the cash would last with all those men to pay?

"Evidently not six months," she said.

"No. If it takes me six months we might keep our heads above water. If I do it in three then I believe we just might be home and dry."

"Can you do it in three?"

"De Hay wouldn't think so—which is why I didn't tell him. So he couldn't tell the bank and panic them into thinking me rash . . ."

"And are you?"

"Yes. Of course I am. Always have been."

Sitting by the parlor fire at an advanced hour of the night, she saw, as he lit his cigar, the taut muscles in his cheeks, the hard mouth smiling with a humor that had always been faintly bitter. "Oriel—you don't know the risks I took in the old days."

"I can imagine."

"I doubt it. Risks with myself and risks with other people too, I have to admit. The difference being that I didn't much care about risk then—or didn't see it. I see it now."

"But you'll take it just the same."

"I will. Otherwise I'll be a small man again, Oriel. Just making a living. A man the navvies don't trust because he's let them down, and a man the railway companies don't trust either because, in a year or two, they won't remember why I couldn't complete—whether it was the bank's fault or mine. And just 'making a living' wouldn't be enough for me, Oriel. It's not my style."

"So you'll do the Midland line in three months." Very carefully she had not asked him if he really believed he could.

"Yes. Three hard months—" she saw he was talking to himself—"bloody hard. I'll have to live on the site . . ."

Leaning toward him, sliding her hand into his, she said, "Would you like me to come with you?"

"Like it?" Instantly his brooding, his mulling over of those back-breaking, possibly heart-breaking months was gone. "Of course I'd like it . . ."

"I'll come then."

"And live in a navvy hut with a dozen randy lodgers?"

"I suppose you could protect me—couldn't you? Although to tell the truth, I was thinking of a room in the nearest town."

Laughing, shaking his head, his hands closed around hers, drawing her toward him. "Or a suite in the nearest grand hotel, which would be nowhere near at all, I do assure you. No. Wait for me here, Oriel. I've saved this house for you and the kids whatever happens. Look after them—and the cash, I reckon. And when it's over we'll go up to Ullswater for a week or so, just the two of us. You with your big new diamond and me more than ready for that herb-pillow—waiting to get moonstruck again like I seemed to be that night . . . You remember?"

"Yes. Three months, then."

Once again she walked with him to the garden gate and waved him off.

"Are you falling in love with that giant of yours?" asked Kate, expecting no answer and receiving none.

"Are you going to talk to your husband?" inquired Oriel blandly.

"Yes, Oriel. I'm going to talk to him."

"And when might that be?"

Kate smiled. "When I can."

"Ah—of course."

"It has only been a few weeks, Oriel. Six at the most . . ."

"Eight."

"Ah yes." Sipping tea lightly flavored with lemon from Oriel's pure white china with its delicate pattern of gold fleur-de-lis, Kate smiled. "Must we be so precise? I will talk to Francis when I can, Oriel. Not because I am a monster of selfishness and depravity, as people say—although, of course, they are fully entitled to their opinion—but because when I do talk to him I must be sure of saying the right things."

"He is a rather wonderful man, Kate."

"Do you think so? I'm sure you are right. Although the truth is I hardly know him. Can you believe that?"

"Easily."

Kate nodded, very pleasantly. "Quite so. I fell in love with a figment of my own imagination. I know that much for certain. And then, when the 'figment' evaporated—which didn't take long—I felt so guilty. Lord—how guilty. Because how could I blame him for not being the man I'd thought he was when he'd never even pretended in the first place? What he really wanted was to go to Mecca. The trouble was, so did I."

"And what do you want now?"

"I'll tell you when I can." And then, jumping to her feet, crossing to the window for the sheer pleasure, it seemed, of exercising her slender, still brittle limbs, she called out, "Oh look, Oriel—there's Quentin coming up your garden path. How lovely. Except—oh damnation, damnation—he has Susannah with him. I'd better run upstairs, I suppose, and hide in your bedroom to deny her the pleasure of not speaking to me. Which is a great nuisance, since I find Quentin has turned out so entertaining. Don't you? Or are you going to tell me that he always was?"

Yet, when the drawing-room door was opened by Oriel's butler only "Mr. Saint-Charles, madam," was announced, Susanah having gone up to Morag's room with a parcel of books she had apparently promised.

"Really," said Oriel, by no means pleased about it.

"Thank heaven for Morag," said Kate, very pleased indeed, her eyes a bright challenge. "Oriel and I have just been saying how entertaining you are, Quentin."

He bowed. "Thank you, Kate. What a pity you failed, so abysmally, in your youth, to form that opinion."

Kate burst into a peal of laughter so uncomplicated, so wholly natural as to leave Oriel in no doubt as to the easy terms on which she and Quentin now stood.

"Well, yes, Quentin, I did think you dreadful once. But that was when you were trying to marry me for my money. As you were, you know."

He smiled. So did Oriel.

"I know," he said. "And why not? It seemed an entirely logical undertaking then—and even now. . . ."

"You mean you would still do it?" She looked greatly

elated, as if she found the theory of marriage, if not its practice, a most amusing topic of discussion.

So too, it seemed, did Quentin. "Let's not be too hasty," he said. "One must first consider the cost of getting your freedom. But—well—let's say that if you managed it with enough of the Kessler inheritance still sticking to you, then yes—we might very likely reach an agreement."

"Quentin Saint-Charles," she sounded delighted. "What a cold-hearted monster you are."

He bowed again. "My dear, it is called realism. What else could induce a man in my position to marry?"

"You might fall in love, I suppose?"

"I might. What has that to do with marriage?"

"So you are a matrimonial predator," said Kate, as if awarding him a medal.

"I dare say I am," he agreed, bowing again to allow the Order of whatever she was bestowing upon him to pass smoothly around his neck.

"And are there no limits to your callous opportunism?"

"I shouldn't think so."

"You hear that, Oriel?" Kate gurgled happily. "It strikes me he would even marry Dora Merton . . ."

"Even?" said Quentin levelly and coolly. "Dear Kate—there is no *even* about it."

"*Quentin*. Surely not?" Now he had really entertained her. "Not Dora. Not 'Madcap' anymore, I fear, just a poor lunatic, all alone in her mansion . . ."

"Kate," he said crisply. "She is richer than you. Not only in money but in property extensive enough to get her husband elected as a Member of Parliament, if that happened to be his fancy. And contacts enough to give him a more than even chance of a seat on some Prime Minister's cabinet . . ."

"Which Prime Minister?" murmured Oriel.

"My dear—it hardly seems relevant. Can *you* tell one from the other?"

She shook her head. "No. I must admit to finding them tediously similar. You would surely grace the office, Quentin."

This time he bowed to her. "Indeed. Which gives me cause not so much to regret Dora's little instabilities of character—hardly lunacy, Kate—as the sorry fact that she will not have me."

"Have you asked her?" Kate and Oriel spoke together.

"Ladies—good Heavens." His expression of shock was, they both felt, quite masterly. "Do you imagine, had I done so, that I would be here to tell the tale? Lady Merton would have had me on a convict ship to Australia the morning after. Or, failing that, a few whispers in powerful ears about it suiting her if my legal career came to an end, and—well . . . Can one doubt it would have ended?"

They were all three laughing easily, companionably, thoroughly enjoying their own wit and one another's, when Susannah suddenly entered the room, her taut appearance taking Kate in particular so much by surprise that she said incautiously, "Oh hello, Susannah, we were just talking about foolish marriages . . ." A remark she realized to be unkind, unwise, probably downright foolish the moment she remembered that Mr. Field, Susannah's recently released fiancé, had just announced the date of his marriage, in his own church, to that winsome, apparently very willing Dessborough maiden of just nineteen.

"Indeed," said Susannah, looking straight at Oriel, it being against her principles either to see or hear or otherwise acknowledge Kate. "And you will be attending Mr. Field's wedding, Oriel, I suppose."

"Yes, Susannah." Oriel saw no reason to evade the issue. "Since he has been kind enough to invite me . . ."

"Oh naturally—naturally . . ." Susannah was, quite simply and quite obviously, beside herself with rage. "How could he be other than very grateful to you, Oriel, for using your influence with your friend, the squire, to get him the living? And the wife, of course, which seems to go with it . . ."

"Susannah," said Oriel very firmly. "When you broke off your engagement to Mr. Field I understood you wished it to be final. Was I mistaken?"

Had life at the vicarage, under Maud, proved more demanding than anticipated? If so, Oriel felt no compulsion to apologize. Nor Susannah, it seemed, to forgive.

"I am ready to go now, Quentin," she said to her brother. "And I feel it only right to tell you—face to face, Oriel—that I shall not be coming to this house again."

"Tell her why," Kate snapped curtly.

"Yes," said Oriel, curt herself in the probable defense of Morag with whom Susannah had clearly quarreled during the past half hour. "You'd better say why."

"Indeed I will. But to the proper person—to the head of this household . . ."

"You'll leave my husband alone," Oriel informed her, knowing she ought to have made this statement years ago. "Good Heavens, Susannah, you must know *something* about the situation he's in. And until he's resolved it you won't bother him—*I'm* telling you."

Susannah ignored her. "We will have to be off, Quentin. You promised Mama you would call in for at least half an hour on the way back. And Aunt Maud has made a chocolate cake."

"Oh—absolutely . . ." he murmured, allowing her to leave the room and then, as Oriel turned abruptly in his direction, a hand flung out to detain him, he smiled at her, his fingers lightly pressing hers and then letting them go. "I know, Oriel. You want me to find out what is the matter with her, and restrain her from annoying your wounded giant. Naturally I shall do the best I can."

Her wounded giant? Since his return to the Midlands she had spent only two days with him in a town she could not remember, the weather being dark, her attention, her energy, her ingenuity, wholly absorbed by her effort to recreate for him, at his giant demand, the moonlit, Lakeland night when she had first made love to him instead of pleasantly accepting the love he had made so often, so vigorously, to her. How was he now? Gigantic, she thought, as both Kate and Quentin had said. Fighting hard and hungry and winning, she believed, ready to take that Midland line in his own hands and wrestle it to completion.

Only a month to go now, he telegraphed to her. Then two weeks. Then—"shockingly" it seemed rather than the much tamer "suddenly"—there he was, striding into the house late one afternoon, with no warning, no message of triumph to say "It's done. Wait for me with your hair down. Prepare yourself for Ullswater," and no air of celebration about him either as, throwing his hat and coat and gloves in the direction where somebody might well be waiting to catch them, he ignored completely the woman of his new, moonlit illusions and, freezing her exultant welcome in its tracks, growled out, harsh and loud, the single query, "Morag—where the hell is she?"

She came to the foot of the stairs, looking, it seemed to

Oriel, like a thin column of ash in the precarious moment of disintegration.

"Here, Father." And it was the toneless, hopeless answer one might give to an executioner.

"Then get in *there*," he said, his hand indicating his study with the ugly, jabbing motion of a hatchet.

"Yes, Father." And she walked before him, her head bent low, so obviously expecting some part of herself to die that Oriel—had she dared—would have barred the way. She did not dare. Nor did Elspeth, appearing around the corner of the stairs, dare to do more than whisper, "What is it? What has she done? Oh Lord—Lord—I've seen him angry before. But not like that."

"She's quarreled with Susannah," Oriel whispered back. "That must be it. Susannah has told him something about her—made some complaint, I expect. Go on upstairs, Elspeth. I'll wait here—and see."

"Oh yes—I'll go—don't leave her."

Elspeth, in her great terror, seemed to melt away, the last thing to disappear being her light voice, eerie with distance. "Poor Morag. Don't leave her. Oh Lord—how I hate that Susannah. How I wish . . ."

But what had Morag done to call forth such anger, to make him leave his Midland line two weeks before completion and stride into his home as if hunting down a mortal enemy? Waiting in the hall, her stomach churning with anxiety, Oriel could not imagine it, even when she heard the study door slam and Morag came running past her, one hand over her mouth, the other pressed to her stomach in the unmistakable pose of nausea.

The girl was going to be sick. "Morag . . ." But then, hearing the snarl that was Garron's voice first giving orders of some kind to the butler and then calling her name, she went into the study, suddenly a room where violence—she could feel it all around her—had been done, and let a moment pass for the good reason that she could think of no words safe enough to speak. A moment more. But then, because his hardness and brutality had such a pit of weariness underneath it, because he looked so like a man, it suddenly struck her, who, having averted one fatal disaster has been driven to something like desperation by another she said "Garron," speaking his name almost as if he needed to be reminded, recalled from the terrible arena in which he seemed, so cruelly, to be struggling. And then, when he did not answer, she almost called out to him, knowing that this matter, at least, could have nothing to do with Morag. "Garron—how is the line going?"

"All right," he said, and what terrified her all over again was that he hardly seemed to care. "Finished near as dammit. They can manage without me now, so I thought I'd come . . ."

"What is it with Morag?"

"Later." Standing by his desk he bent his head, two letters in his hand, his face closed, his jaw set in a line of cold authority. "We'll get to Morag later. I thought I'd come home to settle one or two matters outstanding . . ."

But his voice, somehow, did not—*could* not?—continue and, shocked into hasty speech herself, she caught sight of his greatcoat flung on the chair back and almost cried out swiftly, her nerve—for reasons which could not be obvious to him, since she could not have named them herself—clearly going.

"Are you going out again . . . ?"

"I am. And the girls with me."

"Oh—am I—? May I know . . . ?"

"No. Not yet."

"Then . . . ?"

"*Listen*, first—will you . . . ?"

"Garron?"

"Aye. You see these letters?"

And it was with pure horror, with an anguish unknown as yet but *there*, in every pore of her mind nevertheless, that she saw the two letters shake in his hand, saw the steel-hard determination with which he laid them down on the desk before him, and then, when the raw moment had passed, picked them up again without a tremor.

"These letters . . ." And there was no tremor in his voice now, either, his face set in lines so rigid that it might have been the mask of—what? Harsh Justice? And its accompanying need for Punishment?

"Letters?" And even though she had no reason—surely—for guilt or fear, she could hear both these alarmed voices whispering behind her own. Could he hear them too?

"Yes," he said. "Letters."

"Oh—?"

"Sent to me at the site . . . ." and she realized that although his eyes were fixed on her face he was not looking at her.

"Sent by whom?"

"By your friend Susannah."

Friend? Never. Declared enemy by now, surely? But it was as she drew breath to tell him so, to laugh every Susannah of the world to facile scorn, that the screen upon his vision fell aside, exposing her to the full shock of emotions which her own civilized, so carefully trained nature had, until now, avoided. Pain—his pain—which overwhelmed her, his fury at suffering it, fear—yes, *fear*, she could not mistake it—at the violence such pain and fury might unleash within him unless now—absolutely now—he forced them back within the barriers he had erected around his own heart.

"Garron . . . ?"

"Yes," he said, as if finding it difficult even to acknowledge his own name. And then, blinking hard, "Yes, Oriel. Let's get it over with, shall we?"

"I'm here, Garron."

And it was the anxiety in her voice for him, the offer, all over again, of her support in his crisis—whatever it may turn out to be—that released a sharp, clearly painful laugh in his chest, which set free his voice again.

"Aye. You're here. So it won't take long. And let me say now that I don't want it to take long, either. Two letters. You see them? One from Susannah herself. The other a copy of a letter Morag sent to her, three months ago, from your blessed Ullswater. Morag needing advice—doesn't it stand to reason?—as to what to do about . . . your adultery, Oriel. The railwayman's wife with the squire . . . ? The lady with the gentleman—eh—as soon as her husband's common back was turned—eh? . . ."

"No," she called out, a cry from the heart, knowing what had been done to her; then "I don't understand" although in part she did; then "Garron—Garron—don't" because she could see it was crucifying him: crucifying her. Filling her mind and her vision with so many swift, disjointed images that she did not see the clenching of his fist until it crashed down on the desk top, scattering his papers and overturning the inkstand like a flow of darkening blood.

A flow, a damage to his carefully guarded, enormously valued property, of which it terrified her, all over again, that he took no notice.

"Shut your mouth," he snarled, his own mouth tight enough—surely—to break. "*Shut it*. And listen. I haven't long."

And, his meaning seeping into her like a horrendous flood, she found herself nodding her head. "Yes, Garron—yes," terrified of the violence only a few bare inches, a few fragile minutes away from her, yet wanting to save him from it too, aware—by instinct far more than reason—of the wild pain and grief he would himself endure should his fists smash into the damage so far taken up by the soulless table. There would be her own pain, her own damage, too.

"So listen, Oriel. And don't try to defend yourself—or talk your way out of it. I haven't time. There's no point to it, either. You don't think I'd take that bitch Susannah's word for it, do you? Or even Morag's—without making sure she knew what she was talking about? She knows. I've just had her here, standing in front of me—not liking it, but saying it just the same. Everything she saw the day she came back too early from Watermillock and hid in the garden until you'd walked away—arm-in-arm—you and your squire . . ."

Abruptly his eyes closed on a spasm she knew—somehow—to be part protection, part absolute need to keep his control, images that had once been potent pleasures, now bitterly erupting memories, flashing razor-sharp from his mind to hers. The Lakeland moon. The mattress full of sweet herbs. Her voice, from the windowseat, telling him that this was really their wedding night. His voice, later, warning her in the act of love, *God help you if you try to leave me now. And God help anybody else—man, woman or child—who tries to take you an inch away.* Susannah, who could be sacrificed to his rage with a good will, Francis who could take care of himself. And Morag, who had unburdened what she had seen as adultery to a woman who had used the information—for what? To root the faithless wife out of Garron's house and enter it herself? Oriel knew she could ponder Susannah's motives, and deal with them too, much later. Just as certainly as she knew that now, above all, she must protect Morag, the child who loved her father and who, this past month or two, had started to love his wife.

Morag, who had never realized her mistake about Oriel's supposed adultery, who had never even doubted that it had taken place, but had forgiven her instead.

"She saw you, Oriel—with him."

"No—not as she thinks . . ."

But, gripped wholly by his overwhelming need for haste, to get it over within the space his fast-erupting discipline might endure, he was not listening to her.

"I checked—goddammit—*of course* I checked. You'd hardly expect me to take the word of a frustrated spinster, would you, and a young girl, without making damned sure—without going up there to find out? And I did. Your squire told his housekeeper he was going to Carlisle for ten days. He was there one night. *One night.* And nothing seen of him again until he turned up at Lowther Castle the week after—telling his host he'd come straight from Carlisle, the week, in the hearing of gamekeepers and parlormaids and the like who don't mind talking to a railwayman . . ."

"No," she said, "I can't bear this."

Neither, it seemed, could he.

"Then tell me Morag was lying. Can you? No. I know you can't. Susannah yes—very likely—but not *my* girl. And I reckon you'll hardly be fool enough to ask me to forgive you—which is what Morag thinks I ought to do . . ."

"No," she gasped, pressing desperate hands against her forehead. "No. No, Garron." And what she was really saying, beneath that single, useless, unashamedly panic-stricken word, was, "Don't let this happen to us. Don't throw us away. Don't waste us now. Even if I were guilty I'd be asking you not to waste us. Even then it wouldn't be worth it. And I'm not guilty."

But she had known from the start—more than ever now—that no explanation of hers could penetrate through to him, and, her own mind slipping to the primitive region of domestic violence—of domestic murder—which he too was struggling to hold away, she was suddenly aware, with horror and with sickness, of little beyond the frailty of her own female body, the ease with which his male hands might cause it to break. For if he killed her then—some voice cracking within her mind told her—she would be dead, he a murderer, Morag crucified by guilt that might never go away, Elspeth and Jamie horribly orphaned. She could not allow that. Neither, she believed, could Garron who, through all his menace, still seemed to be pleading with her—she could just hear it—to take her treacherous, but at least—thank God—living body away.

"I'll go," she said, without fully realizing she had spoken

until, incredibly, his hard, taut mouth curved on a smile she would have acknowledged more readily on the face of an imperial inquisitioner.

"Aye, that's what I came to tell you, bonny lass. You'll go."

And seeing the menace visible and well-nigh lethal in him now, she began to back away until he raised a hand in a gesture which froze her where she stood, even her breathing suspended in the absolute knowledge of how, at all costs, she must neither defy, nor even contradict him if she wished to remain whole.

"All right—madam. We know what you've done. And as to the reasons . . ." Pausing, he shrugged impatient shoulders, taking refuge—she almost wished she could not see it—in the pose of a man of extensive business affairs dismissing an employee. "Shall we say never mind the reasons—eh? Unless we just put it down to the morals of your class being different to mine."

And because she dared to do no other she nodded her head in agreement, the swift gesture of "the woman of fashion" he may have been expecting; may even have needed to maintain and justify his contempt for her. Which was better and easier—surely?—than jealousy.

"Good. And you'll understand, of course—being your mother's daughter—that there'd be no point in making a fuss. Not with me. I reckon you'll do as I tell you—eh?"

And hearing the menace in his voice mingled with the faint yet so unnerving plea of "Don't resist me. Take care, for God's sake, not to shatter my self-command," she rapidly nodded her head.

Yes, Garron. Whatever you need to say or do to me now in order to save yourself. And me with you. Anything. Anything to keep your hands from my throat so that at least one day—whenever you can bear to hear me—I shall have a voice left in me to explain—to put as much right to all this as still remains.

And even with those words in her mind she knew she was nodding, bending to him, showing the guilt to which he had condemned her not only because he wanted—needed—to see it, but for the simple, if not pure reason, that she was terrified.

"So there we are, Oriel. I might like to flay you alive, or I might like to forgive you. But there'll be no doing either. I couldn't afford either—could I—with three bairns to consider. Two girls among them—aye—young ladies no less—who can't be allowed to mix with you now—can they? *Can they*?''

She shook her head.

"That's right, Oriel. They can't. But—since they *are* young ladies now—they can't be mixed up in any scandal either. Oriel—*can they*?''

"No," she said, offering the spoken word to him as a propitiation surely—no less—that he would then have no need to shake it out of her.

"So . . ." And for a moment there was silence, a pit of it in which Oriel could feel herself sinking, until, his eyes staring at her once again without seeing, his voice clipped and cold, he went on, ''All right. We know what you've done. I don't want to know why. I want it over with—that's all. I had plenty of time, coming down from Carlisle to decide on that. So this is what you'll do. Are you listening?''

"Yes."

"Then I'm going away again—ten minutes from now, I reckon—and taking the girls with me. Don't you want to know where?''

She nodded.

"What's that, Oriel? I can't hear you."

"Yes." And she had never believed, in her whole, never easy life before, the dreadful necessity of speaking a word.

"Aye," his eyes still glazed, still unseeing, he smiled. "Then I have to tell you it's none of your concern, bonny lass. Is it?''

"No—*no.*"

"So we'll be back—the girls and I—by the end of the week, shall we say? Friday. Which should give you time, I reckon, to pack your belongings and get out of here by Thursday at the latest. *Shouldn't it?*''

She nodded, swallowed hard, and then, driven by his empty eyes, raised at least a whisper. "Yes."

Had he said where? Not, it seemed to her, for the long moment she could feel, throbbing and bare, between them, a heavy moment sinking her into that silent pit again until he pronounced curtly, from his own pit, "Wherever you please. It makes no difference to me. *None.* There'll be money available to you—such as I think necessary, that is. Don't thank me. Consider it as wages for covering your future escapades so as not to embarrass my girls again. That seems reasonable enough, I reckon. Doesn't it?''

But this time he did not wait for an answer.

''We won't be meeting again, Oriel. Send your lawyer cousin Quentin Saint-Charles to me at the Station Hotel in Hepplefield—tomorrow or the day after—and I'll deal through him. He'll let you know where you can afford to live and what you can afford to spend. There'll be no reason, at any time, for you to approach me. Do you understand?''

She did.

''Good. I'll be on my way then.''

But, crossing to the door, his greatcoat around his shoulders, he paused, swung round again and, snapping hard fingers, held out a hand toward her. ''Ah yes—the keys, Oriel. To my cash-boxes. Even my generosity has its limits.''

Yet when, her own hands shaking, she took the keys from the belt to which they had been so securely attached for these three—had she believed them glorious?—months, and held them, rattling against each other, toward him, he did not— could not?—take them from her, remaining frozen into a pose of blank, impossibly distant command until she dropped them on the desk, on top of Susannah's letters, and, scooping them up, he walked away.

Standing quite still, she could see him, through the door he had left open, ramming on his hat and gloves as she had watched him do so many times before, intent on yet another journey, issuing curt commands to half a dozen servants at once, his eyes on the clock, his mind, it seemed, on the road, the train. ''Where the devil are those girls?'' And there they were, coming downstairs one behind the other in their neat traveling capes, new hats and gloves, Elspeth's head bent to hide the tears one did not display—as Oriel had taught her— to the public, Morag staring straight ahead, blank-eyed with her own battle for self-control, her face tight-drawn and gray as early-morning ash.

What now? Hearing the door close behind them, Oriel remained, for a while, quite still by the desk, an inch away from Susannah's letters, feeling no urge—no need—to read them as Garron may well have intended that she should. Letters from Susannah who had succeeded, it rather seemed, in destroying her, certainly in wounding her, in robbing her— could one doubt forever—of so many precise and precious things she had always known to be valuable but had only found possible for herself—or even likely—these past few weeks or so.

And when the shaking of her hands, the tumult inside her chest and stomach had eased perhaps only sufficiently, it was with Susannah deliberately in her mind—Susannah meaning nothing to her and therefore being easier to dwell on than some others—that she went out herself into the hall, Miss Oriel Blake again, well-versed in the concealing of domestic tragedies, emotional dramas, who, pausing a moment to survey the masked but eager curiosity of the servants, continued quite slowly up the stairs, letting them know her requirements on her way. A carriage in one hour to take her to the station. A small traveling valise containing specific items to accompany it. The remainder of her clothing and other items of which she would presently make a list, to be packed, with accustomed care, into the required number of trunks and valises and delivered to a destination to be specified within the next few days.

"Certainly, madam."

"Thank you. Please have my small valise ready not later than four o'clock."

And then, in a state she vaguely knew to be shock, a state of cold distance, apart and almost grateful to be apart from this hot humanity, she entered—for the last time, she very clearly knew—her bedroom, assembled her toiletries, her hair-brushes, such other things as might be termed her personal bric-à-brac, changed into her own traveling clothes and, finding herself ready to take her flight too soon, sat down on the edge of what had been her bed, her well-gloved hands folded lightly, it seemed, but surely upon a bag of pale blue velvet.

Her personal fortune. Her inheritance from a woman who would have shown anger but resilience at finding herself in this situation; and would have expected her daughter to do the same.

Walk elegantly down to your carriage, child, and smile, speak graciously to your servants in conversation as you go, since only you know for certain that they are not really your servants anymore. And take your leave as if you were going off to a royal dinner-party or a pleasure-trip to Monte Carlo. So that they can't be sure whether or not you'll ever be back again. Just in case you are.

So would Evangeline have advised her, and hearing the trill

of her mother's voice in her head, she smiled faintly, quietly, and, waiting for the clock to strike, got to her feet and began—what? Just to move as yet, to walk with a graceful body, a calm smile, a stunned mind, the ghost of Mrs. Keith perhaps, yet moving hopefully in a direction which might lead her back, or even forward, to Oriel Blake.

What else could she hope for? And although, just then, with her hand on the door, her ability to hope appeared to have almost guttered out, it occurred to her—dimly at first, then with an almost irritating persistence—that, alongside the miseries and anxieties, the fears and deceptions, the very personal pains which were none of them entirely new to her, she was, for the first time in her life, very nearly free.

Surely—if only to distract herself from so many things, right or wrong, that hurt her—she ought to give *some* thought to that?

Seventeen

She had set off, of course, to go to Kate. But, emerging from the gloom of Hepplefield station, her back so straight that not a few of Hepplefield's respectable citizens awarded her swift glances of approval, she turned a sudden corner in the direction of Quentin Saint-Charles and—with a certainty far beyond anything she had experienced in her life—tapped, with urgency and relief and an amazing realization of what she could not deny to be pleasure, on his door. Nor—she was surprised to feel—had she doubted for one moment that he, a gentleman of locally famous, much envied, business consultations and social pressures, his letter-box full, every morning, of commissions and invitations, was indeed *there*. Waiting for her, it almost seemed.

"Oriel?"

"Yes, Quentin." Her friend. She was in no doubt of that. A man whose mind, considered by everyone else who knew him to be cold, had, for a long time now, been to her so marvelously familiar. Her own mind, almost: moving so clearly in *her* direction, his vision so quietly, so harmoniously in tune with hers, that no need existed to cry out to him of her disaster. Beneath her calm, habitually pleasant manner he heard the cry of that disaster very clearly, saw it as keenly, as rationally, as he would have observed disaster in himself, waiting—as she would have waited upon him—in a manner which offered silent, but unmistakable support until, taking a chair by the warmth of his fireside, a stool for her feet, a glass of very fine wine—no doubt the finest in Hepplefield—in her hand, she smiled at him, comfortable in the knowledge that he would in no way mistake her smile for anything approaching bravado or frivolity.

She had brought him the most complex and personal crisis of her life, as she hoped—with a flicker she recognized as intensity—that he, in a like situation, would come to her. Two complex minds, two minds much given to self-protection, to personal caution, to emotional restraint, who, nevertheless, for years now, had been open to each other.

"Tell me . . ." And, slowly, almost precisely, she told him every detail she could remember of betrayal and destruction, of Garron's blind, furious pain and what she feared it might still do, not just to him and to herself, but to Francis Ashington who was wholly innocent, and to Morag who must be floundering now so badly unaided in a nervous agony of guilt.

"Fueled," he said, "by my sister, who has caused this. I'm sorry, Oriel."

"Yes. I know. But I suppose she truly believed me guilty of adultery. Do you, Quentin?"

"Oriel," he said softly. "It would not cause me to change my estimation of your real worth even if I did."

"Quentin . . ." She had been about to say how glad she was of his trust, how grateful, and then paused, knowing it to be inadequate.

"There is no need," he said with his brief, brisk smile, "to defend yourself in my eyes, Oriel. And it will give me the most undoubted pleasure to defend you in the eyes of others. Your husband has earned at least *my* gratitude by appointing me as your legal adviser. Although I can do nothing for some hours yet—not until tomorrow morning, I think, when those of us who know about it have slept on our knowledge, and those who don't are poised to hear it. You are reprieved until then."

He gave her another glass of wine, the quietness of the somber, immaculate, quite richly furnished room spreading itself into an oasis around her, its library odors of leather and tobacco, its landscape of dark browns and deep crimsons making no demands upon her rapidly strengthening nerves. The wine was dry and cold and fastidiously chosen, the fire in the polished hearth calculated most carefully to give neither too much nor too little warmth, the heavy mahogany desk, the carved chairs, the books, the expensively framed pictures of sedate Flemish ladies and exotic Latin courtesans all untouched by the hand, breath, or eye of any aunt or mother, his possessions all entirely free—like herself—of the untidy complexities of family life.

"So this is where you live, Quentin."

Naturally, she had never visited a bachelor apartment before, particularly one with a series of handsome housekeepers in residence who had caused such grief to the bachelor's mother. How ridiculous, it seemed now, sitting by his carved mahogany fireplace, her own virtue in ashes, her future certainties extending no further than the contents of the blue velvet bag in her cloak pocket, to have heeded such a prohibition, to have denied herself the rational comfort of this fire, the discreet warmth of this man who had won so awesome a reputation for coldness and yet who was so essentially, so thoroughly, like herself.

"Yes, Oriel. This is where I live."

"Are you happy?"

"No. I am ambitious. The two do not go much together."

"Then do you have what you want?"

"No, Oriel. Something I wanted quite acutely has been denied to me. And as for the rest—well, I *am* ambitious. And wanting more, and then twice as much, is a natural condition of that."

She smiled at him, easing her position in his deep, leather chair. "Well, since you are so very clever, Quentin—which *does* go with ambition—will you tell me why I am sitting here now, having a pleasant conversation, instead of screaming and shaking in my shoes and wondering how I am to hold up my head tomorrow? Or how—the week after—I shall even manage to eat?"

He leaned very slightly toward her. "Perhaps because you know you will manage."

She nodded. Yes, somehow or other, in ways she could not at this moment even imagine, she would manage. As Evangeline had always done. How could it be otherwise now, when she could no longer afford the screen of respectability which her mother, by managing for her, had provided? Yes, Quentin was right. She may never be secure, or satisfied, rarely happy in this new phase of life so brutally thrust upon her. But she would manage.

"Although," he went on, "it seems only fair to warn you that you may not feel quite so much in the mood for pleasant conversation tomorrow."

Where would she even be by then? He told her. "When you are ready, Oriel, I will take you just across the road to Kate. She will be very glad to have you. And it would be putting another hatchet in your wounded giant's hand, rather, if you stayed the night with me."

Of course. She got up very quickly, finding herself close to Quentin who had risen at the same moment.

"Have I troubled you, Oriel, by calling him a wounded giant?"

She shook her head.

"Then why do I see tears in your eyes?"

They were, indeed, standing very close together, hemmed in by chairs and stools on one side, the fire on the other, a disgraced woman alone with a man well-known for his cool philandering, who saw no need to insult him by moving away.

"Because a wounded giant is what he is," she said. "And I don't somehow feel—just now—that I'm much of a healer."

Nodding briskly, he gave her a smile she was aware of greatly valuing, not of man to child, not of man to frail or flighty woman, not of man to a woman he plans to exploit or cherish, but of one logical, steady adult, so deeply familiar to another. "That is a useful attitude," he said. "Try to maintain it awhile longer."

She slept the night in Kate's bed, believing sleep to be impossible yet sleeping—as Kate had warned her she might—so deeply that her waking mind was tranquil and empty until memory tore into it again, nailing her to Kate's extravagant pink silk sheets tucked around the narrow, rooming-house bed, while the shock receded. And then, after the shock and the trembling which succeeded it, she lay quite still, attempting, between bouts of panic and even sharper bouts of anguish, to acknowledge her new reality. And then, reaching nothing beyond the conclusion that no matter what that reality might be, her only real choice was to make the best of it, or not—bleak choice, perhaps, but exceedingly real, nonetheless—she got out of bed and sitting at Kate's untidy toilet table began to do up her hair; and then, her first effort failing to pass muster, did it again until it met her satisfaction.

She found Kate sitting on the hearthrug of her shabby rented parlor, wearing a vibrant but decidedly crumpled robe of black and orange striped satin with no evidence of anything underneath it, her hair hanging loose, a pile of newspapers on the floor beside her, a pen in her hand, a bottle of ink and a cup of strong coffee sitting side by side on the stained but conveniently wide fender.

"Good morning, dear sister," she said.

"Good morning. You look exactly as poor Aunt Maud always said you would. Do you know that?"

It was perhaps a compliment. Certainly it was spoken with affection.

"I know," laughed Kate. "But have some coffee while you're thinking about what a ruin I am. It's over there on the sideboard with bread and boiled eggs and cold ham. Quentin found me a timid little woman who scuttles in every morning to 'look after me,' and looks quite grateful every time I tell her she can scuttle out again. She's left some kind of meat and potato pie in the oven for luncheon. I'll accept your judgment as to when it's done. And she did mutter something about a rice pudding and not leaving it too long. You'll understand rice puddings too, I expect. Good. So have breakfast now. There's nothing wrong with feeling hungry and tragic both together. And we'll be lucky to see Quentin before midnight. He called in very early, while you were still asleep, to say he was going first to High Grange, probably to murder Susannah, and then on to Lydwick. And yes, in case you don't quite like to ask, I *did* receive him in this awful dressing-gown. We even had a pot of coffee together, which seemed to cause my poor housekeeper some pain. She kept looking at Quentin as if she wanted to save him from his evil ways—or mine . . ."

Walking over to the sideboard, filling a cup for herself and another for Kate, Oriel murmured, "How evil is that?" And, walking back to the hearth across a further scattering of newspapers and what looked like half-written letters, possibly unpaid bills, sat down, gave Kate her cup and, putting her feet on the fender beside the ink-bottle, began to sip her own.

"This place is so untidy, Kate."

"Yes, isn't it." Kate sounded as if she had been paid a compliment. "It was bare and puritanical as a workhouse when I came in. Two little bedrooms, this poky parlor, a kitchen that feels two inches wide and three long. A clerk from one of the Hepplefield factories lived here before me with his wife and four children. Lord knows how she kept it so clean, even when he lost his job and then fell ill with one of those awful coughs you hear all over Hepplefield. They got behind with their rent, it seems, the man died, and the landlord threw the woman out, with her children. Of course. My clutter tends to cover it over somewhat, I find.''

Feeling a slight trembling in her hands, Oriel put her cup down on the floor among the jumble of papers, an act of domestic carelessness she had never performed before in her life.

''Are you telling me—little sister—that I could be far worse off than I actually am?''

Kate's smile was one of sheer delight. ''Oh yes—I am bullying you, Oriel. I'm saying 'Don't cry because you have no shoes when I can show you plenty who have no feet'—which is what Maud used to say to me once upon a time. Boring nonsense, of course, because if it hurts, then it hurts. No matter what it is. And should it be worrying you, as it seemed to be last night, that you've been accused of adultery with *my* husband, then please don't worry at *all* on my account. Good Lord—what right have I to complain? And as for Francis—well—unless your Garron is thinking of shooting him—and I expect Quentin will manage to talk him out of that—there's no need to give a thought to *his* reputation. Because the very same people who'll surely condemn you to the social gallows for kissing him in your garden will just think him a lucky dog for getting the chance. They'll be congratulating him with one hand, love, while they're stringing you up with the other. But you must know that.''

She knew.

''I'll just go and look at that rice pudding,'' she calmly said.

And she was halfway to the door, locating the kitchen by her sense of smell, her back to Kate, when Kate said, tonelessly, very much as a matter of course, ''Let's say, shall we, Oriel, that anywhere I am is home to you—and vice versa? Which would make it a waste of time, rather, to wonder where the meal after this one is coming from. Or on which pillow one is next to lay one's head. Pillows and meals, my dear, we can always manage. Thank goodness, of course . . . Even though it does give us so much extra time to think about—well—so many other things. Just like men do.''

They ate the meat pie from plates on their knees like maidservants gossiping around the fire, Kate having changed her exotic robe for a dark, English dress, but not the tone of her conversation, intending—it seemed to Oriel—to distract her from her present troubles until Quentin should arrive to tell her exactly how numerous and troublesome they might be.

"No point in crying over spilled milk," Kate announced, "until you know just how much has gone over. So listen, instead, while I tell you about my mother's pictures. I took two of them to Paris with me on my last trip, and what do you think? A little primitive, my art-dealer friends said, but well—yes, indeed—*promising*, certainly that. Possibly, giving the artist a year or two to develop of course, very promising indeed. And then—do you know—every one of those dealers approached me later, in strict privacy, and offered to buy them. I've rarely been so pleased about anything in my life. They thought *I* was the hopeful painter, of course, and although I can't imagine what my mother would have made of that, I was rather touched by it. She was an artist, you see, and not a madwoman, as Maud kept telling her. I only hope she knew. Although it strikes me she didn't. Maybe her passion for my father was just a wrong turning. She ought to have felt all that burning and boiling for her work—don't you see?—and couldn't, because 'ladies' aren't supposed to get beyond pressing flowers and painting water-color landscapes for the drawing-room. Poor mother. And the Kesslers would have been so proud of her. *That's* the real tragedy."

"Will you sell her pictures?"

"Oh—one day, perhaps. Maybe when Maud and Letty are dead—which is actually very kind of me, since they'd be horribly upset by the portraits she did of them. I'll show you, when you're feeling better. In fact I'll give you the one of your mother. Yes—just think how appropriate that would be, if her work ever became valuable. The jealousy of my mother for your mother converted into a fortune for the daughter who surely wasn't to blame for it. You could sell it and buy yourself—well, whatever you want most."

What, she wondered, did she want more than her cottage by Ullswater, which Garron would have sold to strangers long before the art world could be brought to recognize the talent of Eva Kessler? And to save herself from the draining of energy that too much grieving for her own quiet acre would cause her, she asked, very quickly, "Have you made up your mind to talk to Francis yet?"

Sitting once again on the floor, leaning her back against the shabby but nevertheless warm tiling of the fireplace, Kate smiled. "Yes, of course I've made up my mind to talk to

him, Oriel. Not quite when, of course. And please don't bully
me. Quentin does quite enough of that, forever telling me to
think of Francis, and choosing not to believe me when I keep
on telling *him* that that's just it. I am thinking of Francis.
And that little girl as well. Perhaps I was an unfeeling monster to run off and leave her. Certainly I was unfeeling to
entice that poor young fiancé of Dora Merton's into coming
with me, since I gave him nothing to make his trip worth-
while. And Dora would have been quite kind to him, really.
I might have been unfeeling never to have answered your
letters. And when Francis went on sending me money, and I
went on taking it without a word, he'd be entitled to think
that unfeeling too. Well, I had reasons—excuses, if you like—
which meant a whole complexity of things to me. Excuses I
could live with. But where that little girl is concerned, my
excuses desert me. She has a loving father and a peaceful
home. Did you ever have that, Oriel? Did I? So I'd really be
a monster, wouldn't I, to fly into her life—unless I had something to offer, beyond the sight of me flying out again, that
is. One of my Kessler cousins once told me—after several
bottles of wine, I must admit—that the best thing I can find
to give my daughter may turn out to be my absence. In which
case my absence she shall have. Is she a nice child?''

"Yes. Very nice." But to her great distress, when Oriel
tried to think of the pretty, contented little princess of Dessborough, it was the thin, taut face of Morag—her *own*
Morag—which filled her mind.

"And Francis is always laying his cloak over life's puddles
for her to walk on, is he?'' murmured Kate, as if she had
often imagined it. "A fatherly knight-errant riding off with
her on a new adventure every morning. How happy *I* would
have been with that. Is she?''

"I think so.'' How happy Morag would have been with it
too.

"Good. And he talks to her, doesn't he, and explains
things? Quite deep things, I expect? And *listens* to her? Does
he? Very seriously, picking things out of her chatter that mean
she's exceptionally intelligent or compassionate or has a hidden talent for music or mathematics, or that she's going to
be a famous ballet dancer or ride to hounds better than anybody else? Or so he imagines. Some of the German Kesslers
talk to their children like that. Beautifully, I think. It saddens
me, rather, that the only time my father ever really talked to

me was ten minutes before he went off and shot himself. Because he couldn't live without your mother, I expect.''

''Yes—I expect so too . . .'' But whatever Oriel had begun to say about Matthew—and she knew it had been something—never reached her tongue, defeated once again by a swift series of images flashing in her mind one after the other, the taut plea that was Morag, the taut, so *harsh* plea—but plea nevertheless—that was Garron, his savage hands clamped in their stranglehold around a chairback, the savage, suffering line of his shoulders hunched away from her, containing, with equal ferocity, both his need to murder her and his need to weep in her arms.

Bleakly she did not think he would ever do either.

''Well now,'' said Kate cheerily, ''I suppose I had better get on with my work.''

''What work?'' Morag's pain, Garron's pain, her own, had made Oriel's voice sharp.

''Didn't I tell you? It is Quentin, of course, who is to blame for it. There is a newspaper in Hepplefield called the *Gazette*. No, I am sure you have never seen it. Neither had I. But there are women, my dear, in Hepplefield, who actually write letters to it, asking all manner of questions on *desperate* topics like whether to announce dinner fifteen or twenty minutes after the arrival of one's guests, and whether one is really obliged to have gray carriage horses—which are more expensive—for a wedding, or whether one can settle for chestnut or bay at half the price. Which leads me to wonder if one could get black for even less. Would you think so, Oriel?''

What a ridiculous question. Yet, nevertheless, she found herself shaking her head and, if only faintly, smiling. ''I expect there are people who would try.''

''Very likely. So you see why the poor editor—having asked for all these letters in the first place to boost his circulation—really couldn't cope with them. One would hardly expect a gentleman to know the best way for cleaning fur cloaks, or whether a conscientious mama should permit her daughters to read novels.''

''Do *you* know?''

''Ah well . . . While you were still asleep I constructed a reply to the letter signed 'Conscientious Mama' telling her what Aunt Maud used to tell me.''

''Which is?''

"That one may read authors who write neither for money nor to entertain but only to morally instruct. I thought you might know how to clean fur."

"Hot flour and sand."

"How very drastic."

"Not if you give it a good brushing afterward and a going over with a wet comb."

"Oh good," said Kate making swift notes "Poor editor, you see. All he could think of to do was turn to Quentin—like the rest of us."

"Yes. I see."

"And Quentin solved his problem in a flash. You'll see that too. Told him at once what he needed. A lady of breeding and quality with a high tone and a high reputation. A gentlewoman fallen on times hard enough to arouse her interest in working for a pittance, while still remaining very gentle. 'The very thing, Quentin dear boy,' said the editor. 'You're a brilliant fellow.' So Quentin sent him to me."

Kate's laughter, warm and rich and very steady, seemed to fill the room for a moment and then, as she took up her pen and began to peruse another letter, reduced itself to a wry amusement. "I don't sign my replies Kate Ashington of course. Lord—can't you just imagine the faces of those 'conscientious mamas' if it ever came out they'd been advised by the Ashington whore? My poor editor friend turns pale, at least twice weekly, at the very thought of it. Lady Penelope Peel. That's my *nom de plume*."

"Chosen by Quentin?"

"Of course. Now then, this one is only about morning calls. I suppose I can manage that. How long should they last and should the caller expect refreshment? Oh dear, this lady's husband must only just have made his money if she doesn't know that. A quarter of an hour, dear lady, no longer, or your hostess will start worrying in case you think she's invited you to dinner. No refreshment either, even if it's freezing outside, or you're swooning for a cup of tea. Now what about this one? I have a young lady here who has been engaged for several years to a man she no longer loves."

"Does she know why?"

"Well—it seems, although she doesn't quite say so, that she has fallen in love with somebody else. Can Lady Penelope accept that as a good reason?"

"I shouldn't think so."

"Nor I. In fact I seem to remember there's a definite social rule to cover it . . . ?"

"There is." And, although the images of taut faces and heavy, hunched shoulders, had not quite receded, Oriel smiled and adopted a tone of voice somewhere between Maud and Evangeline. "A young lady in such a position must inform her fiancé of her change of heart. And that, my dear, is all she must do, the rest being entirely up to him. If he chooses to release her from their engagement then she may go off to her new love—if he will have her. But should her fiancé prefer to keep her then he is entitled to do so, obliging her to forget about love and get on with marriage."

"Splendid," applauded Kate. "I remember all my governesses telling me that too. Now then, what does one do about round shoulders?"

"Lady Penelope would recommend a backboard."

"And how should a young lady behave in the street to avoid the attentions of gentlemen?"

"My dear!" And they could almost have given the answer together. "She must not attract such attentions to herself in the first place. She must walk quietly and close to the wall, with her eyes modestly straight ahead and a little lowered. No audible conversation. No laughter. To put it in the simple manner young ladies can best understand, if she does not encourage a gentleman's notice then he will leave her alone."

"Do you believe that?"

"Of course not. But it's what all *my* governesses told me. And I expect it will please your editor—particularly if he has ever noticed a young lady too vigorously himself."

"Oriel—what a cynic you are."

"Kate—if you had been brought up as I was you would have been spared your innocence."

Yet, as the afternoon progressed, even Lady Penelope's letters began to pall, leaving Oriel's mind unguarded once more against the need to know in exactly how deep and dangerous a mire she, and others, now stood.

Where was Quentin?

"He'll come," said Kate. "He always does."

But a cool evening had drawn in, a silence which none of Kate's casual cheer could penetrate had fallen—Oriel's ears strained with their listening for footsteps on the stairs, every other sense strained a bare whisper away from breaking—before he walked into the twilit, still untidy, still oddly nourishing and sustaining little parlor as calmly as if it belonged to him, not even a hint of fatigue or anxiety in his lean, dark face, no travel stains or creases about him anywhere, a cool, immaculate, faintly amused, discreetly competent gentleman whose main concern appeared to be the correct chilling of the wine and the correct serving of the oyster patties, veal cakes, and game pie he had brought with him.

"If you could manage to find three glasses of decent crystal, Kate?"

She gave him a wide smile, evidently—and pleasantly—accustomed to his strictures. "Good Heavens, Quentin, if the wine is superb enough what does the glass matter?"

"Kate, the wine *is* superb."

"Quentin, I would stake my life on that."

He bowed his very slight acknowledgment. "In which case, Kate my dear, being certain of one pleasure, it seems no more than commonsense to add as many others to it as one possibly can. Beginning with a crystal glass. I have told you so before."

"So you have. You see what a voluptuary he is, Oriel? Is that usual, do you think, in the son of a vicarage?"

But Quentin answered for her. "Quite usual, Kate. Clerics who can afford it are every bit as fastidious as I am. So do fetch the glasses and those Crown Derby plates I lent you—hopefully unbroken—so that we may sit down and—well—ease Oriel's mind in as many directions as we can."

The glasses, long stems of diamond-cut crystal, were brought, incongruous in the shabby room yet highly appropriate to both Quentin and Kate, the wine, which Oriel readily assumed to be fine and famous, scarcely penetrating the dryness of her tongue.

"Are we celebrating?" she murmured, as Quentin raised his glass to her. "Or offering consolation?"

"A last supper?" inquired Kate, setting out the oyster patties with a casual hand. "Which might suit the humor, one supposes, of a fastidious cleric like yourself, Quentin dear."

Smiling, he raised his hand to her, not calling for silence, suggesting it rather, and when she, returning his smile, sat down on the hearthrug, her back against Oriel's knees, and began eating her supper, he turned calmly, pleasantly, to Oriel.

"Are you feeling rational and strong?"

"My goodness," said Kate from her perch on the ground,

her mouth full of oyster. "Such *little* things to ask of a wronged and abandoned woman. Of course she is."

"Strong enough," murmured Oriel, her fingertips resting for a moment on Kate's shoulder, their touch saying *And if not, little sister, if it happens that I break or even shatter, then no one could ever pick up my pieces faster and better than you.*

"Go on, Quentin," she said.

"Yes."

He had gone first to High Grange vicarage, not in any way to recriminate—which could, in his measured view, have served no useful purpose—but merely for information, Susannah having confirmed, whether readily or otherwise he did not mention, her part in the proceedings. Yes, she had indeed received a letter from Morag, written from the cottage by Ullswater to which Susannah had never, despite repeated pleas from Morag to Oriel, been invited. A terrible letter, proving the girl to have been in a painfully strained condition, and no wonder—surely—when one took in the shock of all she had uncovered. Was it surprising therefore, that she had turned to Susannah, her trusted confidante, the woman she would have preferred her father to have married in the first place, for advice? In short, by sending her husband's daughters to Watermillock in the full knowledge that Morag, at least, did not wish to go, Oriel had managed to be alone for seven days and nights at her so conveniently isolated cottage. Or had she been alone? Returning before she was expected, Morag had been appalled to see, through the cottage window, her stepmother pressed up against the windowpane with a man she did not recognize until—concealing herself in the garden for the simple reason that she was afraid to go inside—she had witnessed a prolonged embrace of the most intimate nature. And then, when it was over, the further and even more dreadful shock of seeing her father's wife offer another. The letter had been most descriptive, stemming no doubt from the girl's need to unburden herself, going into some detail as to how she had felt, watching the guilty couple stroll away arm-in-arm, the agony she had undergone waiting for the clearly adulterous woman's return, the way Oriel's face had "changed color" when she found Morag in the room her lover had only just vacated, the resulting sharpness of her tongue, her failure to mention that she had had any kind of visitor, her all too obvious annoyance that Morag had dared to come back without her permission. Evidence enough, surely, to convince the poor girl not only of her stepmother's guilt but to torment her, most acutely, as to whether or not it was her duty to inform her father.

No doubt about it, in Susannah's opinion.

"My dears, that goes without saying," murmured Kate.

Yet when Morag had returned to Lydwick some days later she had reacted in a strange, dreamy, downright difficult manner to the advice Susannah had hurried to give her. Not that the girl now believed herself to have been mistaken, or had received an explanation from Evangeline's daughter which had been clever enough to set her mind at rest. Nothing of the kind. She simply—and far too heatedly for Susannah's peace of mind—did not wish to give her father any more troubles, at the moment. An attitude Susannah could appreciate, had "the moment" not clearly run the risk of being forgotten, the intention "to do the right thing" well-nigh obliterated in Morag's mind by Oriel who, doubtless suspecting the extent of what was known against her, had set about defending herself by charm. Exactly as Evangeline had known how to be charming whenever it suited her to make someone who ought to have known better eat out of her hand.

Susannah had spoken several times about it to Morag, pointing out to her that one's moral duty is not intended to give immediate pleasure, that it would not, in fact, even deserve to be called "moral" unless it was extremely hard to do. But Morag had resisted, made excuses, had even demanded the return of her letter in so insulting a manner that Susannah, in her brother's presence, she reminded him, had informed Oriel that she no longer cared to visit her. And returning to the vicarage, she had made a copy of Morag's letter and, after some days of deep contemplation, had sent it, with a note of her own, to Garron.

"A sweet little note, I expect," said Kate, "telling him he needs a shoulder to cry on and, whatever he might think, she knows she can bear the weight."

"Let's not worry about that just yet," suggested Oriel, taking a long drink to ease the parched effort of words.

Quentin smiled at her.

He had gone next to Dessborough, first to warn Francis of the accusation and then to dissuade him from going at once to see the husband he declared he had never wronged, and to champion the lady's innocence.

Laying down her plate and glass, Kate put her hands together in a gesture of applause. "One expected no less of him."

"Quite so," agreed Quentin.

There had then been a convenient train back to Hepplefield and a long wait at the station hotel although, during the strained hour before Mr. Garron Keith would consent to see him, he had managed a few hurried words with Morag.

"Quentin—" Oriel heard, with dismay, the break in her own voice. "How was she?"

"Oh—not well. She looked quite ill, in fact, which I am sure you would expect. Luckily she understood my position as your lawyer and your friend, and was anxious—I think—just to know that you were safe. She and her sister had stayed up all night worrying themselves it seems into a dismal state about you. Missing you, I believe. But I feel it only fair and right to tell you that although Morag pleaded desperately with Susannah to return her letter and then quarreled with her most bitterly when she would not, she still believes her assessment of your conduct to have been true. In her honest opinion, Oriel, she has not misjudged you. She has forgiven you. She has come to believe that you are worth forgiving. When her father came striding into the house last night with her letter in his hand, demanding an explanation, that—I am quite certain—is what she told him."

"I have to see her," said Oriel without realizing she had spoken, both Quentin and Kate reaching out a hand to hold back if not her physical then at least her emotional need for flight, to rush to the girl who could have become, who had *almost* become, her child.

"I'll come with you," said Kate. "When we can."

"Later." And there was no doubt at all in Quentin's voice. "Much later, I think, Oriel. Because her present loyalty, of course, is to her father. He needs her. You don't. And although she might well need you, I don't think she'll allow herself the indulgence."

"You rather like her, don't you, Quentin," said Kate.

He nodded. "Yes. She'll be a strong woman one day, at this rate. And strong women please me."

"Good Heavens." Kate's show of astonishment was no more than disguised amusement. "Then why on earth have you involved yourself so much with me and Dora Merton?"

"If I write to her, Quentin," said Oriel, not listening, "will you make sure she gets my letter?"

"Of course. And having spent some time today with her father, I understand why you think the postal service could hardly manage it."

"Quentin?" This was the moment she had been dreading.

"Yes. Your husband." She saw how perfectly he understood. "Not well, of course. One assumes he had spent the night in drink—a not unnatural refuge for a man with that kind of weight on his mind. And one could see how weight and whiskey had combined in a most painful fashion. He bore it well, of course, neither alcohol nor infidelity being at all new to him—although the infidelity, one assumes, had always been on his part before. I will be as brief as I can, Oriel, which, in fact, presents small difficulty since he was in no mood for any detailed discussion. He accepted me simply as your legal adviser and, as such, made it abundantly clear that he has no intention of taking you back."

"Did she say," inquired Kate, "that she wished to go?"

Raising his shoulders in slight exasperation, Quentin preferred, it seemed, to otherwise ignore her. "Sadly, Oriel, I failed to persuade him even to discuss the question of your guilt or innocence. He condemns you utterly, not only on the evidence of his daughter, who stood before him last night and confirmed, in no matter how heart-broken a manner, her belief in all she had written to Susannah, but on his own investigations. Thorough investigations, I believe. It may be that he set out to prove you innocent and only managed to find you more and more guilty instead."

A great silence descended upon the room, an awareness in Oriel's mind of how dark it was, no moon outside the window, no lamps lit.

"If you are thinking *I* might find you guilty," said Kate, "—of making love to my husband, I mean—then please don't. And even if I did believe it, the only thing I'd feel entitled to do would be to congratulate him . . ."

"Congratulations, dear Kate," murmured Quentin, "are not in order."

"Ah well—just in case."

"Quite so. Your husband—Kate—tells me he spent ten days walking the Roman Wall, which I find easy enough to believe. Although *your* husband, Oriel—being barely acquainted with Francis—merely brushed it aside when I mentioned it. And, since he slept on the ground like a pilgrim—possibly imagining himself on the way to Mecca—one has no means of proving . . .''

"I'd rather we didn't talk about Mecca," said Kate, surprised at the pang it had evidently given her.

"No," said Oriel, "Garron couldn't believe it. He's had to sleep on the ground too many times himself because he couldn't afford a lodging. So he'd find it hard to see why a man should do it for pleasure."

Again Quentin smiled at her. "Particularly a man with money to burn and an invitation to Lowther Castle."

"Yes. But will he leave it there . . . ?"

"Do you mean will he take action against Francis? Apparently not. I gather—from certain remarks of his I could hardly repeat to you—that he rather thinks men are entitled to take their sexual opportunities where they can find them. And having taken such opportunities himself—in the past, of course, with other men's wives, he sees no satisfaction in punishing Francis for doing the same. It's you he wants to punish, Oriel. It may be that he separated himself from you last night from fear of punishing you too much. But having done it, he seems to consider it final. The only matters he was prepared to discuss with me were financial. He had already decided how much, and in what installments, you are to be paid and refused to listen to any suggestions—for improvement, I must admit—of mine. You will have what he calls 'enough'—but with very little to spare. My role is to be simply as go-between and he made it clear to what extent he would lose his temper should I try to exceed it. He has told me to find you a house, at a value he has specified, outside this area. He has also set a limit on the furniture you are to buy. Nor will he release the more valuable of your jewelry, including your mother's. To prevent you, I suppose, from selling it and thus managing to purchase something without his permission. I have the impression he rather wishes you to be poor. I am afraid he has the law on his side. As I expect you know."

"Yes, Quentin."

Kate was less agreeable. "And is there nothing else you can do? Good Heavens, Quentin, did you go to Cambridge all those years just to learn about whose *side* the law is on? Didn't they teach you how to get around it?"

"Kate dear," but he was smiling at her. "One cannot get around the law, only around a man's determination—or need—to enforce it. *Your* husband's need—Kate—was to give you more money than he could, at the time, afford, and rather more than you required, when one remembers how often you frittered it away. Oriel's husband needs to expose her to a financial struggle and there is nothing I can do, as a lawyer, to prevent him. And, furthermore, should she find some means of earning money in the future he will be fully entitled to take her wages away from her, should he feel the need to do that.''

''And Oriel's need?''

''What need? She is his wife and her identity, in law, is identical to his. I can do nothing about it. If she had a child of her own body, I could not even arrange for her to see that child without her husband's permission, much less ensure her right to be consulted on any matters concerning its upbringing. A woman has no such rights. I don't make the law, I merely operate it. Do forgive me, Oriel. I am talking as if you were not here. I tend to seize any opportunity to show Kate what Francis could have done to her had he desired.''

''Ah yes.'' Kate smiled into her wine, reflectively, perhaps sadly, although it was not clear just where her sadness was directed. ''So you do, Quentin. But Francis felt deeply sorry for me. I suppose he still does.''

''Is that wrong of him?''

''No—no. It proves the excellence of his heart—of his judgment. But what you don't know, Quentin—since neither do I—is whether I might have preferred him to come after me with a carving knife. As one rather feels Mr. Garron Keith might like to do.''

''Quite so,'' he said, rather coldly.

''*Quite* so, Quentin. So what is it you now advise Oriel to do?''

''I presume she may stay here, for the present?''

Once again they were talking as if Oriel was not there. And, leaning her head on the back of her chair, half-closing her eyes, it seemed to her that indeed she had slipped a little aside, inwardly retreated, turned off the more inquiring sections of her brain the better to contemplate, the better, quite simply, to take in, to come to terms, to bear the full impact of all she had just heard. And she was tired now, weary to the marrow of her bones and the inner fiber of her heart with the burdens she already understood and would have to find a way—her own way, she rather thought—to carry.

Let them talk around her, for as long as they felt the need, her own need being to recover her damaged strength and get it all healed and improved and—hopefully—doubled at least, by tomorrow.

"She can stay with me forever," said Kate. "We all know that. What we don't know—at least Oriel and I don't—is exactly how much punishment one needs to take."

"From a husband? My dear—I know of no limit."

"And what of divorce, Quentin?"

"Kate—for Heaven's sake—what of it?"

"I am asking you. For my own information as well as my sister's."

He raised his eyebrows. "Very well. The first thing one learns about divorce is that it is impossibly expensive. The second that it is—realistically if not legally—only available to men. The third, that the number of divorces granted rarely exceeds two a year. One begins by obtaining a Private Act of Parliament, if one can, followed by a suit in the Ecclesiastical Courts. If this goes well then the husband is next obliged to bring a case for damages against his wife's alleged lover—a lover being absolutely necessary. If guilt is again proved and damages granted then the husband has won the right to apply to the House of Lords for an Absolute Decree containing permission to remarry. But even if the Lords are convinced, they will do no more than send the case down to the House of Commons again, for their approval which, if granted, leaves the poor husband with nothing more to do than ask for Royal Consent."

"Dear God," said Kate.

"Indeed. And even if you—or Oriel—possessed the wealth and determination and all the friends in high places required to bring this about, I feel it only right to warn you that while a man needs to prove nothing more than adultery, a woman does not get off so lightly. Adultery in a husband, my dear ladies, has never been considered serious enough. Not serious at all, in certain circles. Therefore a wife needs something else to back it up. Extreme physical cruelty, for instance, by which I mean something rather worse than a few black eyes or broken teeth—something so painful that no woman could be suspected of having asked for it. You will follow my meaning."

"Do you think this right, Quentin?"

"No," he said. "In fact no one who actually thinks about

it possibly could. Which does not mean, of course, that they would all be prepared to change it.''

''So you are telling us we have no choice but to stay married?''

''I am.''

Watching them from her increasing distance, Oriel was aware that they had had this conversation before, were having it now only for her sake, to instruct her without any effort on her part, with no need for her to ask questions, Kate asking them for her, Quentin supplying the smooth, sharp answers she most wished to know.

''Thank you,'' she said.

''I beg your pardon,'' they both spoke together and, getting to her feet, she held out a hand to each of them.

''You know what I mean. You have been having an old conversation for my benefit, full of the things I need to be milling over and managing to live with. So, if you don't mind, I'd rather like to go to bed now. I have never felt quite so tired in my life.''

Kissing them both with careful affection, she left them alone together to finish off the wine, smiling from the doorway to reassure them that she would survive the night.

''She *is* tired,'' said Kate.

''Yes. And so am I. So perhaps I can recruit you now to the plan I have made . . .''

''Quentin. A plan. Have you really?''

''Of course.''

''A good one?''

''Certainly. With your cooperation.''

Refilling her glass, squatting now rather than sitting on the rug by the still blazing fire, she gave an inquiring shrug. ''Of course. You have only to tell me . . .''

''Very well. Her husband mentioned to me, in a manner indicating his wish that I should mention it to her, his firm intention of selling her house by Lake Ullswater.''

''What a brute he is.''

''Possibly. But—since he is hardly likely to handle the sale himself—it would be possible for me, through a series of agents *his* agent will not suspect, to buy it . . .''

''For her? Quentin—the very thing. How clever.''

''No—no, Kate. Not for her. If her husband wished her to live there, he would say so. He is selling the cottage—surely— to punish her.''

"Oh Lord—this makes me angry . . ."

"Indeed. But if it belonged to you, of course, then you could permit her to stay there as long as she liked. Until—shall we say—she had decided what else to do? At her own leisure . . ."

"You mean . . .?"

"Yes, Kate. I mean if Francis could be persuaded to use some of the Kessler money to buy the cottage for you. I imagine he would be only too pleased—although you would have to meet him and discuss it with him yourself, of course. And by tomorrow at the latest, I fear, before the cottage is snapped up by somebody else . . ."

There was a short silence.

"Quentin Saint-Charles, what a *devil* you are."

"I dare say. Will you do it, though?"

She sighed. "Of course I will." And then, jumping to her feet, she gave him a wide, brilliant smile. "But just the same, poor Quentin, what are *you* to do?"

Perfectly reading her mind, he smiled back. "About what?"

"About the woman you have been in love with for so long? About Oriel, my dear, who is free of her husband now and might even be persuaded to love you—who knows—in return. She might even come to live with you, one day, and make you so happy—except that such an association would utterly ruin your career. Can you do it, Quentin? Sacrifice ambition for love, I mean?"

He was still smiling. "I don't know."

"But you do love her, don't you?"

He stood up too, his eyes going to the door through which Oriel had retreated. "Oh yes," he said, "with all my heart. Which seems a pity—rather—that my heart, dear Kate, is very far from being the warmest or the gentlest one I know."

"Don't hurt her," whispered Kate.

Leaning forward, he brushed his mouth lightly along her forehead. "Shall we begin by buying her a lakeside cottage?" he said.

Eighteen

The scandal of Mrs. Oriel Keith failed, after all, to titillate Gore Valley drawing-rooms anywhere near as much as her mother, Evangeline Slade-Blake-Stangway had so often done. Perhaps Oriel Keith, although quite beautiful enough to be scandalous, had lacked her mother's delicate skill for arousing envy and a sense of grievance. Perhaps Mrs. Keith's husband, the railway contractor, deserved less sympathy, in Gore Valley opinion, than Matthew Stangway who, despite the disdainful turn of his mind had nevertheless been "one of them." While as for Squire Ashington of Dessborough, even if it were true that he and Mrs. Keith had been caught in some kind of dalliance, the Valley had always hesitated to pass judgment on "gentlemen," the aristocracy being easier to forgive because it always paid so much better to keep on the right side of them, and they were famous, in any case, for living by their own rules and making their own manners.

No. By and large, this was not a first-class scandal, no deaths in suspicious circumstances, no rushing off abroad like Lord Merton who, so far, had shown no inclination to come back again, leaving his wife in her Scottish castle, his daughter Adela in the grip of some Cheltenham religion, only Madcap Dora flitting alone and somewhat disconsolately around their ancient, noble Abbey. A tale of domestic destruction—wrought, of course, by the wicked, wonderful Evangeline—which fired Gore Valley imaginations far more than Mr. Garron Keith whose installation of his daughter Morag as housekeeper was considered quite natural, his dismissal of Susannah Saint-Charles, when she called with suggestions of keeping his house herself, being merely vulgar, phrased, as it had been, in rough words Susannah did not understand but which the servants translated for her, discreetly, as "Go away."

She had gone. And although, for a while, she had shown signs of becoming as distracted and, regrettably, as tedious as her mother, she had—by a stroke of luck everyone admitted to be rare in the life of Susannah—found consolation by the arrival in High Grange of a widow of shy disposition but comfortable circumstances with a delicate daughter of fifteen, both of them not only quickly devoted to Susannah but very happy, it seemed, to depend upon her company and the once again flowing fountain of her advice.

The Squire of Dessborough remained in his manor, waiting to become a very rich man on the twenty-fifth birthday of his wife to whom he had presented a cottage on an isolated fell above Lake Ullswater which she, in her turn, had placed at the disposal of Oriel Keith. A matter, it was decided, of one fallen woman helping to raise another, which caused no comment beyond a certain shaking of heads over Squire Ashington's misguided liberality and some slight sympathy for Elspeth Keith, the younger of the contractor's daughters, who, having just become engaged to a young gentleman of Watermillock, could hardly consider the presence of her disgraced stepmother on the other side of the water to be a blessing.

Or certainly the young gentleman's mother, Mrs. Landon, had not done so, stepping sharply aside without a word one afternoon in Penrith when, coming out of the apothecary's door, she met Oriel coming in.

"Good afternoon, Mrs. Landon," murmured Oriel.

"Oh—good afternoon," came Elspeth's light voice from behind her future mother-in-law's back. "Are you well—are you?"

"Yes. Yes I am. Bless you, Elspeth. Tell Morag the same."

Driving back in her borrowed dog-cart to Pooley Bridge and then along the path below Swarth Fell, a clear summer sky mellowing to autumn above her, Watermillock felt, not seen, on the other, greener side of the lake, she shed tears quite freely as one could in this solitude, the bare brown fells too high and impervious to be troubled by the small sorrow of a human woman for children not even her own. Therefore, until she reached the Buck Inn on the corner of the lake at Howtown to return the dog-cart and pony, she cried as loudly, in the gilded summer silence, as she pleased, walking back the half mile or so to her cottage, her cats, her flowers, with all her weeping thoroughly done.

She had come here in the early spring, very quietly, having expressed her gratitude warmly but privately to those who had made it possible, accepting their assurances that to help her gave them, each in their separate ways, immeasurable pleasure because she could see it was true; accepting her own need of them at the same deep, surprisingly natural level. They—Kate her sister, Francis her friend, Quentin far more than a friend although she had not yet reached a decision as to how much more that might be—all needed to help her. She needed their help. Whenever help became due to one of them she would feel a corresponding need to give it. So simple had the truths of herself become. So simple, too, the strengths which rose in her, almost unbidden, as she repossessed her quiet acre, the keys returned to her by Quentin who had performed acute acts of espionage to obtain them, he and Kate both making the journey north with her to help with the trunks and boxes, to share her joy, Kate staying for three weeks of settling in, settling down, renewing and exploring; Quentin joining them every Friday to Monday to eat her elderflower fritters, her dandelion and bacon salads, to stroll, champagne glass in hand, every evening through her garden in conversation, laughter, warm and easy understanding, followed by the Labrador puppy Francis had sent her from Dessborough, a gift of canine protection for a woman alone, which had considerably offended her cats.

The puppy was waiting for her now as she walked between her quiet lavender hedges and brilliant, golden splashes of marigold leading to her cottage door, startling a pearl-gray kitten as he bounded toward her, the rest of the cats, basking beside the valerian flowers, ignoring him, treating him with the faint contempt deserved, in their arrogant, jeweled eyes, by a young dog of frantic, foolish energy, huge paws leading him astray as continually as his vast and incoherent appetite for love, his potential strength and savagery, his burning desire to lay himself, as often as she would let him, at her feet.

An ungainly, impetuous puppy named ''Glory'' by Kate since she thought him unlikely to win it in any other way, who would, quite soon, be a fighting black giant of a dog, staking out his territory, his possessions, his people, and guarding them without even stopping to think whether they wished to be guarded or not.

"Glory," she called out, knowing her command to be by no means sharp enough. "Do get down—do stop leaping on me—do behave . . ."

But, wagging a hefty tail in eager circles, hanging his head on one side to tell her he knew she did not mean it, he reared up again as she had expected he would, planting two large, clumsy, muddy paws on her dress, earning her—as she began to scratch his ears and submit to the kisses of his rough, scratchy tongue—the patient contempt of the cats who, although quite fond of her, would not, in her place, have put up with such nonsensical antics for a moment.

"Poor Glory," she murmured and, realizing what the elegant black mother cat, a sophisticated adult of at least ten months old, her white and her marmalade sisters, and their lean, tiger-striped brother-lover thought of her dog's far too excited, far—*far*—too sincere emotions, she allowed him to come inside with her, where, totally exhausted by love, he threw himself down before the empty summer grate, concealed by a spreading fan of larkspur and clove-carnations, the sound of his panting and snoring filling the room until Oriel at her writing-desk by the window, grew too lulled by it to hear.

Her days—when Kate was not here filling the house and garden with her visit, or Quentin walking up at dawn sometimes from his lodging in Pooley Bridge—were all much the same. Mornings among the plants; fine afternoons out on the fells; wet afternoons—of which, in this region of high peaks and deep, still water, there were a great many—walking only half her usual distance and then rushing back either to her stone-flagged kitchen to concoct her herbal lotions and her pot pourri, or to her desk where, at least twice weekly, she fulfilled her obligations, taken over from Kate, to the editor of the *Hepplefield Gazette*, a gentleman who was as much amused as she was herself by the high tone and precise nature of her advice. Lady Penelope Peel—the adulteress of Ullswater—expressing shock, written in exquisite copperplate, that any young lady should even think herself entitled to walk out so much as two yards alone with any gentleman to whom she was not formally engaged, and even then only with the express permission of her parents; or advising a series of "conscientious Mamas"—usually with a plate of herb dumplings on her own knee—of the shudder which ran through "Good Society" at the merest glimpse of anything so unmannerly as a young lady enjoying her food, suggesting to these much embarrassed mothers the remedy of sending an ample tray upstairs to a "greedy girl" ten minutes before a dinner-party so that, coming downstairs replete, she would have no difficulty in passing herself off as the spiritual creature, kept alive on delicacy and fresh air, all gentleman wished to see.

"To the spiritual, utterly abstemious Lady Penelope," the editor had written on his card accompanying a case of claret, along with a suggestion that, in addition to her readers' letters, she might care to undertake a weekly column of "social notes," descriptions of a little ball she had given last Friday evening—or whenever it was one gave balls—and of the trips she made "in season" to fashionable flower shows, for instance, or charity bazaars, invitations to expensive boxes at the Opera—London, of course, where "Lady Penelope" would be sure to have friends—and to suitable-sounding country houses to do whatever it was one did there, Hepplefield's matrons being very fond of a glimpse of the aristocracy at play. Surely she could whip up some good descriptions of musical soirées, visits to fashionable hat-makers, "her ladyship's" daily round of paying and receiving calls, fitting in a dinner party, a theater, and two or three dances in one evening while she was taking those long walks of hers on the fells? She had replied that she rather thought she could.

"You can hardly live here alone forever, you know," Quentin had warned her.

"I do know, Quentin."

It had also occurred to her, with a deep, unashamed pleasure, that he might well have an alternative in mind. Yet, until such a moment of decision should arrive, this was a life, nevertheless, suspended in time perhaps but no less vital for that, allowing her the blank repose she needed, the turning-off of her more acute urges to plan, to grieve, to hope too precisely, to examine in too much detail the depth at which she might learn to feel, the direction in which those feelings might go, so that when those busy urges came on again she would be better equipped to consider life—alone or otherwise—elsewhere. For the present, therefore, it was a life. From the editor of the *Hepplefield Gazette*, along with his occasional gifts of wine, she received a parlormaid's wages which had at least enabled her, so far, to buy the few things she could not grow herself—a stock of coal, for instance, against the winter, candles, oil for her lamps, a little game and salmon from a quiet man, somebody's gamekeeper she supposed, who came very discreetly to her kitchen door— as well as paying a woman to come in twice weekly for the heavy cleaning and the heavy laundry, without any need as yet to touch the contents of her mother's blue velvet bag. Her security, known only to herself and Quentin, lying safely upstairs beneath the cashmere shawls and fur wraps brought across the barrier of her other life, also by Quentin and which, at need, she could sell, along with the satin and lace ballgowns—cut far too low for the taste of any Lady Penelope— which Garron's money and generosity had bought her.

In the spirit of one who takes laudanum to ease a physical pain she had, by sheer force of will, drugged the part of herself which might have dwelled too closely on that. But now, her elbows on her desk, her chin on her hands, Lady Penelope's letters waiting in their dozens to be answered, she could not avoid the presence of Watermillock, that green and pretty place just across the water, the lights of its few, scattered houses visible from her window, a garden unrolling like a carpet patterned with conifers and pale lilac, pure white, vibrant crimson masses of rhododendrons, to the water's edge, where Elspeth, possibly Morag, might well be standing. Elspeth, she supposed—narrowing her eyes in an effort to see across a distance she knew to be too wide for accurate vision—walking with Tom Landon or with his mother. Morag, she thought, probably alone. Tom, the young fiancé, who, only a few months ago, she had thought quite good enough for Elspeth, almost inevitable. An only son with a doting mother and a sizable if not spectacular inheritance, quite rich enough and quite handsome enough to flatter a girl like Elspeth who—Oriel abruptly realized—would grow not an inch taller in any direction other than the purely physical from the day she married him.

It terrified her now how much she did not want that to happen, how much, in fact, she wanted Elspeth to find some sensitive, open-hearted, open-minded man to value her, not for the silvery airs and graces Oriel herself had taught her, but as the girl who, refusing to ignore her disgraced stepmother, might be capable of so much more.

And Morag. She had written to Morag through Quentin, not explaining her innocence, simply asking Morag not to blame herself, not to let it burden her, asking her—if she still could—to value the affection which had started, tragically too near the end, to grow between them. Too late, of course. And far too easy to blame Susannah. Far, far too easy when she knew that, had she so desired, she could have sent Susannah packing from the start, as firmly and immediately, if not as obscenely, as Garron had now done. She had smiled when Quentin had told her about that. But now, still staring across the lake, her chin still on her hands, the exasperated pity—but pity nevertheless—she had felt for Susannah no longer served as an excuse for all she had allowed it to do to Morag.

She had made the wrong choice. Convenience, doing what others called the right thing, keeping sweetly out of trouble instead of briskly causing it whenever the cause seemed worthy, as Morag had certainly been. And now, after all her tact and elaborate consideration, after all the years of smiling and understanding and biting her tongue, her achievement consisted of Elspeth rushing into a refuge which, perhaps quite soon, would bore her, Morag keeping her father's house in a mood of rigid penance for the woman she had helped to dismiss, Susannah insinuating herself into the bosom of another family, instructing another woman how to run a home and bring up a child Susannah herself had in no way paid for. And Garron? Could he too be there, across the lake at the Landons, hearing how Mrs. Landon had snubbed her today in Penrith and—much worse—how Elspeth had not? She thought it likely. If not today then some other day, if Elspeth's marriage went ahead. Too young, of course, at sixteen. Although perhaps her mother had not been much older. Kate, after all, had been eighteen, herself just twenty-one. Too young. Would Garron come over here, crossing the lake, it seemed to her in sudden panic, in two colossal strides, to demand how she dared pollute the air that was to be his daughter's, defending what had now become *his* territory as fiercely and fundamentally as the dog, over there, would one day guard his? *This is mine. Kill me to take it. Or I'll kill you.*

Too quickly, already hearing the crash as he burst her door down, she got to her feet, the dog, waking from the blank depths of sleep to instant and acute awareness, leaping toward her with love huge enough to be an invasion, a desire for possession—to claim her yet also to belong to her—massively beyond his control. A young dog still, who had not learned the defense of hiding his passionate heart behind a fighting shield, a block of rough granite, like Garron. Shivering, she sat down again and picking up her pen, holding it a moment until the slight shaking to which her hand subjected it had ceased, began—in her so exquisite copperplate—to write: "Dear Mother of the Bride—One can be in no doubt of your obligation to entertain such bridesmaids as come from any little distance in your home for at least three days, one before the wedding so that the dear young ladies can compose themselves, and two afterward to enable them to recover. Your further obligation to chaperon them most adequately cannot be overstressed, never for one moment forgetting the flights of emotional fancy induced in them by a wedding, made ever more dangerous by the presence of an equal number—one could hardly settle for less—of groomsmen. May I congratulate you and caution you in the same breath." And she was smiling again, quite calmly, as she came with a flourish to the signature "Lady Penelope Peel."

The summer passed, her accounts of the London Season, her descriptions of how any lady "in society" must be up by seven-thirty to prepare for her obligatory ride in the park at nine o'clock, followed by a breakfast party at eleven, luncheon with friends at two, a mad rush to a concert or an exhibition of anything considered fashionable at half past three, an even madder one to a garden party at four o'clock sharp, the usual round of theaters, dinners, and balls between seven o'clock and three in the morning, followed by the scramble to get up for the nine o'clock ride again, winning her an increase in salary to which, sitting out on the fells with a cheese sandwich, writing an account of the Regatta at Henley where she had never been, she felt herself fully entitled.

"I liked your piece about how a girl should never dance more than three times with the same partner," said Kate who had come up to the cottage to celebrate her important twenty-fifth birthday that September. "And your breakfast menus—good Heavens—for people who've been dancing all night, potted shrimps, pigeons in jelly, broiled whiting, deviled chicken, steaks and chops, I seem to remember—as well as all the usual eggs and bacon and muffins and good old marmalade. We never had all that at Dessborough."

"You did at Merton Abbey though."

"Ah yes." Kate sounded almost sad. "So I did. I expect

they still serve it all every morning to Dora who might eat a muffin and then wander off while the servants pack it up and—well, sell it, I suppose, in the village. Or to somebody like that quiet, shrewd man I've seen on your kitchen doorstep—just the kind who'll take Dora's breakfast off to Hepplefield Market while it's still fresh on one of your husband's trains. I wonder if your husband knows he's a poacher's friend?''

''I expect so.''

Kate smiled. ''Yes. So do I. But Dora won't know what's going on, of course. She'll just sit at the dinner table in front of a quarter of beef like the ones she's been looking at all her life—you know, the kind her mother used to order to serve three dozen. Poor Dora. There's no sign of either her father or her mother coming home yet, and Adela never will. I can't think why she stays rattling around that mausoleum all by herself.''

''Can't you?''

''Ah—you think she's still in love with Francis, do you?''

Now Oriel smiled. ''I haven't seen her for a long time, but she used to be.''

''So did I,'' said Kate, very steadily.

Little sister, so did I. But because, at some moment she had never identified, that love had changed to something which made her far happier, she merely said, ''I hope you haven't forgotten Francis is coming here for your birthday?''

Oh no. She had not forgotten. Her birthday morning rising pale gold and tremulous above the fells, a smoky tang of autumn, a lingering sweetness of summer blending together in the September air, a kitten getting beneath her feet as she came down the narrow cottage stairs so that she stumbled into the kitchen laughing, attempting to retrieve and comfort the startled animal which, running for cover beneath Oriel's skirts was startled once again when the two women came together in a huge birthday hug. Oriel scooped it up under one arm, frantic paws catching in the pale, ruffled lace of her collar, while with her other very steady hand she gave her sister the breakfast mug of hot chocolate and cinnamon with its birthday dash of Caribbean rum, waiting on top of the stove.

Kate was a rich woman today; Oriel a serene and, it seemed, very nearly a free one; Quentin, arriving for a mid-morning glass of Old Sercial, which he brought with him, looking his usual immaculate, faintly amused self; even Francis, walking down from the inn at nearby Askham with jars of rare Oriental spices for Oriel, a box of Kessler jewelry for Kate, finding no difficulty in easing himself into this house, this atmosphere which he knew at once—having encountered such things before—to be an oasis.

A necessary interlude perhaps in a lifetime, to be enjoyed to the full extent of one's capacity, for the simple reason, it seemed to him, of discovering exactly what that capacity might be. An interval—no more—when time receded like a tide, leaving one standing on a sandbank of possible wonder and delight, a possible gathering of self-knowledge, not all of it just as one had imagined about oneself or desired, until the water rushed back and carried them all off into the mainstream again.

So that when Oriel's slender glasses were raised, full of Quentin's vintage champagne, in the conventional toast of good health and long life, it was Francis who murmured, "I wonder where next year will find us all, at this time?" Not here, it seemed to him, in this beguiling, calming, so gentle oasis. Not even Oriel.

"Do you not find yourself too isolated here?" he asked her, entirely forgetting that the house was legally his property, having purchased it and all its contents through Quentin's agents who, working in strict secrecy, had taken no greater advantage than to help themselves to some of her best china and crystal.

Although today her luncheon table, pulled out into the middle of her small parlor, was decorated by some half-dozen glass vases along its center each one full of September roses, a velvet stream of pink and cream and apricot—Rose Oriel, he suddenly remembered—flowing between the birthday meal she gave them; scallops, obtained at her back door from the gamekeeper with Scottish connections served in their natural shells in a sauce of wine and chives and tarragon, grouse provided—indeed, shot—by Francis, with vegetables from Oriel's garden, apples puréed with sweet cicely, a plum cake with pink icing, wide enough for twenty-five pink candles which Kate, first declaring the feat to be impossible, just an antic for children, far more than any poor twenty-five-year-old woman could possibly manage, blew them all out nevertheless with a single breath of accurate determination.

Francis had spoken to her only once, so far, an interview

in Quentin's chambers which had begun and ended with
Kate's promise that soon—quite soon—she would talk to him
about his child, his home, herself. He had come today to
claim that promise, meant to claim it, no matter how easy it
was to blend with the calming, lotus-eating mood of this
room, this even more enclosing mood of wit and warmth and
amity, whispering even to him that it was good enough,
surely, intriguing enough, rare and special enough, to last
forever.

Yet when Kate, making a sweeping gesture to emphasize
some point about the scandal of the wounded British soldiers
being left to rot in the Crimea, dipped her sleeve in the bowl
of puréed apples and went off upstairs to change her dress, it
was Quentin who held out his hand to Oriel and, clasping the
hand she gave him—Francis noted—very willingly, said,
"Shall we go out and get some fresh air, a little way along
the fells, perhaps—and leave these two alone?"

Smiling, she got to her feet as if she had been waiting for
his command and, her hand still in his, walked out into the
mellow afternoon, along her garden and down the grassy
slope to the lakeside, her height and Quentin's about the same,
noticed Francis as he watched them from the window, a couple strolling together who—he could see very clearly—had
strolled together many times before, each step in tune with
the other, each movement in harmony, a turning together that
seemed, not passionate perhaps, but entirely natural. A couple indeed. Oriel who could never be free in her husband's
lifetime, Quentin whose professional status could afford no
breath of scandal with a woman of his own class. Yet—nevertheless—a couple, Francis' clear vision showing him an
unmistakable pair of lovers lingering by the lakeside willows
who may never have touched each other—he thought probably not—but whose natural harmony, even at this distance,
brought a warning tightness to his throat.

But emotion would not serve him now. And turning away
from it, he found himself face to face with Kate who had
been standing behind him, in a different, dark red dress with
hints of gold about it, for rather longer than he knew.

"Oh—Kate."

"Yes, that is my name."

He smiled, but nervously, a shade irritably he felt. "Quentin has taken Oriel out walking," he said. "So that we can
have some time together."

Brilliantly, with no trace of nerves in her anywhere, she smiled back. "Is that what he told you? He told me to make some excuse to go upstairs and stay there as long as I could to make it easier for *him* to have some time alone with Oriel. And since I knew how badly he wanted it I thought apple purée on my sleeve a small price to pay."

He waited a moment, allowing her triumph to pass, and then said, quite smoothly, "Nevertheless, we are alone together just as effectively, are we not?"

"Oh yes," she nodded her pleasant agreement. "A matter of getting two birds with one stone, I expect. Quentin is very good at that."

"And does Oriel want to be alone with him?" he inquired, realizing only when he saw her smile that his voice had been somewhat too sharp.

"Sadly—I think she does."

"Why sadly?" And he heard the sharpness himself now.

"Because I think it may be too late for them. Ten years ago they could have married young, right in the teeth of family opposition, and then struggled side by side—very happily, I think—until they succeeded. It seems too late for that now. He has succeeded already, you see, and he'd have to throw it all away—wouldn't he?—if he took her on. While she has that giant of a husband of hers and his rather promising daughter to worry her."

"So it won't come to anything between them, you're saying?"

"Francis—good Heavens." She raised both her shoulders and the extremely elegant line of her eyebrows. "I'm saying nothing of the kind. It may come to a great deal. And though I shall congratulate them both very heartily if it does and do everything I can to help . . . Well, what worries me most is that in *another* ten years—who knows?—she might start spending too much time thinking she's ruined him, as well as the other one—the giant, I mean, and his clever little girl. And Quentin might start regretting the legal practice in London and the seat in the House of Commons that Dora Merton—for instance—could have given him. I expect all that worries him too. He's quite wise enough."

"So are you, it seems, Kate—sometimes."

"Ah yes, but only about other people's business, I expect you mean," she said, folding her hands quite neatly before her, lowering her head like a good schoolgirl as he had seen

her do once before, years ago, when he had taken her to task
for risking herself among the man-traps in Merton Woods. A
world ago. Or, at least, *her* world, into which he had not
even meant to linger. Did he recognize it now as his? He
rarely allowed himself to think too much about it, pacing
himself only to the levels and limits of Celestine.

"Francis, are you actually unhappy?" she rapped out at
him very abruptly.

"No," he said, startled into giving the answer which
leaped first into his head. The right one? He would not, given
the time to reflect, have thought so.

"Are you actually happy, then?"

But now he made time. "My dear girl—are you?"

"More often than not," she said. "Which is quite wonderful—isn't it?—when one remembers how I used to be. All
I really have to contend with now is guilt, you see . . ."

He saw far too clearly. "Good Lord, Kate, not on my
account, I hope . . ."

"Good Lord, *Francis*." And although he could not know
just why she was laughing, it intrigued him. "Of course on
your account. What dreadful things I have done to you. I fell
in love with you far, far more than could ever have been
reasonable, and when I suddenly couldn't feel the full, furious mountain of it anymore I wasn't stable enough to discuss
it with you—to try and work it out as I expect Oriel would
have done. I just went on howling to myself in my own dark—
getting worse—hurting more people and not knowing how to
stop myself—certainly not knowing how to tell them how
much they were all crucifying me. I didn't seem to belong in
this world. It seemed—almost—as if I'd got myself into the
wrong skin, or the wrong species. If this was humanity then
I wasn't human. No—no—please let me finish, Francis—I've
been thinking what I ought to say to you for long enough.
Don't stop me now. When the child was born I couldn't stand
life—humanity—*people*—at all. Lying in bed with them
around me, all I could think was that Maud had got me again.
I was terrified she'd get the child too. You stopped that. But
you couldn't stop me—could you?—from being such a danger
to us all. So I thought, for a while, about killing myself and
ended up—of course—nearly killing Dora Merton instead.
Poor Mertons, really—with me and then Evangeline to contend with. They've never got over us. But never mind that

now. I took myself out of your way, Francis. It seemed the least I could do.''

Watching her as she stood beside the window, her hands no longer demurely folded, her pose taut yet decided, her profile sharp and elegant, older, he saw, in both texture and experience than twenty-five, he felt his throat tighten again. What an interesting woman—damned interesting in fact—she was.

''And now?'' he said, his voice no longer sharp at all.

''Yes, *now*, Francis. First I must apologize to you . . .''

''My dear—please don't.''

''Oh yes. I know, you see, more or less what happened. I have never mentioned this to Oriel but Quentin knows you intended marrying her. Evangeline was already bargaining with him for dowry money and a decent marriage settlement. A wife for Dessborough, so you could go off again adventuring—and seeing no more of Dessborough, I expect, than seemed strictly necessary. So Quentin said. Poor Oriel—I daren't ask her if that's what *she* wanted. I couldn't bear to know.''

''I think, at the time, she would have accepted.''

''Ah—'' She smiled across the rose-strewn room at him. ''I see you don't mean to spare me. Not that I blame you, since you found yourself with me, and then we so oddly changed places—me going off to find myself, which didn't take long once Quentin put me in touch with the French and German Kesslers, and you, who already knew yourself very well, staying in the last place you wanted to be. I'm sorry, Francis.''

''Don't be, Kate. It serves no purpose.''

''Ah but it does.'' And turning her faintly Oriental head toward him, her long eyes half closed, she gave him, once again, her brilliant, almost professional smile. ''We have a child. I may not seem to be aware of it, but—nevertheless, there she is. You have given her six, almost seven, years of your life. I have only given her nine months of mine. And since these lives of ours are not repeatable—neither yours nor mine—and she, the child, with luck has rather longer to go than we have. . .''

''What *are* you saying, Kate?'' He hardly liked the sound of it.

''Just this. The world is still as wide, Francis, and even though Captain Richard Burton has beaten you to Mecca there must be other places you might care to strive, and possibly die for. In which case, it seems only fair that you should do so. And that I should stay at Dessborough—how long? She is nearly seven. Ten years, then—or fifteen—before she is married and has no need of either of us.''

"*Kate.*"

"Oh—don't worry, Francis. I shall get on with her quite well enough. Little girls are easily charmed at seven. I have taught whole classes of them, from time to time, in Paris and Tours and Vienna, and the ones I wanted to like me have always done so. *Your* daughter, my dear, may even be glad to see the back of all those good ladies who keep falling in love with you. And she will be very proud of your letters from faraway places and—well—whatever those places may have in their bazaars for you to send her. And when the Queen makes a 'Sir Francis' of you, for having discovered something really salable which royals tend to like, I can bring the child to watch . . .''

Silence. And then, biting off each word with curt precision, he said, "And if I die in the attempt she can always collect my medals for me.''

Silence again, broken this time by Kate's even, very low-pitched, almost gentle laughter. "Ten years ago, Francis, such a thing would never have entered your head.'

"I suppose you mean something very wise by that, Kate.''

Her smile was gentle now. "I mean that you probably couldn't bear to leave the child and may not want to leave Dessborough now, either. I mean, through my madness—which is often the way things work out, one finds—you are in the place you ought to be.''

"And you?''

"Ah—no—no, Francis. All I want is to assuage my guilt, you see, by convincing you that instead of ruining your life I actually did you a great favor . . . You would very likely have been dead by now in a heap of camel dung somewhere, if I hadn't just *almost* killed you with my nonsense.''

"Thank you, Kate.''

"Or if not precisely dead, you'd have been rather withered, wouldn't you, and maimed, I expect—not at all attractive as one tends to think of you now.''

He swallowed, quite hard, and then, realizing he had never met this woman before, much less ever spoken to her, he smiled and bowed very slightly, his eyes meeting hers with the salute of one pleasantly flirtatious adult to another. "May I know who suffers from this tendency to think me attractive?"

"Oh—a fair number, I would imagine."

"Might you be among them?" He had not said *still* among them, aware more deeply than ever, that this was a first and possibly vital encounter.

"Oh—" she said, making him wait for her answer by the slowness of her smile. "I might. You could bring me another glass of champagne, while I am thinking about it."

Carefully, not insulting her by hurry—as he would have taken care not to rush an intriguing stranger—he poured the wine, neither his hand as he gave her the glass nor hers as she took it, quite steady, her voice sliding into the refuge of light amusement teasing speculation, as, turning away from him to the window, she said, "Oh look how far Quentin and Oriel have gone. Over there, on the fell path. You can just see them. I wonder if he is telling her he loves her?"

Not yet. They had walked, so far, in the companionable silence by no means strange to them, talking intermittently of Kate and Francis rather than each other, of Evangeline and, from her, to Lord Merton who had recently announced his permanent settlement in Monte Carlo, his wife enjoying her refuge in Scotland too much to leave it, Adela only a step away from becoming a nun. And Dora?

Reaching the top of the fell path, the lake far beneath them, the vale of Martindale lying just ahead, the sound of water never far away, rising beneath the tufts of coarse grass, falling fast and ribbon-fine down every slope of the encircling hills, Oriel looked around her for a moment, making a familiar, wholly natural communion, and then, turning to the man who now seemed, himself, so natural to her, said with the smile of calm affection she gave to no one else, "Kate thinks you might marry Dora Merton."

Once again he held out his hand to her. "If I could get the chance, she means?"

"Could you?"

His hand remained firm and cool around hers. "Yes. Amazing, isn't it—and rather sad, I suppose—but I think her father would be relieved now if I made the offer. It is Adela's estranged husband, remember, who inherits the title and the Abbey. But Lord Merton has a great deal more property—a house in London, for instance—and a fortune apiece to leave his daughters. Somebody must administer it. Somebody will have to look after the Abbey as well, since Timothy Merton can hardly settle in Adela's ancestral home with his foreign mistress and a bastard son. Particularly if Dora should be married and have a son of her own by then, who would eventually inherit the title. And since Dora's young men have never done her much good in the past, and she seems to have rather lost her taste for them nowadays anyway, her father is feeling desperate enough to lower his sights to me. The family lawyer—good God. But at least I can be relied on to keep the door well-polished and everything inside it turning over just as it should. And one tends to forget that my father is the cousin—if somewhat distant—of an earl. Which would give Lord Merton something to talk about, at least, in his club.''

But Oriel, of course, knew all this. ''Does Dora like you, Quentin?''

''She trusts me. Rather pathetically sometimes. There are days—not always easy ones—when she hardly likes to take a step without my direction.''

''Do you want to marry her?''

She thought she knew this too, but they walked on awhile longer, tasting the fresh wind, before he said, ''Oriel, I have six brothers and four sisters younger than myself, all of them, at the moment—including Susannah—in need of assistance to establish themselves in life, one way or another. My mother could never begin to supply that assistance. My father ignores it. He always has. And when he 'passes on' and the vicarage passes with him into other hands it will astonish me more than anything in my life if he has made the slightest provision for anybody. No doubt he considers such provision to be the rightful business of his God. Possibly so. That may even be the reason I was born to him.''

''To provide?''

''So it seems. In which case would it be right to neglect one's opportunities?''

They walked awhile longer, the lake now very far behind and below them, the ancient yew tree of Martindale churchyard already in sight, the low stone church looking small yet some how invincible beside it, before she said, ''I asked if you wanted to marry her, Quentin?''

''I know.''

''Yes. I know you know.''

He did not look at her, his eyes on her high fells. ''Oriel, you are the only woman I have ever *wanted* to marry. Do you know that too?''

Not until now. Or not for certain, although, even as she denied it, she knew how right it was, how *natural;* knew—so deeply and totally that she seemed to have known for-ever—his nature to be the one for which her own had been molded; knew—without any need to peer into the past—how serenely they might have moved together, grown together, in friendship and a love that would have been so rich and yet so peaceful. Loving friends, companionable lovers. Had it not been, of course, for the Stangways, and Evangeline, the Reverend Rupert Saint-Charles and his hungry, affectionate tribe of children.

''When?'' she said, walking a step ahead of him and then waiting at the churchyard gate until he came and stood beside her.

''I have more than my share of sisters,'' he said, taking her hand again. ''When I first met you I remember thinking what a pity they weren't more like you. What a pity—at times—that I even had them, since it meant I'd have to marry Kate. Naturally it never once entered my head not to marry her. I merely wished *she* could be like you.''

''I had no notion, Quentin—not then.''

''Of course not. There seemed no point in telling you. You had no money. Neither had I. And did either of us disagree when our mothers said how much we needed it?''

''No, Quentin. We were both so well brought up, weren't we?''

''You were, my darling. I was just naturally acquistive. And then you fell in love with Francis. I was almost glad. It encouraged me, rather, to fall out of love with you myself—if I could.''

''You were very kind to me the night of Kate's engage-ment.''

''I hope so. Yet—sadly—seeing you behave so graciously, with that knife in your heart, made me want you all over again. Marrying you would have done my career no good at that stage, of course, and would have somewhat upset the Stangways . . . But there it was. I wanted to marry you quite enough, by then, to stand all that. A decent interval of time, I thought—my vicarage upbringing making me cautious I ex-pect. But then you went off to see your friend Miss Woodley and came back engaged to your railway baron. Your mother was not the only one to be appalled by that. I almost—almost—never quite—asked you to break off with him and marry me. And please—I do mean *please*—don't tell me now whether you would have agreed to do it, or not.''

They walked through the wooden gate and along the brief path to the church porch, no larger than the entrance to a simple cottage, distinguished only by the one brave bell above it, no decoration within—although they did not go to look— beyond natural strength and solidity, wooden benches facing each other across clean, enduring stone, the House of a straightforward God for the meeting-together of His down-to-earth people.

"Imagine," he said. "If I'd gone into the church and you'd had a mother less ambitious than Evangeline—could we have been happy here, in a country-living like this, do you think?"

"I think so, Quentin. Until you started wanting to be a bishop, that is."

"Yes." He smiled at her. "Are you telling me that now I want to be a cabinet minister?"

She walked away from him once again and then, maintaining the distance, spoke across it. "I'm telling you we could have been happy here. I'm telling you we could have been happy anywhere, in spite of your mother and mine, if we'd had the sense to marry when we could. I'm telling you we were probably made for each other. Why not? I'm Matthew Stangway's daughter and you're his nephew. Why shouldn't we be alike? Why shouldn't we complement each other? I'm telling you we could have been *right* together, as well as happy. For ever after, as they say in the fairy tales. Or 'until death us do part' as you'd say if you'd got to be a bishop.''

Crossing the distance of tufted, fellside grass, he took her by the shoulders. "What else are you telling me?"

"I don't know. Perhaps . . ."

"Yes," his hands tightened. "I know."

"Perhaps that I have a husband. And you really want that appointment as a minister."

"Do you know how much," he said, "how very much I wish I didn't?"

The tree stood just ahead of them offering shelter, concealment, its branches touching the ground to make the dark but living cavern where she had once accepted the proposal Garron had made with no intention of letting her get away with a refusal. She had not thought of him all day. She thought of him now, it seemed, only through mist, the distance from her side of the lake, from her side of life, to his seeming almost—regrettably not quite—eternal.

"Will you go back to him?" Quentin said. "Your wounded giant? He must want you. I suppose he is only waiting until he can admit it."

She realized she had been supposing this too. "I don't know, Quentin. Perhaps if you could sweep me off my feet and carry me away . . . ?"

"Instead of just thinking—like you—of all the reasons why I'd better not?"

They were standing quite far apart, a gnarled six inches of the tree trunk between them, and looking at her for a long moment of rapidly increasing communion, he said quietly, his eyes still on hers, "They have such grand emotions, some of them, don't they? Your wounded giant, for instance. What storms he can generate. And Kate, of course, controlling it better now but catching visible fire every now and then. Francis too. I sometimes think it easier for them than for those of us to whom love comes differently. Calmer. More thoughtful—maybe too thoughtful. But it is love just the same—my darling—isn't it?"

"Yes,' she said, moving two short steps forward, as much as had ever been needed to cover the distance between them. "It is love, Quentin."

And although it may have entered the forefront of her mind a day ago, a week ago perhaps, she knew it had been living and growing in her heart for years. Not the passionate love of a stranger but the commitment, both natural and total, to a man who could be the other half of herself.

Nineteen

She lay awake on her herb-pillow for a long time that night, aware of Kate and Francis below her in the garden, their voices rising intermittently for what seemed several hours after midnight, aware even of the dog heavily patrolling the staircase, throwing himself down with a wheezing thud, every now and then outside her bedroom door, guarding her, she supposed, from the man who remained downstairs, even though he was occupied with another woman, and from the man who had gone away immediately after bringing her down from Martindale but who—in that jealous canine opinion—might always come back again.

They had remained under the yew tree for perhaps half an hour, an act of physical communion too deep for mere sensuality which could be aroused, after all, by so many men, so many women, with whom one had no need to be in love; beginning when she had walked into his arms and ending, after an embrace any observer would have thought quite innocent, with a kiss to which her lips and her heart had opened with happy ease, as if to open herself to him had, through long years of serene loving, become wholly natural.

They had then walked back down the lower slope of Hallin Fell to the lake, darkening with autumn sunset, his arm around her as they bent beneath the willow trees and alders along the water's edge, emerging to the field path to her garden gate where he had left her, saying only that he would come again tomorrow.

She had gone inside, merely smiling at Kate and Francis as she passed them and, having directed the housemaid she had borrowed for the day from the Buck Inn as to the correct clearing away of the birthday luncheon, had taken her dog for a long ramble in the dark along stony paths of tufted grass and ever-present, sudenly emerging water over which she had leaped without need for thought or even too much vision, her mind still open to Quentin, as her arms had opened to him earlier in the yew tree cave of Martindale; as open as her whole body which even though he had never entered it, already knew him with all the impulses of a deep-rooted, tender, wholly welcoming desire.

A revelation she found disturbing mainly because it did not even surprise her as it should have done, her acquaintance with desire so far throughout her womanhood having been mild and good-mannered rather than urgent, troubling her at first by its very absence and then progressing—not far enough, she readily admitted—to a rational, pleasant, but rather less than essential part of marriage. She had never desired any man in his absence, had burned and then grieved far more emotionally than physically for Francis Ashington, had responded to Garron's caresses with no more than good-will and good hope to begin with, leading to sensual pleasures which she had found thrilling and moving from time to time, occasionally glorious, but never addictive. She had never refused her husband, even when the headache her mother had advised her to manufacture had been quite genuine. She had responded, sometimes with real enthusiasm, sometimes with a pretense motivated by affection—by an honest wish that he should have satisfaction even when she did not—to every one of his sexual moods and methods. Yet, on the morning of his every departure, she had put the need for such excitements away as easily as the many other domestic needs his presence created, not even a dream of erotic delight much less any waking languors or amorous imaginings disturbing her until he came home again.

Her desire had always been conditional, entirely dependent on the presence of a far more urgent male desire to direct and stimulate it. She had believed herself capable of nothing more extreme. But now, striding along the roots of Swarth Fell, leaping the puddles, neither the chill night air nor the stern exercise could still the longing at the pit of her stomach, the length and depth of her limbs for Quentin's hand and mouth upon them, a clamorous urgency for the splendors and sufferings—following fast upon each other, it seemed—of her suddenly released sensuality which she had never before understood.

She understood them now, sleep at first eluding her on her return to the cottage and then leading her, as she had known it would, into dreams of love's consummation, the delicate miracle of heart and mind and orgasm blending together as, in her, they had never yet blended, the elements of trust and honest liking, of fun and faith, the fierce heights of emotion and the surfaces of happy, everyday belonging entering her body as Quentin entered it repeatedly through the night, the seeds of all these diverse wonders flowing with the seed inside her and mingling there essentially; waking her early and reluctantly to a cool dawn, a gray hint of rain in the sky, her dog still whimpering outside her door, the cats to be let out and given their breakfast, vegetables to be scraped and cleaned for luncheon, fires—by the look of that steel-colored sky—to be lit.

Yet these normally pressing everyday tasks failed to move her this morning, fading into the category of things to be left for later, things unlikely to tilt the earth on its axis in any case, compared to her need to lie back on her pillow, permitting no nonsensical leaping of heart or the newly liberated pulse of her sensuality to distract her and think, clearly this time, even chastely if she could, about Quentin. An honest intention quickly defeated by the impression of his love covering her against the chill of this possibly difficult morning with a blanket as warm as fur and as fine and subtle as silk; as Quentin himself was both subtle and enduring. At every perilous or painful corner of her life he had stood beside her, discreetly, often at an acceptable social distance, but there, nevertheless, to support her at need, to show her, if only by hints or remarks she might have thought, at the time, to be merely "clever," which way it seemed best to go. On the morning of Kate's elopement she had turned to him by instinct, knowing—without knowing how she knew—that he would not let her down. He had guided her through the day of her mother's death and the days thereafter as no one else could have done, bringing Kate—with an effort she could well imagine—to her side. When her chaste, well-ordered life had collapsed under false accusation his name, his face, had been the only ones to enter her mind.

She had wanted to go to him then just as she did now, the wanting alarming her only because it still seemed so wholly natural, so right, and so inevitable that had he now opened her door she would have felt a familiar, unmixed joy, a sense of who else had a better right, or any right at all to enter her bedroom, although ten minutes or so later it was Kate who came in, wrapped in her exotic Oriental silk, her hair unbrushed, her feet bared, two mugs of cinnamon chocolate in her hands and no intention at all of allowing the dog to follow her.

"Get out," she said, her voice never gentle at seven o'clock of any morning. "You're a male. Go off and rape some poor pedigree greyhound somewhere."

"My word—" Oriel, at both her dog and her sister, was smiling. "What have *you* against well-brought-up young bitches this morning?"

"No more than usual." Sitting down on the edge of the bed, by no means carefully, she handed Oriel a mug with cream, pink-tipped roses painted all over it. "Breakfast, madame."

"My goodness—how kind."

"Not really. An act of sheer desperation, love. Brought on by the gruntings of that damned dog, and those cats scratching all over the place—including my door."

Smiling, Oriel sipped her chocolate, finding it, as she politely murmured, not bad for Kate.

"Thank you, kindly. I got your paper and sticks all ready laid out for the parlor fire too, which I thought very good of me. But just how to light it I'm not certain. One never had to, you see, in France and Italy. And in Germany I always stayed with the Kesslers who are so good to their servants that they have a great many. Thank goodness the kitchen fire kept going all night."

Oriel raised her mug of hot chocolate in a solemn toast to Kate's domesticity. "You mean the fire under the stove, I expect."

"I do. Or you'd have been drinking cold milk, my girl, or spring water. Are you well this morning, Oriel? It seems to have come rather early for me."

"You stayed up late, I expect, doing—whatever seemed good to you."

"Ah yes." Jumping to her feet, her own cup luckily half-empty, she crossed to the window seat and, drawing her knees up to her chin, grinned companionably at the speculating Oriel. "Quite so, Mrs. Keith. And should you be expecting to find Francis when you go downstairs trying to look as if he had just called in for breakfast, then I shall have to disappoint you.''

''My dear Mrs. Ashington,'' murmured Oriel, ''what could I possibly have to say if I did? Since he *is* your husband and this house—remember—*does* belong to him.''

''Oh no—no, no,'' Kate clicked her tongue and shook her head. ''That's just the legality of it. And what can that mean to us? It's reality we're dealing with. And by that reckoning the house is yours and Francis and I are definitely not a married couple. If I'd shared a bed with him last night I'd have been feeling very much a mistress this morning, I can tell you.''

''You didn't then?''

Her arms around her knees, her black and gold kimono slipping aside to reveal thin, amber legs with neat ankles, Kate rocked herself up and down for a moment in a blithe fit of laughter. ''I did not. I sent him away. And I feel certain it never once entered his head to say, 'I am your husband, my good woman. Take your clothes off at once . . .' ''

''Kate—I hardly think he would.''

''Oriel—you don't realize how coquettish I was down there, in the garden—until what must have been the middle of the night . . . Heavens, I set out to tempt him as far as I could and when I got there, to the point that comes just before commitment, I drew back exactly as if we'd just met and it was too soon. And he did the same, knowing better than to rush a woman he's just met, and being all whimsical and sweet and teasing about it. A very polished performance I thought. Just as if I'd been one of those London ladies who dash over to see him all the time from Merton Abbey. He's quite a flirt, isn't he? I suppose he always was. Although never with me.''

Finishing her chocolate, Oriel put her cup down carefully on her bedside table and, smiling, shook her head. ''Is it any wonder? You were eighteen and thought he was Adonis.''

''Exactly.'' Kate hugged her knees again, pressing her cheek against them. ''Poor man. So impossible to live up to. And so unlike him, as it turns out. I didn't know him at all when I went away. You're quite right, I thought he was Adonis coupled with—well, yes, the side of my father you may never have thought particularly charming, but which could have charmed me, I must confess, if he'd ever taken the trouble. That was the image of Francis I took away with me. And although I realized—fairly quickly—that he wasn't Adonis because nobody is, and he wasn't that idealized version of my father either—well, that was as much as I could honestly say about him for certain.''

"In fact you'd lost your Adonis Stangway."

They laughed together. "So I had. Not that it worried me. I soon lost the taste—or the need—for mythical heroes."

"And now?"

She wrinkled her nose. "I came back to meet him as a stranger. I knew I'd have to meet him because of the money and the child, and because of my conscience. I didn't know what kind of man he'd turn out to be. Dull, I may have thought, and getting somewhat pompous as squires do. Willing to split the money with me, perhaps, but not wanting me near *his* daughter. Possibly—in fact quite likely—with another woman he didn't want me to upset either. I was quite prepared for that. But to tell you the truth, what I didn't expect was to find him so attractive."

"Oh dear," murmured Oriel, "dear me . . ."

"You might well say so. Which is what made me take an extra glass or two of champagne last night and end up so flirtatious. Heavens—such *fun*. And that's the last thing—surely—we ought to have been having, a couple with all the agony and desertion and sheer dreadfulness there's been between us? Fun? I was quite ready, if he had another great lady-love, to go abroad and pretend to be dead—so long as he promised to keep up my income . . . Then he could have pretended to be married to her and move her into the manor. Don't laugh. Such arrangements work very well so long as everybody involved goes on properly pretending. It's only to satisfy the 'friends and neighbors'—like most of the things those of us in 'good society' think we have to do.''

"Did you mention it to Francis?"

"Yes. He suggested I might like to change my name and use a foreign accent and move back as his mistress myself. It sounded very amusing last night, I expect, sitting under your willow tree in the moonlight. Flirtation is one of my very favorite things, so long as one conducts it properly. By which I mean verbally, and *cleverly* . . ."

"Of course."

"Yes, Oriel. I suppose Quentin is accomplished in that direction too.''

"Ah well. Are we going to talk about Quentin now?"

Oddly it neigher worried nor surprised her.

"We are. That's what I really came for." And coming back to sit on Oriel's bed, she said, very clearly, "Did he tell you he loves you?"

"Yes."

"Did you know?"

"I did when he told me."

"And you love him?"

"Yes. I love him."

"Oh Oriel—Oriel—I thought so."

"Don't worry, Kate. I also know he wants to be a famous Member of Parliament and have a place in somebody's government—I don't think he much minds whose—and make a lot of money and have influence and prestige, so that he can do what he has to do for his family and a lot for himself. I know he's worth the influence and prestige. The money goes without saying."

Taking one of Oriel's hands in both hers Kate squeezed it gently. "Yes, Oriel. I know all those things about him myself. You're quite right. I also know he wants you too. I've known it for ages. He used to tell me about it very nearly every time he came to see me in France."

"Did he?" It pleased her to imagine it.

"Oh yes. So I know for certain what you mean to him. But Oriel—listen—you're not the reason he's never married. If he'd met a woman capable of financing his way into politics, and upward toward that influence and prestige you were talking about—and which we both know he's capable of—then he'd have taken her, Oriel . . ."

Smiling, she returned the pressure of Kate's hand. "Darling, I know—I know. That's Quentin. It doesn't shock me. It doesn't make any difference, either, to what there *is* between us. No matter what we actually do about it in the end."

"Oriel, just do the right thing, that's all."

"For me? Or for both of us?"

"Oh Lord." Kate shook her head, biting her lip quite hard. "Both—if you can. If not, then you. It has to be. Although he means a great deal to me too."

"Thank you, Kate."

Kate once more shook her head. "You know you'll have to go abroad if you decide to live together, don't you?"

"I do. I also know he'd be unlikely to get any government appointments there."

"And you know if you stayed in England as his mistress

you'd be forever in the shadows of his life—waiting up here while he made his name in London, or wherever he thought likely—and then when you're both forty or fifty he could still marry some young heiress, if he's made his name well enough, and leave you in this cottage, with your cats and that abominable dog—and possibly me.''

They were both laughing, on the very edge of tears, love and the need to defend each other, the need to go on crusade for the other's cause and be ready, with anything that might bring comfort, if it failed, rushing through the air between them, even reaching the dog, still at his post behind the door, who—seeing no reason why anyone else should usurp his readiness to defend—tried to growl it down.

"I know," promised Oriel. "I know. I'll take care. Don't worry."

"Worry?" Biting off a sharp laugh, Kate shrugged her shoulders. "Good old worry. That's what I'm made of, love. Aren't you? We're women, after all, and how many of us managed to escape it? So I'd better say now what I've been sent to tell you . . ."

"Sent? By Quentin?"

"Of course. You *do* know him well, I'm glad to see. All right. He gave me a message for you, yesterday—round about the time he told me to make some excuse to go upstairs and keep out of the way for a while. You remember the apple sauce on my sleeve?"

"Yes. So he told you to tell me . . . ?"

"All right, Oriel. Here it is. He came up on the train from Lancaster to Penrith yesterday with your husband. Quite by chance, of course. Your husband came up to him and said he wanted to see you. Quentin explained your house would be full of guests for the next few days but your husband said he didn't want to come here in any case. He's staying at the George in Penrith and the message is that he'll ride over here to the Buck Inn at ten o'clock this morning and wait half an hour. If you decide not to walk over and see him, then he'll ride back to Penrith. Quentin didn't say whether or not he thought you ought to go, but I expect he does. He asked me to wait until he'd gone back to wherever he's staying—Askham, isn't it?—before I told you. I don't know why."

Drawing her knees up under the bedclothes and resting her folded arms on them, Oriel, although she had paled a little, smiled. "Don't you?" How well, how very well, her mind flowing so smoothly, so surely along with his, did she know herself. "He knew I had to be told. He also knew he was going to speak to me himself, to decide if we could have a future together when the time seemed right. Perhaps meeting Garron on the train convinced him we'd have to make that decision now—or perhaps never."

Of course. Oriel was in no doubt about it, remembering—as she knew he had remembered—that other time when he had waited too long for the *right* moment which, because of his courteous, fastidious delay, had never come at all. Lowering her head to her folded arms, she allowed herself a moment of her own to contemplate that delay of his, those desperate days following Kate's wedding, when, by hesitating to speak to her himself, he had allowed her to come here to Miss Woodley, and Garron. A delay which, they both knew, had made her Garron's wife, not his.

"Naturally," she said aloud, "he couldn't risk another."

"Oriel . . . ?"

She raised her head. "Oh, I'm just thinking aloud."

"And suffering too?"

"Well—yes, so I am. But we're women, aren't we, Kate? It's just part of our stock-in-trade. He left Garron's message with you, love, because he knew I had to have it. He realized he couldn't trust himself to give it to me—that's all—so he committed himself by telling you."

"You really *do* know him, don't you, Oriel?"

"Yes. I know him."

"And your husband?"

"I think so."

"You'll be walking down to the Buck Inn to see him, then?"

Drawing back the bedclothes, Oriel stood up, stretching herself beneath the frilled, immaculate cambric of her night-dress. "What time is it now? Eight o'clock. That gives me two hours. Yes, I expect I'll walk over . . ."

Kate stood up too, clutching her flamboyant, none too well laundered Oriental satin around her, sudden tears in her eyes. "Oh Lord, Oriel—I almost wish you wouldn't. I almost wish I hadn't promised to see Francis again today. Goddammit—dammit—I wish we didn't feel we had to—and might even like it in the end—or think we do . . ."

"Kate . . ."

But the dog, picking up the note of high distress, began to

claw so frantically at the door that Oriel let him in, falling
back on the bed again as his huge body, his huge joy, his
huge desire to save her from everything that was not himself,
overcame her.

"What a *man* that dog is," said Kate, laughing her fierce
tears away.

But not Quentin, never him, it seemed to Oriel as, picking
herself up, she caught a glimpse through the window of the
lean, fastidious dark gray cat in the garden directly below,
his long topaz eyes looking up at her, his casual, elegant pose
in no way betraying that he had been waiting there for some
time—since dawn, very likely—to make whatever checks
seemed necessary to him on her presence, the state of her
health, and the balance of her human and consequently somewhat muddled mind. *Dear human woman, I am guarding
you, you know, in my fashion, just as thoroughly as that fearfully red-blooded, hopelessly ardent savage of a dog.*

She knew.

The Buck Inn was no more than ten minutes away, less
had she chosen to walk briskly, although, having chosen to
wear nothing more elaborate than the garden dress and shawl
she usually wore at this time of day, she saw no reason to
hurry, even pausing, as she reached the water's edge, to look
up, just as she always did, at the fells, veiled this morning in
fine curls of mist, a taste of rain in the air, a single, amber-
tipped leaf taking flight on a sudden, sharp breeze, the first
lovely casualty of autumn coming to settle at her feet and
then, a moment later, two others, one gold, one a burnished,
poignant copper. Bending down, she picked up the gold leaf
and then, having lingered a moment over its color and fragility and its sharp, emotive scent, set it adrift on the lake, a
last adventure which might take it to Watermillock or Pooley
Bridge or straight to the bottom should the rain come on, but
which seemed better, she thought with a smile, than a certain
trampling to death underfoot on the narrow path.

Walking on, abandoning the gold leaf to its fate as she had
usually—so far—abandoned herself to her own, she felt a
surprising lack of anything to which she could give a name.
She felt no fear, no hope, no remorse, no urge either to
defend or to blame, no anxiety as to what she might, or might
not, be asked to give up, take on, explain, suffer, make
amends. That such things would be asked she was in no
doubt. Or some of them. But having decided this meeting

with Garron to be inevitable, the only sensible thing, it seemed to her, was to go and meet him, maintaining her energy and her often fluctuating courage, safeguarding the fine, pale shell into which she knew she had once again slipped, until she discovered in which direction they should be needed. And even when she saw him, his caped greatcoat filling the doorway of the long, low, slate-gray inn, her emotions—of all temperatures and colors—remained obediently dormant, allowing her to walk up to him across the yard and, glancing at his coat with its rich fur lining, to say to him, quite pleasantly, "Are you cold?"

"Yes," he snapped, in order to say something—anything— as she had done, acknowledging, as men of status are apt to do, that one could not air one's domestic grievances at an inn door: a precaution he would have disregarded with some swagger, she rather thought, ten years ago. "Yes, I'm cold. I always am up here. You don't want to walk up those damned fells, do you, and ruin my shoes? There'll be rain coming on, any minute. They've offered to lend us a room at the back and leave us alone—for an hour or two."

It was a small bar-room, low and square, richly timbered with gleaming black wood, red velvet framing a clerical, ruby and emerald window, a red chair on which she sat, an ornately carved bar with an air of a medieval past about it, at which he leaned, pouring himself a glass of the whiskey he had purchased, she supposed, along with their privacy.

"You look like some hill-farmer's housekeeper on her day off," he said tersely, casting an eye that found no favor over her gray wool dress and Paisley shawl, her sensible country boots—in case he *had* wanted to take her up the fells—the absence of the gold chains and rings which, she supposed, he had locked away at Lydwick, or given to his daughters.

"Thank you," she said.

"You've got a better dress than that, haven't you? Or have you sold the good ones already . . . ?"

Seeing he did not expect an answer, she folded her hands and waited, quite comfortable in the deep red chair, noticing, as he took a swift drink, the taunt muscles in his throat, the angle of his hard, fighting jaw which struck her as thinner than she remembered it, his whole face pared down to the heavy bone, covered by a skin still tanned and rugged yet lined, now, she saw, in tell-tale places, with crinkles fanning out from the eye-corners, tense furrows on either side of the mouth from heavy nose to truculent chin; a face that, without its necessary exposure to the sun and wind of his construction sites, would have been pinched and gray, she abruptly realized, and ten years older—she realized that too—than the face she had known—how long was it?—barely six months ago.

"You got the line finished on time then, didn't you?" she said quite gently, his loss of weight and sad gain of years due, she supposed—she hoped—as much to the Milne, Morrissey Bank as to herself.

"Aye—as you'd expect. I got it finished, and the one after—and the next. I'm sound as a bell again."

"I'm so pleased." She sounded no more than polite, her cool air of good manners tightening his jaw with a menace she well remembered.

"Pleased? Aye—I reckoned you would be. The money's flowing in hand over fist again. Which brings me to the reason I sent for you today—no point in beating about the bush—not at the price this landlord is charging me for a place to talk to you. I could stay overnight at the George for what I've just given him."

It was true, of course. Any landlord anywhere would have drawn the same conclusion. Garron knew that even better than she did, or, at least, had known it for longer. She experienced no difficulty, therefore, in answering his scowl with a limpid smile.

"All right," he said. "Leave the landlord out of it."

"Yes, Garron, of course. But he's quite a decent man, really, almost as famous as John Peel when it comes to hunting foxes—on foot, you know, like they do up here because they can't get horses over the fells—and with hounds a bit more wiry than ours . . ."

"Listen to me," he growled, his jaw visibly threatening her again, his grip so tight around his glass that, for a half-anxious, half-amused moment, she thought it would shatter between his fingers. "*This* is what I have to tell you. It's time you came back again. I need a wife. So long as you live I can't take another, and resident mistresses cause more problems than I'm ready to put up with now. In any case the girls seem to want you back. Even Jamie . . ."

"Oh. I'm—so pleased," she said formally, "to know that."

"Aye. So there we are. I'm away to Scotland tomorrow for

ten days or so—time enough for you to pack your bags and make your arrangements. I'll call for you on my way back.''

It was settled then.

''Thank you, Garron,'' she said. ''For your offer, that is. Not—of course—that I can accept it.''

And as her voice trailed away on a slight note of derision, in the exact manner of her mother Evangeline, the small, dark room seemed, for a moment, to retain its echo, filling her not with dread—although thinking of his hard jaw, his grasping fist, she rather wondered why—but *almost* of compassion. She saw that he had suffered, was suffering still, not only from the cause of his pain—herself—but from a bitter fury that *he*, of all strong, fighting men, could sink so low as to feel it.

She knew he loved her, as the dog who so often knocked her down and trampled on her in his passion loved her too: and the lean, gray cat—she did not for one moment forget him—arching himself fastidiously at her window to take note of her sanity and then gliding just as fastidiously away. None of it was a revelation. There was nothing here that she had not turned over and over in her mind these past months, during which she had drifted not always willingly toward the decision she knew to be right, and good, and quite inevitable, although by no means necessarily the one she might—just *might*—have made. Had she been harder—that is—or frailer, less acquainted with the truths and needs of love. Her own. And theirs.

''I expect you know,'' he said, ''that all I have to do is ask some High Court Judge to order your return—which means I can take you by force if you won't come.''

''I know.''

''And what do you think of that?''

''I think it's nonsense, Garron. I think it means you'd be getting a woman you'd have to rape every night and who'd lie there, while you were doing it, thinking how best to stab you in the back. She might mellow with time, of course, and settle for your money, cheating you of the odd hundred pounds or so whenever she could, and wishing you'd hurry up and die so she could have the rest. That's what I think . . .''

With an abrupt, yet heavy movement he turned away from her, his caped greatcoat draped around his shoulders, making a massive menace of him in the bar corner, reminding her painfully of the last time he had been unable to look at her, until—somewhat to her relief—he swung round again, his face taut but no longer a threat, and said dryly, "Yes. That's what I think too."

Finding her own throat very dry, she swallowed, rather quickly. "I didn't expect you to do it, Garron. Force me, I mean."

"Is that a compliment?"

"Yes." She was half smiling. "Because . . ." and now her smile fully broke through, "there'd be nothing in it for *you*, would there? Not really. It wouldn't be worth your trouble."

There was a pause and then, the sigh wheezing in his chest—too many cigars, she supposed—he gave a brief movement of the lips that she thought it best to accept as an answering smile. "I reckon not, Oriel. Not in your case, anyway. Oh—make no mistake—there are women who'd rather put up with conjugal rape than starvation, and make the best of it. But they're usually the ones who have nowhere else to go. And your friends will always look after you, won't they? I know that. I even knew it the night I threw you out. Or I did the next morning, when I'd come round—yes, sobered up—enough to know anything. And then your clever Mr. Saint-Charles came calling to reassure me—he said—that you'd come to no harm and never would, so long as he had anything to do with it. I don't know why this matters—I don't know why the hell I should care—but I'd like you to know something. I put that damned cottage up for sale because it was the worst thing I could think of to do to you. It even struck me—that night—to come up here and burn the place down. Christ—there was a minute when I say myself dragging you with me and making you watch. Making you go through the kind of loss—I reckon—you'd forced on me. Sometimes I still wish I had. But even so, when your Mr. Saint-Charles put his men in touch with my men to buy it, I knew. I'd thought of it already, you see. I'd worked out what I'd do if I wanted to help you, and since buying that bloody cottage would have been it, I knew. And I let it happen. Do you believe me?"

Yes. Without any hesitation, she believed him.

"Why, Garron?"

He shook his head and, beneath the voluminous black fox lining of his coat, shivered. "God knows. You do understand—don't you?—why I walked out of the house that night and left you alone . . . ?"

"Yes, I understand."

"I could have killed you otherwise. It might have come to that—believe me. And even if it hadn't you'd have been a mess . . . You've never seen a navvywoman, I reckon, after her man's caught her in the wrong bed. Christ—even then I couldn't do that to you. And don't thank me, for God's sake, or I might just do it now. It's what men *do*, where I come from—except the poor, bloody fools I never had any time for. Until I turned into one myself."

Getting up slowly, walking carefully as if any sudden move- ment might startle him either to terror or to terrorize, she crossed the room to stand beside him, his body slumped heavily against the bar, hers tall and arrow-straight, poised—she was well aware of it—half in compassion and half in flight.

"All right," he said, scowling at the whiskey bottle as he refilled his glass. "All right. I didn't expect to impress you with a court order. Maybe I just wish I could. But this is your fault, Oriel—all of it—this grief you've caused to Morag, and Elspeth—and to me as well."

"All my fault?"

"Yes—it bloody well is. Because if you'd been the woman I thought you were—the woman I bought and paid for—the luxury I treated myself to as soon as I could afford it—if that's *all* you'd been, and for a long while I thought it was, then I'd have just evicted you out of your squire's bed and mine both together and never given you much thought again. Goddam- mit, I was willing to let you go your own way—wasn't I?— when the bank failed, with as much money as I could scrape together to pay you off. I'd have wished you luck. I meant it. You surely knew that."

She nodded in what looked like pleasant agreement. "Oh yes. But what I couldn't decide was whether it was because you were generous and brave in adversity, a truly perfect gentleman. Or even that you rather cared for me. Or whether you just thought me an expensive nuisance it would be cheaper to get out of the way—like the pedigree hunter one sells to get the stable roof repaired . . ."

There was a short, very silent moment and then, with a familiar, defensive sneer he rapped out, "You aristocrats always have to make light of every damned thing, don't you— Oriel Blake? Such little matters as earning a living and keep- ing what you've slaved your guts out for . . ."

"Ah well," she smiled once more. "Could that be why we coped so well with the guillotine?"

"What the hell does that mean?" he inquired curtly, a working man no longer but an industrial grandee responsible for the living wages of a thousand others, emptying his glass with an almost brutal sweep of the elbow but hearing, nevertheless, as clearly as she did, his own voice speaking to her on the night of the bank failure, the night she had refused his offer of a comfortable escape and given him herself instead. Or so he had believed. *God help you if you try to leave me now. And God help anybody else . . . who tries to take you an inch away.* And how many had tried? Susannah, the frantic, frigid woman who desired him but would have screamed rape and murder—he'd always reckoned—had he tried to touch her. Morag, his favorite child, who loved him too and was withering now, day by miserable day, before his eyes in her need for Oriel. As he was—goddammit . . . Withering, wanting her and ready to kill her for it, except on the days when he was even readier to fall at her feet. Or have her lay her body, once again, over his in the moonlight, as she had on that black night of crisis, pouring herself into him with what could have been love, *would* have been love—surely—at the end of those hard months of near bankruptcy when she had kept the keys to his safe so faithfully, defended his back, given him that extra reason, that extra spark, he'd needed to endure. The woman he'd played with and used for his purposes only for so many years, the woman he'd purchased as an indulgence, the cool and cultured luxury who had stood beside him more steadfastly in his time of need than any woman he had ever known or could imagine. His woman. And what he now wanted, urgently and essentially—vitally, he knew it—was to force himself to forgive her for what he had established as one night of sin.

"Listen," he said roughly. "I've had women enough all my life—a few of them after we were married, I admit it . . ."

"Of course," she murmured. "But men are allowed that, surely? Do many women complain?"

Was she asking a question?

"Don't be clever," he said. "For God's sake, don't provoke me. I'm not boasting. I'm just admitting I wouldn't want to be blamed for the rest of my life for something I'd done in a few hours—and which may not have meant much to me at all, or not more than those few hours could cover . . ."

"That's very wise of you, Garron."

"And if that bloody woman hadn't sent me that letter we'd have been happy now, I reckon. Wouldn't we?"

"Yes, Garron. And so would Morag. And I don't think Elspeth would have been engaged to poor Tom Landon. I might have put a stop to it."

He reached out a hand to his glass and then, changing his mind, gave her a hard stare. "You'd be a fool, Oriel, not to take me seriously."

But her smile was undimmed. "I know, Garron. I've always taken you seriously. I've always respected you. I didn't much like you when we first met because I'd been taught to set too high a store by "good social behavior." But that didn't last. And even from the first I felt I'd like to know you better. Well—not from the *first*, perhaps—but soon enough. I felt there was a great deal *to* know. Yes, your money did matter when I married you. If you hadn't had any I'd never ever have met you, would I? And there have been times— yes—when it seemed to me you quite liked having bought yourself a 'lady of quality' as a housekeeper."

"Maybe I did. Maybe I used to look at 'ladies of quality' in my laboring days, and wonder just what made them tick over."

"Girls like me? Half of them as feather-headed and silly as half the girls in your navvy camps, and the other half just as nice and clever."

"Aye, I know. And I've always known which half you came in, Oriel. I got what I paid for, I admit it, even in the days when the only real thing between us was the money. You did everything I asked, and more—things I hadn't even known I'd wanted until you gave them to me. You were a perfect wife. A perfect woman. I'd have taken an oath there wasn't a fault in you. And—I'll tell you now—in anybody else so much perfection would have bored me—made me suspicious—I'd never have trusted it. I tend not to do much trusting in any case. I trusted you . . ."

"Then I can tell you . . ."

"What? That it only happened once with your squire?"

"Oh—is that what I was going to tell you . . . ?"

But in the sheer effort of speaking about it, thinking about it, admitting that it had happened, he was not listening to her.

"Don't tell me. I believe it was—just once. Oh no—it's not a question of having faith in you, Oriel, nothing so damned fool romantic as that. I've never been much acquainted with faith anyway. I hired a detective who accounted to me, eventually, for your squire's movements around that time—except on the day Morag saw him with you. And the night before.''

Feeling the tension in him, the tight-clenched pain, she began to say, ''No, Garron—please let me . . .'' but shaking his head, making a gesture of absolute refusal to hear, to learn, to be tormented by any more than he *knew* already, he silenced her. ''No. Let me say this, Oriel. It's not easy. I know Kate was supposed to meet him at your cottage and canceled at the last minute. Which means what happened between you wasn't planned. I know he'd been up on the Roman Wall but came down one night before he turned up at Lowther Castle. I know he didn't spend the night at any inn or hotel in this region. I know there was something between you before he married Kate. I know what Morag saw. So it was one night. Wasn't it, Oriel? One night and never again. I have to believe it.''

She could not answer.

''Oriel—you have to say it—you have to tell me. If it was more, then I swear I won't lose my head—I won't touch you. All I'll do is walk out and go away, I swear it, to work it out on my own—if I can. But I have to know.''

Still she could not speak.

''Oriel . . . ?''

And on a strange wave of something that seemed partly resignation, partly something else, she understood the uselessness of trying to prove her innocence, realizing, at a deep, vital level of her judgment, that he had spent so long coming to terms with her guilt, even longer striving to forgive her, that he was blind now to anything else.

''Oriel. One night. Tell me. I'll never ask again.''

Lowering her eyes against the pain in his, she whispered, ''Yes Garron. Once. Only once. No more—because—because more would have been impossible—always . . .''

''Christ,'' he said and, hearing plainly in his voice the cry that meant, ''I can't bear it,'' she held out her hands to him and said what she knew he needed to hear: ''Garron—what did our marriage really mean before then? Where was the real feeling between us until we had to face disaster together and found we could? The bank failure broke other couples apart, but surely it brought us together. Which must mean something too important to be thrown away? I was your wife then—truly your wife—you must know that. I felt you valued me and I know I valued you—so much, so constantly. And Garron—believe me—had you failed then we'd have failed, truly, together. I'd have matched what strength I have with yours and worked with you—*wanted to be with you*—please understand . . .''

"Aye," he said, and with a heightened, most precisely disturbing vision, she saw him wince, his eyes narrowing against the painful tumult behind them which he had struggled so continuously, these past months, to control. "Aye. I've worked all that out myself, Oriel. You were a perfect wife. And then suddenly, by God, you were *my* wife. And there was one hell of a difference. The first six years were what I'd ordered. The last three months were more than I'd ever believed in—much less realized I wanted—until you gave them to me. Love—if that's the word—I've never given much thought to, Oriel. Responsibility—yes. That I understand. That's what I felt for my first wife. Responsibility, generosity, a fair measure of sorrow when she died. But I didn't need her. Needing you has been the hardest thing I've ever had to come to terms with. Needing. And wanting. So what do I do—tell me that—to get you?''

The whiskey bottle stood between them, and carefully moving it aside with the tips of her fingers, she touched the back of his hand which abruptly closed around hers, their arms twisted together to the elbows like a pair of stern and silent wrestlers. And then, the tension leaving him, he pulled her forward against his chest, his coat coming around her, wrapping her into the urgency of his need for the woman who may not have been the whole and absolute Oriel Blake but who, nevertheless, for those three splendid, perilous months, had been his wife.

"Come back to me, Oriel. Christ—when I think of half the things I've done I'd be a fool to go on blaming you. There's no reason to talk about it again. Just come home.''

He paused, breathing heavily into her ear. "Come home, Oriel. And let's be faithful to one another. Listen to me, my bonny lass—listen—I think I'm asking you to marry me.''

Twenty

Walking back alone up the field path and through her garden gate, she found the three of them meandering, glass in hand, among her autumn flowers, the day having turned fine, and looking straight at Kate, said, very pleasantly but not intending to be disobeyed, "Why don't you take Francis for a drive in the Buck Inn's gig? I thought you might like to spend the afternoon in Penrith. There's so much to see there. The landlord will have his horse ready by the time you walk down there."

"Oh—what a *wonderful* idea," cried Kate, clapping her hands together with obedient enthusiasm. "Just what I should like. Wouldn't you, Francis?" And hardly waiting for his reply that nothing could please him more, she dashed inside, returned in no more than half a minute with her hat and gloves and, planting a kiss on Oriel's cheek, took the arm Francis smilingly offered and strolled off with him, exclaiming loudly about the sudden beauty of the day and how clever of Oriel to know that for ages now—simply ages—she had been longing to explore the ancient glories of Penrith. So ardently, in fact, that she could not imagine being back again a minute before—should one say?—six o'clock?

Oriel watched her until the chattering, loving voice had died away and then turned to Quentin, watching and waiting as fastidious and elegant and as apparently aloof in his caring as the cats who were themselves scrupulously aware of her, blinking their gold eyes at her in muted anxiety, immaculate, understanding, from their basking place beneath the valerian. Only the dog showing so fundamental a need to grapple with

434

whatever might be troubling her, to chase it out of her and worry it to death between his murderously adoring teeth that she was obliged to lock him up in the kitchen, leaving him to sulk by the fire while she took her trouble, and herself, to Quentin.

He was waiting by the parlor window, a glass of wine already poured for her, Quentin's wine, tasting dry and subtle and valuable on her tongue.

"You saw your wounded giant then?" he said.

"Yes. He has gone to Penrith now, on his way to Scotland. His daughter Morag is coming over from Watermillock to stay with me tomorrow. And on his way back, in about ten days, he will call to collect her here."

"And you too?"

"I think so."

"You're going back to him then?"

"Ah—yes." And only because she knew him as she knew herself, her brother and lover who was actually neither, always both, did she glimpse the pain behind his subtle smile.

"Am I wrong, Quentin?"

"To go back to him? No, Oriel. Had I thought it wrong I would never have allowed you the chance to do it. I would have claimed you for myself by now—had I been able."

"Quentin." Her smile was as subtle and painful as his own. "You would have been very easily able—very happily, I think. If only to begin with."

He smiled again, although very briefly this time. "That knowledge may comfort me eventually, I suppose. And I accept your judgment, of course. 'Happy—if only to begin with.' Yes. That strikes me as an accurate opinion of our chances together. I wish I could deny it. I do love you, Oriel. Indeed—I have loved no one else in my life. I grew up thinking it an affliction for fools— believe me—in no way applicable to any decent, intelligent man. From a young age—a fearfully young age—I looked at my mother and shuddered. With pity, of course, mixed in with the confusion, the boy's fear of getting caught and smothered, spurred on rather by the sight of my father forever locking himself away behind his study door. Yet what respect could I ever feel for a man whose sole contact with his wife was the one that made her pregnant—again—and again—with children he barely seemed to recognize in the street? Then there was Maud, who wanted to live through me and soon turned away when she realized she couldn't. As Susannah does. I understood all that fairly soon. I understood Matthew Stangway and your mother. I understood life well enough—to my own satisfaction. I understood the direction I wished to take, and why. Love had no part in it. Until I loved you, Oriel, so naturally and inevitably that it never even surprised me. Indeed—nothing in you has ever surprised me. You've been the other half of myself, my darling—the better half. And what would we ever have known but joy in each other had our lives permitted it—if so many other lives, not all of them foolish ones, or grasping ones, hadn't come between us? So that now you are chained by others who love you, quite hugely, I know. And I am finding it best to be just ambitious.''

Putting down her glass, mainly because her hands were shaking, she moved slightly away from him.

"Oriel—would you prefer me to leave now?''

Looking at him for a moment of perfect stillness, she smiled and shook her head. "No, Quentin.''

"I'll stay, then . . . ?''

And going back to the window seat where he was still sitting, she leaned over him, taking his lean, so finely, so familiarly molded face between her hands and kissed him, her closed mouth touching his lightly to begin with, offering the love of her mind, her intuition, her careful heart, and then, as her mouth opened, following it naturally—so naturally—with the potent maturity—so natural still—of her body's need, blending with her mind, to love him.

"Oriel,'' he said, almost groaning. "Don't let me hurt you . . .'' But laying a finger across his lips, she shook her head.

"No, Quentin. Please don't talk to me of guilt and shame and all the things I have suffered quite long enough already. Just tell me this. I am a convicted criminal in any case, surely, am I not, my darling? I have been charged and found guilty and quite thoroughly punished for an act I never even thought of committing. I have even confessed to it. Oh yes—for good reasons, I think, necessary reasons—I really didn't mind. And through all the turmoil of being branded as a fallen woman these months past I have made as little fuss—you must admit—as I possibly could. For the sake of the people who were branding me, of course, rather than mine. I suppose I would do the same again . . .''

"Yes. I think you would.''

"So would you, Quentin. So will you always. The right things, in accordance with your role in life—whether it was your first choice as a role or not. As I will. Happily, as things have turned out for me, I think. Perhaps very happily."

"I hope so, Oriel."

"I know you do. But is it too much to ask now—for ourselves—to take one afternoon out of a lifetime? I told my husband I had been unfaithful to him only once and would never be so again. I never will, Quentin. But that once—you know . . ."

"I know," he said. "Is it waiting for us? My darling, Francis said this house was an oasis—do you remember . . . ?"

An interlude, he had said, the tide of reality, of necessity, receding, detaching the whole of that afternoon entirely from the mainstream of their lives, a time they knew to be short but which, nevertheless, had space enough to contain the progress of their love, following them through courtship, declaration, the outpourings of youthful romance to the final joining of mature bodies, every emotion she had dreamed of the night before entering her body as he entered it, and remaining, within and around her as his pleasure embraced hers, and grew with it, seeding the heights and depths of her joy.

"My darling, you have committed your crime."

But she shook her head. "I will remain criminal, I think, until the end of the afternoon."

It passed; and Kate, returning not one moment earlier than the hour she had named, found Oriel alone, talking to the cats by the valerian flowers, the dog prowling a jealous circle around her, as immaculate in her appearance and manner as ever, except that her eyes were a trifle heavy and her pale hair hanging loose down her back.

"Oriel," said Kate, her own manner flurried as a March wind, blowing from good cheer to no cheer at all and back again. "I suppose Quentin has gone?"

"Yes. To Hepplefield, if he can catch the train."

"You're going back to your husband, then?"

"Yes. Are you?"

"Yes. I am."

"Darling—what do you feel about it?"

"Oh Lord—" Kate shook her head, her hair escaping a little from her elegant chignon, her long jet earrings dancing. "So much of everything I can hardly name it. One minute

it's so much more than I've ever dreamed of I can't get over
my luck, the next minute I can get over it only too well. You
know. It's glorious, then it's a disaster, then it's half one and
half the other. Let's hope the glory wins.''

"Shall we have some supper?''

Sitting at the kitchen table, the dog keeping a close eye on
them, they ate bread and cheese, chocolate cake and ginger-
bread, drank several cups of tea, love, as Kate pointed out—
if love it was—playing unreliable tricks on the appetite.

"First I'm dying of hunger, then I can't eat anything. Francis wasn't too hungry today, either. He says he wants to look
after me. How odd. Now that I don't need looking after, the
idea rather pleases me. I hated it before, when I did. It was
one of the things I most ran away from.''

"Take care,'' said Oriel, refilling the tea-pot, "not to run
away again.''

Kate smiled, her elbows resting lightly on the table, her
head, despite the tumbling curls, suddenly elegant again, few
doubts, if any, to be glimpsed in her eyes.

"My dear, a woman of my age doesn't run away. I am at
least one hundred and five, as you must surely know.''

"I do. Does Francis?''

They were laughing together. "Darling—absolutely not. I
have never met a man anywhere who could cope with that.''

The supper dishes put away, the kitchen tidy, they walked
out in the twilight down the field path to the water, Oriel's
hair still hanging smoothly down her back, Kate's very elaborate again until, suddenly snatching out the pins, she shook
it free.

"How beautiful,'' she said, taking a deep breath of the
night air. "What are those lights on the other side?''

"Watermillock. Morag and Elspeth are there tonight.
Morag is coming over here tomorrow. Mrs. Landon won't let
Elspeth come, of course. She won't want the girl who is
going to marry her son in contact with me—or you either—
just in case our sins are catching. I don't think she much
liked me even when I was a good woman. But never mind.
I'll be seeing Elspeth soon enough.''

"My word,'' murmured Kate, "is this what motherhood
does to us? Will the day come, I wonder, when I shall be
judging some poor Tom Landon or other nowhere near good
enough for my Celestine?''

Stooping to set another gold leaf afloat on the water, Oriel smiled at her. "That's the first time I've heard you speak your daughter's name."

"I dare say," she shrugged. "That's what Francis said. And I had to agree it sounded quite odd talking to him about "your daughter" when she's mine as well. Except that she isn't. No—no, not really. It takes more than those months of being sick and those few hours of straining and pushing and all the rest to make a mother. Don't argue with me, Oriel, because you've never done the pushing. Does it worry you?"

"Oh—it used to. No more."

"You've done the caring though, haven't you?"

"No, Kate. I've taken the responsibility, that's all. And it hasn't been enough."

"So now you're going to make amends?"

She nodded. But with her eyes on the lights of Watermillock it was neither Morag nor Elspeth who rushed into the forefront of her mind. Only Garron was there, his presence, his voice filling her head. *I'm asking you to marry me, bonny lass.* He was only ten days away and when he returned, *then*, with a true and happy heart, she knew she could be his wife.

"You're quite fond of that giant of yours, aren't you?" murmured Kate. But fond had never been a word in any way applicable to Garron and laughing, taking Kate's arm, she shook her head. "You don't *like* giants. You either can't stand them at all, or you can stand them very much. But let's talk about your newly discovered Celestine instead."

"My dear, I haven't seen her yet. She was a toddling little scrap who terrified me. Now she's a young lady of seven who may look me up and down with absolute disdain. Or may class me forever as the wicked witch come to steal her father. I shall take it all very steadily. And try never to take too much of Francis either—or not when she's looking. Even then she may never love me. But what right have I to complain? I'll do the best I can, and so will Francis, which is something we have no right to expect of her. She didn't ask to be born, did she? And certainly not to a mother who had to run away—if not precisely on a camel to Arabia—just to learn how to grow up."

"Might you think of giving her a brother or a sister?"

Shivering quite violently, Kate laughed. "I dare say Francis might think of it. A son for Dessborough. Unless, of course, he decides it might upset Celestine."

"I dare say you'll know how to convince him it might."

"Very likely, my dear—very likely, as any woman worth the name does."

Turning, they began to walk slowly, arm-in-arm, back up the field path.

"You loved your mother, didn't you, Oriel?"

"Very much. Worth has nothing to do with it."

"Lord—you don't have to tell me that. I loved my father, even on the days when I couldn't find a scrap of worth in him anywhere. We ought to meet on Sundays, now that we're going to be married ladies again, and put flowers on their grave. They might think it amusing."

They walked on, close together in the dark, slender, minute shadows of humanity disappearing among the fells.

"Do you know," Kate said. "Francis forgave me all my lovers. And I said that was very fair of him and I certainly didn't feel entitled to go on too much about the lovers he's had, since it was my running off that put him in the position of needing them in the first place."

"That seems fair to me, too."

"Well—yes. But these lovers of mine, you see—what I didn't tell him was that, really, I haven't had so very many . . . Not in the way he means, at any rate. There have been men around me all the time, that's true enough. Men who've loved me quite a lot, and men I've absolutely adored on occasion. But what Francis thinks of as a love affair doesn't altogether suit me. He's had his little ladies from Merton Abbey for a night or two and then never thought of them again. Well, I've learned a lot about the sexual act since I grew up, without feeling the need to do it in any way that might be taken for granted . . ."

"Kate, you'll have to do it with Francis."

"Darling," she chuckled, "thank Goodness for that. The prospect delights me. But I don't think I'll confess my relatively mild promiscuity to him, would you? He likes the exotic and the exciting, and although I could never compete with the pilgrimage to Mecca, I'm ready to do my best."

"Does he still want to go there?"

"Oh—I think he likes the idea of it. And perhaps the idea is all he needs. One learns the trick of that. I believe we call it 'compromise.' The very wisest of my friends all swear by it, Oriel. Don't you?"

Opening the garden gate, they stood for a while looking

down at the lake and the reflected path of moonlight in the water.

"I'll take the dog with me,' said Oriel. "He'd pine otherwise. The cats will make their own way—splendidly. I'm sure of it." As Quentin would do.

"And the house?"

"Yes. I think we should sell it. Garron will never want to come here and I wouldn't come, now, without him."

"I see." Kate laughed, pressing her cheek against Oriel's shoulder. "The lengths to which some women will go to get rid of Mrs. Landon's son, the fiancé."

And they stayed for a long moment in companionable silence, Oriel's arm around Kate's shoulders, their heads close together.

"No," Kate said. "Your cottage doesn't want to be sold. It's just told me so. Francis will never want to come here either. But all we have to do is keep on that good lady of yours to feed the cats and do whatever has to be done. And who knows? At least it's here. And ours. We have a place of our own. And I seem to remember solitude as a great luxury in even a happy married life."

"Just be happy, little sister," Oriel said. *And if it ever happens that you're not, then there's no need to run any further than to me. As I ran to you. As I know I can always do again.*

But he was only ten days away and now, waiting for him already with an eager welcome and—she was glad to discover—a clear conscience, she did not envisage any likelihood of flight. For her freedom had come hand-in-hand to her with choice and she believed that now *her* choice—how magnificent—had been made.

About the Author

After living in Paris and London, Yorkshire born Brenda Jagger returned home to live in Bradford, one of the mill towns she writes about.